Edge of Ruin

The Edge Series: Book Two

Lennan Daniels

Because consent matters...

While far darker works exist, The Edge Series may be too intense for some readers. We use p-words and c-words here. Every character has a backstory, and the sex leaves marks.

Please visit LennanDaniels.com for a list of content warnings specific to each installment in The Edge Series.

For specific questions or to recommend additions to the list of content warnings, reach out via social media or the author's website.

Devon isn't here. I am.

For those impatiently waiting...
Demon will see you now.

HOPE

Hope stared across the sea of milling bodies to where Devon, Nix, and Lucas juggled glass and alcohol for the masses. Two times in as many hours, Devon had abandoned their table for the business side of the bar. *They're in the weeds*, he'd say, foot bouncing on the bottom rung of Hope's chair until she vibrated with his restraint.

Shit. Lucas dropped a glass...

Shit. That guy is mouthing off to Nix...

Shit...

A veritable play by play until the vibrating stopped because Devon had bolted for the bar.

Considering he hadn't taken a New Year's Eve off since opening the place, Hope wasn't holding his need to help against him. Idleness wasn't his nature when something needed to be done. And here—in *his* house? Despite his *tendencies*, Devon didn't possess that level of control.

Hope sipped her wine and waited, seconds piling on top of the fifteen minutes he'd already been occupied. At least she had an excellent view. The rolled shirtsleeves, ink covered forearms, and self-assured competence... Delectable. Devon grabbed a bottle with the same confidence he grabbed her, and that got Hope tingly in all the best places, two glasses of Cab Sauv or no.

Her thoughts circled things she'd always fantasized while watching him work. Her legs around his hips. Yanking his shirttails free of his jeans. Mouths meeting with scorching passion, a prelude to the hot slide of his flesh into hers.

And there were the newer additions—the ones she'd never dared dream of before him, now inspired by their reality. Shivers and floggers and that time he'd wrapped one hand around her throat and the other around his—

"...out early?"

Hope's wine missed her esophagus as her brother's voice broke through the daydream. Eyes watering, she hacked a full-bodied red out of her lungs.

"I'm sorry, what?"

"I asked if you all were staying for the ball drop or heading out," JJ repeated at a patronizing volume.

Chloe chortled. "Hope might have to kiss Devon across the bar at midnight. Isn't he supposed to be off?"

Swiveling toward their high-top table, Hope intentionally ignored the view of the dark street framing her friend and brother.

"I think this is as *off* as he gets," Hope said.

"Speaking of work," her brother, JJ, cut in as he rested a hand on the back of Chloe's chair. "When do you start at the nonprofit?"

"Next week."

"Excited?" he asked.

"Thrilled, tickled, grateful... I finally get to use my degree, and I'll be...less broke. It feels too good to be true."

"Aw..." Chloe pouted. "No Team 3F?"

Hope laughed. "While I love you to pieces, I'm not so hot on the idea of listening to you screw my brother from a room away."

Chloe cut a sidelong glance at JJ. "With how thin our walls are, I'm pretty sure you can already hear it."

"Maybe that's why she spends so much time at Devon's." Smirking, JJ continued, "Trying to give us privacy, while getting some of her own. Emphasis on the *getting some.*"

He wagged his eyebrows; Chloe giggled, leaning closer to him. She did something with her face that made her lips scream *insert dick here,* as she angled herself for optimal cleavage display. Hope respected the effort; she wasn't exactly flat-chested, but she could never pull that off. JJ stared into the depths, as he toyed with a lock of Chloe's hair.

"Do you all need a room?" Hope asked.

"Funny coming from you..." JJ reached for his tumbler, then lifted it toward the bar. "You two are a heartbeat from ripping each other's clothes off at any given second. It's kind of disgusting, actually."

"We are not."

Chloe nodded. "It's Hope's fault."

"What?"

She gestured with a hand tipped with sparkling white nails that matched her ice queen look. "I mean, look at her. How could any moderately straight man or less-than-straight woman resist?"

"I'm moderately straight, and I don't find it difficult," JJ declared. "But Chloe's right. You do look nice tonight, sis."

Hope tugged the hem of her navy-blue dress. It was too short, too expensive, and had too many sequins... But this was the start of her best year yet, and that deserved celebration.

"Thanks," Hope said. "Means a lot coming from the girl who could make Aphrodite swoon." She blew a kiss at Chloe. "And...*you*," she added for JJ, who laughed.

"I meant to ask," Chloe said, "are things still quiet on the Aaron front?"

An unnamed sensation skittered down Hope's spine at the mention of her ex's name.

JJ raised his glass again. "Fastest mood-killer of the night award goes to..."

"Sorry." Chloe glanced at him. "Curious."

Hope forced a smile. "Nothing new to report. Sydney's lawyer magic did the trick."

"So everything is great?"

"Yep."

"No worries at all?"

"Not a one," Hope said.

"Interesting." Chloe watched the bubbles float lazily to the top of her glass. "Is that why the bouncers are targeting all the blond guys?"

Hope whipped her head toward the door, where Alex loomed over a customer.

"Your boyfriend doesn't know anything about sports," JJ said, "but he covers bases."

"Alex is just doing his job. It has nothing to do with…" Hope trailed off as the bouncer waved the guy inside, let two more people pass without interruption, then stepped in front of an approaching blond man, peering at him from the shadows of his hood.

Chloe laughed. "We had a running bet on when you'd catch on."

"Which I just won," JJ added.

Chloe whacked his arm. "You did not! I said by New Year's."

"But you *told her*. Cheaters forfeit."

"That wasn't a rule." Chloe's pitch climbed with mock offense.

"It's always a rule, cheater."

As her brother and best friend traded jibes, Hope ran her fingers over the rope bracelet on her wrist, her focus drawn to the inky window at their backs. It was coincidence, she decided. Alex and Mark kept an eye on things at the bar in general; they didn't need to pay extra attention to men who happened to look like her ex. Why would they, when she hadn't heard a peep from him in weeks?

Beyond the window, darkness folded and rolled, the effect of her mind's struggle to rearrange the imaginary into the tangible. Hope knew what was coming; staring into the shadows while thinking of Aaron was a bad combination. Her pulse feathered in her throat, stuttering in her chest. She resisted the urge to look away as a mass materialized in the void.

Not real, she reminded herself. *Nothing but shadows.*

Hope breathed through the unease rising like a crescendo inside her; letting it hum in her bones until it fizzled into the sound and warmth of the bar. With an unsteady hand, she sipped her wine and willed her racing heart calm.

Pareidolia. The human tendency to see a recognizable shape, even when there wasn't one. The evolutionary quirk made babies smile at their mothers and helped those same mothers spot a threat in time to run. Hope found the phenomenon fascinating, and Aaron's silence had given her ample time to study its intricacies.

One would think that his absence would be reassuring; instead, her anxiety inched upward day-by-day. The longer she waited for the other shoe to drop, the more faces she saw in the dark. It had gotten to the point where she had resorted to a sort of *exposure therapy*—letting her brain manufacture monsters, only to remind herself that they didn't exist, in hopes that she would stop seeing them so often.

She had no intention of revealing that to anyone else.

"Well, I'm glad you aren't worried about him anymore," Chloe said. "He's taken up enough of your time."

"I couldn't agree more," Hope said. Placing her wine glass on the table, she spun her stool.

When Devon locked eyes on her, mid-pour, Hope lifted her chin and pursed her lips. She watched his brow furrow, an unspoken *What are you up to, darling?* written on his face. Uncrossing her legs, she parted her knees, pressing them wider until a burst of cold air tickled her barely-there knickers. Devon's nostrils flared; his throat bobbed. His eyes raked down her body. Clear liquid flooded over the rim of the glass and pooled on the bar, as Hope primly tucked one ankle behind the other.

Devon shook his head at her, righting the bottle and grabbing the towel over his shoulder. He turned to the waiting patron, mouth moving as he sopped up spilled liquor. The man replied—probably something about the overflowing shot glass—and laugh lines crinkled the corners of Devon's eyes.

As the customer claimed his spoils, that heated, hazel gaze centered on Hope again. She felt powerful when he looked at her like that—like he couldn't stay on the other side of the room if he tried. Yes, he looked like he might eat her alive when he got to her...but only because she let him.

He handed over one last drink, signaled Nix, then headed back toward their table like a predator stalking prey. Walking straight to Hope, he cupped her chin in a hand and tilted her head. The scent of cedar and sandalwood melded with spilled vodka as his lips skimmed up her neck. "I see you," he whispered, nipping her earlobe. "And you distract me, darling."

"Sorry, Sir," she murmured.

Devon made a sound deep in his throat, somewhere between laughter and pleasure. "You know exactly what you're doing, impatient little thing."

Hope bit back a guilty smile.

"Sorry, Sir," she repeated...and then remembered that they weren't alone.

Hope nearly knocked over her drink in her rush to look toward their company, but she found JJ and Chloe lost in their own conversation—as oblivious to her mortification as they were to what she'd said to Devon. Twice. His eyes sparkled with amusement.

"Nervous someone will hear you, kitten?" he chided at a volume not meant for secrets. Leaning back to her ear he added, "Maybe we should leave before you get louder, hmm?"

"Yes—"

Hope halted, taking in his wicked delight. She shifted under his gaze, unnerved by the gnawing desire to follow through. Devon would never demand that of her in front of her brother and friend; but the thing simmering between them...? Sometimes it asked things of her that Devon never would, and as hard as she tried, Hope hadn't yet gotten her head around it—not that she'd had time.

Between her shifts at Silver Sassafras, group meetings and brushing up for her impending counseling debut at Redact and Recover... Holidays, family drama and obligations, finances, and figuring out how Devon fit into it all... Analyzing her compulsion to call him *Sir* sat lower on the list than getting that hit of relief each time she did.

Having escaped the fray for a moment, Nix, Devon's friend and assistant manager, sidled up to the table. "We're slammed," she said, dewy sweat covering her skin, her dark eyeliner smudged.

Devon straightened, resting a hand on the back of Hope's neck. "Don't worry. In about two hours, it'll be Tuesday. *Poof!* No more crowd."

He raised his tumbler of mostly melted ice in a toast, then downed the dregs with a grimace. Nix laughed as she worked her fingertips through her spiky pixie cut, coaxing it upright.

"They get half an hour after the countdown, then they better get gone." She turned to Chloe and JJ. "Hey, guys. If you get bored and want to head out, I can meet up with you after I get off. I'm leaving as soon as it calms down enough for Lucas to manage alone, but that'll be after midnight."

Hope watched this interaction play out with fascination. She was a solid seventy-percent sure that Nix and Chloe had a one-night thing a few weeks before JJ and Chloe started...whatever they'd been doing since Christmas. There had been a night that Devon walked Hope home, but Chloe stayed back at Cleary's with Nix—who showed up to work four hours late the next day.

Hope wondered how much her brother knew about her best friend's amorous personality. Did he realize that his sister had made out with his current fling at least half a dozen times? Well, *stepsister* anyway, but still... Had Nix mentioned to Hope's towheaded brother during any of their tattoo sessions that she had a thing for blonds of *all* varieties?

"We can wait," JJ offered.

Nix shook her head. "Nah, you two go. I'll catch up."

"Well... In that case..." Chloe got to her feet, JJ close behind. "Devon, uh... No offense, but take another shot or three, dude."

"I think I'll pass for tonight."

"You're supposed to be off." She moved in for a hug, and he wrapped an arm around her.

"If you want him off the bar, adding alcohol definitely won't help," Nix mumbled. Devon gave her a dirty look.

Hope kissed Chloe on the cheek, hugged her brother, and passed out the requisite *I love yous* and *Happy New Years.* Then, Chloe and JJ headed for the door. Nix ran her tongue ring over her teeth, as she returned her attention to Hope's favorite bartender.

"I'm doing rum shots for the toast," she said without preamble.

Hope suppressed a giggle as Devon's hand spasmed against her nape.

"Rum shots?"

"Don't." Despite Nix's voluptuous, pint-size, faerie-goth appearance, the word came out with as much authority as Devon would have crammed into it. "You keep saying we aren't moving the rum." She gestured to the packed bar. "Here's your opportunity."

"But..." He looked around. "Isn't it supposed to be a champagne toast?"

Nix crossed her arms and widened her feet; Hope ignored her body's response to that action. "We can blow through the bubbly with one Sunday mimosa special. At this rate, that rum will be here when we die."

"Look who's complaining about the rum now," Devon grumbled.

"Don't start with me. You got your head up your ass making an order, and my shins have been paying for it since *May.* You aren't even on the schedule. Not your scene, Dev."

"This is always my scene."

Nix pinned him with a cold stare, but his tone left no room for argument. They'd likely do this until the ball dropped, Hope realized. One would pass out champagne; the other would pass out rum. People would vomit, and she'd never get laid.

Devon exhaled sharply through his nose.

"Fine," he said.

Nix and Hope both narrowed their eyes at his easy forfeit. Devon looked down at Hope with blood-sizzling intent.

"I've got better things to do than argue about rum," he said, rubbing a thumb behind her ear, staring unapologetically at her mouth.

"Right." Nix laughed. "You two going by Edge when you leave, then? I thought I—" She stopped short.

"Uh..." Hope looked between the two of them. "*Edge* is...?"

Above his collar, Devon's neck was the color of a ripe strawberry. "It's nothing—"

"It's the local dungeon," Nix said at the same time. "It's in that—"

"Fucking hell. Really, Nix?" His eyes widened and the blush overtook his cheeks.

"What?" She held out her hands like she didn't see the problem.

"The local BDSM dungeon..." Hope said, looking to Devon as her brain untangled their overlapping responses.

"He has a yearly tradition," Nix announced.

"Shut up, Nix," Devon warned.

Hope grinned up at him. "A tradition, huh?"

"No."

"Come on, it's New Year's." Hope rocked on her seat, bumping him with her shoulder. "It's not even ten-thirty. If you want—"

"I *want* you slicked with sweat and unable to remember your name by the time I kiss you at midnight." He pulled her black woolen peacoat from the back of her stool and held it out.

"I wasn't trying to stir anything up," Nix said. "Edge after work is a New Year's Eve tradition and..." She glanced at Hope, then back to Devon. "Do you think it's a good idea to skip this year?"

"Hope's making me go to the luncheon at R&R tomorrow and a family dinner on Sunday. Can't get more masochistic than that."

Hope snickered, despite herself. Nix's brows pinched with worry.

"Dev, you aren't a masochist, and none of that is going to—"

"We really need to go," Devon said.

Nix pulled herself up straighter. The gravity in her demeanor urged Hope to her feet. "You need to tell her."

"Tell me what?"

Devon bared his teeth and glared a searing hole through his best friend. "I swear I will fire you right now if you don't shut your mouth."

"*Bull. Shit,*" Nix countered.

Hope put a hand on his arm, but he ignored it.

"I'd have to help Lucas close. Do not ruin my evening."

"You promised to talk to her, Dev."

"*Hello,*" Hope said. "I'm standing right here. Talk to me about what?"

"Nothing. It's nothing." Devon rounded on his friend again. "I do talk to her. She's one of the only people I talk to."

"But not about the shit that matters, dickhead."

"Stay out of it," he spat.

He turned to Hope and held out her coat. "The only place I'm going is between your thighs." He said it like a promise. "So, unless you want me going there in front of all these people...Coat. Now." He said *that* like a promise too.

Hope sank her teeth into her lower lip and slipped her arms into the sleeves.

"Stubborn bastard," Nix said under her breath.

Turning Hope to face him, Devon straightened her lapels. "Don't act surprised."

"Unbelievable..." Nix leaned around his larger torso to regain a line on Hope. "He's going to tell you he's fine," she said, "but I'm telling you right now that he is a fucking liar."

With a sarcastic *Good luck, genius* aimed at Devon, she spun and stormed back toward the bar. Patrons with nearly a foot on her hustled out of her path.

"Champagne!" Devon barked at her back.

"Rum, jackass!" She shot her boss a two-handed, one-finger salute as she strode away.

***

Hope stared after Nix in horror. "What was that about?"

"Don't worry about it." Devon put a hand on her lower back and guided her toward the exit.

"You threatened to fire her."

"Trust me, it's fine."

But he didn't sound fine. He sounded agitated and tense; and Hope didn't understand what had triggered their fight. She was used to their verbal sparring matches, but what just happened felt more heated.

"I fire Nix at least once a year; she quits twice as often." He opened the door for her, and Hope walked through, another question about the exchange with Nix already spilling out of her mouth.

"But... *Ah!*"

Devon shoved her behind his body before her squeak faded, his head whipping around. The hulking man with a skeleton face—the one who had startled the crap out of Hope—unhitched himself from the wall. His massive body uncoiled, and something in Hope eased; taller than Aaron, and his vigilance mirrored her boyfriend's.

"Oh, Alex..." She brought a hand to her chest. "Shit."

The bouncer reached up and pulled down the skeleton face, which Hope now realized was a gaiter. "You screeching at me?" he said.

"Yeah, sorry." Hope cringed. "You just...startled me."

Devon relaxed the arm holding her at his back. "Aren't you on the door?" he said to Alex.

"That door?" He hooked a thumb over his shoulder as Devon huffed out a stream of white steam.

"You know what I mean, Alex."

The big guy shrugged. "It was getting feisty in there."

"I hired you to back me up when things get feisty."

"You hired me to protect your business and family," Alex corrected. "*Me*, because sometimes *you* are your biggest problem."

"Well, tonight my problem is a pissed off cupcake."

Alex crossed his arms over his broad chest, eyes shamelessly tracking an approaching patron until they made it inside. "That's Mark's territory," he said. "I'm not getting on her shit list over you and your mouth."

"You're like ten feet taller than her," Devon pointed out.

Alex scoffed. "You can't measure Nix like that. It's got to violate some kind of labor law, leaving me here after riling her up."

"Pretty sure we violate all kinds of laws that work in your favor," Devon grumbled.

Hope's brow pinched, but Alex stepped toward the door.

"Meant to say, have a good night, boss." He turned to Hope and tipped his head. "Happy New Year, ma'am. Sorry I scared you. If I can make a suggestion—"

"Don't," Devon warned.

Alex grinned. "Didn't ask you. Now, if I can make a suggestion in the spirit of protecting this bastard from himself—don't let him near the whiskey." Pulling open the door, he stepped inside.

"No respect," Devon muttered. "No fucking respect in this place anymore."

Thirty seconds later, he deposited Hope in the passenger seat of his black Charger, slammed his own door, and fired up the engine. Hope fumbled for her seatbelt, as the rumble of a whole lot of horsepower vibrated under her feet and rear. He navigated out of the lot and onto the street.

"Devon?"

"Hmm?"

"Why is everyone acting like you're about to explode?"

"Because I am. Maybe on your face..." His eyes flicked to hers, then lower, before returning to the road. "Or your tits. I love coming on your perky little tits."

Hope pressed her thighs together. "You know that's not what I'm talking about."

"It's what I'm talking about."

"You threatened to fire your best friend in the world, and you apparently have a New Year's dungeon tradition and some looming catastrophe that you aren't telling me about."

He swore under his breath. "Nix and her big mouth..."

"She's *worried* about you. If something's going on—"

"Nothing is going on." He flipped on a turn signal and made a right. "At least, nothing new. That video they passed around of Kelly..." He wet his lower lip.

"I remember," Hope said, sparing him the need to elaborate on the evidence of his sister's assault.

"It was taken at a New Year's Eve party." Hope studied his profile, the tight set of his jaw as he stared through the windshield. His throat bobbed and voice softened. "She had been gone for weeks by the time I saw it, but you could tell when it was taken. There was one of those noise makers on the coffee table. Someone stuck a party hat on her partway through, which everyone found hilarious." He shook his head, shifting gears with more force than necessary. "I don't enjoy drudging that up at the start of every year, so I look for a *distraction*. Nix means well, but this... This is the opposite of distraction."

"If it's still triggering you, it sounds like something you need to work through; not shove down for another year."

"Therapists and bartenders aren't so different, you know. If you want to hash out my triggers," he said, a tone of warning in the words, "I might start bringing up yours. Like the way you screamed the moment you saw Alex leaning against the wall."

Hope tugged the hem of her dress, brushed her fingers over the bracelet on her wrist. "It was more like a squeak."

"You *squeaked* so loudly that we both thought you saw Aaron gearing up for a drive-by."

"So, you *did* put the bouncers on Aaron-watch."

He chuckled. "Of course, I did. He's an asshole, and I don't want him anywhere near you."

Hope sighed. "I don't want to spend our first New Year's Eve talking about my ex."

"And I don't want to spend it talking about my dead sister." He looked at her meaningfully. "Look, I appreciate the concern. I love you for it. But not tonight, okay? If I need help airing out my feelings, I'll let you know."

"Promise?"

"Uh huh."

"Because if you ever needed to..."

Releasing the stick, he slipped a hand between her thighs. The streetlights illuminated her legs in waxing and waning pulses as his hand disappeared to the wrist. Hope gasped as he hooked a finger under her panties. Devon smirked in the glare of passing headlights, that wicked grin she recognized.

"I know what I need, love." Unhurried, he probed her already slick pussy, sending tremors of pleasure along her nerves. "I need to ruin you in a dungeon."

"But... Oh God..." Desire set Hope's teeth on edge, strained her voice. Her hips rolled, pressing her clit against the heel of his palm. "I th...thought you said you didn't want me at Edge, Sir."

There was that *Sir* again—the one he pulled from her effortlessly. Her head lolled against the seat, hips scooting forward and legs spreading to grant him access. Devon rewarded her effort with another finger, and her body flushed with warmth.

His laugh was a deviant thing when he pulled his fingers from her with a wet, squelching sound. He took a moment to appreciate the light glinting off the gossamer webbing connecting his digits, then reclaimed the gearshift.

"Edge isn't the only dungeon in town, darling."

HOPE

Hope lay belly-down on something that resembled a padded sawhorse. Her legs dangled off the back. The mood lighting set Devon's preferred vibe—dark, ominous, a sensual promise of pleasure and pain. The toes of her *fuck me* heels brushed the floor, and low music thrummed through the air around her. Wearing only black cargo pants, Devon crouched in front of her, a pair of leather cuffs in hand.

"Safewords."

The reminder served as a single word warning that sped her pulse, as he affixed the cuffs first to her wrists, then to the eyebolts on the horse.

"Red and yellow, Sir. I remember."

"There's a good girl."

He pressed a kiss to her cheek, then stood and circled behind her, where his open palm connected with her backside without warning. The fabric of the dress he had insisted she keep on softened the sound of the impact, but the shock of it squeezed the air from her lungs in a gasping-wheeze all the same.

"Oh…" He clicked his tongue. "You weren't ready for that one." He smacked her bum a second time, and Hope yelped in earnest. Devon hummed his appreciation. "Better," he said.

She couldn't remember why she wanted in this room so badly.

"We're improvising tonight. See, usually," he went on, "I would scoot you forward. Spread your legs. Give myself unobstructed access to all of your soft places." He lightly kicked one leg of the horse, sending vibrations through her. "It's what this thing is designed for."

Warm fingertips brushed the backs of her thighs. One hand skimmed higher, grazed her lace panties. Lust swirled in her belly. "Christ, you're a mess. It's a wonder you haven't soaked the back of your dress." He hooked a finger under the sodden scrap of fabric. Hope let out a ragged exhale. "How did you do this, darling?"

"I didn't—"

"One."

One? Why did he say *one*? Devon pushed a finger deep in her pussy, and the thought fizzled into raw need.

"Sir…" She pushed back into him.

"You're only making this harder on yourself, you know. It's a simple question. How did you get so wet?" he repeated, enunciating each word. "And *two* because you made me ask twice."

Hope panted as Devon leisurely penetrated her sex. The memory of him behind the bar surfaced, the hunger in his eyes when she'd flashed him. "It just ha-happened."

Devon clicked his tongue. "Liar, liar…Three and four."

Holy fuck, he's counting. Fire had nothing on the heat that raced up her spine.

"In the car... You were fingering me in the car."

"Are you blaming me, love?" His voice was a playful, satisfied dare.

"N... No." She swallowed hard and shuddered, the ceaseless movement of his fingers making concentration impossible.

"Of course not," Devon agreed. "You wouldn't do that; not when *you* thought about me taking off this dress from the moment you put it on. But let's call it five anyway, just to be safe. And six, for the way you spread your legs in front of everyone without permission. All those people... Anyone could have seen."

"No one saw." She tried to catch her breath, to stop her head from spinning, but her body felt like a spiraling vortex of need. One that he toyed with at his leisure.

"But they could have. Why does that make you so wet, darling? Why are you dripping off my wrist right now?"

Hope's answer came out as a choked sound of desperation. She wanted his cock so badly that she was half a second from begging.

"You need it, don't you kitten? It's why you squirmed so much when I pulled my fingers out of your greedy hole in the car. It's why that hole was already wet when I checked how bad you'd been."

Hope took tiny breaths through her nose, hyper-focused on the feel of him owning her body. "Yes, Sir." Then his fingers were gone, and his palm slammed into her butt again.

"Naughty exhibitionist," he said over her yelp. "Maybe I should have taken you in the office. Let everyone in the bar hear what comes out of your mouth when I fuck you." Hope jerked on the horse as he ripped down her panties. "Then again," he said, reaching up her dress to rebury his fingers in her scorching depths, "filthy girl like you, you might like that."

Hope tried to tilt her hips, but she couldn't get enough leverage.

"Or behind the bar," Devon mused. "What do you think, darling? Bend you over and pull this tiny dress up? You'd look just like you do now—dangling off the edge—but with an *audience.*"

Heat licked through her as embarrassment stained her cheeks. Devon pulled his hand free again, leaving her achingly empty. Scooting her short dress up around her waist, he stepped closer. The fabric of his cargo pants brushed her bare legs.

"You make such pretty faces when I pound you from be-hind." His voice went down like a shot of hard liquor. Hope pushed her hips back as much as her restraints allowed, her body begging. "Greedy," he growled, backing away again. "You're such a filthy, greedy, insatiable, little slut for me."

Those words ricocheted through her brain so violently that Hope registered neither his grabbing the flogger, nor his swing.

THWACK!

The tails connected with her ass as she emptied her lungs, morphing what would have been a surprised shout into a desperate inhale. Jarring pain faded into a dull ache as she pulled in air. Devon wasted no time swinging again.

THWACK!

On the second blow, her wail rattled the gear on the wall. Hope smashed her face into the padded top, dampening the last of her shout.

"This room has a ton of sound proofing, and I get off on the way you scream." His voice was all whiskey and gravel. Hot and rough, without the honey-sweetness softening the edges. It felt like he'd poured gasoline on her arousal, then struck a match. "Now, get your face off that horse and count, or I will."

"Count?" Her mind somersaulted.

THWACK!

The flogger lay a searing path across her thighs, dragged a pained *OW!* from her throat.

"*Count.*"

THWACK!

"One!"

Devon chuckled like a fucking sadist. Goosebumps erupted across Hope's skin, and her chest heaved against the bench.

"Seven," he said, adding another blow as he continued counting-on.

"Ah! Please, I don't understand," Hope managed.

"Seven," Devon repeated. "Because you forgot to say *sir.*"

He swung again—vicious and without warning; Hope dropped into subspace like a stone through still water.

"I'm sorry, Sir. One, Sir."

Her words sounded funny and far away, but she spoke as clearly as she could for him. Rounding the horse, Devon took her chin and swiped a thumb over her lower lip.

"So good that time. Just perfect." Hope smiled up at him. "Six more and we'll move on. Mess up, and we'll start over. Expect marks either way because your ass is already looking gorgeous."

"Yes, Sir. Thank you, Sir."

Cotton filled her head. Devon's mouth twitched. He moved out of sight. Then, delivered the final six lashes with an intensity that had tears streaming down her face. *Two, Sir, three, Sir, Four...*

Putting the flogger back on the wall, Devon stroked from the top of her head, down her spine, his fingers jostling the fabric of her bunched dress before finding her flesh. Hope's body quivered uncontrollably. Stepping around behind her, he rested his hands on her hips and knelt, nuzzling his face against her burning cheek.

"So good," he said, lips brushing her. "Good enough to eat."

Hope screeched as his teeth sank. Stars danced across her vision and a fresh layer of sweat broke out on her skin. Devon laved his tongue over the pain.

"I told you there would be marks," he said, straightening. Hope numbly registered the sound of a condom wrapper tearing. "Just so we're clear, I rather like the idea of you dangling over the side of my bar." His legs flanked hers, pressing them together, as he pushed at her opening. "They'd want you, but I'd have you, and that... Well, that sounds exciting. As much as that fantasy makes you drip—and it *does* make you drip, love—it makes me hard."

His thick head popped inside, and Hope moaned.

"*Fuck*," Devon groaned, digging his fingers into her hips. "You're so tight like this."

He fucked her slowly, entering and retreating, keeping her thighs shut as her body fought to open them. The futility of struggling against his hold burned through her blood like an addiction. No one had ever given her this...this safety to be exactly who she was. To drag it out of her because that's what she needed.

"Look forward, darling."

Lifting her head at his command, Hope stared into the large mirror propped against the wall in front of the horse. Her core tightened at the sight of her dazed expression; but the view of Devon towering behind her, taught muscles bunching and relaxing as he thrust into her, nearly tipped her over the edge.

"I'm not going to last like this tonight." He stepped back, pulling out of her. Hope whimpered at the loss as she was again left wanting. "Hush, now, I need to grab something." Devon reached under her, pushing the head of a wand against her clit, and then clicking it on. "Settle down, darling," he tutted, when she squirmed away from the overwhelming sensation.

"I c... can't, Sir."

"You can. Breathe for me. Big deep breaths. There's a good girl." She did her best to comply. "Grind your pussy on it, baby. Just like that."

"It's too much, it's too much, it's too..." She chanted, helplessly doing exactly as he asked. Devon laughed.

"It is set pretty high, but fuck me... You should see what I see right now. The way your ass tightens and hips roll. The way you suck in a breath only to hold it because your brain wants to fight the inevitable—and it is inevitable, darling. This is going to happen. You can feel it building already; I know you can. You can't stop it. You can't hold it in. You're going to come for me right about…"

The building climax tore through her, pulling a guttural moan from her throat.

"*There we go.* So gorgeous," he said, pushing his cock inside her still clenching pussy.

"Sir…"

The second he stopped pressing her legs closed with his own, Hope spread them, bending her knees, her heels digging into his ass.

"That's it, darling," he gritted out. "Rock on it. Grind on it. Fuck, you're such a good girl." His words were strained, movements erratic as his control slipped. "I'm about to come so goddamn hard, and you're doing all the work with that tight cunt of yours."

"Oh… Sir…"

Her legs tensed, locking him in place. The muscles in her pelvis grabbed on like they had no intention of ever releasing him. Rhythmic flutters undulated low in her belly, gripping him as she came again.

"*Fuck*, Hope." Devon groaned.

The wand hit the floor, buzzing against the leg of the horse, as he snatched a handful of hair at the back of her head. Hunched over her, pumping into her, he chased his own re-lease, until he bottomed out hard, cock jerking inside her.

Then, his hand in her hair loosened, and he backed away. The music stopped and the vibrator switched off, leaving the room silent. Devon yanked up his pants and hustled to the front of the horse.

Hope stared out at him as he fussed with her restraints. His cheeks were red and hair damp with sweat.

"Do you need to go clean up first, Sir?"

Devon's head snapped up, like he hadn't expected her to speak.

"I need to unfasten you."

DEVON

It was a dream.

Devon slipped down the hallway, less concerned over waking her with every passing step. The distance bolstered him. You couldn't hurt a person you couldn't reach, right? Not physically, anyway.

A stupid fucking dream.

Breaching the living room, he turned for the basement stairs. More and more, the isolation of the dim, stifling cave beneath his feet called to him. With Hope in his bed, it felt like the one place he could go to get away without leaving or waking her. He reached a shaking hand toward the knob, hesitating when a low rumble vibrated through the still night. The sound teased every hair on his already sensitive body to primal awareness—a sensation that had crawled across human flesh for millennia.

"Apollo."

The pup's growl cut off in an apologetic whine at the censure in Devon's voice. Tags jingled and muffled paws padded closer, until Apollo walked out of the shadows. Devon sighed.

"What are you doing out here, bud?" He stroked an unsteady hand over the dog's cinderblock head and down his flank, the sweat on his palms catching against silky fur. "Fireworks scare you?"

Apollo cocked his head.

While Devon appreciated that his neighbors had never interrupted a scene in the playroom by calling the cops, he found the organized lawlessness of his neighborhood a bit annoying on the first and the fourth—especially when it scared the shit out of his otherwise docile dog.

"They should be finished now. Why don't you get to bed? Go on, buddy. Place."

With a disgruntled snort, Apollo retrieved his battered teddy bear from the cushion in the corner of the living room and waddled down the hall toward the bedroom where Hope slept. After watching him go, Devon opened the basement door and flipped on the light. He descended into blessed privacy.

Bare feet reaching the concrete floor, he sank onto the second step from the bottom. The warmer temperature heated his sweat-slicked skin, but the tremor in his hands remained. He sucked in a breath as another snippet of the nightmare that woke him surfaced, assaulting his senses with the scent of leather and blood. The sound of her pleading in his ears. The feel of—

His cock twitched in his sweats, and Devon swallowed bile. *Not real.*

As if his subconscious had taken the anemic defiance as a challenge, the next image that flashed in his mind showcased his sister's eyes—half-lidded, unblinking—more memory than nightmare.

"Christ," he said on a shuddering exhale, scrubbing his face as if he could erase the past. Bracing his elbows on his knees, he held his head in his hands.

Numbness was a slippery slope for someone with an alcoholic father and a sister with a pill problem, but Devon craved peace. He wanted to stop feeling everything, all at once—just for a few hours. And maybe that was weak or selfish, but he was so tired. Glancing over his shoulder to assure himself that Hope wasn't standing there judging him, he reached beneath the bottom step and pulled out the tin.

An assortment of flowers and peace signs decorated the lid, painted in various shades of chipped nail polish. He traced lines of white-out that spelled *Desperate Times* in his sister's loopy cursive, each curve painfully familiar. The metal chilled his fingertips, and Devon reminded himself that the goosebumps dotting his flesh were normal...at least until the furnace kicked on. The ghost of moving air ruffled his hair, and he startled like a five-year-old.

"Jesus fuck..."

The tin originally contained elementary treasures—notes from fourth grade girls, lip balm that he wasn't allowed to touch. Later, it held cash for an escape that would never come. They'd sat cross-legged on Kelly's twin bed, while their mother cried on the other side of the wall; and she had promised to take him with her.

His chest ached at the memory of it. At the tragedy of two children holding onto doomed hope and each other.

Kelly added the writing later—around the time the cash vanished.

"I miss you," he said into the stillness. "So goddamn much. I couldn't even talk to you about this shit because it would be so weird. Hell, maybe I wouldn't need to talk about it if you hadn't done what you did." He shook his head, staring at a lop-sided daisy. "That sounds like I blame you, but I don't. I just...miss you."

Not knowing why he talked to her like this when she was nearly twenty years in a grave, Devon flipped open the tin. A small white pill sat in the bottom, and he pushed it sideways an inch with his index finger, listening to the distinctive scraping sound. Next, he pulled out the lighter and one of two joints he'd gotten from a part-time server at the bar—tip jar green, traded for another variety on a Saturday night.

People don't talk about it, but there's a connection for almost anything if you work in a restaurant or bar. Better to have it and not need it, than need it and not have it, Devon figured. He knew who he'd ask about a variety of illicit substances, guns without serial numbers, and a bunch of other crap he didn't need. He even knew who he'd call if Hope's ex had an accident—Alex. Definitely Alex for that last one. Actually, the big bouncer could probably arrange said accident... Devon smiled.

On a more mundane front, Mark had a truck if you needed to haul something, and his wife, Stacy, made jewelry. One of the cooks ran a fantasy football league that Devon would never voluntarily join, and if you wanted to get high, someone always had a weed hookup.

His thumb rolled over the lighter's wheel. Sparks crackled in the darkness, before catching flame. He sucked in heat, until the familiar flavor coated his tongue and smoke burned in his lungs. Devon held his breath as his heartbeat slowed. And when he couldn't stand it any longer, he exhaled in a rush.

"Happy New Year, Kelly."

Smoke curled around the words.

HOPE

The following afternoon, Hope entered the bustling group space of Redact and Recover with Devon trailing two paces behind.

Folding tables lined one wall, loaded with crock-pots, foil-covered trays, and casserole dishes. There were disposable plates, flatware, and off-brand two-liter bottles. A pile of cookies towered atop the biggest platter she had ever seen, telling her that Betty was in the building. The woman, who attended Survivors Circle religiously, made the best cookies on the planet. Hope smiled over her shoulder; Devon deliberately turned up his own mouth in response.

"Come on." She urged him. "It'll be fun."

He glanced toward the door. "I need to patch that wall if I'm ever going to get it painted."

"At least, eat first."

He looked around the room with a sour expression.

"There's nowhere to sit."

Hope pointed to the small clusters of shoddy seating pushed off to the side. "I think people want to mill around."

"Yeah, but—"

"Well, look who decided to come!" Monique drowned out the end of Devon's sentence. She pulled Hope into a firm hug. "Ready for next week?"

Hope's smile hurt her cheeks, but she couldn't tone it down. "I can't wait."

"You already fit right in."

Hope got the fleeting sense that she'd forgotten something important but lost the thread when Monique flashed Devon a dazzling smile.

"You gonna paint my bathroom this year?"

"I'm patching it today, but Hope insisted that I come to this first."

"Good for her. You need to eat your beans and greens for luck."

"Yes, ma'am."

"Devon didn't tell me there would be such a big turnout. There are so many people here, Monique."

The counselor eyed Devon. "I suspect he didn't know."

"But," Hope looked between the two of them. "I thought you all did this every year?"

"They do, but this is my first one," Devon mumbled.

Monique's expression softened. "This time of year is hard for people." She reached over and squeezed his forearm. Devon tucked his hands behind his back when she released her hold. Hope's brow pinched as he shuffled on his feet. "Gotta make sure they remember they aren't alone," Monique went on, with thinly-veiled concern. "You know Cleary's Christmas Eve parties inspired this.

We skip the dancing and drinking, but people still come. Oh!" Her face lit up as her gaze fixed on the door behind them. "Here's someone I want you to meet."

Hope turned to see a Black woman striding into the room, her face framed by dozens of tiny braids. "Officer Neely," she said.

The woman smiled at Hope as she put an arm around Monique. "*Detective* Neely. Hey, Mom."

"Detective?" Hope said. Neely grinned and nodded.

"You two know each other?" Monique asked.

"*Detective* Neely comes into the shop sometimes." Hope gestured to Neely with a flourish and a smile. "Congratulations on the promotion, Detective."

"Well, I call her Imani." Monique looked delighted in the way only a proud mother could.

"Aaron's partner." Devon's unease vanished as he crossed his arms and inched up his chin.

Neely arched a brow. "You must be Devon. For the record, I was never Aaron's partner; we just used to work the same areas pretty often. Currently, he hates me because I got what he wanted. Can't say I'm sad about it."

Devon relaxed his stance and chuckled. "Sounds like we have some things in common."

"Just a bit."

"Is it good or bad that you already know who I am?"

"Mostly good. Why, is there something I should know?"

"Pretty sure I have the right to remain silent."

"That's the first time I've heard that joke...today." Neely laughed, sounding like her mother. "Don't worry. I came for lunch." She squeezed her arm around her mom's shoulders.

"Now, that's what I want to hear." Monique rubbed her palms together. "Go get a plate. You two should eat too, before those cookies are gone."

"There's a mountain of them," Devon said.

Monique chuckled. "Ah... look again."

"Wha...?" He stopped short at the sight of the platter; the *mountain* of cookies reduced to a single spotty layer. "How is that even possible? That was like...a million cookies."

"Clearly, you've never had one of Betty's cookies." Hope tugged him toward the table and snatched two before they vanished. "Here, guard these with your life." She pushed the treasures into his hand.

She poured soda into a paper cup and handed that over too, then piled a plate with beans, greens, cornbread, and various delicacies ranging from coleslaw to fruit salad.

"Let's find a spot," she said.

He studied the room again. "On the floor?"

"That or we could lean over there against the wall." She pointed. "I don't mind either way."

"Let's get in a corner, so no one tramples you." He stepped into the throng with dogged determination. Hope fought the urge to roll her eyes.

They ran into a guy named Josh on the way. He had *Locker Room*—the men's support group Devon attended bi-weekly—written all over him. Stiff, uncomfortable, unlike the Ladies Night and Survivors Circle members with whom Hope was already acquainted.

It broke her heart that many of the guys had such a hard time connecting. A staggering amount of social conditioning lay between them and healing—something they would each have to dig out from under before they could begin the climb toward *whole*. Little boys forbidden to cry grew into men who lacked the ability. By the time they hit adolescence, half of them had no idea how to safely offload feelings.

They knew how to bury a thing and let it rot, though.

They knew how to light the fuse and watch it explode.

Hope chewed her lip, staring at the back of Devon's head. The urge to roll her eyes shifted into something else.

When they reached the corner, Hope lowered herself to the floor. Devon followed her down and balanced the cookies on his knee. They cleaned the plate in under five minutes, and then, Hope headed for the trashcan. She waved at an arriving Dre as she headed back over to where Devon leaned against the wall—standing now—with most of a cookie crammed in his face.

"This is the best cookie I've ever eaten," he said around the mouthful.

Hope laughed. "Good thing I grabbed you two."

Devon stopped chewing. "I can't eat your cookie."

"I'll get more at group."

His eyes widened. "You're serious? You love me that much?"

Hope leaned close and spoke low in his ear. "I'm letting you eat this cookie now, so you'll eat my other cookie later. I love the way you eat it, Sir. You're so good at it."

Devon coughed, eyes watering and cheeks going crimson. After a few hearty thumps to his chest, he was stepping into her space.

"I take it back." Chocolate and brown sugar breath, mingled with cedar and sandalwood. "This cookie is a distant second. No offense to Betty, of course. My *favorite* cookie... My *very favorite* cookie in the whole wide world—"

"Devon, my man!" Hope caught a case of the giggles, as Dre walked up and clapped a hand on Devon's shoulder. "Didn't expect to see you today."

People kept saying some variation of that, she noticed. Monique, the Josh-guy from the men's support group, and now Dre.

"The warden made me come in here. I wanted to head straight for that hole in the bathroom." Devon smirked. "But she is letting me eat her cookie, so I forgive her." He winked at Hope, adopted a wickedly innocent expression and took a huge bite of *her* cookie. Hope's face went twelve shades of red.

"Hey Dre," she squeaked.

"There's the woman of the hour," Dre said. "Fist bump? Hug?"

"Definitely a hug." Hope opened her arms.

"Next week is the big R&R debut, right?" he asked as he stepped away. "The daytime one, anyway. Are you excited?"

"Yeah, nervous too," she admitted. Devon's hand brushed the small of her back.

"You'll be great. I heard you rocked those groups with Monique. In case you didn't know, we've been desperate for you for years. You are a lifesaver."

"You're too kind, Dre."

"Nah, just honest." His gaze swept the room. "I don't know how Monique does this. Even Baker and Josh came."

"Hold up." Devon cut in. "We ran into Josh, but *Baker*? It took months for him to show up for group consistently."

"I know, right? And he says he'll be at Locker Room tomorrow."

The men's group counselor looked as pleased as Monique; Hope could see why. There was a deep satisfaction in watching everyone talking and smiling together. Scarfing down home-cooked food. Safe. Supported. Even if the guy beside her did so begrudgingly.

"This community is something else," Dre went on, resting a hand on Devon's shoulder. "Monique will be tickled you made it this year. She can check that off her bucket list."

"We already ran into her," Hope said. "Devon got to meet her daughter, and I found out that I already know her."

"Keisha's here?"

Hope shook her head. "Imani."

Dre nodded. "Ah... the new detective. I bet Monique is over the moon. She loves showing off her kids and her work."

"She would've liked it better if I'd finished the bathroom first," Devon said, brushing invisible cookie crumbs from his shirt. "I'm going to head that way, while you talk to everyone," he said to Hope.

Dre forced a laugh. "Can't that wait, man? Eat."

"We did," Devon assured him. "I even had two award-winning cookies."

"Then wind-down for a minute."

"I want it finished tomorrow. Can't paint a hole, so it's getting patched today."

Devon shrugged, shifting sideways. Hope wasn't sure if Dre intentionally put himself between Devon and the door, or if the action was coincidental, but he matched Devon's movement with a smooth step to the side.

"You'll make it to group though, right? I'd rather have you in the meeting this week than have that bathroom painted."

Intentional, she decided, as Devon glanced at her.

"Yeah..." He nodded at Dre. "Shouldn't be a problem."

The counselor grinned. "I'll see you tomorrow, then. I'm going to make the rest of the rounds, see if I can catch Imani before she takes off. Hope, we'll see you bright and early Tuesday morning."

"Wouldn't miss it."

Devon's knuckles grazed her spine, and his chin settled on her shoulder as Dre left.

"I need to get out of here," he said.

Hope turned to face him, looping her arms around his shoulders, as his hands found her waist. "Devon, what's going on?"

"There's a hole—

"That hole has been there over a month. A little longer won't hurt anything."

"Darling..." Devon caught her jaw, turned her head, and kissed her cheek. "You want to visit with everyone; I want to sort out this patch job. I'll come get you when I finish."

Unease crawled through her belly. She ran her fingers over her bracelet at the back of his neck.

"Do you think it will take long?"

"Mmm... Not too long." He pressed a kiss to her forehead.

"Okay."

Devon gave a curt nod and then beelined for the door. With nothing better to do, Hope moved through the crowd, looking for familiar faces. She grabbed another paper cup and filled it with soda, wondering where her mood was coming from. Hormones? Seemed a tad hormonal...

Idling beside Betty's empty platter, she pulled out her phone and navigated to her period app. She frowned at the notification predicting the Sunday arrival of the red tide. *PMS week. Fabulous.* She'd get to bleed right through her first R&R shift. She sighed.

"Hope!"

She looked up to find a middle-aged woman with a perfect-ly executed balayge, hand-knit sweater, and designer jeans, flag-ging her down. *Laura.* Hope knew her from the Survivors Circle group that Monique hosted every other Thursday. Laura was one of R&R's few clients who could afford to pay Sydney's normal rates, proving that while financial security might be an excellent deterrent for trauma, nothing was foolproof. With a disturbing lack of support available, victims of the sort of crimes that R&R specialized in ended up in the same boat, despite the differences in their day-to-day lives. Kind of a crappy way to meet people outside of your social circle.

"Hey, Laura. Ben." Hope inclined her head.

Standing behind his wife, Ben nodded and smiled.

"Monique told us that you brought your boyfriend." Laura ratcheted her brows up to her hairline and grinned. The expression struck Hope as carefree; something she doubted the woman could have managed a year prior. "We have to meet him."

"Oh, well... he brought me, technically."

Actually, without Devon, she would have never made her way to R&R at all. The nonprofit was another example of one of his spaces where Hope had entrenched herself. She rolled her bracelet between her fingers, thinking of Devon on their first date, assuring her that, between the two of them, he had more to lose because he couldn't stop going to Cleary's if he decided to back out.

Now, it wasn't only Cleary's. Hope visited the bar, sure, but she'd gotten a job at the nonprofit that he helped start. She had slept in his bed more often than her own for weeks—at first because Aaron was being Aaron, and then because she didn't want to stop.

What if Devon didn't want something so serious? What if he didn't know how to say that, so he kept carving out moments away from her in the middle of the night or...

"He's, um, patching that wall in the bathroom," Hope said, remembering that Laura and Ben awaited her response. "He volunteers here. I'll introduce you if he makes it back in before we head out."

Because she couldn't leave without him, could she? Devon drove, so he was stuck chauffeuring her home.

Hope mumbled some pleasantries and excused herself. Clutching her paper cup, she meandered between guests. The crushing sensation in her chest swirled and ached, feeling sad and empty and too big for her body, all at once; but it was different from the run of the mill anxiety to which she had grown accustomed, and Hope couldn't put her finger on how or why.

DEVON

This was new.

More than that, this was a BDSM thing, *and* it was new. The surprises kept coming with Hope around.

Devon's *fuck me* moment arrived approximately two seconds after she burst into R&R's bathroom with tears streaming down her face. At first, he stood there, hands dripping into the sink, staring at her like he had no idea what was happening—because he hadn't. He asked her the only thing that came to mind—Aaron's name, barked out as a single word question.

Hope shook her head, managing to look both devastated and ashamed—a state that gutted Devon as he tried to figure out the cause of her distress. It was when she begged him to take her back to her apartment, to her car, that the other possibility popped into his head. Once it did, he kicked himself for not thinking of it sooner.

He wasn't sure how he had extricated her from the building without getting half of R&R involved. Freaking miracle, right there. Try explaining that one to a couple of therapists and a gathering of sexual assault survivors and their loved ones.

Don't worry, I just edged her on the ride home, cuffed her to a horse, spanked her, gave her a few lashes, then bit a full set of dental impressions into her ass, before fucking her senseless. Totally normal. She's fine...

Thanks, but no.

Ignoring the whole lot of warm, slippery, and naked going on down his stomach and between his legs, Devon kissed the crown of her head and wrapped his arms more snuggly around her. Christ, he was an ass.

"I'm fine," Hope said for the sixth time, since the crying stopped.

Devon rested his chin on her shoulder. "You will be."

"You don't have—"

He nipped the curve of her neck, savored her answering shiver. "I want to. What do you want for dinner? We'll have something delivered."

"Anything's fine."

"Italian? Sushi?" he prodded.

"Whatever you want."

Devon suspected there was a silent *sir* at the end of her response. Did he mention he was an ass? He sighed again.

He'd do the pasta-seafood-cream-sauce deal, he decided. Not original, but Hope loved it on their first date; the comfort would do her good. And cheesecake, definitely cheesecake. As soon as he got them out of the tub, he'd put in an order. Assuming the restaurant wasn't closed for the holiday. Devon worried over the possibility briefly, then saved that bridge for later.

"It's sub drop," he said, "or...it's playing a part, anyway." Pulling a curtain of sopping wet hair aside, he kissed the back of her neck.

Devon loved doing that—pressing kisses to all the soft, warm parts of her without stopping to wonder if he could or should. That was new for him, too. He had kissed plenty of lips of the oral and non-oral varieties over the years, but kissing foreheads, shoulders, napes, and knuckles? All new. Every time Devon indulged and she shuddered or sighed in response, he thought that maybe this could be *something*...for a while.

"Another BDSM thing?"

"Yeah." He returned his lips to the curve of her neck because he could. "If subspace is the what-goes-up, drop is the must-come-down. All those hormones and chemicals get dumped in play, but you can't stay up forever."

As he said it, Devon wondered if he had missed her dropping from the start. Hope had already been in a fragile emotional state the first time he'd taken her in the playroom. Aaron left those pictures at her apartment, Silver Sassafras, and the bar—mortified her in front of nearly every important person in her life. If she dropped in the days after that first scene, Devon had overlooked it, assuming Aaron's behavior triggered any dysregulation.

He swore internally. Then, when Hope shifted, and his treacherous cock—not giving a fuck that he had more important concerns—stiffened against her back, he swore for another reason.

"Like a sugar crash?" she asked, innocent as a lamb. He kissed her shoulder.

"Clever little thing. I'm sorry it hit at the luncheon."

"It's okay."

Her words nearly cut off his own in her hurry to placate him. Devon's molars ground together. It wasn't *okay*. It was an oversight, and he had no excuse for it. Devon was more than competent. At Edge, he doled out aftercare with the best of them, especially when playing with someone who didn't have a regular partner taking over when the scene ended. When he had a sub in the playroom, he always got them sorted before they left. He took that responsibility as seriously as safety during a scene—but that was for the *immediate* drop. Shakes, shivers and a need for grounding.

That other drop—the one that could sneak up a day or two later—hadn't crossed his mind because Devon never stayed around long enough to see it. Who put his unattached partners in a hot bath and fed them cheesecake when they dropped? Who tended to the marks he left on more than bodies?

"There's also the depleted reserves thing," he said, pulling himself out of his own dark headspace. "Your body reaches for those chemicals, but you're running on empty. I think that's what happened today."

"That makes sense." She skimmed a hand over the surface of the water. The image of his legs flanking hers distorted with the ripples, while their knees remained a quartet of static islands. "Is there a dominant version of sub drop, or are you all immune?"

That memory of her—battered and begging in his nightmares—flashed in his mind's eye again. His foot slid across the bottom of the tub with a groan. Hope's bum lost traction, sending her forward several inches. She squeaked, bracing a hand on his thigh, as Devon righted himself.

"Sorry," he mumbled, pulling her back against him.

Could that be it? He had never suffered an identifiable case of Top drop...Dom drop...whatever, but he didn't have a better explanation for his desperate desire to get her out of the playroom that first time, nor the sickening nightmares which followed. Even now, exhaustion plagued him; the dreams having returned as soon as he risked it again. It hadn't mattered that he had gotten her up and out of the playroom. Showered, fed, put to bed... Roughly an hour after sleep claimed him, he'd startled awake—covered in sweat, with a throbbing cock and a guilty conscience.

"Not *immune*, exactly."

Hope resumed trailing her hand through the water.

"So, you're curing my deficiencies with a bath?" A welcome playfulness warmed her words and detoured his attention.

"Is it helping?" With the outside of her thighs brushing the inside of his own, and her legs going on for days, Devon's answering question came out more seductively than intended.

"I think so." She nestled closer. "I'm sorry for interrupting you today. I keep doing that."

His brows drew together. "You aren't an interruption."

"But you need to paint tomorrow." She sniffled. "You can't paint a hole; that's what you told Dre."

"That damn wall is miles behind you on my list of priorities." Hope scrunched down, and he sighed. "I was done, anyway," he said. "The only thing you interrupted was some hand washing."

"So, you can paint before group tomorrow?"

She swirled a finger over the water as she spoke, spelling her name. The action had no point beyond her simple pleasure; and unlike his pleasures, it left no trace beyond a few anemic ripples that soon faded as if they had never existed.

Devon inhaled, exhaled.

"That's the plan."

In truth, he had zero desire to get looped into the trauma-porn, bromance situation known as Locker Room this week, but he was painting that bathroom if it killed him.

"Would it help if I came by to let Apollo out? I could pick up dinner."

"I...wouldn't want to put you out," he said, wanting very, very much to put her out if it meant finding her in his house when he got home.

Hope shrugged, her shoulder blades slipping against his chest. Devon's heart pounded into her back. Why was he so nervous?

"You're feeding me tonight. It's the least I can do. I can head home after—"

"No, stay," he said. "Stay tomorrow. It doesn't make sense driving home that late when you could sleep here."

"I thought you needed a break from me."

His brow furrowed. "You thought that I needed *a break* from *you*."

The back of her head canted away from him an inch as she dropped her chin. "Maybe? I don't know."

"Hope..."

"Then I somehow got around to thinking I shouldn't be at R&R. I'm only there because of you. You drive me around, let me sleep over, feed me half of the time. I got a job at your nonprofit—"

"Whoa. Cleary's is mine; R&R isn't." He sighed, stroking a thumb down her bare arm. "I fix the occasional leak, but you...you can help people heal. You're meant to be there." He squeezed her. "They need you more than they've ever needed me. You are going to be a perfect fit."

Hope jerked and rolled, water racing from one side of the tub to the other, as she settled against him—belly to belly, with his now annoyingly rock-hard erection sandwiched between them. Devon's breath came out in a hiss, but the look on her face distracted him from that fact in an instant.

"Hope, what's wrong?"

Her eyes widened with panic. "That's what I forgot."

"What?"

"The suit fitting for Ashley's wedding!"

Devon tucked a strand of wet hair behind her ear. "I thought they pushed that back."

"They did. It was supposed to be last week, but one of the groomsmen went out of town for Christmas. They moved it to Thursday."

Devon blinked down at her, pieces of her frantic babbling tumbling into place. "*The-day-after-tomorrow* Thursday?"

"Yes! Oh shit. Shit. Shit. Shit." She started to push up from him, so Devon wrapped his arms around her waist. "I was supposed to find someone, and I freaking forgot."

"Okay, don't panic. You've had a ton going on. You've been working full-time at the shop, while doing groups with Monique, plus the holidays." He didn't mention her now-quiet stalker, though Aaron hovered, ever-present on Devon's own list of concerns. "We'll figure it out."

"How? I have two days! I told my mom to get rid of Aaron. I told her I would find someone."

She looked up at him, anxious eyes the color of a calm sea, and Devon cursed the problem that had her riled up all over again.

"Let's think. Do you have any cousins?"

Hope shook her head. "Ashley has a cousin, but he's already in the wedding. The rest of the guys are Greg's friends."

"Chloe?"

She laughed. "There's no way. Mom wants that traditional *guys in suits* and *women in dresses* nonsense."

"Hmm...What about your brother?"

Hope tilted her head as she considered it. "I mean... I guess it could work. Ashley's met him several times and likes him well enough. My mom would hate it, but at least he wouldn't be you."

"Really, darling?"

She cringed. "Sorry."

Devon pressed his lips to her forehead, chuckling. "I'm kidding, love. Why don't you ask him tomorrow? Stop by the shop after work. You're hard to say no to, in person."

"Am I?" She caught her lower lip between her teeth, and Devon became very aware of his erection again.

"If he can't make it work," he managed, "I'll leave Lucas alone for a few hours, and go make a terrible impression on your mother."

"Thank you." She inched up his torso.

"For what?"

Rosy-pink painted her cheeks and the tip of her nose—likely from her earlier tears as much as the heat of the bath. Warm lips brushed his. Devon's cock had a heartbeat.

"For always trying to give me what I need."

"Do you feel better?" he asked, lids going hooded as she nodded her response. "Then, roll over." His voice sounded husky in his own ears. A tiny V appeared between her brows, her head tilting. "This is where you say *yes, sir.*"

"Yes, Sir," she said, doing as he ordered.

Devon looped an arm around her and pulled her into his lap. With his other hand, he parted her knees, flexing his own up between until she sat, spread wide, with his cock nestled snuggly in the valley of her ass cheeks. Hope squirmed atop him, tightening his sack with flashes of pleasure.

He looked down her wet body, watched the rise and fall of her breasts as water ran off her in rivulets. Her nipples budded in the cool air, tempting him. Reaching around, he rolled one pebbled tip between a thumb and forefinger. Her breath caught.

"You'll feel better after this," he promised.

"A...after what, Sir?"

He chuckled at her incessant curiosity, pinching until she sucked in air. His other hand rested lazily on her hip. "After you come for me."

She started doing that delightful panting thing—the one that betrayed her crumbling composure. Devon loved that sound.

"Show me," he said against her ear. "Show me the naughty things you do when you think of me."

The wordless sound she made was simultaneously needy and embarrassed. Devon's head canted; Demon's probably did too.

"It's not a suggestion, darling."

"Okay, Sir." Her hand inched lower, rippling the water, before she froze. A protest bloomed on her lips as prettily as the color on her cheeks. "I don't think..."

"Did I tell you to think?"

"N...no, Sir."

"You want to show me," Devon said, "because you're a good girl. *My* good girl." Her panting shifted to a stilted inhale, her breath catching before its ragged release. Oh yeah, he thought, his greedy little darling was *so* into this. "Let's start small. Touch it a little, for me."

Soft limits earned their name; tie a ribbon of trust around a few *my's* and *for me's*, and they turned to putty. Hope swallowed, trailing her fingertips over her mound. The water alternately distorted, then magnified Devon's view, teasing him.

"Use your words," he said into the shell of her ear. "Tell me how it feels."

"Soft. Smooth. *Tingly*."

Breathy voice; whispered words.

Saliva pooled in his mouth. He imagined hoisting her onto the rim of the tub, scooping his tongue through that delectable cunt and slurping down everything dripping from her—while she writhed and squealed.

"Are you a wet kitten?"

Hope chortled. "I'm in a bathtu— *Ow!*" He tightened his hold on her nipple, digging into her supple flesh without mercy. She bucked.

"Careful," Devon warned. "Smart mouths earn punishments." There was no hiding his heady delight in the prospect, with his cock pulsing like mad. Christ, he wanted her to fuck up way more than he should—a sentiment that never seemed to fade.

"I'm sorry, Sir."

Hope collapsed back against him; Devon stopped torturing her nipple.

"That's better, but I think I should check for you." He slid the hand on her hip between her legs, probing her pussy as she mewled. "Oh, yes... Just as I suspected. You are wetter than this tub, baby." He loved the viscous slide of her thick juices on his fingers. Unable to help himself, Devon shifted his hips, feeling the slip of her ass against his cock. "And definitely slicker," he added, returning his hand to her hip. Hope whimpered, as his fingers left her heat.

"Now, be a good girl, and show me," he repeated. "I want to see how you touch yourself, when I'm not around to do it for you."

"Okay, Sir."

Head resting back on his shoulder, Hope reached for her clit. Devon's heavy breaths washed over her chest, further tightening her nipples under his gaze. She rubbed her fingers over the nub, wincing.

"Are you sore?" He rolled his lower lip between his teeth, craving her response.

"Not bad," she said, breathing deeply as she got into it. "From last night. The good kind of sore."

Devon's cock twitched at the reminder, aching to bend her over and pound into her like he had in the playroom.

"Can I use both hands, Sir?"

"Fuck, yes," he said on an exhale, ravenous eyes fixed on the show.

Her other hand slipped beneath the water and spread her labia. Possibilities ricocheted through his brain. Clamps and crops. Teeth. Fucking toothpaste. Pull back her hood and run his tongue over her until tears streamed down her face, and she begged him to stop using every word except the one Demon would obey...

But Hope only rubbed in rhythmic circles. *One, two, three, pause. One, two, three, pause...* Devon found himself curious about the vastness that had to lay between their thoughts. Hope was keeping time, while he was fantasizing ways to torture her clit, for fuck's sake.

"What's in that pretty head?"

"I... uh..." She licked her lips, panted. "That time in your office, when you wanted to teach me a lesson, so you wouldn't let me come... The way you grab my throat when you fuck me. Your *teeth.*" She gritted her own, and Devon's brows rose in surprise. "When you spank me, or flog me, and I *hate* it," Hope ground out, rubbing faster. Nothing about her body language aligned with those words, and that dichotomy set his blood on fire. "Except, I don't want you to stop," she cried, "and I don't understand why."

She might not know why, but Demon did.

"Slower," he ordered, his voice taking on that other timbre.

With the flushed heat of her feverish skin against him, and the desperation in her movements, her words, Devon couldn't help himself. He wrapped one arm around her waist as Hope slowed her ministrations, her legs trembling against his own. Snaking his other hand up to grip her throat, Devon rocked her body up and down, his cock sandwiched between her cheeks and his lower belly. He could come like this, he realized. It wouldn't even be hard. Pump her body like a rag doll and spurt up her back.

"Such a good girl," he purred, squeezing harder, fearing that if he loosened his hold, he might slip inside her bare.

Devon didn't know how long he'd last if that happened—with Hope spread and needy atop him, massaging her clit like he ordered. His obedient little fucktoy. Would he make it minutes? Unlikely. *Seconds* seemed the better bet at present, and given the taut nature of her under-utilized ass, Devon suspected that any such slip would land him in the hole that came with consequences.

Fuck, he'd love it, though. Ram himself into her, feeling every glorious stroke in high-def, before shooting his load somewhere near her goddamn diaphragm. Get in her so fucking deep that she had to swallow him back down when he finished.

Devon was full-on bouncing her now—the water coalescing into a single rolling wave that lapped up the far end of the tub before sluicing back over her glistening breasts on repeat. The sights... The sensations... The way she whimpered with need, while he sated his own... Too much.

An electric buzz tightened his balls, climbed up his spine with the promise of ecstasy. He could stop using her like a fleshlight and make this last, but she felt so goddamn good that the hedonistic bastard in him laughed at that idea.

"May I come, Sir? I need to come!"

The need in her voice—as razor-sharp as his own—undid him. But the way she *begged*? Even Demon hit his knees.

"Oh fuck, yes. Come for me, kitten. Come for me, like a good little slut," Devon managed, thrusting hard against her.

Hope's body arched. Her legs stiffened and toes curled. Devon felt the muscles of her thighs, ass, and back clench, as they slipped against his own. His spend exploded up her lower-back, smearing between them.

Good little slut...

My darling girl...

Mine...

Mine...

Mine.

HOPE

Shoving down another intrusive thought of the night before, Hope opened the door to *Inky Things*, the tattoo studio her brother owned. She didn't need the memories bouncing around her brain while visiting JJ because...*eww*. But given her inability to squash them during her shift at Silver Sassafras, she didn't anticipate them dissipating now. Even as her geriatric coworker, Francis, incessantly complained about the dreary weather, Hope hadn't stopped sporadically shuddering with remembered pleasure. At one point, Francis asked if she were coming down with something...what with the red cheeks and all.

Hope waved at Layla, the purple-haired woman with acres of ink at the desk.

"It's going to be April before he has that kind of opening," Layla said into the phone propped on her shoulder as she mouthed *Oh, hey!* at Hope. Her fingers flew over the keys of a laptop wallpapered in faded tattoo flash.

Hope headed down the hallway, toward JJ's room. She leaned against the jamb, thinking of the person she had been falling asleep beside more often than not for the last month. She and Devon had fostered deep intimacy and vulnerability in such a short time, but that sort of fast attachment came with drawbacks. Like a blade without proper tempering, it carried the risk of snapping without warning—a failure that usually happened under pressure, when you needed it most.

She had to stop inviting herself to sleep in his bed. Devon could let his own dog out; he'd been doing it for years.

"Uh... Hey, sis?" JJ's white-blond brows pulled together. Hope blinked at the sight in front of her—her brother leaning over a sprawling back, tattoo gun in hand.

"Oh JJ, I'm so sorry." She turned and side-stepped out of the doorway, but it was too late. She'd walked right in without considering the privacy of his client.

"Fine with me if you wanna come in," a gruff voice said. "I'm not shy."

"You're good, Hope," her brother, past his initial surprise, called. "Matt doesn't give a damn. Hope, Matt. Matt, Hope. She's my sister, so don't get any ideas."

Hope eased into the room and chose a spot against the wall, while Matt chuckled. She couldn't see his face, but she had an eyeful of the lush vegetation, interspersed with patches of line work covering him from shoulders to waistband as he straddled the specially designed chair.

"JJ, huh?" came the rumbling voice again.

"Jameson to you, unless you want me to get sloppy back here. I have a reputation to maintain." Mechanical buzzing signaled his return to work. "So has Aaron tried anything stupid since the last time I saw you?" he asked, never diverting his gaze from his living canvas.

"That was Monday."

"And now it's Wednesday."

"Are you going to ask about him every time I see you?"

Her brother's blue eyes flicked up to her then back down. "If you show up unannounced at my studio, I'm going to start at the top and work my way down. Stalker first."

Hope eyed the stranger. Deciding that Matt Whoever-he-was was probably safe enough if JJ trusted him, she answered her brother.

"Still good."

"I didn't expect him to let up." JJ dabbed a gauze to Matt's back, before putting his needle into a well of vibrant red ink.

"He isn't stupid. He knows what he can get away with, and he sticks to that unless he's pushed."

Her brother cleared his throat and homed in on a hibiscus. "At least this solves the issue with your mom. You can't be in a wedding with someone you're threatening to... What's the threat?"

Hope shrugged, fingering the hem of her pullover before reaching for her bracelet. "An order of protection, if I could get it. Reporting the stalking and harassment. Any of it could be a problem for him with his job."

JJ didn't know about the pictures. For some reason, Hope would rather tell Back-Tat-Matt about them than her brother.

"Things good with Cleary?" JJ asked, inking life into the unfinished flower on Matt's shoulder blade.

At the mention of him, Hope flashed straight back to the memory of Devon humping her ass like a rutting animal while she rubbed one out. Hormones, man. Distracting buggers.

"Uh, yeah."

JJ nodded. "He working?"

"He worked the bar this morning, and he's painting at the nonprofit this afternoon," she said. "I'm taking takeout over to his place after I leave here." JJ raised his head and popped his brows. "It's not a big deal," Hope said. "Keeps him from having to run home in between for the dog."

Her brother shook his head. "Rolling right along, aren't you?" he said on a rhetorical. "I like the guy, and your mom will shit when you tell her you're walking down the aisle at Ashley's wedding with him. Does she know yet?" He grinned with a satisfaction Hope could feel in her bones. JJ didn't know her mother well, but he found her as frustrating as Hope did—and without the obligation-inducing blood tie.

"Well, that's a problem. She's made it crystal clear that she can't have a stranger in the family photos."

"Lopsided wedding party it is. There's no fucking way Aaron's walking you," JJ all but spat.

"There's one other option." Hope watched her brother press his mouth into a tight line while he worked. "Any chance you're off tomorrow afternoon?"

He chuckled. "Is the wedding tomorrow?"

She forced a strained smile. "The suit fitting is."

Unfamiliar laughter reminded Hope that her brother's canvas was attached to a human. JJ pulled his hands away, as Matt vibrated with boyish giggles.

"What's so damn funny?" JJ asked.

"I could be wrong," Matt said between fits, "but it sounds like Mom wants your sister to be in a wedding with a guy that's stalking her. And she's dating a bartender that the old broad wouldn't approve of, but sis thinks fucking *Jameson James, of Inky Things,* is going to suit up and stand in... Like that's going to be better! Man, y'all got some bullshit going on." He sucked in a breath and shook his head.

"But wait, Matt," JJ said to the back of his head. "There's more. Her stalker ex is a cop, who followed her here when she moved, and her mother is my stepfather's ex-wife."

"So, Miss Hope here's not really your—"

"Shut your mouth, Matt." JJ swiped away smeared ink; Matt sucked in a breath. "Hope's mom married into silver spoons and doesn't like her perfection bubble popped—ever. She *loves* the fine upstanding pig, even though Hope booted him a year ago; and they both *hate* me." JJ grinned. "What time is the fitting?"

Hope cringed. "Six?" An evening favor was more than a minor sacrifice to a guy who owned a busy tattoo studio.

"Layla!" JJ called. Footsteps echoed in the hallway, and a head of amethyst pinup curls popped into view.

"Whatcha need, babe?"

JJ glanced up at her, then refocused on Matt's jungle. "Call that three-hour block I have tomorrow and see if they can push it up an hour, then call the two-hour after them and ask them to push it back an hour. I need to ingratiate myself to my sister by tormenting her mother."

"I got you." Layla turned toward the sound of a ringing phone and disappeared again.

Hope sighed in relief. "Thank you."

Her brother made a *pshhh* sound. "I'll wear a monkey suit to piss off your mom. Keeping Aaron away from you is icing. But check with Ashley so we don't crash her wedding stuff. She's cool. I bet she'll be fine with it."

"I owe you one."

"You have to go with me tomorrow though. I'm not hanging out with your mother by myself."

"It's the suit fitting. She wouldn't—"

"You know she'll be there putting her two cents in." He caught his lip between his teeth and pulled a line, nodding. "I'm an artist, Matt. You are so damn lucky." Matt snickered. "Bring coffee."

"At six in the evening?"

Her brother nodded. "I'd like to preemptively ward off the headache that is Beth Barrow."

"It'll take more than caffeine to counter my mother," Hope said.

DEVON

Fuck Dre. Fuck his creepy therapist sixth-sense and his annoying need to make sure everyone got the support they needed, whether they wanted it or not. While he was at it, fuck Baker too.

Devon had spent several hours at the bar, on the pretense of clerical bullshit, before dragging his feet through two neat coats of pale blue behind an *Out of Order* sign at Redact and Recover. He had a plan. Carefully crafted and beautifully executed, right up until Dre stuck his head in the door five minutes before Locker Room's scheduled start.

Given that Devon had been sitting on the immaculate counter, scrolling his phone, all of his supplies cleaned and organized in the corner, he'd lacked an excuse to miss group. Admitting that he didn't want to attend meant explaining *why*, so he'd gone to the stupid meeting, even though he knew better.

Devon shook his head as he passed under a traffic light.

"Christ, I'm such an asshole."

Dre was not the problem. Neither was Baker, the thirty-something volunteer firefighter, with dead eyes and anger management issues. Baker's only sin was showing up to group, leaking the same emotions that they all shoved down daily—which was the point of a support group. Baker was processing shit. Painful, *painful* shit that tied Devon's head in messy knots that no set of shears would ever gnaw through.

Devon didn't need Baker's description of warm lips pressed to cold or the futility of chest compressions on a corpse. He'd *lived* it. The firefighter's desperation tasted as bitter on Devon's tongue as his own had that day on Kelly's bedroom floor. He'd do almost anything to make that sensation go away.

His attention snagged on the massive, beige warehouse that housed Edge as it flitted past the passenger side window. He bristled.

Nothing stopping you from—

"Not that."

Wetting his lips, he accelerated. Then, remembering that he was a mess and Hope was waiting for him at home, he down-shifted. The engine whined its submission.

It wasn't that Edge was bad, only that Devon sucked at being good for extended periods of time. Especially when he had a head full of things better off ignored. The dungeon offered mental and physical distraction without judgment or obligation. More fulfilling than anything in his basement; less-complicated than what he shared with Hope.

Edge could be anonymous, if he wanted. No one asked why he wasn't sleeping after a scene or what had him so edgy. No one asked if he was okay. Devon was Demon there. Negotiate, dominate; rinse, repeat. Tonight, the prospect of letting his darker side out to play, to test if it could work again, enticed him more than it should; but only because it was January, and Baker had a dead fiancée. He didn't *need* to go.

One fast scene. In and out.

"It doesn't even work."

It does for a while…

"No."

Maybe Hope was right, and this *trigger* kept popping up for him because he did everything in his power to avoid dealing with it. What if he…talked to her instead? *Really* talked to her, in the way Nix kept pushing. Even if it didn't work, with the anniversary of his sister's suicide fast-approaching, and Devon's historically negative reactions to that grim milestone, his girlfriend deserved more warning than a passing mention of Kelly having been assaulted on New Year's Eve.

"Can we talk?" he said, almost silently. "Christ… That sounds like the breakup talk."

Maybe if he had a drink, he thought, hands tensing on the wheel. A few shots of liquid courage to get the story about Baker's fiancée out of his head and loosen his tongue. The idea triggered a memory of his father's ruddy cheeks. Of Hope's ass the last time he'd flogged her. His sister's bottle-red hair, his mom's red-rimmed eyes. A montage of *red*.

The steering wheel groaned.

"Jesus fucking Christ. It's been years and has nothing to do with her. Get the fuck over it, you worthless…" He trailed off, swallowing another man's words.

Pulling in a slow breath, he tried again. "You know how I told you that I'd let you know if I needed to talk? Well, I think I do."

He hadn't even spoken to her yet, but the tiniest scrap of tension drained from his limbs. The shift was marginal, the effect consuming. Parking beside Hope's Prius, he got out, and headed for the porch, his steps lighter, despite the weight in his chest. If he gave her the invitation, she'd guide the conversation. Hold his hand until he got somewhere better. She was good at that sort of thing.

The outside light wasn't on, so the sliver of light between the door and the jamb stood out like a neon sign. Devon's stomach lurched as he took the stairs at a jog. Glancing at the disengaged deadbolt, he pressed a fingertip against the flat plane of the door. The latch gave with a quiet, metallic, scraping sound. He stepped into an empty living room.

"Hope?"

Devon turned toward a rustling in the hallway, but instead of Hope, Apollo loped into view and plopped down beside him. His heart rate doubled.

"Hope?" he called again, locking the front door.

"Where is she, buddy?"

Apollo stared up at him, silent. Passing a hand over the dog's head, Devon moved deeper into the house. Walking to the patio door, he found it locked tight. She wasn't in the kitchen either, but her keys, purse, and two takeout bags sat on the counter, the contents warm. Aaron hadn't bothered her in weeks; she had to be here somewhere.

Baker did chest compressions so hard that Nina's ribs cracked. You're big enough to crack ribs now, aren't you?

"Hope!"

He moved back through the living room and down the hall, passing the closed playroom door, the open door of the guest bath, before entering his bedroom. Apollo's tags jangled behind him, like his nerves. Devon stood in the emptiness for an agonizing second, heat flushing his face and ears. Then, it was a handful of quick strides to the master bathroom, flipping on another light and peering into another empty room.

"Hope!"

Apollo side-stepped out of his way, as Devon sprinted to the playroom. Flinging the door open on a room dark as pitch, an icy chill sluiced over his skin. All semblance of his control crumbled, and her name tore from his throat loud enough to startle the neighbors.

"HOPE!"

Devon had been so consumed by his own thoughts of that ridiculous anniversary that he'd grown complacent over the real, present threat to the only thing that mattered. If Hope wasn't in this house he'd—

A rhythmic thumping noise, soft and muted, reached his ears, followed by the opening of a door. Devon bolted, skidding to a halt in the living room as Hope emerged from the basement with a basket of towels propped on her hip.

"Hey, what's all the yelling about?"

He stared at her, panting. Her smile switched off like a light bulb, and blue-green eyes caressed a path from his face to his feet.

"Devon, what's wrong? Did something—"

"What are you doing?"

Hope gestured to the basket, as if it should be obvious. "Um... laundry? I figured I'd run a couple of loads so you didn't have to do it when you got home. Did you know that your basement is basically a noisy sauna? Between the furnace and..."

Soaking in the details of her flushed cheeks, the baggy t-shirt she'd snatched from his drawer, Devon lost track of her words. Laundry... He had panicked that she was missing or worse, while she was downstairs, wearing his clothes, folding his fucking towels.

Hope's brow pinched. "Are you okay?"

"You didn't shut the door."

Her gaze shifted that direction as he said it, then she shrugged.

"Oh, sorry. After I went to see JJ, I picked up the food. Apollo wanted out as soon as I got here. I already fed him, so don't let him convince you otherwise. I guess I forgot to finish locking up after I set everything down. JJ said he can do the wedding thing, by the way, and Ashley is fine with it. I'm going to the fitting tomorrow, so he doesn't have to deal with my mom alone."

Devon didn't give a damn if her brother walked her down the aisle naked, while Apollo ate a metric-fuck-ton of fillet. The door was the problem.

"You have to shut the door, darling. You have to lock it."

"Okay..." Hope chuckled. "It's shut now, right? Are you hungry? I got Pad Thai." She walked past him, dropping the basket of towels on the couch.

Over the armrest.

No, over the knee. Feel her body jerk.

Devon's boots inched wider as parts of him too close to the surface demanded her attention. Every other thought in his head, the things he needed to tell her, turned to dust. Reaching out, he hooked a finger through the bracelet he'd given her for Christmas and tugged. Hope stared at the point of connection, fighting a smile that Demon wanted to wipe off her face.

"Your ex was stalking you as recently as a few weeks ago. The locks are a priority."

"He was annoying me more than stalking me," she said, "and right now, dinner is the priority."

Devon imagined her bracelet five inches longer and fastened around her pretty little throat. Maybe yanking *that* would get her attention.

"It sounds like we have different priorities," he said. "How about we see who comes out on top?"

A seductive grin spread across Hope's face.

"Threatening me with a good time, Sir?"

Her expression shifted to delighted surprise as he snatched her.

"Devon!" She squealed, but he was already dropping into a chair, wrestling her down across his lap. "What are you doing?" She giggled.

"Making sure you rememb...*errr.*" He grunted as her elbow grazed his balls.

A few jumbled moments later, Devon had her draped over one knee, his other leg running across her thighs to keep her from flailing. His forearm ran the length of her upper spine—elbow between her shoulder blades, hand restraining her wrists at her lower back. A thin layer of sweat cooled on his skin, while his dick jabbed her flank through his jeans. Shoving her pants down revealed the fading flogger stripes and bite mark he'd left on New Year's Eve. Hope twisted in his hold.

"Are you going to *spank me* for forgetting the locks?"

"No." Devon rubbed a hand over her bare ass, traced his own teeth prints with his fingertips. "I'm going to spank you for scaring the shit out of me."

"Not if I stop you," she said.

Devon chuckled. "You won't."

He counted to three in his head on the off-chance that she surprised him, then brought a hand down on her creamy backside with a vicious smack. Hope shrieked, the sound skidding along his nerves, smoothing the chaotic static that had arced beneath his skin a moment prior. He exhaled his relief.

She was there. She was safe. She was his enough to squeal for him.

"Hush, now. You're being all mouthy and bratty. You need this as much as I need to give it to you. Say it."

Some of the tension ebbed out of her, her abs relaxing against his thigh. "I need it, Sir."

Devon nodded, popped her again—the kind of swat that left marks on top of marks.

"You can use the handprints I leave on your ass to size my next set of bag gloves. I'll need them, after I finish working off how terrified I was when you *didn't fucking answer*."

"Sorry, Sir," she whimpered.

His laugh felt a tad unhinged, a little far away; and Devon should be wary of that, but he had to get his point across first.

"Not enough, but I'll fix that," he ground out. "Lock the door, Hope."

Impact number three followed a moment later, and with it, her vocalizations changed pitch. The frenetic staccato of unadulterated pain faded, leaving something new in its wake. Something *delicious*.

"Lock the goddamn door."

Devon's hand crashed into her rear on a tireless quest to drag that magic out of her—all while he reminded her of what got her over his knee in the first place.

Lock the fucking door.

Hope's husky, keening voice spoke of potent pleasure threaded through her pain. Even when her body jerked and his hand hurt like hell, that underlying moan told Devon everything he needed to know.

Not enough.

"Pants off. Get up here," he growled, shoving his jeans down as Hope scampered to her feet.

She left the pajama pants in the floor, then straddled him. Devon grabbed her hips as she descended, aligning his cock to her entrance and groaning when she sank to his balls. Slick... so damn slick.

"Don't move."

"Yes, Sir," she stammered, eyes glassy.

"I need you to listen, darling." He hooked a hand behind her neck and pulled her forehead to his. "I need you to obey."

This was pushing it. Hope had no issue kneeling for him or calling him *sir*, but something defiant flashed in her eyes at his blatant use of the word *obey*. It faded as his cock twitched against her walls. Hope's lips parted, her breath mingling with his own, and he had her.

"When I'm not with you," he said, feeling his own pulse thrum inside her, "your first priority is your safety. If I'm not there, I am trusting you to take care of that for me. Understood?"

"Yes, Sir."

Her voice, breathy with restraint, sent the last pint of blood in his body racing for his pelvis. Hope arched her back in answer, further tightening his balls.

"Fuck. I said don't move," he gritted.

"I'm sorry, Sir. I can't help it."

Hope rolled her lower lip between her teeth, and all Devon could see was her mouth. Her warm, wet mouth which *wasn't* a landing strip for her uterus, when he couldn't reach the condoms.

"Then get off."

Her eyes went wide, and her pussy tightened around him.

"Wh... what?"

"If you can't follow orders like a good girl, you'll get on your knees like a bad one." He hooked his arms under hers and plopped her on the floor as he pushed to his feet. Burying his fingers in her hair for control, he pressed the head of his cock to her lips. "Don't make me ask."

Hope opened her mouth on what might have been a gasp, but it didn't matter. Devon slipped in the moment there was an opening.

"Apologize again," he said, watching his cock disappear down her throat.

Hope gagged something that sounded like *guy gant*, so Devon thrust harder, watching tears gather along her lower lashes.

"I don't fucking care. Apologize for bouncing on my cock like a fucking whore, two seconds after scaring me half to death, and one second after I told you to sit still."

His tone was rough—more Demon than Devon. Hope's eyes rolled back, and she pressed her thighs together, which did nothing to calm him. Spit trailed to the front of her stolen t-shirt, leaving dark spots on the heather grey fabric, while Hope mumbled incoherent words around his shaft in a ceaseless stream of apologetic submission. Everything about her was addictive, and Devon found himself chasing something he couldn't name—something so much more than an orgasm.

"Don't you swallow. Don't you dare swallow, and don't lose a drop, understood?"

She nodded around him, tears streaming, squirming her ass against her heels. Devon slammed deep until electricity inched up his spine; then, he pulled her head back and came on her tongue. Hope kept her lips around him, tongue laving his tip for the last drops. As soon as he pulled out, Devon caught her jaw in his hand and tipped her chin up.

"Not until I tell you," he said, panting.

Hope nodded and blinked up at him, as Demon faded into the background, leaving Devon staring down at his girlfriend—cheeks flushed and a mouthful of cum.

"I need you safe more than anything in this world, darling. So, I need you to lock the door. After you swallow, you're going to tell me that you understand how important that is."

To his pleasant surprise she linked her hands in her lap and nodded again, waiting for a firmer command before cleansing her palate.

"You try so hard to be good, don't you?" Hope's puffy mouth quirked up in a smile. "You may swallow in three... two... one."

Her throat bobbed on cue; she licked her lips, and said, "I'm so sorry for forgetting to lock the door, Sir. I promise to be more careful."

HOPE

"**Y**ou are my favorite brother."

Hope handed JJ a to-go cup of mocha something-or-other, as she bumped her car door closed with a hip. Halfway through the action, she wondered if the marks on her bum might protest, but they didn't. Hope smiled, thinking of the watercolor bruising, the purple impressions of Devon's teeth, and lingering dappled spots from the tips of the flogger tails that she'd collected in recent days. She had spent her shift at Silver Sassafras distracted by the thought of those marks, by the confusing sense of pride they instilled. Eventually, she got brave enough to snap a few secret pictures in the restroom but deleted them ten minutes later, when she thought of Aaron and his envelopes.

"I'm your only brother," JJ said, leaning against the passenger-side of his SUV. "Which is why I'm stuck at a suit fitting for *your* family wedding." The streetlight illuminated his hair and face a ghostly white as he sipped his coffee.

"Thank you for doing this for me," Hope said again.

"Come on." Her brother grinned. "Let's get it over with."

The shop sat in a strip mall storefront. Nothing said *high-end* like a strip mall. The sky had cleared after lunch, but they dodged puddles on the way to the door. An artificial holiday tree stood in front of the curtained off window, its sagging garland begging for retirement.

JJ scowled at the wonky decorations. "Are you sure we're at the right place?"

Hope reread the sign up top. "Right name and address."

"Yeah, but *your mom* chose..." He gestured to the unlikely destination. Hope shrugged. "Okay, then." JJ pulled open the door. "After you, ma'am."

They entered an expanse of gleaming floors and mahogany woodwork. Expressionless mannequins dripped fashion, under lighting that made the existence of Photoshop gratuitous.

"Swanky," JJ murmured.

"Never judge a book," Hope replied, wishing she had changed out of the sweater and jeans she wore to work and into something more appropriate—like a ball-gown.

"Welcome to the Golden Cuff." An older man in a suit, measuring tape flopping around his neck, strolled toward them. "You must be with the Barrow/Nice party."

"That's us," JJ said.

The man's eyes widened as JJ swigged from the paper coffee cup.

"Can I offer you bottled water? Champagne?" he said.

"I'm great, thanks. Hope, you want the bubbly?"

"No, thank you."

"You sure?" JJ put a hand in front of his mouth that did nothing to hide what he said next. "Your mom is here. Take the free booze."

Mr. Tape Measure wrinkled his nose.

"So, um…" Hope smiled. "The rest of the party?"

"This way, please."

Hope glared daggers at her brother, as they followed their guide through the store. Toward the back, they found Hope's mom, Beth, chatting with Ashley, Dr. Gregory Nice, and four men that Hope presumed to be the other groomsmen. The bride and groom-to-be gave genial waves when they spotted her and JJ, alerting the ever-frustrating Beth Barrow to their arrival. She rushed over, intercepting them.

"Why are you here?" she whispered.

"For the fitting." Hope gestured to JJ, who grinned.

"Hey, Beth. Good to see you, too."

"I couldn't make him come alone," Hope said. "He barely knows anyone."

"I barely know anyone," JJ parroted, doing his best impression of a lost puppy.

Her mother's cheeks reddened under meticulously applied blush.

"You can't be serious."

"Exciting, isn't it?" JJ went on. "You think they have any sleeveless shirt options? I want the ink on full display when I ditch the coat and tie at the reception."

Hope swatted his arm.

"You said to get someone. I got JJ."

"You didn't tell me," her mother hissed. "Avoid my calls all you want, but I saw you at Christmas; and you didn't say a word about this."

To be fair, Hope hadn't mentioned it at Christmas because she'd only cleared it with JJ and Ashley...yesterday. She was not putting that weapon in her mother's arsenal, though.

"Ashley's fine with it," she said, focusing on what mattered. "Last time I checked, it was her wedding."

Her mother surveyed the store, brunette bob flicking. "I cannot believe you've done this," she muttered.

"*Me?*"

"Yes, *you*."

"Um... ladies?" JJ said.

"You told me to find someone, Mom."

"No, I didn't. You *told me* you would find someone because the perfectly respectable option wasn't good enough for you. Then, you didn't even bother to follow up. You never do, Hope. You leave everyone else to clean up your mess. And now, because you're a *therapist* who can't even speak to her own mother about important family obligations, Aaron is going to show up here expecting to be fitted. Do you have any idea how embarrassing this is? Oh wait... You do. You just don't care."

"This can't be happening." Hope brought her fingers to her temples. "You can't be this oblivious. I told you to get rid of him over a month ago, the very first time you mentioned including him. He's my ex, Mom. You had no business asking him in the first place."

"Excuse me, sir." The man with the tape measure appeared at JJ's side like something out of a Houdini act. "We're ready for you. This way, please."

Of course, they were ready. The rest of the crew arrived first, but JJ came with the drama, so the staff wanted him out the door ASAP. Adrenaline flushed through Hope, but she caught her brother's gaze and nodded him on. Mr. Tape Measure was right; the sooner they left, the better.

"He won't show up," Hope said under her breath, as JJ disappeared.

Her mother huffed. "Unlike some people, Aaron is very dependable."

Hell yes, he was dependable. You could depend on him to call and text until you blocked his numbers. To show up at your job. You could even depend on him to take clandestine photos and then toss them around until they ended up in your hands, with the implied threat that they could turn up anywhere. Hope took deep breaths through her nose, swallowing her desire to scream.

"When did you last speak with him?"

Dependable or not, Aaron wasn't an idiot. He'd left Hope alone since Sydney doled out those legal threats, and there was no reason to think that he would break that streak on a Thursday evening. Maybe if he were drunk one night, or they had a chance encounter, but not like this.

"Last week."

"Last..." Hope blanched.

"On Christmas, of course." Her mother lifted her chin. "He called to wish us a happy holiday. Said he was looking forward to hugging me. I swear he enjoys spending time with this family more than you do. You've barely spoken to us since you broke up with him. You devastated that boy, Hope, and he's never been anything but good to you. He uprooted his life to make room for your nonsense."

"I didn't ask him to follow me here."

"You didn't have to," her mother countered.

"There is nothing romantic about him refusing to let me leave him, Mom. That's not only toxic, it's dangerous."

"Dangerous?" Her mother scoffed. "You're dating an alcoholic, covered in tattoos. A near-stranger. And you think a decorated officer, who postponed his own dreams to follow you, is *dangerous*. He was up for detective in Charlotte, Hope. Did you know that? They offered him his dream on a silver platter, and he picked you."

"He was…" Hope trailed off. If her mother had meant to stir guilt, she'd succeeded in stirring fear. Hope didn't give a crap about whether Aaron made detective in Asheville or Charlotte; but she doubted he would say the same, especially on the heels of losing an expected promotion to Detective Neely. "Okay, putting aside the fact that you haven't even met Devon, you sound like a weird Aaron-disciple right now," she said. "He doesn't deserve that kind of devotion. You have no idea what he's like."

Brushing her fingers over the bracelet Devon had given her for Christmas, Hope waited with a tainted optimism that her mom would ask why she had run far and fast from her ex. That she would care enough to wonder, instead of assuming that Hope's personal flaws caused their split.

"It wouldn't matter if I'd never met Aaron," her mom said. "I know you."

"Mom..." Hope took a step back.

Her mother straightened her spine and lifted her chin. "Like I said, Aaron is incredibly dependable, and he values this family."

Ashley locked eyes with Hope from deeper in the store, then fixated on some spot up toward the entrance. She reached for Greg's hand and tugged, pulling his attention from his conversation with a groomsman. Hope could imagine doing the same to Devon—a tug to get his attention if he were chatting with a friend and she needed him—and she wished more than anything that he was with her.

"Aaron dear, it's so good to see you," her mother said.

Hope's stomach lurched as she turned.

"Beth, looking ravishing as ever." He had on that leather jacket again, his blond hair clean-cut, but uncharacteristic stubble on his face. He wrapped his arms around her mother, while staring at Hope. "Didn't expect to run into you here, babe."

The weight of attention pressed into her. *Play nice, speak softly, don't cause a scene...* She chewed her lip, her fingers dancing over the bracelet on her wrist.

I need you safe, more than anything in this world, darling.

"No," Hope said, tasting salt and promises.

Aaron's brow pinched; his head canted. "What was that?"

"No, I am not doing this again."

Then her feet were moving.

"Where are you—" Her mom called after her, but Aaron cut her off.

"It's alright, Beth. I'll talk to her. Hope..."

"I said, no, Aaron."

DEVON

"I'll be there," Devon said into the phone at his ear. His mom hated texting, so any conversation requiring more than a few words earned a call. He walked to the schedule and skimmed the list of names, already knowing the contents. "No, Friday nights are busy. I couldn't take off, but I put myself down to close. We'll go before my shift."

Nix stepped up to the bar. "*Your mom?*" she mouthed.

"No, no." Devon said quickly, even as he nodded to Nix. "Don't worry about dinner next week. I'll see you Friday, anyway. We can get lunch, if you want. Yeah, Hope's great, about to start working shifts at R&R. I'll tell her. Love you too, Mom. Bye."

Pocketing his phone, he downed half a mug of black coffee in a single, gluttonous gulp. Nix cocked an eyebrow.

"Needs must," he told her, turning toward the pot for another in a string of innumerable refills. While he was at it, he poured a second cup and held it out to her.

"Thanks. I'll need the boost to make it to closing." Fixing dark eyes on him over the rim of the mug, she blew across the surface. "You know, I don't mind closing with Lucas next Friday."

"Thanks, but I already filled out the schedule."

He grabbed an empty glass and placed it in the tub, nodding a silent farewell to the regular heading for the door.

"What's Hope up to this evening?"

"Suit fitting for her stepsister's wedding. JJ's going to be a groomsman."

"JJ in a tux…" Nix raised her brows. "Wait, I thought Hope was his only sibling."

"He's not related to the bride. Ashley is Hope's stepdad's bio-kid. Her dad and JJ's mom married when Hope was fourteen, I think. Her dad's…JJ's…that's the side of the family that I met over Christmas. They're pretty low key—sports and barbecue sort of deal."

"What's her mom's side like?"

Devon shrugged. "Ski resort vacations and exclusive memberships? We're having dinner with her and the stepdad at the bride and groom's on Sunday. Something about wanting everyone to get to know each other before the wedding shower next month." He put on his most horrifying serial killer smile. "They live on the edge of a golf course, and the wedding shower has a color scheme that applies to guest attire."

Nix grimaced, and Devon sighed. Reaching beneath the bar, he tossed a towel over his shoulder.

"Her dad hated me. I own a bar, and he still disappeared to the den before we got to dessert. I can't imagine her mom being easier to please than a guy with a beer gut."

The pattern of unpleasant expressions flashing across his friend's face supported his suspicion that he was screwed on that front. Devon had never had reason or opportunity to care if a woman's parents liked him. He wished he didn't care now.

Nix sipped her coffee. "Maybe it's one of those *daddy's little girl* things. No one is good enough."

"Aaron was," he said. "At least, from her parents' perspectives. Her dad sees a good ol' boy with a gun who cheers for his favorite football team. Her mom sees a *prestigious* future that she can brag about to her social circle."

"I didn't realize hauling in drunks was such an elite profession."

Devon's mouth quirked into something resembling a smile.

"His grandfather was a police chief; he has an uncle who spent over a decade on the force, then went into politics. He's a representative in..." He searched his memory but came up blank. "I forget what state."

"Dev..." She narrowed her eyes. "Tell me you did not have the R&R tech team do a deep dive into your girlfriend's ex."

"Didn't have to. I kept my ears open, then poked around online." He lifted a shoulder, tense muscles protesting. "It was as easy as figuring out why her family already hates me. Aaron is a prime example of the respectable American male, while I am a bartender, who doesn't give a shit about football."

"*Business owner*. This place is pretty great, and it's not like her ex is a brain surgeon."

Devon chuckled. "I don't need an ego boost, Nix. I know what we have." He downed more caffeine and considered that maybe a part of him didn't hate her incessant prying.

"Well, good. Did you finally talk to your girlfriend about next week?"

A very small part. Tiny, like microscopic.

"Is that any of *your* business?"

"Like it or not, dickhead, you are my boss and my friend, and therefore," she pulled in a breath for dramatic effect, "my business."

"We could go back to me firing you."

Nix laughed.

"Please, tell me you did the big boy thing and talked to her. If your mom is calling to make sure you're off work for your annual respect paying, it's past time, dude."

"I did."

Nix gave a relieved sigh. "Oh thank—"

"Sort of."

Devon felt the color creeping up from his collar. He reached for the towel and swiped roughly. Nix put down her coffee.

"Dev—"

He heard the *snap* of fabric against wood, before he registered his movement. Nix straightened, eyes widening, as Devon stared down at the towel clenched in his fist, the length of it swaying. *Breathe. Pause. Get a fucking leash on it.*

"What was I supposed to do? Her ex was stalking her, basically blackmailing her until Sydney got involved. Then, that asshole settles down, and the holidays roll in. I might not be a romance guru, but I've seen enough chick flicks to know that you aren't supposed to ruin Christmas. I have a mom and a sister, remember?"

Bracing a hand on the bar, he sucked in a breath. His muted reflection peered back at him from the glossy surface.

"I'm trying, Nix; I am. You tell me to talk to her, and sometimes that's all I want to do; but then something else happens, and I can't put that extra weight on her. *My* extra weight. I came home from Locker Room a mess last night—one that Hope had to deal with because I fucking lost it over an unlocked door."

"Hold up." Nix pressed her palms to the bar. Her short nails were painted the color of an oil slick—a Gothic rainbow. "Devon Cleary went to group *in January.*"

Devon looked around for something to do. "It's not a big deal."

"It's a huge deal."

"I couldn't get out of it."

"There's a snowball fight happening in Hell right now, Dev."

"Nix..."

"Pigs are literally flying."

"It's not that weird." He fiddled with his mug.

"A bear just shit in the woods."

Devon chuckled, despite himself. Nix grinned, propping her tongue ring in the corner of her mouth. His chest warmed—not *hot*, like embarrassed or angry; pleasantly warm. "What in the world are you talking about?"

"It's a saying."

"One that doesn't apply here."

Devon went to sip but found his mug empty. As he topped it off, Lucas ushered Brandy through the door.

"Boss Lady! Boss Man!" the chipper young manager shouted. Devon rolled his eyes as they disappeared into the hallway to stash their stuff.

"I don't want to be some horrible version of myself around her," Devon said, studying woodgrain he knew by heart.

"You would whip out the heavy shit right as the kids arrived," Nix noted. "So, what happened last night?"

He ran a hand up his face and through his hair. "There's a guy at group, a firefighter. A couple of years ago, he came home to his fiancée's dead body. Last night, he wanted to revisit that nightmare in detail."

"Shit."

"Yeah." Devon swallowed. "It got in my head a little."

Nix raised a brow.

"Maybe *a lot*," he admitted. "I was going to talk to Hope about it; really, I was. She already knows why New Years is difficult."

"So, you told her about Kelly and the party?"

"Yeah, I just...didn't tell her the rest."

Nix swore under her breath.

"I promised her that I'd talk to her if I needed."

"Then why didn't you? You went to group and had a chat about some guy finding *a body*. You needed to talk."

"The front door was open."

"Okay..." Nix scrunched her face like she didn't get it.

"I couldn't find her, and I thought... It doesn't matter." Devon rubbed at the buzzing sensation in his left ear, as understanding filtered into his friend's face. "By the time I realized she was downstairs doing laundry..."

His brain flashed a tantalizing image of Hope on her knees with a mouthful of cum, staring up at him like an obedient little... The memory of his latest nightmare slammed into him, narrated by his own personal Demon, and shattering the fantasy of her making promises around his cock.

Mottled bruising.

Lines and stripes and gaping flesh.

Your seed, tinged red, dripping down her thighs.

Red, like the word you ignored.

Devon's coffee mug tipped; dark liquid flooded toward Nix's side of the bar.

"Christ. Sorry." He tossed the towel down, creating a dam. "It wasn't rational, I know that. He hasn't bothered her."

He reached for a second towel, but Nix caught his wrist. Devon stared at her hand, the way it left a creamy relief against the inked knots binding his forearm.

"Dev." Sympathy softened her features. "For someone who has been through everything that you've been through, *that is normal,* but you have to talk to her. You are not okay."

Pulling his arm free, he went back to mopping up coffee.

"I've got a handle on it. I'm fine."

"Is Demon?" she asked. "Because he's eventually going to want out for real, and your shiny new sub is an unlikely match for all that."

"Really, I'm good."

"You're playing a dangerous game."

"Sure am. It's called *stocked-before-it-gets-busy*." Devon grabbed his notepad, turned his back, and clicked his pen, ignoring his closest friend in the world swearing behind him.

HOPE

Ignoring the flurry of chatter, her mother's protests, Hope marched away from the wedding party with the singular goal of reaching her car and leaving. She pushed into the open air, stomach churning, legs unsteady because of the fast-rising fury that ducked out the door a few paces behind her.

"Hope, stop!"

His voice cracked at her back, the increased speed of his feet hitting the ground sending a surge of panic through her. Hope broke into a run, pressing the unlock button on her fob over and over. Every light on her car flashed in time to the sound of locks releasing. Skidding between her Prius and JJ's SUV, she could see her way out. Gripping the door handle, she could feel it.

And then, like always, Aaron ripped it away.

The handle tore from her fingers. The door slammed shut with jolting finality—the metallic snick of handcuffs magnified into the metal crunch of another escape denied. Hope ducked and covered her head. Her body quaked as she tucked herself into a ball. *Not again. Not again. Not again. Not—*

"Stop," Aaron bit out.

He planted his feet wide, creating a wall between her and the rest of the world. Not a safe wall; not a Devon wall. Instead, Hope found herself in a prison that she'd already fought her way out of once.

"You look like a fucking idiot. Stand up before someone sees you."

Unless she learned to phase through her car door in the next few seconds, getting up was a requirement of getting away from him. So, heart thundering, she did as he said.

"Obviously, I had no idea you'd be here," Aaron said. "I came because Beth asked me. Because I didn't want you to be humiliated when you came to your senses. Your mom has thanked me a dozen times for doing this, and because I still care about you for some insane reason, I haven't told her that you lost your mind, again." He glanced around like cops do, checking the perimeter, then refocused on Hope. "I'm guessing you haven't told her either, since you know it's all bullshit."

"Back up and let me leave," she said, pressing against the side of her car for any inch of space she could manifest; Aaron shuffled forward, eating up her breathing room before it existed.

"We need to talk."

"You need to leave me alone."

"We have to fix this. Let's go to my place or your apartment..."

Leave? He expected her to *leave* with him? Aaron had asked her out dozens of times since they broke up. He'd showed up at her home or work and expected entry; but this request felt dangerous.

"Somewhere private so we can sort this out."

She shook her head. "No, I'm not going anywhere with you, Aaron."

His hand smacked the glass of her driver's side window. Hope held her breath as he wrestled for control.

"Those threats you made are serious," he gritted out. "Career-ending serious. Go-to-jail serious, if you keep telling lies. You know that detective spot I was promised? They gave it to Neely. Fucking *Neely*."

"Maybe they decided to wait until next year. You've only been there—"

"They blacklisted me because you had a legal complaint delivered to *my job*," he snarled, looming over her.

"I'm sorry that you didn't make detective this time. I know how much you've wanted that promotion." Hope rattled off validation, while her fingertips scrambled over slick paint behind her back. "I swear that I'm not trying to get you in trouble." The smallest scrap of relief seized her as her fingers dipped into the depression beneath the door handle. "I didn't file anything about the pictures or the stalk—" Realizing her mistake, Hope froze.

Aaron blew out a breath and shook his head. "Whoa."

"Aaron, please..."

"Please what? Throw away my whole life for a lying cunt, who won't even give me a chance to explain myself?"

When I'm not with you... I am trusting you...

Hope spun toward her car and pulled until her fingers protested; but with her hip against the door panel, nothing happened beyond the useless oscillation of the handle. Aaron clamped her upper arm in a steel grip, yanking her around. Her pained squeak cut off as he slammed her back into the side of her car with stunning aggression. He hovered an inch from her face—his visage transmuted into a black void, backlit by the streetlight.

"L...let go. You're hurting me."

"Stalker..."

He leaned against her—fingers biting into her flesh. The familiar scent of his cologne filled her nose and tears flooded her eyes. Hope might not be able to see his face, but she could hear his fury.

"Add it to the list of shit you say about me, I guess. Leaving me isn't enough; you have to play the goddamn victim until you fucking destroy me."

With each pained whimper from her lips, he squeezed harder. Anger and embarrassment seared trails down her cheeks; bile rose in the back of her throat, as she shoved against him.

"I bet you'll turn this into another imaginary assault, huh? Well, how about this? I dare you to try to take me down." His grip tightened. White teeth and frigid blue eyes flashed in the darkness. "It will be the last—"

The impact came out of nowhere and nearly took Hope off her feet. On its heels, came a thud, a scramble, and a lot of grunting and cursing. She whipped toward the tousle but couldn't process the absurdity.

JJ had been in one fight, back in middle school. He got his ass kicked. Broken nose, busted lip, two black eyes... The whole nine. Given the endless bullying he'd endured and his penchant for annoying the crap out of people way bigger than him, Hope was surprised it had only happened once.

Despite this limited and uninspiring brawling experience, Aaron lay flat on his back under Hope's scrappy little brother—who was shirtless. JJ straddled him in ill-fitting suit pants and untied sneakers. Tattoos of varying artistic skill were everywhere, and in the harsh lighting, his halo of close-cropped hair and what bare skin he possessed glowed like an avenging angel. *Surreal.*

But then shit got very real.

"Not this time, motherfucker!"

"JJ!" Hope screamed, but it was too late. Her brother reared back and decked Aaron square in the eye.

Aaron stared up at his unexpected opponent, oozing hatred. A heartbeat later, his fist connected with JJ's face. Blood spattered the silver paint on Hope's car, as her brother's head snapped back. Before she had time to worry if he was even conscious, there was more scuffling. The pair got upright, slammed into the rear quarter panel of JJ's SUV, then hit the ground a second time, with Aaron coming up on top.

"No, Aaron! Stop!" Hope wailed. "Stop it!"

"Cheap shots are for pussies," Aaron snarled, drawing back a fist.

"Better a pussy than whatever the fuck you are," JJ spat.

Lunging forward, Hope caught the back of Aaron's jacket and yanked with everything she had. The knowledge that she would have an up-close view of her brother's face caving in under the pounding fists of her enraged ex if she failed fueled her effort until

Aaron tipped like a domino. The sudden slack as he succumbed to gravity sent Hope onto her butt, too.

With both hands fisted in his jacket, she hit the ground with a bone-rattling crunch, Aaron's torso landing between her legs. Hope scrambled back, pulling and scooting; dragging him with her and screaming for help. If she were alone, she could stay quiet; she could calm Aaron down without making more of a fool of herself. But this time JJ had gotten involved, and Aaron had always hated her brother.

An ear-splitting whistle sliced through the evening, silencing the disorienting din of insults hurled by the two men, along with Hope's frantic pleas. Greg, Ashley, and the rest of the party stood over them—faces visible above hoods, whole bodies at the head and foot of the vehicular valley they occupied. Aaron stopped struggling. Hope stilled on the wet ground, chest heaving, heels dug into the pavement by her ex's shoulders. Her aching fingers clenched his leather jacket like JJ's life depended on it.

"I come here as a favor and get attacked by a psychopath." Aaron touched his bruised eye.

JJ tried to stand, but landed back on his rear. "I'm not the fucking—"

"From my understanding," Dr. Gregory Nice said in an authoritative tone that Hope never would've anticipated from the mild-mannered pediatrician, "you weren't supposed to be here at all, Aaron. The future Mrs. Nice already signed off on Hope's escort. It wasn't you."

"Well, maybe someone should have told me that before I wasted—"

Greg crossed his arms. "Were the legal threats not enough? I've never been in that position myself, and of course, I'm a doctor, not a cop. Perhaps I'm out of my lane, but I feel like a woman threatening to take out a restraining order would give me some indication that I shouldn't expect to participate in a family wedding with her."

"I think, it would be a protective order," Hope said numbly.

Greg's brow furrowed; he tipped his head. "Get her, Ash."

Ashley's hands covered Hope's, loosening them. "Come on, honey," she cooed. "You can let go."

Ashley helped her to her feet, but Hope stumbled against the side of her car.

"I need my phone," she said to no one in particular. A door slammed nearby, and she jerked.

"Okay, hon." Ashley patted her back. "Where is it?"

"I'm so sorry about this." Fresh tears blurred her vision. Hope tried to blink them away, but they kept coming.

"You didn't do this. This was all Aaron. Well, mostly." Ashley aimed a withering glare at her stepmother.

"I didn't know," Beth protested. "How could I have known? And now poor Aaron—"

"I need to call Devon," Hope mumbled, ignoring her mother. "No...wait. He's at work."

Maybe her hard landing jumbled the pieces in her head because, right now, the steps of the plan she'd formulated with Sydney a few weeks earlier felt as scattered as those pictures her boyfriend had shoved off the coffee table the same night. Hope reached for her bracelet. Not immediately finding it, she dug deeper into her sleeve.

"I'm supposed to call Sydney," she said, remembering. "But..." She scanned the parking lot. "Where's Aaron?"

"Bolted like a coward." JJ, on his feet, took up the side of Hope opposite Ashley. He wrapped an arm around her, staunching the bleeding from his split lip with the back of his free hand. "Called me a pussy after grabbing you like that." He shook his head. "What a piece of shit."

"I'm sorry." Ashley looked between them. "Who's Sydney?"

"The attorney. She's awesome." JJ's words were muffled by his hand. "I met her at a Christmas party."

"Sydney Malone?" Awe transformed Ashley's face. "Your attorney is *the* Sydney Malone?"

Hope's mother put a hand on her chest. Her eyes widened. "*Attorney?*"

Hope shrugged. "She donates time to my new job. She wrote up the papers to try to get Aaron to leave me alone."

"Can I help?" Ashley asked, shelving her inner fangirl. "I haven't graduated, but it's after hours and—"

"Oh, no." Hope felt for her bracelet again. "I've ruined enough of your evening. And yours..." she added to JJ. "JJ can get fitted, then head back to meet his client. I'll figure out the rest after. If you still want us in the ceremony, that is. I understand if you don't." Hope took in Ashley's stricken expression; the irreparable suit pants her brother wore; and struggled under the crushing weight of it all. "I know this is awful."

Desperate for something solid, familiar, she abandoned her tactile approach to jewelry finding and pulled up her sleeve. Dirt and a vicious red stripe stared back at her from her otherwise bare wrist.

No...

She hadn't taken it off since Devon put it on her—sitting on his bar, under multi-colored holiday lights. That bracelet had become her go-to fidgeting outlet. When Hope was anxious or sad or upset... When her dad tried to talk sports over Christmas dinner, while her boyfriend tried to keep up...

The night before, it had morphed into a symbol of that other relationship dynamic when Devon hooked a finger through it and pulled her to a stop. And it was *gone*.

"Oh, Hope—"

Hope hardly heard Ashley speaking. She scanned the poorly lit ground, until the gleam of silver caught her eye. Hope bolted to where her precious gift had landed during the tousle, half-submerged in a puddle. She crouched and fished it from the mire, and then her heart sank all over again.

Muck dripped from the misshapen clasp. The springy bit flopped, and on closer inspection, the silver bale that gave away the bracelet's location with its metallic wink had been crushed underfoot. She closed her fist around the length of rope, pulling in a ragged breath as puddle-water squished between her fingers.

"Sis?" JJ stepped in behind her.

Hope pocketed the bracelet, wiping her hand on her jeans before looking up. She glanced at Greg herding the other groomsmen back into the shop. Mr. Tape Measure had come out at some point, which made things that much more embarrassing.

"I'll call Sydney and see what I need to do."

JJ's eyes darted between her and Ashley.

"If that's how you want to handle it," he said.

Hope nodded and pulled out her phone. Instead of the usual slick surface, a fine mesh of shattered bits comprised the screen. She tapped like normal, then blinked at the mostly white surface, devoid of any useful information. Her chest constricted.

"I...I don't know numbers," she said.

"Hope, honey—" Ashley held up both hands, as if approaching a frightened animal.

"I don't know anyone's number," Hope repeated, inching toward hysteria. "I don't know Sydney's. I don't even..." A pained sob stole the end of her sentence.

"Hey... Don't worry. My phone's in my jeans. I'll go grab it and look up the number," JJ said, all *no big deal* as he headed for the store.

DEVON

Fifteen minutes later, Devon scribbled the word *Crown* on his notepad, as his newest bartender and most reliable server chatted a few feet away. One of the two had a crush. The other only had time for one baby boy, and that was the four-year-old at home.

"Okay, but... If you could go *anywhere*," Lucas said with a grin, "Cancun, Paris..." He put on a sorry French accent and wagged his eyebrows at poor Brandy like he planned to fly them there on his own propulsion. Devon threw a clean towel over his shoulder, so he could wipe the dust off the necessary bottles in the stockroom, stifling a laugh when Brandy responded.

"I'd go wrap this silverware before we run out." Then that girl was gone. Gone, like they sing in country songs.

"That is the most beautiful woman I have ever seen," Lucas said, staring after her, slack jawed.

"Lucas, have you ever heard of *human resources*?" Devon chuckled when the question earned a confused expression from the young manager.

Nix breezed behind the bar with an empty tray. "How about *Don't shit where you eat?*"

"Hey," Devon turned to her, "you got that one right."

"I don't think I got the last one wrong. Where else is a bear going to shit?"

"That's my point. You put bears shitting in the woods in the same category as flying pigs."

"I don't think I said it that way." She ran a card through the reader.

Lucas nodded, tapping his temple. "I hear you, Boss Lady."

"Wait..." Devon pinched the bridge of his nose. "You understand her point, but not mine?"

"Yep. I'll ask Brandy out, but like...*not* here."

"See." Nix headed back for the floor, card and receipt in hand, and a self-satisfied smirk on her face. "I make perfect sense."

The phone behind the bar rang, as Devon swiped a hand over his face.

"Cleary's. This is Lucas. How can I help ya?"

Whoever was on the other end of the line could probably hear the cheesy grin. Devon had never seen the guy *not* cheerful. His default setting was big-ass-smile, even when people forgot to tip.

"Sorry... This is *who*?" Lucas said.

The shift in tone caught Devon's attention more than anything. People rarely called the bar line, but when they did, they didn't inspire the level of concern that he heard in Lucas's voice. Devon looked over at his newest manager at the same time Lucas's eyes flipped to him. Devon held out his hand.

"Yeah, he's here. One second." He handed it over.

"Devon Cleary."

"Hey, man. Everything's okay," began a somewhat muffled voice that he couldn't quite place, until...

Devon dropped the notepad on the bar.

"*JJ?*"

"Yeah, hey... So uh, sorry to call you at work. We...um—"

Devon's inner alarm system pealed wildly. "Where's Hope?"

Where was Hope? Why had JJ called instead of her? Why did he call the bar line instead of Devon's cell? They were supposed to be together at a suit fitting, so where *the fuck* was Hope?

Go get her.

Having no clue where they were, Devon ignored the voice in his head, and instead focused on his girlfriend's brother.

"She's—uh, I already said she's okay, right?"

Fuck. You need to go get her, that other part of Devon repeated.

"You said *everything* is okay," Devon reminded him, a muscle twitching in his jaw.

"Right..." JJ said.

Molasses in winter...

"Okay, so no need to worry..."

Too fucking late...

"But we had some trouble over here."

Trouble. Trouble. Trouble...

"Hope's pretty shaken up."

Aaron.

"Is he still there?" As he asked, Devon stormed toward the step-down that would get him closer to the exit; because he was going to get her...as soon as he had a location.

"Dude, how did you know—"

The receiver jerked backward as Devon reached the end of the cord, cutting off the end of JJ's sentence.

"Fucking hell," he grumbled, regaining control of the phone. "Educated guess. Where are you, and is he still there?"

"Nah, he took off when the rest of the family came out to break up the fight."

Devon fumbled the phone a second time.

"The fi... *Fucking Christ*. Where are you?"

JJ's exhale *whooshed* across the line. "In the fitting room. Hope was trying to call Sydney, but her phone is fucked. She didn't have any numbers, so I came back in to—"

Get in the goddamn car and go get—

"Jameson," Devon snapped, cutting off Hope's brother and his own internal chatter before anything important ruptured in his brain. "I need directions. Where the fuck are you?"

HOPE

"**I**'m fine. Go change." Despite her protest, Hope's feet remained rooted in place, her arms linked around her brother's torso.

"This is ridiculous," her mother said.

"Yeah, it is." Greg, having returned from getting the other groomsmen settled, agreed. "I have no idea why you invited that asshole, and even less idea how he was stupid enough to show up."

Beth Barrow huffed.

"Ash," Greg said, ignoring his soon-to-be-mother-in-law, "we may need to split up to get everyone's vehicles home."

Hope winced. As if her drama weren't enough, now they were dealing with some transportation issue. The bride and groom should not be dividing and conquering such things. Unfortunately, the only bridesmaid present needed to get her own crap together before she could offer help, and JJ had to get to work as soon as his face stopped bleeding.

"Sounds like a plan," Ashley replied. "It's on the way."

"JJ," Hope said, focusing on something she could fix, "it's freezing out here. Go inside. Get fitted. Then, get changed, so you can meet your next client, and I can work on…"

Well… She didn't know. Hope needed to do something, but she kept clinging to her brother—who was supposed to be scribbling permanent doodles on someone in an hour. A bizarre numbness settled in her aching bones.

"I'll wait for reinforcements, thanks," JJ said, over the pulse-spiking sound of a revving engine, the bark of rubber on cement.

"Maniacs these days," her mother grumbled.

Hope flinched, then went rigid. Her brain spat out an image of Aaron, sporting a shiner and whipping out his Glock. She sucked in a breath and clung to JJ.

"It's okay." He gave her a quick, tight squeeze. "Just the cavalry. Here, look."

Loosening his hold, he peeled Hope off and turned her around.

A still-idling Charger sat on the closest available slice of pavement, blocking the thoroughfare. The driver's side door swung wide, and Devon surged toward her. His face was lined with worry, steeped in white-hot rage. Hope panted through her nose, too many emotions warring within her to do more.

"Darling," he said, all whiskey and honey that cut through the numbness.

Hope threw herself into his arms, inhaling the scent of cedar, sandalwood, and *safe*, as relief flooded her system. "You're here," she whimpered into the towel over his shoulder.

"Of course, I'm here," he said roughly. "Let me get a look at you, sweet girl."

Ignoring their audience, he stepped back, grabbed her chin, and turned her head left and right under the streetlight. His thumb brushed her lower lip, hands skimmed down the sides of her throat, tucking beneath the shoulders of her jacket, grazing the sides of her breasts, then splaying over her stomach. Hands and forearms... Hips and thighs...

"Why is he touching her like that?" her mother said. "Hasn't even bothered introducing himself, but he's pawing all over her. She's fine, whatever-your-name-is," she called. "You can see that she's fine. No need to cop a feel in front of the whole town."

"Shut up, Beth," Ashley hissed.

Devon either didn't notice their interaction or didn't care. His focus was singular. *Consuming.* As if his entire universe had crammed itself into Hope's skin, and he meant to explore it right there in a strip mall parking lot.

"Nothing broken," he said to himself. "Christ, you're filthy. Is any of this blood yours?"

Hope looked down at herself. "I...I don't think so."

She chewed her trembling lower lip, as Devon took her face in his hands, hazel eyes locking on hers. Again, she thought of the night before, apologies uttered around his cock and promises made with the taste of him on her tongue. She had failed in under twenty-four hours, and all she wanted to do was sink to her knees, but he had a hold of her.

"JJ said there was a fight. Are you hurt?"

"I'm so sorry. I tried to leave when he got here."

Devon closed his eyes and took a slow breath. Then, he scooped his arms around her and crushed her to his chest.

"What the fuck happened?" he said.

"Aaron came, so I tried to leave. I'm sorry. I really did try." Her body twitched, and Devon tightened his hold. The pressure squished out more shaky words. "He hit JJ. He hit JJ hard. There's blood on my car."

"It's on more than your car," Devon said.

Hope sucked in a ragged breath, swallowed through the burning in her chest, as his head pivoted toward her brother. JJ snagged the bar towel and pressed it to his busted lip.

"See." He motioned with his other hand. "That's why I called you. She needs a ride. Even if she could find where she needs to go, she's too shaken up."

"That's what happened," Hope said. "You asked, and I told you. I don't need a ride; I need to talk to Sydney. You called the wrong person, JJ."

JJ shook his head. "The fact that you are oblivious to how right I got this is certifiable proof that I called the right person. Beth *invited* Aaron," he told Devon.

"Finally, an introduction." Hope's mother pushed forward, chin in the air. "It's like dealing with a pack of wolves. Beth Barrow." She extended her hand, her features a mask of mild disgust.

"Mrs. Barrow..." Devon's tone sank deep, furling around the part of Hope that answered to him, alone. "You don't want to make my acquaintance ten seconds after I found out that you had a hand in my girl's assault."

"Good lord, she wasn't—"

"*You do not want to make my acquaintance tonight,*" he repeated. Hope snuggled closer. Her mother dropped her hand and took a step back. Even beneath the harsh lighting, color flushed her cheeks.

"Right..." JJ said with a laugh. "So, Beth invited him; and because he's Aaron, he came. When Hope bolted, he followed her to her car. I was in the fitting room, but I ran out when I heard people talking. Never trusted that guy... Found him yanking her around and not letting her leave, so I pulled him off her."

"JJ tackled him," Hope corrected. Maybe she was too shaken up to tell the story properly, but she knew a full-body tackle when she saw one.

Her brother shrugged. "Fine. I tackled him. We went a round, then Hope saved my ass by pulling him off before he could crack my skull like a walnut."

"I sat on my phone," Hope said. Everyone glanced at her, then kept talking.

"Ashley and Greg came out about that time." JJ gestured to where Ashley stood in Greg's embrace; the couple nodded an acknowledgment. "Greg called Aaron out on his bullshit, and he took off while Hope and I got off the pavement."

"Thank you," Devon said.

JJ waved him off. "Eh. It's nothing. Not like he started shooting up the place."

"Jameson." A tremor ran through Devon's body—one that Hope felt in every point of connection. He pressed a kiss to her forehead before continuing. "You look like shit, and she looks like she tripped and fell on her ass." His throat bobbed. "*Thank you* is the best I can do right now, and I am well aware that it's not enough."

Hope watched her brother scuff the toe of his sneaker against the pavement. "Thank the baby-brother-wiring. I didn't think about it; I just did it. Might have gone better if I had taken a second to come up with a plan, though."

"Can you drive?" Devon asked.

Hope nodded; Devon stared down at her like she had lost her fucking mind.

"I was talking to your brother," he said.

"As long as we don't trade rides, I'll be good." JJ gestured toward Devon's Charger. "I'm going to need one hand to apply pressure and the other to steer."

"I was more worried about the blood-loss than the shifting," Devon said, the corner of his mouth quirking up. "Are you a fainter?"

JJ chuckled. "If I took Greg up on his offer to sew me up without numbing it, probably. But I'm not going to pass out on the way to the ER."

"Wait, the ER?" Hope's fingers clutched the back of Devon's shirt.

"Baby, that split is clean through," Devon said. "He needs stitches."

"I...I can take you." As soon as she worked out the logistics of managing both of their vehicles on top of getting in touch with Sydney, getting to... somewhere downtown...

JJ's expression softened. "I'll manage."

"But it's my fault you're hurt. Devon, tell him."

JJ looked between her and Devon, whose hand slipped up her spine and encircled the back of her neck.

"Darling," Devon said, his grip a gentle, grounding pressure that slowed her breathing and soothed her nerves. "It isn't your fault. You also can't take him to the ER."

"Why not?"

"Because you'll be with me. We have to call Syd, then see if we can get you an order of protection." Hope stared at him in disbelief. "Hope, you don't think I'm going to get back in the car and leave you here, do you? Now, come on. JJ will call and update us, won't you?"

JJ nodded, pulling out his phone. "Absolutely. I want updates too."

"Yeah." It was Ashley speaking, as she and Greg moved closer. "Can we get a number too? I think Hope's phone is out of commission, but we want to check in after we drop off her car."

***

Hours later, Hope sank onto the edge of Devon's tub and winced.

"Everything hurts."

Devon looked at her over his shoulder as he fiddled with the shower controls. The white noise of spraying water echoed off the walls. "You hit the ground hard. The meds should take the edge off soon."

He'd fed her dinner from a vending machine and bummed two ibuprofen from the woman who took her statement. While Hope wanted to believe she could handle herself, in truth, she didn't know where she would be without him. Literally. Devon had been the one finding the right parking garage, the right building, saying the right things until they found the right person. And on the way out, he had been the one with a hand on her lower back and a soothing word in her ear when she balked twenty-feet from the car.

Her cheeks heated. Was she afraid to get in cars now?

"Why am I so tired? I've been sitting around for hours, while you did all the work."

"Shower, then you can sleep," he promised.

Hope grasped the hem of her sweater, but the fabric weighed a ton. Seeing her struggle, Devon dried his hands on his jeans.

"Arms up, if you can."

The muscles in her shoulders sang as he eased the sweater over her head and tossed it in the hamper. Hope ditched her bra, got to her feet, and fought with the snap on her jeans.

"I should trash these," she said. "They'll never come clean."

A whispered curse brought her head up. The nape of her neck tingled as she took in the expression on Devon's face. Tracking his gaze to her upper arm—the one Aaron had grabbed when he spun her against the car—her blood chilled.

"I...I didn't realize it was that bad." She crossed her arms, but it didn't cover the bruising.

"*That bad*?" He stepped toward her. "Hope, that's a..."

Her hands came up, as she took an involuntary step back, calves bumping the edge of the tub. Devon froze, a look of pained horror on his face.

"Sorry, I'm..." She trailed off.

"Flinchy." He blew out a breath as he scrubbed a hand over his face. Hope's heart did a weird fluttering thing.

"I didn't mean to back away from you. I don't know why I did that." Her sinuses burned with the threat of more tears.

"It's okay." Eyes on hers, Devon inched forward. He reached for the front of her jeans and unfastened them. "I know why you did it, and I know that you can't help it." Hope hissed as the denim waistband scraped along the massive bruise on her butt cheek. Devon tsked. "No wonder your phone didn't make it. Foot," he ordered, dropping to his knees.

Hope lifted one, and then the other, resting a hand on his shoulder for balance as he finished removing her clothes. Shoving her filthy jeans aside, he skimmed his hands up the outside of her legs. Hope looked down into his upturned face. His throat bobbed.

"What are you doing?" Her voice came out in a whisper.

"I can smell you," he said. "From this close..."

Hope pressed her thighs together. Embarrassment flushed her skin as his fingertips traced her hips. "If we're taking a shower, I shouldn't be the only one naked," she reminded him.

"In a minute."

He put one hand on her lower back, used the other to scoop one of her thighs over his shoulder. To her horror, he shifted on his knees and nuzzled against her. Hope caught the fabric of his collar to steady herself.

"I don't want you down there if you think I stink."

"Didn't say that," he murmured. There was something undeniably erotic about the sight of her naked thigh draped over his clothed shoulder. Even in her exhaustion, her blood heated. "I said I can smell you. Stress and pain." He pressed kisses low on her belly between the words. "Fear," he said, his voice husky. "You smell like fear, darling." Gripping her tighter, Devon ran his tongue through her lips and over her clit, then inhaled. "When I make you smell like that, it's layered with arousal. With desire. With need so potent that I can *taste* it."

"Devon..." Her body hummed with pleasure.

"He had no goddamn right," he growled. Hope jerked at the suppressed rage in his voice, but his tone immediately softened to one of pleading. "Let me take care of you."

Hope groaned. "I'm tired and everything aches. I can barely stand, much less—"

"I know." He leveraged his arm around her lifted thigh to better spread her. "I'm not asking to fuck you, and I'm definitely not asking you to fuck me. Let me make you feel good. Or better yet, stop me the moment I'm not."

His talented tongue went to work, turning Hope's brain into a buzzing din of emptiness, as the shower ran beside them. His fingers gripped her thigh. His face burrowed deeper, finding her pleasure and stroking it.

"Sir..." Without conscious thought, her hands slid from his collar into his hair, steering him where she needed.

"Like that." His lips moved against her when he spoke. "Need to make you feel good..."

Hope caught sight of the stripe of red on her wrist—the one injury he hadn't cataloged yet. Guilt twisted in her gut alongside her building orgasm, but she pushed it away, as his knees widened, sinking his body lower. She could feel his breath against her pussy—the frenzied way he laved his tongue over her sensitive nub. His fingers dug into her skin, urging her on. She mewled, clenching his head against her; Devon made no effort to throttle her.

Hope felt dizzy, unsteady, and even with his support, the leg supporting her weight trembled. Devon tilted his face for her; then, when that wasn't enough, he eased himself back, guiding her down as he went.

"We're on the bathroom floor," she protested, trying to push up from him.

Between her thighs, Devon's head shook. An unintelligible sound of censure came out of him, as he hooked an arm around each of her legs and pulled her more firmly to his mouth. Breath rushing out of her lungs, Hope toppled forward, bracing her hands on the wall behind his head.

"Fuck, Sir..."

She rocked against him, sending jolts of pleasure through her core. Devon hummed his approval, caressing his hands over her hips and thighs in rhythm with her movements. Hope couldn't stop rubbing herself over his face. Back and forth. Grinding against nose, mouth, and chin... The flat of his tongue... He was a slick and soaking mess between her thighs, staring up at her through possessive, hazel eyes.

The energy inside her coiled in on itself with every roll of her hips. She had to stop. This was ridiculous. How could he breathe with... Devon grunted and even with the angle, with him on his back, eating her while she helplessly rode his face, Hope heard the order in it.

Come for me.

It settled in her bones.

Come for me.

It crawled through her belly and tightened her core.

Come for me because I *need it.*

"Oh... God..." Her nails dug crescent moons into the wall. "Yes, Sir. Yes, Sir." Her aching muscles convulsed in slow, delicious waves, while Devon's grip kept her seated; the pleasure inescapable, as the orgasm rolled through her like a storm. "*Yes, God, yes.*"

Legs shaking, Hope scooted off the moment he released her, smearing one shoulder of his black button-down in a trail of her arousal. Face coated, Devon turned his head toward her.

"Ready for that shower, darling?" he said, breathlessly.

Covering her pussy with one hand and her mouth with the other, Hope nodded. Devon got to his knees, lumbered to his feet. He held a hand out to her, and Hope took it.

"There's a good girl," he said, helping her off the floor.

DEVON

She looked small—a towel-cocooned wisp of a thing, sitting crisscross between his sweat-pants-clad legs. The desire to feed Aaron his own teeth reared its head; Devon tamped it down again, running the brush through Hope's damp hair.

He had gotten through the tangles a while ago, but he enjoyed the smooth glide—the way the remaining water traveled to the ends, before rolling into the fluffy terrycloth. It wasn't all that different from wiping down a gleaming bar—unnecessary, but grounding.

Hope put his phone down on the comforter. "I'm going to fall asleep, if you don't stop." Her words distorted with a yawn. Devon smiled and kept brushing.

"Did you get everyone squared away?"

He had received a string of text messages by the time they got home; only the one from Nix had been for him.

"Mostly... I filled in Ashley and Greg." Hope shook her head, and Devon caught the flush of color on a cheek. "Chloe calmed down after we texted for a bit, and Margo is going to cover my shift tomorrow. JJ made it home."

"That's good."

No mention of her mother, he noted. Beth hadn't wanted his number, but he'd hoped she would ask Ashley for the contact...have them pass along her concern...*something*. He knew they had their struggles, but you would think she would at least check. Then there was her dad... Devon wasn't even sure he knew what had happened. Hope hadn't said a word about wanting or needing to talk to him. If Devon hadn't dragged her back to his place, he had a sneaking suspicion that she'd be holed up at home, planning to work in the morning.

Blue-green eyes fixed on him over a slender shoulder, soft and sleepy, but then the towel slipped. Devon stiffened, biting the inside of his cheek until he tasted blood. Tearing his gaze away from the angry purple handprint encircling her upper arm, he climbed out from behind her and grabbed the tube of arnica from the nightstand.

"Let's coat you up."

Hope readjusted the towel, hiding the visual that had seared itself into his retinas the moment he'd helped her out of her sweater behind a layer of innocuous white terrycloth.

"I need to see it, darling." He didn't want to, but he couldn't treat it otherwise. Her head swiveled back and forth, while Devon struggled to keep his tone neutral. "This will help the pain and fade the bruising faster," he explained, feigning patience he did not possess.

"It's okay," she said. "You don't have to—"

"You have a cellphone imprinted on your ass and his god-damn handprint on your arm. Nothing about that shit is *okay*," he snapped.

Hope straightened, eyes widening. She didn't say a word, and Devon wanted to kick himself for that, but he was too busy scrambling for enough self-control to avoid scaring her. He let out a shaky breath.

"Sorry. I'm just... tired." He wet his lips and tried again. "I need to take care of you, right now." Because if he didn't, he might end up doing something he would regret. Finding a blond-headed, blue-eyed bastard couldn't be that difficult.

Hope glanced at him from the corner of her eye and sank her teeth into her lower lip.

"You get mad when you see them."

"Perceptive little thing..." He moved closer. "I am mad. Beyond mad. *Livid*." Her hand tightened on the towel. "But not at you. You know that, right?" She nodded minutely. "Arm first." He blew out a breath, then added softly, "Please."

Hope stared at the bedspread but lowered the towel. Devon swallowed his rage as he rubbed the cream over her soft, discolored skin. A handprint. *Aaron's* goddamn handprint...

"We'll get you a new phone in the morning," he said, mostly to distract himself from the task at hand. Hope groaned.

"I'll have to put it on a card. I was finally getting on top of things."

"We'll sort it out," he promised.

She picked at the towel. "Do you think it would be awful to ask if R&R could push my start back a week? I don't know when court will be, and I'm kind of..."

"I'm positive they will be fine with that."

She pinched an invisible speck of lint from the terrycloth. "Some way to start a new job, huh?"

"They've waited forever for you, and they already love you. They aren't going to hold something like this against you. If any-thing, your ex just got himself on more shit-lists than he realizes; and trust me when I say that you do not want to be on the R&R shit-list."

"Thanks." She gave him a wobbly smile that unsteadied him.

"Here." He handed her a t-shirt. As she pulled it over her head, a stripe of red on her wrist caught his attention. "You've got—"

Hope yanked the shirt down and shoved her hands under her ass. Devon and Demon bristled in tandem, something that hap-pened often with her around.

"Darling." He held out a hand.

"It's nothing," she said, like a little liar.

"*Now.*"

She shrank away from his tone, but his regret faded as she offered the hidden wrist. Say what you like about the rougher edges of his personality; they got the job done. Devon rubbed a thumb over the mark that cut across the back of her arm and around under-neath, as Demon chuckled in his head like a sadistic madman.

Well, look at that...

"Hope... this is..."

He looked from the mark to her face and found her trying to avoid his gaze.

"Where did this come from?"

Tears welled in her eyes and tumbled down her chapped cheeks.

"Hope, baby... This is fresh. I've only used cuffs on you for weeks." Not to mention, outside of his nightmares, he'd never be so goddamn careless.

Her lower lip trembled.

"Hey..." He cupped her chin and nudged it up. "I'm not mad at you, but you're hiding a stripe of meat-deep rope burn on a day that I took you to get an order of protection. You didn't mention this to a soul." He dipped his head, trying to reestablish eye contact. Hope scrunched down further. "I've looked you over dressed and undressed. Christ, I ate you out in the bathroom floor before getting in the shower with you." She made a throaty sound of discomfort, but Devon continued. "There's a reason I didn't see this. Explain where it came from, Hope. Now."

"I'll show you."

She tugged free of his grasp and shuffled to the bathroom. From his spot on the bed, he watched her dig in the pockets of her filthy jeans, then tiptoe back.

"Here." She handed him something dirty and wet, covered in the same grit that had covered her when he got to her. A cord and metal and— Devon looked to her face, as he realized what he held.

"I don't remember it breaking. I found it in a puddle." She snubbed. "I love it, and it's broken because I didn't keep my promise."

A queasy sensation hovered somewhere between Devon's throat and gut. "What promise?"

Hope sniffed. "To be careful and safe. I promised last night, and I already screwed up."

"You think it's a...*punishment*—one you somehow *earned* by being the victim of a jilted asshole?" Hope said nothing, wringing her hands. "That's not how punishments work, love."

"You gave it to me," she said, voice wobbling.

"And I can give you another. I'm more worried about your wrist than a bit of rope and some findings. If you need a bracelet, Stacy will make a new one."

"But it won't be the same."

Devon looked at her quivering lower lip, then back to the ruined bracelet. A pair of needle-nosed pliers could open the crushed bale enough for function, assuming the metal held on. The misshapen o-ring on the other hand... It had nearly cracked through under the force of being wrenched apart. He glanced at his dresser, then back to Hope.

"I'll fix it."

"Really?" She reached for the towel, wiped her nose. "Can you?"

He nodded. "I think so. It won't be perfect, but it'll be yours." *Mostly,* he added to himself. "If I can't, I'll have Stacy rework this one with new metal."

She surged toward him, nearly toppling him. Devon stroked her back with one hand, the bracelet's sharp edges biting into the other. He wanted to sink into her, hold her close until there wasn't an end to either of them. But he couldn't.

"Roll over so I can do your butt."

Hope backed away with a gasp. "That sounds kinky."

An unexpected smile tugged at his mouth.

"Too bad we're tired. Be right back."

"Where are you going?" she called, as he headed for the bathroom.

"Arnica is for bruises." He pulled open a drawer and found the small yellow tube. "Broken skin gets an antibiotic."

He dealt with the wrist first. A quick swipe of ointment, as Hope lay waiting on her stomach, eyes heavy-lidded. Lifting her shirt to take care of the rest, his heart stuttered in his chest.

He had seen it all before, of course. Getting her undressed for the shower had been a show and tell of infuriating and arousing proportions; but now—with every mark well and truly blooming on her fair skin—

"It's cold," she mumbled, as he slathered cream over cellphone bruises, handprints, teeth and flogger marks alike.

Devon's heart Morse-Coded something about who was allowed to leave marks on a person, and when, and why—an endless stream of rationalizing bullshit that he had trouble believing as he looked at Aaron's damage layered over his own.

"I'm sorry."

But for what? Hurting her? Not being there when Aaron hurt her? For the dark thing roiling beneath his skin, demanding satisfaction? He tossed the cream on the nightstand and pulled the blankets over her. Hope peeked up at him.

"Are you coming to bed?"

"Not yet, love."

His voice was too rough, but she didn't know that.

"Will you lay with me until I fall asleep?"

Sighing, Devon eased in beside her, and she snuggled into her usual spot—temple to his collar bone, chin to his chest. The heat between her thighs sat against his left hip, so close that on any other night, his cock would inch its way through sweats or barbed-wire to say *hello*. She'd come on his face already; she'd be wet, warm, ready for him. Maybe if he got inside her, he could drown out some of the noise in his head screaming about how she'd spent hours begging for a *temporary* piece of paper armor that wouldn't stop a fist—much less a bullet; and, she was covered in bruises—half of which Devon had inflicted.

Only half.

***

When her breathing evened, and the tension melted from her limbs, Devon seized his chance. Slipping out from under her, he crammed a pillow in his place—a technique that he had nearly perfected. Exhausted as he was, his cock still twitched at the sight of her leg hooking over, hips twisting and rocking into the softness until she settled.

Do you get it yet? Why he'll never be done with her...

Yeah. He did, and his skin had morphed into plastic wrap, housing an otherwise naked fifty-thousand-volt wire. Everything itched, twitched, *needed* an outlet—a problem to solve that came with a satisfying conclusion because nothing felt satisfactory when he thought about her fear and injuries and the way he hadn't even known she was in trouble until it was over.

Devon was cleaning up another man's mess, but that mess was *Hope*; and Hope was *his*.

He didn't notice his head canting, feet shifting wider—until something sharp jabbed his thigh. Devon reached into the pocket of his joggers and pulled out the bracelet he had promised to fix. It was a safer point of focus than the idea of what he would do to her ex, given the opportunity. Apollo hoisted himself from his bed and followed him into the hall before looking back toward the bedroom. He whined. Devon couldn't fault the pup for his divided loyalties.

"She's fine, buddy, but you can stay if you want."

The dog reluctantly trailed him to the bathroom, where he waited as Devon rinsed the bracelet. With the muck removed, they headed for the garage. He flipped on the lights, illuminating a space filled with kitchen cabinets he had yet to hang and tools that stirred up ugly memories of his father.

"Don't tell anyone, but we're fixing a collar." *A collar.* He sucked on that word, savored it for the barest moment before he laughed. "I'm kidding." Apollo cocked his boxy head, as Devon located a small pair of pliers and worked them into the crushed bale. "It's a bracelet, obviously. If it were a collar, she'd know, wouldn't she?" He caught his lower lip between his teeth, as he manipulated the delicate metal. "But she's awfully attached to it, huh?"

Running his thumb over the bale, he decided that, despite the imperfections, it wouldn't cut her. He consoled himself with the knowledge that Stacy could fix it for real at any time. Next, he pulled the stabby o-ring out of his pocket for another look. The mechanized bit flopped uselessly, the spring lost somewhere in the strip mall parking lot. Devon frowned. Even if he managed to make the thing round without breaking it in half, it would never function.

"Like the majority of today, this part is beyond my skill level." Apollo huffed an agreement. "Yeah, let's give it a shot."

Returning to the bedroom, he eased open the top drawer of his dresser. Using the flashlight on his phone, Devon dug beneath pairs of black cargo pants until his fingertips brushed velvet. He hadn't *lied* to Hope on Christmas Eve, when he mentioned second-guessing the length of her gift after Stacy finished. He had, however, neglected to tell her *why* he reconsidered his original purchase or the part about commissioning the bracelet, an entirely different piece of jewelry. In short, his girlfriend didn't need to know that he had impulse-purchased a custom collar before they made it to their one-month anniversary, or said collar had been hidden under his cargos ever since.

Opening the box, Devon removed the pristine clasp—once an identical match to the one Hope had worn for over a week. He passed the silver circle through the bracelet's damaged bale, relieved when it slid cleanly. His moment of calm did not last.

"*Ge hm...*"

Devon jerked to attention, spinning toward the bed at the first frightened notes of her voice; but Hope slept on her side, as he'd left her. He waited, listened. When she remained quiet, he wondered if he'd imagined it, if his fragile sanity was finally starting to crack.

Pocketing his phone and her bracelet, he re-hid the box and closed things up. But as the drawer slid home, another unintelligible mumble erupted behind him. A few quick strides later, he reached down and stroked her cheek. Instead of settling, Hope flipped to her back and swatted at him. Her legs thrashed under the covers, her body fleeing something happening in her mind.

"Hope, baby..."

Her eyes popped open, the whites ringing obsidian pools in the darkness. Shoving upright, she grabbed his hand.

"Get him," she pleaded. "Get JJ! *Please...*"

Her last word came out on a sob that ripped through Devon like a black hole, sucking him inside out, before dumping him into a room filled with sunshine and chaos and...*Kelly?* Blemished skin and lanky limbs of barely-thirteen. Begging their monster of a father to stop.

Stop, Daddy! Please!

Devon looked up at the man towering over him, too terrified to breathe, much less run.

"He'll kill him..." Hope whimpered.

You'll kill him... Kelly cried.

"He's going to..."

You're going to...

His father lurched forward. Devon threw up his arms to shield himself from the inevitable, but as he did, he yanked against something solid—a lifeline that hadn't existed when he was nine. It was that sensation of Hope's hand in his that saved him.

His brain followed details like breadcrumbs. *In the bathroom, the garage, at the dresser...* All the steps he'd taken while keeping his promise to fix a thing she loved. *Walking toward her when her nightmare started...*

Christ, his old man would love this. Seeing his wimp of a son fully-triggered by someone else's nightmare. *Soft*, he'd always said. *A fucking embarrassment.*

"*Shhh...*" he soothed. "JJ's at home. Your brother is fine. Everything is...fine."

Hope stared myopically. "JJ's at home," she mumbled. Then, as if coming out of a trance, she looked around the room. "We're at home."

"Um...yeah, we are." Devon eased her back against the pillows, laying down beside her. "You just had a bad dream."

And his own now spilled into his waking hours...which was fucking great. He could limit trips to the playroom or grab sleep in bursts when he couldn't, but how did you get away from nightmares that happened when your eyes were wide open? Devon's heart surged and muscles twitched, as he considered the possibility that this new hell could be permanent.

"Sir?"

He looked down at her tucked against his side. "Yeah, kitten?"

"You're breathing hard."

"That seems to happen to me when you're in distress."

She snuggled closer. "Can you hold me?"

"Sure." Devon pulled his arm more snuggly around her as she yawned.

"Sir?"

"Hmm?"

"Can you hold me more?"

"I don't know what you..." Her entire body was pressed to his flank, and his arms encircled her. There wasn't really a way to hold her more than... *Oh...* "Like this?"

Slipping his hand around her wrists, Devon found that sweet spot that let you restrain a sub's arms, while keeping a grip on their throat. Except instead of pinning her to a bed or a wall, this time he held her hands to his chest. When he squeezed, she melted.

"Yeah... That's good." Her breath came in slow pulls and sweeping exhales. Devon relaxed into the rhythm. "Thank you, Sir."

"Anytime, love."

An hour later, with her nuzzling into his neck, he dug her bracelet from his pocket and refastened it around her wrist, running a finger around the clasp before sinking into sleep.

HOPE

Hope crammed both bags into the floorboard by her feet as the driver's side door slammed.

"He turned my phone into a tracking device, then let you pay for it."

Devon rolled his eyes at the accusation in her voice, then offered his own version of events. "He showed me how to turn on location sharing, showed you how to turn it off anytime you'd like; and he made an assumption ringing us up because we came in together. You'd wandered off."

"I was killing time while you all set up the Cleary's line. I was right there."

He studied the emblem at the steering wheel's center and said, "I didn't realize it would be a big deal."

"Well, it is." Hope yanked up the sleeves of her sweater, her temperature rising with her temper. "Why would he do that?"

"You'd have to ask Pim," Devon said.

"Travis."

Devon's head pivoted her direction. "Huh?"

"The sales guy with the crush on you..."

"He didn't have a—"

"Are you oblivious? He was tripping over himself. When he finally managed to get his name out, he introduced himself as *Travis.*"

His eyes widened, then brow furrowed. "What did I say?"

"You called him *Pim.*"

"I meant *him*," Devon said. "You'd have to ask *him*. Sorry, I'm...tired." He sighed. "Look, I don't know why he suggested setting up location sharing, but I wish I'd had that option yesterday. Your brother couldn't give me an address. He said to look for the dry cleaner sign."

Hope searched her memory. "I didn't see a dry cleaner."

"Really? It's a block down and has the least visible sign on the street. I thought for sure you'd have noticed it." He pulled in a breath, his effort to tone down the sarcasm written on his face. "Sixteen minutes," he said, "from the time he called to the time I laid eyes on you. Sixteen minutes of wondering how badly you were hurt, if your brother was downplaying the situation so I wouldn't panic." He wet his lower lip. "I couldn't even call him back because he called the bar line. I didn't have his number."

Hope tugged the hem of her sweater. "That's why you got a cellphone for the bar today."

"The phone we have was fine until it about jerked me off my feet when I tried to go get you." The corner of his mouth lifted. "Ran out of cord a few miles short."

"You want me to leave the tracking—"

"Location sharing."

Hope rolled her eyes at him. "You want me to leave it on."

"Honestly?" Devon chuckled. "I *want* to strap a locking GPS on you. Something that pings your location on a schedule and couldn't be ripped off the next time you're assaulted." His gaze flicked her direction, and he started the car. "But I know that's irrational."

"Would you want me using a stalker app to see where you were all the time?"

"*Location sharing*," he bit out. "You have a stalker; it isn't me."

"You know what I mean."

He put a hand on the back of her seat and twisted, looking behind them as he backed out of the space. His proximity, the flash of ink-marked skin in her periphery, sparked sensation at the base of her skull. His eyes found hers as he shifted from reverse to first and pulled forward. "I turned mine on when Travis, The He-Him-Pim Sales Guy, did yours."

"Fine, I'll leave it on."

He closed his eyes for a fraction of a second. "Thank you, darling."

Hope reached into a bag and fished out a phone in an aggressively neon pink case. She looked to Devon, horrified.

"That one's for the bar. Hard to steal when it's that easy to see."

"I'll say. I'll still see it when I close my eyes."

"It's also sturdy." He grinned as she shoved it back in the bag. "Have you seen Nix's screen? It's a wonder she didn't need to tag along today."

"It was nice of her to get the bar covered for you."

"Yeah. Having both her and Lucas on staff is coming in handy." As he spoke, Hope dug out the second phone—this one in a pretty rose-gold case. She groaned, and Devon huffed.

"Now what?"

"You got the case."

He down-shifted, signaled, and slipped into a turn-lane. "You loved that case."

"Not at those prices. All of this needed to go on a credit card."

"I remember."

Hope blinked over at him, annoyed. "Then why did you let him ring it up together? Paying off my boyfriend at fifty bucks a month is embarrassing."

Devon shrugged. "So, don't. Let me buy you the phone."

It sounded so simple when he said it like that, but in her experience, simple solutions had hidden costs. Hope shook her head.

"None of this is your responsibility."

"It shouldn't be yours either," he countered. "He keeps putting hurdles in front of you; this one is easy for me to remove."

"Right. So easy for..." Hope trailed off as the flash of silver caught her eye. She stared, disbelieving, at the length of rope running parallel to the red stripe on her wrist.

"Just noticed that did you? You've been playing with it under your sleeve all day."

"You fixed it."

"It's not perfect," he said. "I can still have Stacy make you another."

Hope smiled down at the misshapen bale. "I want the one you gave me."

"Yeah, but—"

"It *is* perfect. Thank you." She looked closer, running her fingers over the unmarred silver ring. "How did you fix the clasp?"

"Magic." When she smirked at him, he laughed. "That's the one part that isn't original," he said, tipping his head her direction. "The spring part's delicate; Stacy said I might need a spare if you ended up wearing it a lot. I'd ask her if ten days is a record for jewelry destruction, but given the kind of jewelry she makes..."

Hope rolled the familiar bit of rope between her fingers. "I'm paying you back for the phone."

"Stubborn... You paid me back when you agreed to leave on the location sharing."

"Devon—"

The phone in question vibrated in its rose-gold case. They both glanced at the screen, and Devon put a hand on her thigh.

"Better answer," he said.

"Oh, good," Sydney said when Hope received the call. "I was hoping you'd be able to pick up."

"We're leaving the phone store. Devon's taking me by my apartment to get my car and clothes. I'm putting you on speaker, if that's okay."

"Great. I need to be quick. I'm on a break. I want to fill you in before I get called back." Sydney's words came, fast and crisp. "I talked to Aaron's attorney."

Hope touched the back of Devon's hand, where it rested on her leg. "Aaron has an attorney?"

"*The* attorney," Sydney said. "Brent Carlson. The guy you hire to make something like this go away. Your ex has had him on retainer since we sent that letter last month."

The speedometer inched higher; the engine begged to up-shift.

"Devon..."

"Oh." He eased off the gas. "Sorry."

Hope refocused on the phone in her hand. "What does that mean?"

"It means this might not be as open and shut as we hoped. This situation is *messy*. You broke up over a year ago. There's no record of you filing anything against Aaron before now, and without cameras in that parking lot, it's all your word against his."

"I tried to report him in Charlotte."

"But you didn't. From a legal standpoint, it doesn't exist. Your ex is a respected public servant with a spotless record. He did a favor for a family he was intimately involved with for over a year and was assaulted for his efforts."

"Are you his attorney now?" Devon snapped.

"I'm good at my job," Sydney countered.

"Sorry, Syd. It's just..."

"I know," she said.

"Do you? Because JJ didn't tackle him for fun. Hope has a handprint on her arm."

"I knew he grabbed her, but…" Sydney cursed. "Get pictures. They'll be useful if Carlson threatens to enter the images of Hope."

Hope's attention bounced between the phone screen and Devon's profile. He took her hand and squeezed.

"The… what? I thought they could only talk about the stuff in the order."

"You put that he was making repeated visits to your work and home, he left items, and that he attended this appointment after you sent a legal letter asking him to stop contacting you. The pictures are on the table."

"But why would he draw attention to those? Why would he want anyone knowing that he took them?"

"Carlson could spin almost anything to his client's benefit. He already has an angle, I'm just not sure what it is. He's trying to scare you into saying this was all a misunderstanding. If you don't pursue the permanent order, the judge will toss the whole thing. When I assured him that wasn't going to happen, he reminded me that—while you claim the images were taken without your knowledge—the…" Sydney cleared her throat, "*positions* were consensual."

"So, what?" Devon's tone was lethal. "If she doesn't play along, they show pictures of her naked? They're going to let him *blackmail* her *inside a courtroom*?"

"Not if I can help it."

"But why do the pictures matter at all?" Hope asked. "This is about what happened yesterday."

Sydney's exhale distorted in the speaker. "I have a feeling that's the part we're going to figure out in court. We're scheduled for Thursday. We'll get your brother to testify too. Devon, I know you'll want to go, but..."

***

"Are you sure you don't want me to stay here tonight?" As they approached the front of her building, Hope dug her fingers into her lower back. "Aaron knows about the order, so it's not like he's going to drop by."

"We're getting your stuff, and I'm following you home. Nothing about that plan has changed."

"But you're kind of..." Hope gestured to his fuming form stalking over the sidewalk.

"Trust me when I say that leaving you here alone overnight will not improve my mood." His expression softened as he opened the door for her. "I'm just frustrated. I don't give a shit how badass *Susan, the bailiff* is. It's not the same as having eyes on you myself, especially when Aaron is in the same room."

"I'd rather you be there too, but it's for the best." Hope walked past him, and Devon followed her up the stairs. "Like Sydney said, you're all intimidating and broody. Besides, you can't keep missing work for me."

"Actually, I can." His voice echoed, hollow as the empty stairwell. "At least, as long as I keep the books caught up and the bar stays... Um..."

"Okay," Hope said, filling his pause, "but what are you getting out of all this?" They turned at the last landing and continued the climb to the third floor. Her legs burned, the three flights of stairs feeling steeper than usual.

"I think you—"

"All the missed hours, the running around." Not to mention the phone that she was definitely paying him back for... "You're supposed to be at work right now." She reached for her purse before remembering that Ashley and Greg had locked her keys in her apartment when they'd dropped off her car. "Crap, I don't have—"

Another resident sprinted up the stairwell and kept going. Hope startled at the rush of feet, but the fear morphed into suspicion when Devon's chest brushed her shoulder blades. She looked at him over her shoulder, found him holding up his copy of her door key.

"Keys..." she said, plucking it from his hand. "You're awfully close."

"You're bleeding," he said without preamble.

"I'm...*Shit*. Of course, I am." Opening her door, she pushed inside and dropped his keys beside her own on the coffee table. "Thanks a lot, period app..."

Devon smirked as she turned the locks. "What?"

"I have an app to track my period."

He shook his head. "They make an app for everything..."

"That's not the point. I'm not supposed to start until Sunday."

"Better early than late, right? Whoa... Where do you think you're going?" he said, stepping in front of her.

"Isn't that obvious?" She pointed to her pants.

"Not until I take a look around."

"Do you expect Aaron to jump out of a closet? Hide in my shower?" Hope shoved those thoughts away before they had time to bloom into another irrational phobia.

"Darling, stay."

Hope's face was a furnace. Her bottoms were plastered to her body, and her boyfriend had stared directly into the stain on her ass the whole way up the stairs. You couldn't *unknow* a thing like that, so she wanted to at least erase the evidence, ASAP.

"But..."

"*Stay here.*" He took off down the hallway, returning twenty seconds later.

"All clear. See? Super fast. So, what do you need? You'll have Silver Sassafras on Monday, unless you call in." His head tilted, voice lilting up in inquiry.

"I'm not dropping those shifts unless I have to," she reminded him.

"Can't blame a guy for trying... You need something to wear to dinner on Sunday and court, too. And, you know..." He gestured. "Tampons or whatever."

Hope blew out a breath, slowly dying inside. "Don't worry about it."

"Don't worry about what, exactly?"

She forced a strained smile. "I'm going to stay. Save the effort of packing things up."

His brow bunched as he studied her. "Why?"

"You're in a shitty mood because of what Sydney said."

"That is far from the only factor."

"And I'm bleeding two days early, straight through my second favorite pair of jeans. Do you know what happened to my favorite pair? They're in your trashcan."

"So...we need to stop somewhere and get you jeans?"

Hope put her face in her hands and groaned. "I need you to leave," she said.

"Unless you produce Sydney's armed bailiff friend, that's not happening—and even then, I'm going to complain about it."

She peeked out at him, then dropped her hands when she saw that he wasn't joking.

"Look, you're amazing, Devon. So great. But I am not your responsibility. I'm tired and achy. I'm snapping at you right now, and you don't deserve it."

His answering smile was too wicked. "You are a vicious little thing when you're at your limit."

"Then, you say stuff like that!"

"Like what?"

Hope caught and held his gaze. "You *know* what. You aren't even going to get laid tonight. You didn't get laid last night."

"I remember last night well enough."

She fidgeted with the bracelet around her wrist, the one he'd missed sleep to fix for her. "You don't want me there. You think it's the right thing to do; and because you're...*you*, you'll take me back to your house and let me ruin your weekend like I've ruined the last twenty-four hours."

Devon straightened. His feet inched wider.

"I'm not sure which part of that is more insulting, darling. The part where you think I only want you in my bed if I can fuck you, or the part where you think a bit of blood would stop me."

Hope ignored the tingle at the base of her skull, the blooming heat between her thighs. "I'm not trying to insult you."

He smiled at the floor. "Oh, I know you aren't." His eyes flicked up to her, and she swallowed.

"I'm going to go change."

Devon caught her wrist, tugged her to a stop.

"I'm not a relationship guy, you know, but I pay attention." He scanned her face. "You have this habit... You *push* when you desperately wish someone would *pull*." He hooked a hand around the back of her neck and brought her lips to his. Instead of kissing her, he trailed his mouth along her jaw, toward her ear. "This is me pulling, darling."

He snatched her up and hauled her to the couch.

"I need to ch—"

"That's a slipcover. If it stains, I'll buy you a new one. You can add it to your imaginary tab, if you want." He dropped her atop it.

"Wait!" Hope squealed, scrambling backward.

"Not a safeword."

Devon grabbed one of her ankles and yanked her flat, then swung a leg over her body, settling on her hips. Panic ricocheted through her, but his hands cradled her face a moment later, his forearms pinning her shoulders deeper into the cushion.

"Hope, look at me. Take a breath."

She inhaled, exhaled, staring at the golden flecks in his hazel eyes.

"I am not going to hurt you, and you know how to stop me. Yes?"

She wet her lips, nodded. Devon nodded too.

"I'm not leaving you here, love. People in the stairwell scare you. You'll barely sit on this fucking couch, and I'd bet money I know why."

"I..." He lifted one dark brow. Hope swallowed her argument.

"Do you think I'll sleep, knowing you're here alone, flinching every time someone on the next floor opens a door? You don't want to stay, darling; I know you don't. So, why are you so hellbent on it?"

"I don't want to be a burden," she whispered.

"Do you think you're expensive?" he asked softly. "Too much effort and not enough reward?"

Yes.

Hope said nothing as he eased her shirt over her head, wedged a hand in the front of her bra and pulled it down, pushing her breasts skyward. They felt so achy and heavy. Every brush of his fingers tingled through the sensitive tissue. The swelling length of his erection pressed into her thigh, as he lowered his head and nuzzled her.

"You're wrong." The words tickled her tightening nipples. "You are *all* reward, darling. So soft and warm..." Voice husky, he skimmed a hand down her belly to the waistband of her jeans. "These are in my way." Unfastening the snap, he worked them lower, yanking off her shoes when everything bunched at her ankles.

"Wait..."

"Still not a safeword," he murmured. Removing the last of her bottoms, he slid his fingers home. "Oh, kitten..."

Hope's eyes widened as he held up red-slicked fingers. Despite her horror, the tingle of arousal pulsed through her clit and deep into her groin.

"Sorry."

"For what, love? You're adorable when you blush, and right now, your face matches my fingers."

"But it's... I mean, people usually think it's gross."

Devon pressed her thighs open.

"Oh, don't—"

"Hmm... No safewords detected. I see slick and wet." Hazel eyes found hers. "Two of my favorite things. I don't see gross, though." Hope swallowed. "How does this feel?" He scooted down her body, pressed a kiss to her clit that would have been chaste if not for his target.

"F...fine, Sir," she squeaked.

An amused smirk flashed on his face. "What about this?"

He circled the sensitive bundle of nerves with his tongue, dragging a ragged exhale from her lungs. Devon chuckled, slipping two fingers deep into her pussy.

"Your shame is delicious," he said against her. "You taste like everything they taught you to hide."

Hope panted, one hand busying itself in an unguided search until he caught it with his own. Something tacky glued them together, and she tried not to think about it. He crawled up her body with a smudge on his chin, shoving his jeans down on the ascent.

"You taste like mine," he growled, mouth finding hers.

Copper zinged across her taste buds, filled her nose, as his tongue and cock claimed her in tandem. Her womb ached, and her spine arched. Devon caught the back of her neck, his thumb brushing her cheek. He kissed her harder, swallowing her moans as he rocked into her. It felt so good—this taboo mixture of pleasure and pain.

"*Mine.*" He bit the word out. "Every fucking inch."

"Yours, Sir."

She knew the wetness for what it was, but it didn't change how good he felt inside her. Devon's pace quickened as he chased his own release. Wild eyes scanning her face, he pulled out and rocked back on his knees, preparing to finish on her stomach.

Hope grabbed his wrist, and they both froze; Devon staring down at her, as Hope looked up at him. His throat bobbed.

"What do you want, kitten?" Lust choked his words. "You have to ask for this one."

Hope's breaths came in gasps; her weeping pussy spread wide, begging him.

"Please, put it back, Sir."

Devon tilted his head, his chest rising unsteadily.

"Please, Sir. I'm so empty."

His mouth parted, as he slid the head of his cock against her entrance, circled it over her clit.

"I need it so bad, Sir," she whined.

"Say it. Say what you need."

"Your cock, Sir. Please, my pussy is so empty." Devon pushed in; Hope groaned her pleasure. "Fill me up," she begged. "I need it."

Devon seated himself deep and let her grind into him. He winced—a visual tell. His head enjoyed the show, but with nothing separating them but her blood, his body longed to thrust to the finish.

"God, you're so gorgeous when you're greedy," he said through clenched teeth.

"I need to come, Sir."

"Do it, darling." Devon pressed a thumb over her clit, circling. Hope was about to explode. "Let me see you shatter with my cock in this bleeding cunt that I own."

Tingling sensation scaled her spine, yanking the muscles of her pelvis higher and tighter in its wake.

"Then, I'm going to shoot my load in your face."

Something in Hope recoiled.

"Or maybe down your throat. Let you taste what a naughty, greedy, insatiable little slut you are for me. Come, kitten."

"No, Sir."

Devon's brows rose in surprise as she shoved upright, pushing against his chest until he toppled.

"What are you..." The question died on his tongue as she straddled him, sinking onto his throbbing erection.

"Fill me up," she demanded, raising her hips only to lower them back down.

Devon hissed.

"Hope..." His face went deathly serious. "I won't last like this. So, unless you mean what you're saying, then we're going to need—" She bounced again, cutting him off. "Holy fuck."

"Should I beg, Sir?"

Devon shuddered beneath her. *"Jesus-fucking-Christ-don't-beg."*

"Please, Sir. Please, come in my pussy."

His zipper scraped her bruised butt with every bounce, a stinging reminder of a cadence she could hear in the wet slap of flesh on flesh.

"Goddamnit, Hope. I—"

"I love the way your cock stretches me when I ride you like this," she drawled, shoving her hands beneath his shirt, scoring her nails down his stomach. "It feels *so good*. Doesn't it feel good?"

"Hope, b...baby—" Now, it was Devon begging, stuttering, coming apart.

"Remember your safewords."

"Fuck." He groaned, eyes rolling white.

"Fill me up. Come in me. Please, come in me."

Her own line was so close that the next bounce might get her there, but the idea of him flooding her as she squeezed every last drop from him was too delicious to miss.

"Come in me, while I come for you," she managed, voice hitching. "Think of how good it will feel—my tight pussy gripping your cock. You like that, don't you? The way I squeeze while you come."

His gaze flipped up to hers. The world pitched, and Hope landed on her back with Devon between her thighs. The sound coming out of him was a carnal growl as he slammed home.

"Is this what you want?" he snarled, fingers digging into her hips. "You want me dripping down your fucking thighs?"

"Yes." Her vision blurred, his vicious treatment pulling tears into her eyes and setting her on fire. "Please, God, yes."

A near-agonized moan tore from her throat as he bottomed out, nails raking her hips with his release. Every muscle in her body pulsed with pleasure so potent she could taste it on her tongue. She detonated; and the walls of her pelvis fisted Devon's length, as he delivered those last punishing thrusts before collapsing atop her, panting.

"Can you please put some stuff in a bag now?"

With his face shoved into the corner above her shoulder, the question came out muffled. Hope giggled.

"I think we're going to need a shower before we do anything else, and unfortunately, mine is nothing like yours."

He lifted his head to look at her.

"I would hose off on the sidewalk, as long as you slept in my bed tonight."

HOPE

"Apollo, sit." Hope glanced between the dog—rear hovering above the hardwood floor—and the door. She cracked it an inch, revealing a sliver of her friend's smiling face.

"You gonna let me in?"

"Yeah, it's just—" Apollo shoved his giant head toward freedom.

"Oh my God." Chloe dropped her bags and pounced on the pooch. "You are adorable." She scratched behind his ears, babbling baby-talk as the dog's chocolate-brown eyes filled with insta-love. "What a doll-baby."

"Did I mention him?"

Apollo had become such a normal part of life that Hope may have forgotten to include him when inviting her best friend to hang out at her boyfriend's house. Tonight. Alone. While he worked a Saturday closing shift at the bar...

"Nope."

Apollo donned his best sloppy grin.

"Chloe, Apollo. Apollo, Chloe." Hope's gaze traced the scars, so obvious, once you knew where to look. "He...had a rough start, but he's very sweet. Wouldn't hurt a fly unless he accidentally squished it cuddling." Parroting the same sentiment Devon had laid on her when first meeting Apollo, she felt a pressure in her chest. The idea of someone judging the big, goofy mutt for his battered appearance felt like a personal attack.

"Obviously," Chloe agreed. "Anyone could see that this is the goodest boy ever." She planted a kiss on his silver brow, grabbed her things from the porch and headed inside. "So, this is where the infamous Devon Cleary lives." Traversing the living room with Apollo on her heels, she glanced toward the nineteen-seventies kitchen. "Not sure what I expected, but it wasn't a mash-up of blast-from-the-past, modern craftsman, and..."

"Clean?" Hope finished for her.

Chloe shook her head. "No, that one doesn't surprise me. We've all seen him at the bar." She deposited her haul on the dining table. "So, have you talked to Ashley or your mom since...you know?"

"Ashley called to check on me last night. I mean, she texted Thursday too, for updates and to let us know they'd dropped off my car and where to find my keys; but last night she called my phone. She was all giddy about us coming to dinner tomorrow."

"And you're still going?"

Chloe's face said she didn't think that was a brilliant idea. Hope pressed her mouth into a smile.

"Ash and Greg have every right to be upset about what happened, but they've been nothing but gracious and concerned. Dinner isn't a huge ask."

"It is if your mom is going to be there. What's she saying about all this?"

Hope shrugged. "I assume Ashley is filling her in."

Chloe's brow pinched. "You haven't talked to her?"

"I'm sure she's busy. You'd think it was her wedding, instead of Ashley's." Hope shook her head. "It doesn't matter." She looked around the house that wasn't her apartment—a place that felt comfortable right up until her neighbor-bestie showed up. "Would you like a drink or something?"

"You know it." Digging a packaged cheesecake and a bottle of wine from the shopping bags, Chloe headed for the kitchen. "I still don't get why you don't skip tomorrow."

"I thought about it." Hope pulled two glasses from a cabinet. "The idea of facing everyone... Trying to shield Devon from my mom..."

"He doesn't strike me as someone who needs shielding, especially anytime you're involved." Opening the avocado green fridge door, Chloe whistled. "Look at that. Bachelor-boy has actual food in here." She moved a carton of eggs to the side and shelved the cheesecake. "I'm pretty sure Devon would jump in front of a bullet for you with a smile on his face."

Hope grinned. "Actually, I suspect he'd look really pissed off."

"You're right." Chloe nodded, grabbing the wine. Hope pointed to the opener hanging on a magnet on the side of the refrigerator, and Chloe reached for it. "That tracks. So, your mom wasn't enamored with him, huh?"

"You mean when Devon informed her that she didn't want to meet him right after he learned she'd caused my assault?"

Her friend's eyes widened, hand freezing on the handle of the half-buried corkscrew. "He didn't…"

"Oh yeah. Then he *repeated* himself."

Chloe wrenched the cork out. "Again…" She gestured with the skewered cork. "You might want to let that situation simmer down before having a family dinner."

"Honestly, I expect it to be weird and uncomfortable anytime I deal with my mom. That's normal. *This*," she said, gesturing between them, "is weirder."

"Us hanging out?" Chloe pouted. "Why?"

"My boyfriend's at work, and I'm receiving company *in his house*."

Chloe laughed. "He knows we're here, Hope."

"I know, but it feels funny."

"The part where he's letting us eat cheesecake on his couch without him? Or the part where you took him up on that offer?" She poured and handed over a glass. Hope studied the wine's burgundy hue.

"I offered to stay at the apartment yesterday."

"Why would you do that?" Concern tainted her friend's voice.

Hope lifted a shoulder. "I've been here every night for over a week."

"Which he doesn't mind."

"I know. He's the one who convinced me to come back."

"How did he manage that? You're one of the stubbornest people I know."

"Not as stubborn as my boyfriend. His weapon of choice was period sex and a hot shower." Her friend laughed, and Hope went on. "I'd be lying if I said I wasn't relieved. I feel safer here than I do in my own apartment. I don't like feeling that way." She worried her lower lip. "Reliant on someone else."

Chloe's face softened. "Aaron shows up at your apartment. You proved what a brave, badass woman you are by filing for protection. You don't have to stay somewhere you feel unsafe, right?"

Hope nodded. "Yeah."

"So...Are you staying here until court?"

Chloe raised her brows and sipped her wine. Hope scrunched her shoulders.

"Yes? It's not like we don't have time apart. My shifts are early, and Devon's at the bar late. We'll both be here alone with Apollo for several hours a day."

"I wasn't fishing for a justification," Chloe said, giggling.

"It feels like I'm supposed to give it anyway. JJ mentioned how much time I spend here when I stopped by the shop the other day."

"Yeah well, that's a sibling for you." Chloe sipped. "Your brother was joking, not judging, and his face is held together with stitches now."

Hope winced. "He keeps *forgetting* to send me a picture."

"He doesn't want to worry you."

"I figured that much. Does it look bad?"

Chloe dangled her glass from her fingers. "Depends on who you ask. Half of his jaw is black and blue. I got Graves to sew him up. Prettiest stitches in the ER—but it's going to leave a scar. He's lucky he kept his teeth."

"Shit."

Chloe nodded, then grinned. "So naturally, JJ thinks it's cool as fuck. He says he can't wait to rip Aaron a new one in court next week."

Hope rolled her eyes. "Good grief, no more ripping, please." Her friend laughed and Hope rubbed her temple. "I feel awful about every part of this."

"Your brother feels like a superhero, and says the scar adds to his image."

"The *scrawny blond kid, who had to transfer schools due to bullying* image?"

Chloe fixed her with a stare. "The *lean, taut—*"

"*Chloe...*" Hope grimaced. Her friend's grin widened.

"Fine. Renowned tattoo artist, with a penchant for rescuing women in distress, even if it's going to get him hurt and not going to get him laid." She raised her glass. "Don't worry about JJ. And as for sleeping arrangements, as your best friend, I prefer you stay here. Your ex is terrifying, and I've only heard him through a door." She sipped again. "Are you going to work your shifts?"

Hope nodded.

"The Silver Sassafras ones. We pushed back my R&R start until after this is settled. I'd love to avoid Francis for a week, but I can't refold tapestries remotely, and I need a paycheck."

"Do you think Aaron would bother you at the shop?"

"No, Sydney says he's trying to make this go away, which means he isn't going to do anything stupid." She lifted her glass, pausing when Chloe asked another question.

"Fair enough, but what happens after court? Will you go back to your apartment?"

"Why wouldn't I?"

"I just thought, with your lease running out..."

Hope let out a breathy laugh. "Don't worry. Aaron won't run me out of my apartment forever, and I won't interrupt your naked canoodling with my baby brother by crashing at one of your places."

"Oh, we weren't worried. We'd get our privacy, no matter who got custody of you." She winked. "But I'm curious why you'd go back when you have other options." Chloe gestured to the house around them. "Are you really about to sign another lease on an apartment that you're using as a storage unit?"

"Whoa." Hope put up a hand. "I'm not moving in with Devon. If the OP stands, I'll hang out here for a few days after court; but I'm going back to my apartment once things settle. I have to."

"You mean *if they toss it.*" Chloe's head canted, and her forehead creased. "You'll stay here longer if they throw it out."

"Oh, sweet summer child." Hope laughed at her friend's naiveté. "If they toss it, he'll gloat. I can handle Aaron's gloating. It's like...a foundational aspect of his personality. But if they extend the order..." She rolled her lower lip between her teeth. "He already blames me because he didn't make detective. I can't imagine what he'll come up with if he loses his job."

"So, you're more afraid of him if this goes your way, than if it doesn't."

"Just until he calms down." Hope forced lightness into her tone, forced her shoulders to rise and fall.

"He's thrown you around twice already." Concern etched her friend's face.

"And I'm sleeping here until after court. Aaron isn't going to try anything, but I'm being extra careful anyway. It's fine, hon." She patted Chloe's arm. "I promise. Let's talk about something else. Something fun."

"Okay…"

Hope sipped. Lips parting, she inhaled, letting the familiar scent and flavor inundate her senses. Chloe's worried expression faded into a mischievous smile.

"Your boyfriend packed the wine, while Nix boxed up the potato skins," she said.

"We have potato skins?"

"Extra sour cream, just like you like. I already had the cheesecake, but Dev had Nix text me to grab dinner on my way here."

Hope blinked, her eyes stinging with a familiar burn as she salivated. Good grief, every part of her was leaky these days.

"Oh, don't cry. It's just dinner. Now, go get on some comfy clothes, babe. We're going to relax if it kills us."

"Okay."

With a deep breath, Hope deposited her glass on the counter and brushed past Chloe. Apollo watched her head down the hall, opting to stick near his newest pal. Wiping her damp eyes on the sleeve of her sweater, Hope closed the bedroom door and opened the dresser drawer above the one she'd overtaken. She grabbed a t-shirt and a sweatshirt for good measure. Ditching her more restrictive clothes, she tossed on sleep shorts and her pilfered tops, trying to ignore the bubble in her chest.

People shouldn't get teary-eyed over potato skins. It was ridiculous...

But it wasn't just potato skins. It was her favorite comfort foods and her favorite wine, gathered by people who loved her, and shared in a home that felt safe. It was an invitation to be comfortable and vulnerable, without the burden of shame or judgment.

Hope didn't want to need these people, but she did; and they came through for her over and over, often without her even asking—often when she told them she didn't need them at all.

Footsteps thumped and Apollo's tags jingled down the hallway. Murmured words about the floors, the dog, filtered into Hope's ears, as she tried to compose herself. She heard a door open.

"Holy fuck." Even through the bedroom door, Chloe's words were clear. "This isn't a bathroom."

Hope bolted out of the bedroom, skidding into the hallway. She stared at her friend who, in turn, peered into the playroom.

"That's... It's..."

Each collection of words that came to mind felt more useless than the last, so she gave up. Chloe turned to her and grinned.

"It's *magnificent*. But I need to pee, and I don't see a toilet in here."

Hope pointed with numb fingers. "Other side of the hall."

"Sweet. Grab the food. We'll move the party in here."

"You… No… We can't…"

Chloe's grin widened. "You aren't even using complete sentences. Will he spank you if you get crumbs in the big, scary, cage-bed?"

Hope froze in horror; Chloe cackled.

"Grab the goods, babe." Then, she ducked into the bathroom.

DEVON

"Excuse me, I ordered a soda."

Devon did a double-take at the pint glass on the bar.

"Lightweight D.D." The man tapped his chest. "If I drink that, we'll all need a ride home."

Nix snickered as he replaced the rogue beer.

"Sorry. This one's on the house."

"Thanks, man." The customer snatched the soda and turned toward his party.

Nix ran her tongue ring across her teeth. "You keep giving away drinks, and we won't make payroll."

"Like you don't screw up the occasional order?"

"Haven't tonight." She batted her lashes and smiled. "We both know your head isn't in this bar, Dev."

He grabbed a towel. "This is the first time I've left her alone."

"She isn't alone; she's with Chloe and Apollo."

He gathered a couple of empties for the bin, then began wiping down the bar. "Not sure which of those would be more useless if Aaron dropped by."

Nix laughed. "The obvious answer is your dog."

It should probably annoy him that she responded without hesitation, but Devon had long made peace with the nature of his particular rescue pibble. Banged up as he appeared, Apollo was a dense, silver, marshmallow, and nothing would ever change that.

"You're right. At least Chloe could call the cops...the *other* cops." The towel cut a rough path across the wood. Devon took a breath and swiped it more gently on the next go. "Apollo is the derpiest pit in the history of the breed. Hurts like fuck when he steps on your toes, though."

Nix nodded her agreement. "I swear he puts all his weight on whatever foot is on top of yours."

"Right?"

"So..." She made a show of examining the limes, of all things. Devon braced for impact. "What's the plan for this mess?"

"Keep her safe. Keep him away from her."

"But how? He showed up at her family thing. It seems as if he doesn't have many boundaries with her."

Making a mental note that the serving staff had finished their meal breaks, Devon tipped his head to Brandy as she emerged from the hallway, tying her apron strings on the move.

"I convinced her to stay with me until court," he said, "and *my* boundaries include beating the ever-loving fuck out of anyone who can't respect hers."

Nix snorted a laugh. "Having seen JJ's face after her ex got a hold of him, I'm surprised she needed convincing."

"It was a period thing. Hormones and shit. I got it sorted."

His friend fought hard to tame a smile, then her expression turned serious.

"JJ said he's supposed to testify."

"Yeah, Aaron is contesting all of it. He hired some fancy lawyer, and there's no video footage." His gaze bounced between the additional cameras that Alex and Mark installed after the incident on the dancefloor. "It's a bunch of her word against his."

"And JJ's," Nix said. "Surely, the stitches in his face count for something."

Devon's pulse thrummed behind his eyes. "Aaron will claim self-defense."

"But how?"

"Because he was invited, and JJ hit him first."

"*Invited*?" Nix said incredulously.

"Yep. Hope's mom... She invited him a while ago, and apparently never uninvited him, despite Hope telling her to cut him loose."

"You're kidding."

Devon rolled his shoulders, but it didn't relieve the tension.

"I wish. Syd is worried about it, which worries me. It's like he's trying to make himself out to be the victim."

"So, make him the victim," a gritty, unexpected voice suggested. At the sound, Devon and Nix both looked up.

Nix's laughter rose above the music when she spotted Alex. "Yeah, Dev." She bumped his arm with her shoulder. "If Hope's ex wants to be the victim so bad, help the guy out." Acknowledging a waiting patron with a lifted hand, she grabbed a clean glass. "I'll be right back."

Devon's eyes locked with Alex's across the bar, as Nix left. "Mark on the door?"

The bouncer cast a quick glance over his shoulder. "For a minute. I'm grabbing a break before he heads out. Heard Miss Hope had some trouble the other night." His eyes flicked to where Devon's hand tightened on the towel, then back up. Like every conversation with Alex, half of this exchange wouldn't be spoken aloud. "Just wanted to see if y'all needed anything."

Moving the towel in a gentle arc across the bartop, Devon kept his tone neutral. "I think we're alright for now, but thanks for checking on her."

Alex tipped his head and turned to walk away.

"Hey..." Devon swiped the towel the other direction, as if it mattered. "You still up on the mountain?"

When Alex turned back, one side of the bastard's mouth had hitched up, furrowing the scar that cut from his temple to his throat—the one partially covered by scruff. Devon had no idea how he got it, but he'd bet a week's pay that the other guy got worse.

"Til the day I die." His dark eyes glinted. "Good place to get lost up there. Peaceful, you know. Nobody around for miles."

A muscle feathered in Devon's jaw. "I might have to come check it out sometime."

Alex smirked. "Drop by whenever you like; you know the way. If I'm not here, I'm home. Takes me a while to get back down to the cabin if I'm up the hill, but I'll show up if you look like you're looking for me." His eyes didn't leave Devon's. "Better get back on the door."

"Right." Devon said. Alex tipped his head and turned away.

"Plotting a murder?"

Devon startled, pivoting toward where Nix had materialized at his side.

"What? *No.*" He shook his head. "No." Her face pinched in a *chill, dude* expression, and Devon, realizing how guilty he sounded, forced a smile. "Can't get close enough," he said, aiming for the kind of playful that didn't sound like scheming—which he wasn't, anyway.

"What's that mean?" Nix grabbed an empty glass and turned for the plastic buss bin.

Devon shrugged. "Syd says I need to stay out of the courtroom. I guess, Hope's fear is *unreasonable* with me brooding beside her, and the judge has a sweet spot for law enforcement because his own kid is a cop in a different county."

"That's... Shit."

"Tell me about it. At least they scheduled her for Thursday." He slapped on a saccharine smile. "I can check this disaster off the list before moving on to the next."

"Dev, you can't..."

"I can't what? Cancel court? Cancel my shitty yearly field trip with Mom?" He laughed. "Yeah, I've noticed. I can't seem to *rewrite history.* So, Hope gets to go to court on Thursday, and instead of calling up my sister and asking if she wants to meet the person I fell in love with, I get to take Mom to visit her grave on Friday."

Pity filtered into Nix's eyes. "Did you talk to her?"

"I already told you—"

"There's a big difference between *I don't love New Year's because my sister was assaulted at a party*, and *Did I mention she killed herself a week and a half later, and I found her body?*"

Devon flinched.

"Should I fire you again?" he managed, swiping the towel over the bar. "Gonna make quota early this year."

"So, that's a no. Look, you're putting on a decent show. You're joking around with Alex and waving at Brandy, but you've also dumped out three wrong orders in the last two hours. You aren't fine; you are this close to climbing on this bar." She held up a hand, thumb and forefinger parted by a millimeter of empty air.

Devon scoffed. "No, I'm not." And even if it were true, that sliver of breathing room would have to do. It was all he had.

The silver ball appeared in the corner of Nix's mouth as she crossed her arms. "The second you slip," she said, "you're going down hard."

Devon scrubbed a hand up his face and through his hair.

"Then, I better not slip, huh? If Hope can do what she's doing, I can handle some decades-old bullshit."

"She has a whole support system, dingbat. And unlike you, she's relying on it."

"Not willingly. She thinks she's a *burden*."

"How do you think she's going to feel when she realizes that you've been in shambles for weeks, and you hid it from her?"

"Why do our conversations always go this way? We'll be having a perfectly normal talk, then it goes to hell in a handbasket."

"That's on you, dude. I'm not the idiot hiding from the person I claim to love."

"I don't want her upset over me right now, okay?"

"No, that's an excuse, and if things were different, you'd find another because you don't want her *picking* at you. You do the same shit with all of us, and we tolerate it because we already know. We've had years to piece it together."

"Drop it."

He scoured the bar.

"Handle it," Nix countered.

Devon opened his mouth, but closed it when his phone vibrated, Hope's name and face illuminating the screen. He opened the text and read it aloud in stunned confusion.

"*Am still aloud to kiss Chloe when I'm drink Sir?*"

Nix leaned over the screen. "You're fucking kidding me," she said.

"I'm not imagining this, right?"

"Oh, no. I see it too." She giggled. "Wasn't she an English teacher? Oh, I know! Tell her *pics or it didn't happen*."

Devon pinched the bridge of his nose. "There's no way that's going to work."

"Try."

His friend pushed out her lower lip, and because women were too damn good at that technique, Devon huffed out a breath and typed a message.

Permission granted, darling, as long as you send proof.

Ten seconds later, his phone buzzed again. His girlfriend and her best friend filled the screen. Hope clutched the bottle of wine he'd packed for her by the neck. Chloe's tongue was halfway down her throat. The blond's mouth ticked up in a smirk, one brown eye cutting sideways, into the camera.

"Damn." Nix's voice had gone husky.

"Uh huh."

Desire, masked as hunger, fanned through Devon, spiking his pulse. It wasn't jealousy; he loved Chloe. She'd met Hope first. She'd kissed her first. And seeing them...made him want to kiss Hope *more*. Spread her thighs... Kiss her lower...

Kiss her now.

Metal zinged on his tongue, a visceral memory from her apartment. His mouth watered.

They'd cleaned up in her shower after. Devon watched fresh crimson and semen run down her thighs, swirl into pink and brown eddies around their feet. And around the time Demon reminded him of his nightmares—her blood and his spend and words he would never, *ever* ignore in the waking world—Hope had dropped to her knees. *To clean you, Sir...* she'd said, having no idea how desperately he'd needed her in that moment. The next thing he knew, he was pumping into her mouth, turnaround be damned.

Hope took his darkest fears and morphed them into something sacred—something he didn't deserve but wanted so badly it hurt. She resurrected that eighteen-year-old boy, with a cargo pocket full of condoms and a tentative belief in possibility...in *hope*.

Back when he and Demon were almost the same person.

Before Devon had fully managed to crack himself in half.

You did that for a reason. You work better this way. You survive *this way.*

I know... I know.

He refocused on the screen.

"I might head home early," he said. "She can be a handful when she's tipsy. It's not that busy..."

The door to the bar opened, and a horde of college kids in pajamas, onesies, and barely street-legal lingerie filed in, partaking in the most poorly timed pub crawl in history. Dozens of them. With each body through the door, Devon's dick twitched against his jeans, pouting.

Christ...

He sighed. "Grab a marker. Let's start checking IDs."

"Wait a second." Nix's voice pulled his attention from the party breaking out on the dancefloor, the swell of bodies approaching the bar. She leaned closer to the phone in his hand. "Is that the playroom?"

"What?"

"Look." Nix pointed to a spot behind Hope's shoulder, where light sparked off a metal ring. "Isn't that..."

An eyebolt. The same one he'd hooked her cuffs to the first time he'd taken her in his private dungeon. One Devon hadn't even noticed in the picture because of his inability to look beyond Hope and Chloe.

"Goddamnit."

"Yeah..." Nix sucked a breath through her teeth. "I'll just...uh...go find that marker now."

***

The driver's side of the Charger dipped off the pavement and into the grass of his front lawn, as Devon parked alongside Chloe's car. A faint glow lit the front window from deeper in the house, telling him that the kitchen light was on; but otherwise, the house was dark. Making his way to his small porch, he let himself in. His vicious lump of a guard dog grumbled from his bed in the living room corner, unsettled from the excitement of having two pretty girls to himself all night.

"It's me, buddy."

As Apollo quieted, Devon slipped off his boots and headed for the hall. He should change, run the dog out one last time, do the dozen post-work, nighttime things that came with adulthood. But first, he had to assure that niggling voice in his head that nothing horrible had happened; and that meant laying eyes on them.

Low light painted the floor in front of the playroom door; Devon crept toward it, as unease simmered in his gut. The moment of *unknowing* stretched and stretched, slowing his steps as if it were a tangible barrier—something thick and sticky that bogged him to a stop three-feet shy of the threshold. His pulse pounded in his chest, his throat, his left temple, for some reason...

"*Psssst...* Devon? Please say you're Devon..."

He closed his eyes and took a shuddering breath, as Chloe's strained whisper doused his nerves in relief.

"Yeah, it's me." He crossed the remaining space to the doorway.

The scene was almost...*cute.* Chloe sat with her back to the headboard, Hope sacked out beside. One arm draped across Chloe's hips in the same position she'd taken against Devon as he surfed his phone that morning. A quarter of a cheesecake and a stack of takeout boxes sat on top of the dresser. He snagged the empty wine bottle from the floor and put it beside the rest to deal with later.

"Thank God, you aren't a murderer." Chloe wooshed out a relieved sigh. "Get me out of here. I'm stuck."

Devon grinned at her. "You're also sober."

"I'm driving to JJ's."

"*If* you escape," he said, grinning harder.

"Devon, it's not funny."

"It serves you right for taunting me with pictures of your tongue in my girlfriend's mouth."

"You know how she gets."

Devon sighed. "Yeah... Give me a second."

It took forty. Chloe ducked out of the playroom in front of him, while Hope snuggled into the pillows he'd used to orchestrate the hostage release. As they reached the living room, Chloe turned on him, and Devon's hope that they could avoid an awkward conversation spluttered and died like every other shred of his optimism in recent days.

"Right…" He braced himself. "So, um…"

Chloe put up a hand to stop him. "Yeah, yeah. Dungeon playroom. You *usually lock it*, except you never remember. Bathroom's on the right." She waved him off.

"Not the reaction I was expecting, but I'll take it."

"What did you expect?"

"I thought you'd be worried."

"I'm worried as fuck," she said, "but not about your kinky sex room. You taught her what a safeword is; her ex doesn't seem to grasp the meaning of the word *no*. You don't need to explain your sex life to me. Only thing I care about is Hope."

Devon let out a breathy laugh. Getting outed for his deviant nature was becoming more anticlimactic with every pass.

"So," she went on, "let's discuss something that I am worried about. I know she's all hormonal, but she cried about the potato skins—or maybe it was the wine and sour cream." She made a face. "Let's pretend I didn't lump those into the same sentence."

The bone weary exhaustion weighing on Devon pressed harder. "You're her best friend. How do I fix…" He gestured to everything and nothing. "That?" He scrubbed his face, his hair. "It didn't have to be something from the bar; we could have called in whatever—"

"Dev…"

He glanced at Chloe, who looked at him with the same sympathy Nix kept displaying. "I think," she ventured, "that Hope isn't used to people taking care of her."

Devon straightened. "I'm trying."

"I know." She fetched her shoes, sat on the couch and slipped them on. "I think it's good that she's staying here until court. She needs that; maybe you need it too."

He nodded at the floor. "I, ah… I do."

A smile whispered across Chloe's lips, as she got to her feet.

"Let's teach her how to count on people. On *us*." Her shoulders popped up, then lowered. "Before, she only had JJ, and there are some things a girl would never tell her brother, no matter how close."

But brothers should know, Devon thought. That's why JJ ran outside at the fitting—because he *knew* Hope needed him. And if you couldn't pick up on something so important as a brother, who's to say you'd be any better equipped as a partner?

"You have boyfriend privilege; I have bestie privilege; JJ's the sibling. Between us, we could pry about anything out of her, and she'd never get stuck handling shit on her own." She leaned toward him, as if letting him in on a secret. "That's when people get in trouble."

A familiar stream of images flashed through his head. Roses and unwelcome visitors. Marks that he didn't cause on her body, tears on her face.

"I like that idea."

Chloe's smile was 3 a.m. sunshine—beaming so brightly that it hurt his eyes.

"Great."

She grabbed him in a hug, and Devon tentatively put his arms around her.

"Wait, are you wearing my clothes?"

"Package deal," Chloe reminded him, patting his back. "Tipsy-Hope says your clothes are the *most cuddly*, and they smell like you." She sniffed his collar, tickling the side of his neck. "Clean-you," she amended. "You need to wash off the bar."

Devon groaned. "A pajama-pub crawl rolled in when I tried to leave early. If I ever have to make another cosmo, it'll be too soon." Her laughter chipped away at his reservations. "Did she, uh, tell you anything else?"

He wasn't sure he wanted the answer to that question. He didn't hate the idea of Hope talking to Chloe—people needed connections like that, and Devon had the same sort of relationship with Nix. But tonight, with Hope passed out in the playroom, waiting for Chloe to divulge how much she already knew felt vulnerable.

"Hmm... Did you have braces as a kid?"

"No." He couldn't think of a single reason she'd ask that question. "*Why?*"

"The teeth marks on her ass were really straight..."

Devon's eyes widened. "How did you even see that? It's been an unidentifiable smudge of..." Chloe giggled, and he trailed off. "Never mind. I'm not explaining that."

"You think I'd need an explanation about how men are animals that mark their territory?"

Devon's laugh was no more than a puff of air from his nostrils. Somehow, Chloe still had her smaller frame pressed to his chest.

"You bought her a flogger before you started dating." The reminder dragged up an image of Hope offering him said flogger from her knees. "You have a fuck-uniform."

"Christ..." He dropped his forehead to her shoulder. She smelled like Hope every time she wore his clothes, but with an undercurrent of some other flavor of feminine. Vanilla, he decided. Nix looked like a cupcake, but Chloe smelled like one.

"No, *God*," she corrected. "She said you get off on her calling you *God.*"

"You didn't get her tipsy; you got her drunk." Losing more of his restraint, he squeezed.

"Not enough for a hangover. She'll be good for dinner tomorrow." Her laugh vibrated in his bones...then faded. The hairs on the back of his neck stood on end in anticipation, as she pulled in a breath. "Hope said something bad happened to your sister."

A million unwelcome emotions cascaded through him; and thanks to his exhaustion, one slipped out as a sharp inhale. Devon pulled away.

"I don't know why she'd bring that up."

"Because she's worried about you."

"She shouldn't be. It was a long time ago." He walked to the kitchen table, pointed to the bags atop it. "Is this everything?"

"Yeah." Taking the hint, Chloe joined him and grabbed her things. "I'm sorry if I wasn't supposed to know about your sister."

"It isn't a secret." He took a grounding breath. "I just don't like talking about it, and right now, I have more important things to worry about. My girlfriend's stalker put his hands on her. Tomorrow, we're going to dinner, where there's a solid chance that her mother—who hates me, by the way—will say something horrible in support of that bastard. I have no idea what I'm doing, *who* I'm supposed to be. I don't even know if I need to wear a tie."

Chloe patted his arm. "Why would you need a tie?" she said through giggles.

"I don't know... They're rich."

"And rich people wear *ties* to boring, Sunday evening dinners with family?"

Devon scrubbed his hands over his face, then closed his eyes. "Okay, yeah... I sound like an idiot."

Chloe's voice drifted into his self-imposed darkness. "Just be you, Dev."

But which him? Devon? Demon? Neither knew how to handle this situation. Both felt angry and emasculated, and so goddamn tired. Maybe he needed a third personality. A stable one...

"Thanks for letting us crash at your house this evening," she said.

Devon dropped his hands and looked at her. "You say that like I did *you* a favor."

"There are crumbs in your massive cage-bed."

A smile got the better of him. "Given that I couldn't have survived that shift with her here alone, I don't get the luxury of being pissed about that."

She glanced toward the living room. "Well, I better go bang her brother."

Chloe walked over to Apollo in the corner, kissing his head and ruffling his ears, before heading for the door. She paused with a hand on the knob.

"Take care of her. She's been through enough, and her mom is going to make tomorrow a nightmare." Devon nodded. "But take care of yourself too. Air masks and pouring from empty cups and all that—" She hesitated when he grinned. "What?"

"Thanks for coming, Chloe."

She laughed. "Night, Dev."

"Drive safe."

She disappeared out the door. Devon hustled to the window, watched her get into her car, wearing a Henley from his dresser. After ensuring she made it out of the drive, he started the closing duties. Checking locks, running Apollo out for one last potty-break, topping off his food and water rations... He gathered the remnants of Hope and Chloe's evening from the playroom, then circled back for Hope. Devon plucked her out of the nest, inhaling the sweet scent of her as she wrapped her legs around his waist, snuggling close.

"Chloe found your dungeon," she mumbled.

He kissed her shoulder through a layer of knit fabric. "I need a neon sign for that bathroom."

"I missed you, Sir."

"I missed you too, baby."

So much.

He tucked her into bed, then headed for the shower, turning on a single can-light set dimly enough that he could leave the door open without rousing her. The line of sight meant little when the room beyond was dark, but there was comfort in knowing that she lay in the void.

Hot water sluiced over his aching body, rinsing away the grime of a long night slinging drinks to twenty-somethings in nighties. As he worked bodywash into a lather, Hope's silhouette moved through the doorway. Devon caught himself watching her dig under the cabinet, shuffle to the toilet to handle the necessities of owning both a bladder and a uterus, before flushing and washing her hands.

The water temperature inched higher—all the cold in the lines diverted to her cause. Then, she brushed her teeth with the tap on, like the greedy little thing she was. Heat wrung sweat from his pores, but the shower washed it away as quickly as it appeared. Devon smiled.

It was only when she finished that things regulated—degree after degree, ticking ever-lower. She disappeared into the darkness, and the shower settled at the once perfect temperature. Devon stared after her, goosebumps blooming on his skin.

She'd had the same effect on his entire life.

Everything was *just right* before that girl strolled into Cleary's and ordered the worst wine he stocked. Seeing her across the bar each week, hearing her laugh or politely tell strangers to fuck off, wanting her so badly he could taste it... Everything got...*hot.* Addictively hot. He'd had no say in the matter; no control over the way his heart thawed into a gooey mess that beat for her.

He'd known it for longer than he'd known that he loved her—since that emotion existed as an overwhelming sensation so alien that he hadn't yet given it a name. It would never stop terrifying him—the gift he'd never wanted—the one too precious to lose. Without her, Devon would freeze. And unlike before, he'd feel every agonizing second.

HOPE

Sunday evening dinner at Ashley and Greg's had gone better than expected. Hope and Devon arrived—bottle of Cleary's bubbly in hand—to find Ashley in an over-sized sweatshirt with *Bride* emblazoned across the chest. Hope's mom and her husband Joe stood around uncomfortably, as Greg—wearing a *Kiss the Groom* apron—plated up eggplant parmesan and salads from takeout containers.

Over the meal, Greg and Devon fell into conversation about the house's original woodwork and the efforts Greg's father took to preserve it during restoration—something Devon related to on a personal level, having fallen in love with the building that housed Cleary's for all the same reasons. Joe became less *holier-than-thou* upon realizing that, while his wife was right that Devon was a bartender, she had neglected to mention the part where he carried out that profession in a business that he owned. It shouldn't have made a difference, but it did.

Meanwhile, Ashley and Hope discussed Hope's impending start at Redact and Recover, and Ashley's excitement over the near-completion of her studies. Both women were moving forward in their fields and grateful for the opportunity to do what they loved.

"This is all very informative," Hope's mom said, as she dipped her spoon into her dessert, "but your father and I need to be heading home soon, Ashley, and I assumed there was something you wanted to discuss about the wedding." She tipped her head toward Hope and raised her brows.

"Oh... well..." Ashley looked to Greg.

"Yeah, Ash... Tell them the very important thing." He urged her on with a smirk.

"If you say so..." She thrust forward her left hand, where a band of sparkling diamonds sat tucked behind her engagement ring. "Surprise."

"You eloped?" Hope stammered.

"We eloped." Greg flashed a self-satisfied grin, as his mother-in-law's dessert spoon clattered against plate, table and floor, leaving a trail of tiramisu in its wake.

Squealing, Hope jumped up and rounded the table, grabbing Ashley in a hug. "You eloped! Holy shit, Ash. Congratulations!"

"You can't be serious..." Beth looked from face to face. "Joe... They can't..."

Ashley's smile faltered when her father cleared his throat.

"Ashley, honey... Beth is right. This isn't funny."

"That's because it's not a joke," said Greg.

The bride's father and husband stared at each other, the tension in the room palpable. This wasn't the reaction you wanted when you announced you'd gotten married, and Hope's heart hurt for Ashley, standing there with fast-fading happiness. She looked at Devon and found him staring at her fingers rolling the rope bracelet around her wrist. Realizing what she was doing, Hope stopped. His eyes flicked up to hers the moment she released it. He nodded once, clapped his hands, and pushed to his feet.

"Champagne? Or I guess, technically it's sparkling wine." He hooked a thumb toward the door to the kitchen, where Ashley had stashed their hostess gift. "Feels like we should pop that bottle and toast the love birds."

Ashley grinned. "That would be wonderful, thanks. There are glasses above the wine cooler."

Devon ducked through the door, and Greg continued speaking in a calmer tone.

"After we dropped off Hope's car the other day, we decided to pop into Cleary's. We grabbed a table and a string of buy-one-get-one rum and Cokes, and we decided we were over the whole mess."

"While drunk at his bar," Beth bit out. "Are you hearing this, Joe?"

"We weren't drunk. We were decompressing after a tough evening."

Hope winced. "I'm so sorry that you had to cancel your plans because of—"

"No." Ashley put up a hand. "We've been talking about this for weeks. I'm sorry we didn't pull the plug sooner." She looked at her husband, her expression softening. "The alcohol might have sped up the decision making, but the choices were all ours; we were extra sober at the courthouse on Friday."

"You two are being hasty," Joe said, shaking his head. "That business at the fitting was unfortunate but—"

"*Unfortunate?*" Ashley raised a brow at her father. "Hope was assaulted, Dad. JJ ended up with stitches."

"Jameson deserved what he got," Beth snapped. "Aaron was attacked. His career is in jeopardy for simply showing up to help when I asked. I feel terrible for what we've done to him."

Hope recoiled. "To him? Mom—"

"Now, calm down," Joe snapped. "No one knows they're married, and what would it matter? People want to attend the events. There's no need to cancel those."

"We scheduled a mini-moon," Ashley said.

"A what?" Joe looked to Beth, who looked as confused as he did.

Greg reached for his wife's hand and tugged until she landed in his lap. "We figured we might as well take a quick honeymoon, since the week is free now. Ash is calling it a *mini-moon*. We're still doing Paris after her graduation, but we'll be in Greece for spring break. Feel free to party without us."

Joe's face reddened. "Greg, there are some of the most influential—"

"I don't care about them, Joe. I care about your daughter." He squeezed Ashley.

"Dad, I've been begging you all to tone down the wedding this whole time, but it kept getting more and more elaborate."

Beth tossed a napkin on the table. "People expect a certain aesthetic, and we needed the space of the bigger venues."

"But what about what we wanted?"

"You wanted to get married in front of a dozen people in the woods!"

"Which was *already* a compromise." Ashley's eyes glistened. "You kept pushing and adding. It got bigger and bigger until Hope and JJ got hurt."

Greg's hand made steady circles on his new wife's back. "We might do a small reception, but *small*. From here on, we're doing this Ashley's way. No more pressuring her into putting on a show for your friends and colleagues. That's over." He spoke with all the authority of a man who had run out of patience.

"The deposits are gone." Joe jabbed a finger at his phone screen. "At least twenty grand for nothing, and don't forget that dress."

"I already had a dress!"

"You had a *doily*," Beth snarled.

Hope's mouth fell open. "Mom..."

"Oh, don't you start. Some people might be willing to lie to your face, but this whole thing is your fault. You threw away the best thing that ever happened to you, and for what? So you could ruin everything for everyone else?"

Devon returned juggling glassware and a bottle.

"Thank goodness we have Devon," her mother said. "We might not manage to open the bottle without a professional."

His brows went up, but he said nothing as he popped the cork and began pouring, handing out glasses as Hope's heart thundered behind her ribs.

"That everyone?" he asked, then grabbed his own glass and slipped an arm around Hope.

"Would either of you like to go first?" Greg said to Beth and Joe.

"Cheers," Joe managed.

"Best wishes on your happy union," Beth bit out.

Hope sighed, then lifted her glass, leaning into Devon's side. "Um...I know this wasn't in the plan," she smiled down at Ashley and Greg, "but I'm starting to see that the best things in life often aren't."

"Oh, come on..." Her mother scoffed.

"I don't think she was finished, Beth." Devon's voice skittered up her spine as his thumb skimmed down. "Go on, darling."

Hope wet her lips and started again. "You both deserve every unplanned adventure and a life bursting with love. And I am so happy you get to have that with each other, because I couldn't think of a better match."

"Oh... Now I'm going to cry again."

Greg handed Ashley a napkin, then lifted his glass. "Thanks, Hope."

Devon pressed a kiss to her cheek, then winked. "Sláinte, love," he said in her ear.

***

"Well, that was exciting." Seething, Devon pressed the accelerator, and they pulled onto the main road.

"I thought it went pretty well until—"

"Your mother followed us to the car to ask you to drop the order of protection." He gestured with an irritable sweep of his hand.

Haven't you caused enough damage?

Why do you have to be so extreme?

Let it go, Hope. You can hardly fear him showing up at canceled *events.*

Hope sighed. "Her mental gymnastics were astounding, but you didn't let me finish. I was going to say it went well until Ashley and Greg dropped a bomb. Mom's endless love affair with Aaron came after; it doesn't count."

Devon grunted.

"What?"

His eyes were dark when he looked her way. *"Stick her in a short skirt and she'll pull tips?"* He cocked a brow. "Your stepdad is a—"

"He's not my stepdad. They married when I was grown, heading off to college."

Devon shook his head. "Eighteen isn't grown." He slipped a hand onto her thigh. "If you ever do want to work in a bar, please tell me."

"So, you can be my boss?" He chuckled at the flirty invitation in her voice.

"Be lying if I said I hated that idea. I could sic the boys on anyone who showed too much interest in your *short skirt.*" He squeezed her leg. "Your mother is a real piece of work, and she married a pervert."

"The gross kind," Hope agreed.

"Are you trying to say something, darling?" Hope smiled at him, and he smirked as he continued. "No wedding, huh? I didn't see that one coming."

"Yeah." She watched the lights passing her window. "We still have the shower, though."

"The one with a color scheme." He shuddered, and she giggled.

"It was my mom's ultimate trial run. Catered, open bar... They rented out the entire Blue Lark." She shook her head. "I suspect Ashley will add a DJ and call it a reception since they won't be in the states for the original wedding date now."

"You're describing a prom," he said.

"What? *No...*"

"Really? What's the difference?"

Hope decided to play along. "Well, for one thing, the open bar will eliminate the need to spike the punch."

His eyes widened. "And I was planning to sneak in a fifth of cheap vodka." Hope snickered. "I'm kidding. Knowing Beth, the punch bowl will have a punch-attendant with the eyes of a hawk."

"You're kidding, again," she said, giggling.

"Of course, I am. You think your mother would let them put out a punch trough? Are we peasants? Well, I mean I am, but..."

Hope laughed again. "At least we only have to do it once now, and my date can dance." She wiggled in her seat.

"I manage," he said.

"That's an understatement." She studied his profile, curious. "Where did you learn?"

"To dance?"

"Yeah. I'm assuming that's one skill you didn't pick up in a BDSM club."

He flashed her a smile full of innocent nostalgia. "In the kitchen. Mom and Dad would partner off, and Kelly and I..." His breath caught, body stiffening. "Um..." Darkness bled through the innocence, and Hope felt a pang of guilt at his palpable discomfort. "What were we talking about?" He bit his lower lip, then nodded. "Oh... Proms... So dancing, booze... Anything that actually differentiates this shower/reception from a prom?" he asked, shutting down any reminiscing over little Devon learning to lead in the kitchen of his childhood home.

"Why don't you come up with one?" she said.

He checked the mirrors, then pulled his hand from her leg to shift. "I'm guessing most proms aren't held in a country club."

"Well...I went to a private school and half of the student body were Blue Lark members. The prom queen's dad still runs the place."

"Your prom was at the same venue housing this *not a prom*? You're making my case for me, darling."

"It was still the quintessential prom experience. Flashing lights, spiked punch, and all. Where was yours?"

His forehead creased. "The gym?"

"Did your school have a cheesy theme? I think ours was *Under the Stars*."

He hitched a shoulder and checked the mirrors again. "I don't remember. I had to work."

"They wouldn't let you off *for prom*?"

His answering look bordered on apologetic.

"I left home the day I turned eighteen. I limped through the last half of senior year on caffeine and adrenaline, and I wasn't wasting rent money on a tux."

"But it was *prom*."

"Mom would've killed me if I skipped graduation. That was the next week, and Saturdays were my best nights for tips. I couldn't skip two in a row." His eyes flicked to the rear-view again, then over at her. "It wasn't that bad."

"You sure? Because that sounds pretty depressing."

He flashed her a grin. "I bet I had more fun on prom night than you did. Ten bucks says you had mediocre sex with a rich kid in a cheap hotel room—and he finished first."

"His name was Cory, and the hotel was really nice."

"Makes sense, I guess—being that he was a rich kid and all." Devon smirked. "Do you think us poor guys fuck better because we're willing to work for it, or is it Mother Nature's way of keeping us in the gene pool?"

She whacked his shoulder. "He was really nice!"

He laughed. "That's the second time you've said *really nice*."

"They brought in a chocolate fountain with cheesecake bites and fruit and..." Hope trailed off as Devon chewed his lower lip to keep from cackling.

"I'm... ah... glad to hear that the room service... made up for Cory finishing first during the mediocre sex," he managed between chuckles.

Hope wanted some witty response, but he'd hit the nail squarely on the head with a battering ram. The highlight of her prom experience remained the perfectly cooked fillet and the chocolate fountain they'd put on Cory's father's card. They'd been sleeping together for three months at the time, but Hope was another two away from her first partner-induced orgasm—that one came from a college guy, three years older than her. Cory was long gone by then.

You don't know you're clueless at that age. Hope suspected that even the delectable Devon Cleary hadn't gone into his first intimate experiences as some sort of sex deity.

"Well, what did you do on prom night?" she muttered.

His smile was slow and wicked in the glow of oncoming headlights. "I made bank in tips with my sob story about missing an important adolescent milestone, clocked out at midnight and went to Edge. I mean, it wasn't called Edge back then, but—"

"Is that *legal*? A high schooler in a..."

Devon shrugged. "Legal enough. I'd been eighteen for six months, but I didn't show them a student ID at the door."

"So, you went to a BDSM club on prom night and had great sex." Her *chocolate fountain* prom story withered with every word out of his mouth.

"Oh no. I watched." His expression turned thoughtful. "I went back the next night. I did a scene, but it wasn't..." Wetting his lips, he tugged at his collar. "I didn't hook up with anyone."

Hope's brow pinched. "Like a spanking or something?"

"Uh huh."

"You know I want to go with you sometime," Hope said picking at her bracelet.

His gaze passed from one mirror to the next again, then landed on her.

"You've mentioned it; but right now, if you're still planning to work in the morning, I need to get you home and to bed."

HOPE

In the lot behind Silver Sassafras, Hope bit back a smile. Beside her, Devon parked and climbed out of his car.

"I thought you were going to Cleary's early."

He hitched a shoulder, as she smirked at him. "I realized I'd never seen where you work; it was on the way."

Hope raised a brow. "Because you followed me."

"The bar doesn't open for two hours. I can spare a few minutes to see where you'll be all day." He looked around, frowned.

"Well, here's the back parking area." Hope swept a hand toward the assortment of faded paint lines and the desiccated remnants of summer weeds poking through pavement. "Very glamorous."

Gaze snagging on the ugly metal door set into the brick wall, an awkward five inches from ground-level, Devon pointed. "Does that lead to the shop?"

Hope nodded. "We're on the end, so everything from that gutter over there to the edge is ours."

"Do you have keys for that door?"

"No." She kicked a pebble, then hooked a thumb over her shoulder. "Margo is the only one who comes in the back, usually. She lives about a half a mile that way. My keys open the front."

Devon caught her hand and started walking around the side of the building. "You leave out the back?"

"Not usually."

"Hmm... Might be a good idea this afternoon. It's dark before you leave." He craned his neck. "There's not much lighting back here."

"You aren't wrong." Hope blinked back the memory of careening headlong into Aaron as she'd walked around the corner on the way to her car back in August. The idea of doing that in the dark, now...

"You okay?"

"Hmm? Yeah." She pointed to the single light on the side of the building. "That one doesn't work. Margo has been on the property manager about it for months." A muscle feathered in Devon's jaw, but he didn't say anything. "I'll text you before I leave and when I'm in the car."

"And one more time when you get home?"

Hope winked. "That one was a given, Sir."

"There's my girl."

Rounding the corner to the front of the store, Hope slid the key into the finicky lock, grabbed the door handle, and gave the necessary tug in preparation for the *jiggle and turn* opening maneuver. Devon hovered half a foot behind her.

"Your nerves are contagious. Are you going to..." She was about to say clear the store like he had her apartment, but she trailed off when the door dislodged before she turned the key. "That's weird."

He scooped an arm in front of her. "Me first."

"Devon..."

"Darling."

He stepped around her and walked through the door, with Hope tight on his heels.

"Anyone in here?" he called over the sound of the bells.

"Good morning. How can I..."

Margo swept out of the back room, then paused, brought up short by the sight of the unfamiliar man standing in her shop first thing in the morning. Hope stepped out from behind Devon before his sour expression riled her boss.

"Margo, I didn't know you were working."

The older woman glanced between her and Devon, raising a brow. "When my favorite employee has to take out a restraining order and take a day off, I prefer to be around the shop. This is the bartender, right? Daylighting as a bodyguard?"

Hope laughed. "Margo, meet Devon. He panics over unlocked doors."

Margo inclined her grey head at him. "Seems rational, given the circumstances."

"Sorry to burst in." He scrubbed a hand through his hair, then looked down. "Oh... Hey guys." Kneeling, he scratched behind ears and stroked backs until the shop's two cats were purring like it was an Olympic sport. "You must smell Apollo."

Hope and Margo locked eyes, wearing matching expressions of confusion as Devon straightened.

"I'm glad to meet you, ma'am." He put out a hand, and Margo took it, her brow pinching at the contact. "Extra happy to see you here today. I was worried about Hope working alone, what with everything going on."

Margo nodded again. "Apollo is your cat?"

"My dog." Devon shifted his feet as Silver and Sass took turns throwing themselves against his calves. "A pit mix about the color of this fella, but huge." He bent again, petting Silver. "Don't worry. I have two hands," he told Sass when she shoved her brother out of the way. Eventually, he stood again. "Wouldn't want Apollo in a place like this. He'd knock everything over."

Margo's head tilted one way then the other, studying him. "Sassafras knocks things over because she can." She gestured to the black cat. "It's intentional."

Devon hummed and nodded. "Apollo's a good boy, but he's kind of like a cuddly bulldozer. Not on purpose, but the damage is the same. Maybe worse, since you can't even be mad at him. Anyway, I'll, uh, head to the bar. Didn't mean to interrupt. This is a nice place you have."

"No interruption." Margo walked to a shelf, let her fingers dance over the selection of stones displayed there, until she found what she was looking for, and held it out to Devon. "None at all."

Hope looked on as Devon studied the smooth, milky-clear stone in Margo's palm, shot through with black, needle-like inclusions.

"Oh, I..."

"Take it. I insist. You should have a souvenir from your first visit." Margo dropped the stone into his hand. He shifted his weight from one foot to the other.

"Thank you. I don't think I've ever seen a rock like this."

The older woman smiled. "We have quite a few rocks around here."

"I'll have to get Hope to bring me by some time when she isn't on the clock." Devon looked to her, something uncertain in his eyes.

"We can do that," she told him.

He flexed his fingers, and the stone rolled. Hope could feel the cool slide as surely as if she'd been the one holding it.

"Don't forget to text when you leave," he said.

Hope nodded again. "All the texts, and I'll use the back door and avoid the scary side of the building."

"I'll still be here," Margo chimed in. "I'll watch until she's in the car."

Devon exhaled in a rush. "That means a lot. I guess I'm a little... Well. I'll leave you all to it. Thanks Margo. It was nice to meet you."

"Nice to meet you too, Devon."

Hope stepped into him and pressed her lips to his as his arms came around her, one hand still wrapped around the stone Margo had given him. "I'll see you when you get home," she promised.

"Don't hide in the basement."

Hope laughed and kissed him again, then they were saying *I love yous,* and Devon left out the front door. Hope tracked his head as it bobbed above the front window displays. Beside her, Margo did the same. Hope waited until he was out of sight to speak.

"Tourmalated quartz?"

Her boss shrugged, crossing her arms and bunching the fabric of her linen tunic. "It's what he needed."

"Let me guess…" Hope wiggled her fingers. "*Dark aura*. You know I don't really believe in all that," she added when Margo chuckled.

"You should play along anyway. We work in a metaphysical shop."

"I wouldn't knock it to a customer."

Her boss pressed her lips into a firm line which accentuated the wrinkles bracketing her mouth. "You already know his aura is dark. You also know it's nothing like the cop's. This one is…" The white strands of hair that had already escaped her bun danced with the movement of her head. "Drawn to you." She glanced over contemplatively, as if she saw more of Hope than what was there. "As you are to him. And yes, his aura is dark." Margo shook her head. "But it isn't supposed to be."

Hope brushed it aside. "You're good at reading people; you've made a living at it. Devon is a little off, but it would be weird if he wasn't after last week."

Margo's face pinched. "No, no… That's a problem, but this wound is…*older*." Despite the cozy temperature in the shop, the sunlight pouring through the prisms in the front windows, splashing rainbows across the floor, a chill skittered over Hope's skin. "Something with its claws in him." Beneath a furrowed brow, the old woman's light brown eyes stared into nothing. Hope's heart pounded. "I don't think he knows how to—"

"*Margo—*"

Her boss snapped out of her reverie. "Sorry. I get carried away." She smiled, and patted Hope's arm. "Too many years in this shop. The customers like the drama and mystery."

"Yeah..." Hope shuddered.

Margo grabbed the broom and began sweeping it across the floor.

"Margo?"

"Hmm?"

Her thumb stroked the rope around her wrist. "Did you like him?"

"Oh, yes. Very much. And your aur... Well, it doesn't matter." Margo shooed the thought away and continued sweeping. "I have a feeling that you two are just what the other needs."

"And tourmalated quartz," Hope added.

Margo leaned the broom against the counter and grinned. "You know what they say... Any stone can keep negative people away when thrown hard enough." Hope laughed. "So, how was your weekend?"

"We had dinner with my family. Apparently, Ashley and Greg eloped on Friday."

Margo's face brightened. "You're kidding!"

"Nope." Hope bent to pet Silver. "My mom and Joe were horrified, but they couldn't do anything about it. After that surprise announcement, my mom tried to get me to drop my *baseless accu-sations* against Aaron."

The old woman swore. "Your bartender should throw that stone at her."

***

Later that evening, Hope stuck her head out of the shower. Shampoo stung her eyes as her heart beat a dizzying staccato in her chest. Her muscles twitched. The desire to reach for the controls and kill the spray before it could drown out her approaching demise nearly won out. She stared at the open bathroom door, water and suds dripping down her body and cool air teasing goosebumps along her skin.

"Apollo!"

A faint jingle punctuated the sound of running water, and then, Apollo appeared in the doorway, cocking his head. He lumbered over, and Hope dropped to her knees in the shower floor, peppering him with pats and kisses through the opening in the glass.

"Good boy." She struggled to slow her respirations. "Good boy, Apollo. Oops..." She laughed a shaky laugh, scooping a rogue dollop of suds off his ear. The action plastered his fur with water. "Apollo, down."

The dog flopped beside the shower, staring toward the open doorway. Hope relaxed a fraction. Without bothering to stand, she scooted under the spray, rinsing the shampoo now burning her eyes and coating far more than her hair.

She could have waited for Devon to get home, taken a shower knowing he was in the house...but that fed the beast. So yeah, she'd called the dog in at the end, but it was a step in the right direction. When she went back to her apartment, she'd manage a shower alone. Just...maybe not with hair washing the first time. More exposure therapy.

Getting out, she released Apollo from duty and dried off before heading to the bedroom. She donned a pair of period panties to handle her waning flow and pulled a shirt over her head as the front door opened. Devon's voice filtered down the hall—warm as whiskey and sweet as honey, tinged with something uneasy.

"Hope?"

Apollo took off for his master at a steady lope.

"I'm back here."

Tossing her towel in the hamper, she met him in the living room. He wrapped her up, smelling of sweat and Cleary's, and kissing her hard. When their lips parted, he left his forehead pressed to hers.

"No trouble?" *I love you.*

Hope shook her head.

"You do okay alone?" *I love you.*

She nodded.

"I missed you." *I love you.*

"I missed you too," she said, inching away to smile up at him. "Even though I've texted with you half a dozen times today."

Devon shrugged. "Did you give Apollo a bath?" He tucked damp hair behind her ear as he said it, let his touch linger on her cooling skin. "He's wet."

Hope giggled. "He stuck his head in the shower."

Releasing her, Devon side-eyed the dog. "You voyeuristic traitor…"

Apollo's tail thumped against the hardwoods; his face split into a sloppy grin that could only be construed as *pleased with himself.* Hope's giggle escalated, and before she knew it, she and Devon were both sucking in breath between side-stitching laughter—something neither had managed in days.

Devon snorted, and it was over. Tears poured down Hope's face. She could barely breathe.

"You…sn…"

"Don't say it," he pleaded.

"Snorted!" She cackled.

"Christ."

"Like a little piggy." Her pitch was somewhere in the stratosphere.

He snorted again, then groaned, clutching his sides. "Why can't I stop making that sound?"

"Okay, okay…" Hope put up her hands in defense. "He's not a pervert; I called him in there."

Devon passed a hand under his leaking eyes. "What?"

"Apollo." Hope sucked in another breath. "I called him into the bathroom."

He inhaled and held it, as if trying to squish the laughter into submission with internal air-pressure. "Why in the world would you do that?"

Hope wiped her face on the front of her t-shirt. "I kept hearing imaginary noises. I bet he smells great. I dripped shampoo on him."

She laughed harder; Devon stopped. His forehead creased and his spine stiffened. The change in him extinguished Hope's laughter.

"What is it?"

"He's wet because you were afraid."

"Well, yeah, but that's the funny part. I'm like the kid that watched *Psycho* and can't take showers. No... What's another horror movie? One with parking lot murderers or like... tailor shop murderers? Why do all the murderers pop in your head the moment you're trying to take a—"

Devon caught her face between his palms. He opened his mouth, closed it again. Hope looked into his eyes.

"What?"

"It's not funny that you're afraid, is all."

"It's not rational fear. In a few days, I'll be sitting in a courtroom. It's just anxiety, you know?"

He blew out a sharp exhale. "How was work?"

"I got to listen to Margo talk about your aura after you left."

He chuckled. "What was the verdict?"

"Take one tourmalated quartz, and call her in the morning."

He laughed harder. "It's so bad that I need intervention? Great." Devon stepped away from her and went to check Apollo's food situation. "So, tourma-what?"

"Tourmalated quartz."

Hope crossed her arms and watched him work, the fabric of his button-down pulling taut. She had spent as much time with him dressed as naked over the last month and a half, but she still caught herself staring.

"Have you looked at that thing?" Kibble rattled into Apollo's bowl. "It has these black lines in the middle."

"That's the tourmaline. It's supposed to be protective."

"Is that so?"

"Margo says any stone is if you throw it hard enough." He chuckled and she went on. "The spiel is that it wards off the bad stuff that soaks into you from other people, and clear quartz is kind of a MacGyver stone—multipurpose, if you will."

"You know a lot about rocks."

"I know enough to help customers who know nothing."

He picked up the water bowl. "So, your boss thinks I'm fucked up and need protection? I'll give her the first, but, respectfully, I'm not the one with a stalker."

"She thinks you're wounded," Hope said, remembering the faraway expression on Margo's wrinkled face. "Some old, deep, dark injury."

On his way to the sink, Devon hummed a response. Hope gave into a niggling desire to give him an opening other than Margo's musings.

"Oh, Monique's daughter came by too."

"The detective?"

He gave the bowl a quick scrub, then refilled it.

"Yeah. She said she needed incense, but I think Monique put her up to stopping in."

"Sounds like something Monique would do. She loves you, and all of R&R is worried."

"That seems excessive."

Replacing the bowl, he cocked a brow. "You realize what they do for a living, right? Even if they didn't know you, you would qualify for their services."

He moved toward her. Hope rolled her bracelet between her fingers and wet her lower lip.

"Neely said they put him on restricted duty. Forty hours a week on a desk until this is settled."

The corner of his mouth crooked up. "So, good news for a change. Forty hours a week that he *isn't* a threat to you."

Hope continued worrying her bracelet. "If the protective order sticks, they'll fire him. Even with his family connections, they don't have a spot for a cop who's been here less than a year and can't carry a gun. I can't imagine he'll take that well."

Devon cast his eyes down for a moment, then nodded. "We'll handle it."

"We don't even know what *it* might be."

"Doesn't matter," he said. "We'll figure it out. Did you eat?"

Hope looped her arms around his shoulders and pulled herself flush, pressing her lips to his. "I love you, Devon Cleary."

DEVON

A *rabid sloth on coke.* Devon nodded, passing a clean white cloth across the surface of the bar in a doomed attempt at self-hypnosis.

A five milligram melatonin had Hope sleeping like a baby overnight, while Devon spent more time in his basement than his bed. Every inch of his body ached from lack of sleep and dark hours filled with relentless abuse. He preferred the pain to the nightmares, though, to old memories that refused to stay dead.

Despite his exhaustion, the handful of miles between the court-house and Cleary's stoked his anxiety, until it arced like electricity beneath his skin. Exactly how a rabid sloth would feel after a weekend cocaine bender, he suspected. Especially, if the sloth's girlfriend were in a court hearing with her stalker ex-boyfriend, and Sydney Malone had barred the sloth from attending because she knew said sloth too well.

Maybe Syd was right, but it didn't help Devon sleep at night—or the sloth. Whatever. The analogy sucked, but spend the hours between midnight and dawn wailing on a bag instead of sleeping and the brain was bound to come up with some weird shit. Devon had found himself in that position more often than not over the past week…what with Hope's insistence that she work her shifts at the shop and his mom's helpful check-ins about their yearly plans—which were now less than twenty-four hours away.

At least his hands were clean-*ish*. He used those gloves Hope gave him religiously. Great when you considered the repercussions of bleeding all over a food prep area, but he missed the sting a little. Not all the time, but when disquieted thoughts filled his head and he needed distraction—Devon missed it then.

Sighing, he glanced at his phone screen for the millionth time. When it gave him nothing, he kept polishing. Nix approached the opposite side of the bar. She checked on him as often as he checked his phone, it seemed, and Devon wished she'd stop.

She rested her forearms on the wood. "Any word?"

He didn't look up. "Nothing since they headed back in."

The last text from Hope said that lunch was over, and they were about to get started. For all he knew, she was already telling her side of things. Twisting the *definitely not a collar* bracelet on her wrist and blushing, while he stood 3.7 miles away with a pretty rock in his pocket, wiping down a clean bar and checking a silent phone—employees standing damn-near on top of each other.

If he left in a rush, they were covered, but he didn't love the audience. Everyone but Nix spoke in hushed voices and steered clear of him. Devon was volatile today, and they all knew it. Cleary's was *home. Family.* He didn't want his crew walking on eggshells on his account, but he couldn't face the mind-numbing insanity of waiting alone. He'd never felt like this, and like so many other feelings Hope stirred in him, he didn't know what to do with it.

Christ, he needed this to work for her. After the pictures, the stalking, the violent altercation at the fitting, and her own mother's stalwart support of the man who'd hurt her... Hope had earned her reprieve—but it was more than that.

As selfish as it might be, Devon needed her to catch this break because *he* was tapped out. Brain stuck in overdrive. Voraciously chewing over shit from thirty years ago, when he was too little to remember more than flashes of pain and fear. And twenty-five years ago, when he thought he was as big as his anger but was so, so wrong.

Stop, Daddy! Please!

Devon shuddered.

Twenty years... *Fuck.* That one gutted him every time it went through his grey matter, and this time of year, that shit stayed on loop.

Kelly died, and the world collapsed; only the terrible parts kept going. Kelly died, and the world collapsed; only the terrible parts kept going. Kelly died, and the world collapsed—

Stop it.

He's passing around pictures, just like they passed around that video.

Not anymore.

He put his hands on her just like—

Fuck.

He took a breath, focused on the towel in his hand. Bright white. Enough texture for scrubbing, but not enough to scratch. An excellent bar towel—which was why they had about a hundred and fifty on rotation and a backup box in the stockroom. And JJ had proved their efficacy in staunching bleeding.

The muscle in Devon's jaw ticked. *Circles,* he reminded himself. *Circles are soft...*

This time, his brain made its way back to fifteen years ago, when a car crash put a stop to his bastard of a father hurting his mom. Nothing Devon did made a damn difference, no matter how grown he'd gotten, but that oak tree got the job done. And sure, the old man wouldn't have ended up in a tree that night if Devon hadn't sent him stumbling off trashed with blood spurting out of his nose, but that wasn't his problem. It wasn't. And it *definitely* didn't bother him.

His mental tires grabbed for traction but spun in the mire instead.

One year ago, even though he hadn't known Hope then. *Slammed her against a door, pinned her to the floor... He was never going to let her go.* Five months ago, when she should have been safe on his dancefloor. Devon was in the same room, for fuck's sake. Looked away for fifteen seconds, and Frat Boy slid a hand right up her skirt.

Face burning, he scrubbed harder, as the more recent shit with Aaron drifted in.

Six weeks ago. *Showing up at her job, her apartment.* Five weeks ago. *The fucking flowers.* Four weeks ago. *The goddamn pictures.* Three—

"Dev?"

Devon flicked his gaze up as Nix's voice sliced through his countdown, reminding him she was standing in front of him.

"You okay?"

Breathe.

"Fine."

Nix shook her head. "I'm going to make a loop. Let me know if you—"

She quieted as his phone blared. They locked eyes across the bar for a split second before he dropped the towel to go for it. Spotting Hope's name on the screen, he brought it to his ear and turned his back on the floor, on Nix.

"Hey..." He cringed at the unease in his voice. Her hiccuping breath set off alarm bells in his head, and his phone groaned under the pressure. With effort, Devon relaxed his grip. "What happened?"

"I just..." As she sniffled, his back molars ground together. "Oh, there it is..."

"There what is?"

"My car. I'm in the...the parking garage."

"Are you alone?" Where in the world was Sydney or JJ? Who let her walk out alone and crying?

"Yes. I needed to get out of there."

Devon cursed under his breath. He should have gone. Even if he'd waited outside, he should have been there for her, no matter what Sydney decreed.

"Lock that, darling," he said on impulse, as her slamming door echoed in the background.

"Yes, Sir," she mumbled. "Can I head to your house now?"

Devon frowned. "Of course, you can." She had a key, and she didn't need permission. She'd been using his house like her own since before the fitting, and even though she swore she was going back to her apartment, Devon had no desire to change that. "What did the judge say?"

"Don't worry. I'm okay."

"Hope."

"It's going to make you mad."

Fury billowed through his body, flickered at the edges of his vision. Devon pulled in a breath and swallowed it down.

"Not at you, love."

"We'll talk about it when you get off."

Yeah, no, he thought. "I'm heading out."

"Oh, no. I don't want—"

"*No,*" he snapped. They weren't wasting time on this bullshit where she told him to stay at work because she felt guilty. Not this time. "I'm leaving now." Ten minutes ago, if he could figure out the logistics of it.

"Okay."

"Hope, I..." He squeezed his eyes shut, hating every inch of space between them. "I love you."

"I love you, too." She sniffled.

"Straight to my house. Straight inside. Lock up. Understood?"

"Okay, Sir."

"I'll be right behind you," he promised.

Ending the call, Devon shoved his phone into his back pocket and stared at the wall of glass in front of him—his eyes landing on the remainder of a bottle of Dubliner. He told himself that he needed a second to breathe. That's all. Calm down and breathe; so, he could go take care of her.

"That her?" Nix asked, stepping behind the bar. Devon kept staring.

"Yeah."

"Bad news?"

"She doesn't want to talk about it until I get off because it's going to *make me mad*." He mentally measured the kick of three-hundred milliliters of Irish courage—not that he had any plans of picking it up when he finished his breathing exercise.

"You leaving or drinking?"

Devon broke off the intense eye contact with the inanimate object to glare at his friend. "It's not even three in the afternoon."

She shrugged. "Easier to get you down when we have enough staff. We're tripping over each other today, so you might as well get it over with."

"I'm leaving." He stalked past her.

"Dev..." When he paused, she continued. "I know you'll be focused on Hope tonight, but you've got your own stuff going on tomorrow."

"Your point?"

"You wanna talk for a few before you go? You seem...in your head."

The concern in her voice was the auditory equivalent of rubbing a cat's fur the wrong way. It *irritated* him. *Open up, Devon. Show everyone the broken pieces with their slicing edges. The blackened, festering, waste in the pit of you... You'll feel better.* Thanks, but no.

"Be glad of it," he said, and stormed to the office for his stuff.

Devon ducked out the back entrance, a door he rarely used because he hated its proximity to the dumpster. He was behind the wheel heading for home, for *Hope*, a moment later. On the drive, he focused on breathing. *Inhale, hold, exhale. Inhale, hold, exhale...* as if it might help him get a handle on it. If he cracked under the pressure, his worst traits would spill out on people who didn't want or deserve his wrath—and he didn't know how to fix it.

Whether it was over a decade of habit or sheer coincidence, Devon again glanced out his passenger side window as he passed the sheet metal warehouse that housed Edge. A lone, cherry-red Mercedes sat by the door—Maeve and Minnie, inspecting rigging and crunching numbers before evening brought the crowd.

For the first time in months, a pang of something other than fear or arousal lanced through his chest at the sight. *Sadness.* He *missed* them. So, he shoved it down with the rest and kept driving. Day or night, Devon didn't need to go in there, and right now, he had things to take care of at home.

No one met him at the door. Instead, Hope and Apollo sat cuddled on the couch—Hope with her back to him. A black skirt hugged her to the knees, and her collared shirt reminded him of the color you got when you back-lit her favorite wine. Murmurs and sniffs punctuated the silence. Her heels lay in the floor, where they'd fallen—simple pumps, instead of the strappy numbers he loved to fold up by his ears.

Apollo stared at him over her shoulder, unsmiling for once. The dog's brows pinched, and his big boxy head cocked a fraction. *Pleading.* Apollo expected him to fix this situation because he was the human, and that was his job. Devon hated to be the bearer of bad news, but he wasn't sure he was any better suited for the task.

"Hey." He moved to Hope's side. "Got a cuddle for me too?" Loosening her hold on Apollo, she looked over. Devon would do anything to erase the hurt on her face. Lower lip trembling, his beautiful girl slipped off the couch and settled at his feet.

"My mom wrote a letter for him—a whole letter about how wonderful he is and how he came because she asked—how I wasn't supposed to be there at all."

"Hope—"

"They asked him if he wanted to file assault charges against JJ. Like *he* was the victim. Like *he* was the one who needed protecting."

All the blood in Devon's body shunted through his head in one dizzying pulse. He lacked words, but his mouth moved anyway. The roughness of his voice, the way it sounded like a command even though he hadn't meant to issue one, surprised him. The way the thing he tried to shelve slipped out so effortlessly the moment she needed someone stronger than him.

He stroked a hand over her hair and said, "Tell me what you need, love."

"You, Sir."

A siren song, a dog whistle...call it whatever you like. He'd never had a choice when it came to her, not really.

"Go get ready, darling. I'll be with you in a minute."

HOPE

"Yes, Sir," Hope managed through chattering teeth.

She watched Devon press his mouth tight, shake his head, and prowl toward her. Black cargo pants sat low on his hips, unbuttoned, unzipped, and barely covering anything south of his navel. Hazel eyes skimmed down her body, and that relentless tingle at the base of her skull announced where they both were. Devon's dominant side had Hope's submissive on her knees—even as her body sagged against the restraints that held her upright on the St. Andrews.

Mind-numbing perfection.

He cocked his head, his gaze taking another trip to the floor and back. "I don't believe you." Reaching above their heads, Devon laced his fingers with hers, stepping in until his warm body pinned her to the wood more firmly than the restraints. The heat of him made her shiver harder. "Your hands are like ice." His lips brushed her temple, her cheek as he spoke. "Your teeth are chattering."

"I'm okay, Sir."

She breathed against his neck, pulling in the cedar and sandalwood scent, layered with his unique flavor of male arousal—a combination that she'd come to crave like she craved the rest of him.

"Did I ask if you were okay?"

Warning whispered through his words—the kind that sounded more like a promise than something to fear. Hope's breath came out in a rush, and her already needy core pulsed. *Think, think, think...* Her brain felt like tangled yarn in her skull. Knots of her day gobbing up the flow. He was so close. The front of his pants rough against her bare skin. His arms pinning hers. Her breasts shifted against his chest with every quick and shallow breath she took; every controlled, measured respiration of his.

Wait, what was the question? Oh... Right.

"No, Sir."

"And what *did* I ask, darling?"

"If I was c-comfortable, Sir."

Devon pressed his body harder against her for a beat, rocking himself free with the momentum. Hope shivered alone.

"And you *lied*." He crossed his arms over his chest and shook his head in disappointment that Hope didn't buy for a second. She wasn't in trouble; he just didn't want her distracted by the threat of hypothermia. "What am I to do with that?" he asked, clicking his tongue.

Hope could think of a whole host of things she'd like him to do with it. She batted her lashes, bit her lip, and aimed for coquettish—but the kind that was already naked and restrained in a sex dungeon.

"I didn't mean to lie." She pouted. Devon's expression shifted toward amusement, but his stance didn't change. "You asked if I was comfortable, and I said yes because I didn't want you to stop. I'm so sorry, Sir. It won't happen again."

"Stop what?" he asked, eyes glittering wickedly.

Hope's cheeks flushed, but at least, the sensation warmed her. "The...uh... *This*, Sir."

The corner of his mouth twitched. "Be more specific. *Darling.*"

Hope blinked, everything around her getting clearer as unease pulled her down. She shivered hard, felt the cold wet coating the inside of her thighs, and jerked against the cuffs.

This was meant to be a distraction. Devon enjoyed the game, but silencing all the mental commentary on her day was his goal. Because today was court day, and court had not gone well. Hope's breath quickened. She grabbed for the edges of the floaty, beautiful headspace already beyond her reach. She didn't want to be back in reality. Tomorrow, she could do it, but tonight, she didn't have it in her.

Devon stopped grinning and stepped toward her. "You're struggling again, but I'm going to fix that."

Reaching into a pocket, he pulled out her blindfold and buckled it in place. Plunged into the sightless void, the rest of Hope's senses heightened. The music swirled around her. Every shift in the air caressed her flesh. She focused on each sensation, hoping that one or all would save her, take her back to that magical place removed from reality.

"Now—" He was close at her ear again, his body near enough that Hope could feel the warmth radiating off him. Teasing, not touching. "Tell me all about the things you didn't want me to stop. You got distracted, and I need all of your attention right here..." He trailed a fingertip up her inner thigh, through all the dripping wet. "Right now."

"This, Sir," Hope said on an exhale.

"Freezing? You like to be cold?"

"I like to be what you want me to be." Her ears strained for input beyond the rhythmic instrumental beat droning around them. She got nothing. "Sir?" she added with an edge of panic when she realized she'd forgotten.

Devon cleared his throat from very close. "Don't worry, kitten. I'm here." He kissed her lips then pulled back a fraction. "You were afraid I wouldn't let you come again. You've had so many, but you're a greedy, greedy little thing. Aren't you?"

"Yes, Sir," she managed, shrinking into herself.

"You were afraid that I wouldn't—"

"Please," she whimpered. Her mind quieted and need drowned out everything else.

"*Please,* what?"

Hope could hear the self-satisfied grin in his voice, but she didn't care. Or she did...but only because it meant he was getting what he wanted, and that felt good to her too.

"Please, God, I need you to..."

She panted hard, twisted her hips from side to side looking for relief. The most she got was the occasional maddening graze against the fabric of his cargo pants and more darkness. *So close...* Every nerve ending in her body terminated in her sex, and he knew it. No matter how many times she came on the head of that wand, it wouldn't fill the empty aching need for him tonight.

"Hush now." Except for the vibrating energy coursing through her, Hope stilled at the decadent command in his voice. "Tell me what you need, and you can have it."

"Devon, it's hard—"

He chuckled like she'd made a joke. "Oh...it's easy, darling. Just say it. Remember last week on your couch? You knew how to ask then. Maybe you need help, hmm? A reminder..."

She felt his hand on her hip, the blunt head of him brushing between her thighs, as she remained spread on the cross. Whimpering, she tried to wiggle lower. Devon circled the tip of his cock at her opening, taunting her.

"Is this what you want?" He pressed only enough to breach her before retreating. Hope groaned, desire peaking near agony. "Oh, baby... It's alright," he cooed. "Do you want me to put it back?" She nodded. "Okay," he agreed, barely pushing into her soaking wet pussy. "But just a little. It's going to help you learn to say it."

Her chest pumped, and her legs trembled.

"Darling girl," Devon said, close at her ear again. "You know how to make it stop. Tell me what you need."

"You, Sir. I need you."

Devon inched deeper, but not deep enough.

"Me? Inside this aching hole?"

"Yes, Sir. Please, Sir," she begged on a sob.

"Use your words, darling. You know I love your filthy mouth."

Hope felt...delicious.

"Yes, Sir. Please put your cock in my pussy. I love the way it feels. Please fuck me. Fuck me hard, Sir. I need it. Please, I—"

Devon pulled off her blindfold, hooked one hand behind her neck, and held her with a stare.

"There's my good girl," he said, all honey and whiskey. "I knew you could do it." She stared into the slivers of gold in his hazel eyes, as he slid in to the hilt. A ragged breath tore from her; tears of relief slipped down her cheeks.

Sex had never been like this before him. Like *connection*. Like *safe*. Like...*home*.

"I have to get you down from here," he said, pumping inside her. "You've been such a seductive little thing, with that filthy mouth. I need to fuck you properly."

"Thank you, Sir."

DEVON

Devon padded barefoot into his basement, balled up a fist and—pulled the punch. Gloves... He needed gloves. All the effort he put into appearing cool, calm, and stable enough for Hope to lean on would go out the window if he showed up to breakfast with bloody knuckles. Not to mention, his mom would notice in the morning. She'd ignore bruising, but she'd have something to say if he split them, and Devon didn't have the bandwidth to comfort two women over the state of his hands on top of everything else.

He yanked them on, strapped them tight. Then it was hit the bag, hit the bag, hit the bag again. Each blow sending a welcome echo of the impact through his arm. The muscles in his back, neck, and chest engaging. Everything in his core and lower body twisting and tightening, throwing power at his target.

If he hit Aaron like that...if he hit *anybody* like that...lights out, asshole.

Holy hell, it took every ounce of self-control in him to not lose it when she slid off the couch and settled between his feet... When she wrapped her arms around his calf and rested her head on his thigh... It gutted him.

Devon had seen her naked on her knees with his cock in her mouth. Hell, he'd seen her naked on her knees with a flogger offered up to him—watched her grab a bar, spread her legs, and trust him to swing. But he'd never seen her submissive side laid bare quite like it was today. Like on the floor between his feet was refuge. He'd stroked a hand over her head, while Demon *writhed*.

Devon swung harder and got the same dull *thud*, the same creak of chains that did nothing to take the edge off—which meant no sleep again; and come daylight, he'd need to make himself functional enough to pick up his mom.

"It's one day," he whispered, brushing his fingers down the bag's worn surface.

But what if, this time, it wasn't a day he had to face alone? The first step to staying off the bar might be avoiding Cleary's altogether. Devon could go to the cemetery, take his mom to lunch; then let Lucas close, while he and Hope had a quiet dinner.

He could talk to her.

Or maybe, if he told her over breakfast, *she'd* call in. Margo was working alongside her anyway and would understand given the way court went.

He imagined standing beside his sister, Hope's hand in his, and the weight-bearing empathy she'd wrap around him like a shield.

Selfish...

Devon shuddered, blinked.

"Hit the damn bag. You can make it through a day."

He swung until perspiration beaded his brow, and his mouth felt like ash.

It's not working.

"Shut up," he whispered.

Running his hands through his hair, fingertips scraping his scalp and sweat further dampening the palms of his gloves, he let out a ragged exhale and side-eyed the bench he'd hauled down weeks prior. Not the best idea when he was running on caffeine and rage, but hey... It wasn't like he had another option.

Weight on the bar. Back flat. Grip it and go.

This required control. It demanded he find focus. Down to his chest, push it up, down again.

Not working...

"But it will."

He had to give it time. Slow, intentional, so his brain could take notes on how to behave, because this was the last idea he had that didn't involve liquor or slipping back into his cargos and leaving. *Leaving.* How could that thought even cross his mind?

But it did, and the urge got stronger the longer he tamped it down. The side of him that was too Irish, too much his father, whispered. *Demon* whispered. Devon wanted to drown them out, but they were in his head with him because they *were* him.

It's not enough.

"Shut up."

Weight up. Weight down. Ignore it. Ignore *them*.

The playroom was a terrible idea, but she needed it. Devon would always find a way to give her what she needed. *Just a little*, he'd promised himself. *Just enough. I'm fine.*

Until he walked in and found her in nothing but sheer white panties, with the flogger, *her flogger*, held up for him.

How did he explain that he couldn't be trusted to swing a flogger tonight? That he might trade it for a belt or a cane the moment he knew she was too far gone to stop him?

It didn't take much for her. By three strokes, her ass was a shade of rosy-pink worth lapping up, and by twelve, she slid into subspace so deep that Devon didn't trust her to safeword. You could smell the chemical cocktail pumping through her; see it in those glassy blue-green eyes.

How could he tell her that every time he took her in that room, he spent night after night dreaming of her bound up and flayed, murmuring or screaming *Red* over and over? About looking down in horror to realize the strange sound echoing in his ears was her blood dripping off the falls, and that no matter what his heart said, his body had no intention of stopping?

That it made him *sick* and *aroused* at the same goddamn time.

Devon shuddered, pushing the bar up with a groan.

No, he couldn't tell her that. There weren't words for *that*.

So instead, he'd hung the flogger back on the wall. And when she looked up at him like she'd done something wrong, Devon told her that her panties reminded him of powdered sugar. He told her how filthy that was and watched her breath catch as he said he wanted to lick her clean. He pulled them off with his teeth before strapping her to the St. Andrews and strong arming her back into subspace every time her brain came back on-line. All the while keeping a tight leash on his anger, and his disappointment, and *Demon*—who wanted to hear her say *Red* as much as Devon loved hearing her say *Please.*

He pushed the bar up, lowered it down. Breathed and breathed and *breathed... This has to be enough*, he thought.

Demon laughed.

Devon thought of her anxious gaze, her tight, pink nipples, her *trust.* Hope handed him everything, and he kept glancing sidelong at a wall of whiskey and the public dungeon on a day she needed him. The day before...

"Hedonistic asshole," he spat.

The center of his chest constricted, burning with every forced inhale until he wasn't sure he could push the bar up again. But it was that or do something loud and self-preserving that would wake Hope, and he didn't want her here.

Grunting and sweating, muscles shaking, Devon pushed with everything he had. Two more inches... One... He slid the weight onto the rack, his arms flopping down with relief. He panted under the invisible boulder on his chest. Covering his face with numb hands, he squeezed his eyes tight and gritted his teeth.

"What the fuck is wrong with me?"

HOPE

An arm hooked around her waist, pulled her back into the mattress.

"Hey, now."

"Stay," he murmured against her hair, snuggling closer.

Hope closed her eyes, relishing the heat of him, the solid strength that held her so carefully. She inhaled cedar and sandalwood and safety—and then, she disentangled herself. Devon shoved upright, rubbing the back of a hand over bleary eyes.

"Your alarm won't go off for another hour; lay down."

Ignoring her suggestion, he swung his legs off the side of the bed, as Hope dug through her commandeered drawer and pulled on her only available pair of jeans.

"Where are you going?" he said, the words full of sleep.

Hope smiled at him.

"Work."

"Oh…right."

She headed for the bathroom, brushed her teeth, and wrestled her hair into a bun. When she returned, she found Devon standing, hair disheveled, wearing only boxers. He looked around the bedroom as if he were too tired to grasp reality. If he was trying to distract her by being adorable, he was doing a decent job of it.

"You could call in," he said.

Hope walked past him. "I'm not hiding, Devon."

He grabbed a pair of joggers from the floor and pulled them on. They didn't help with her adorably-sleepy-Devon issue much, but there was less visible skin.

"Give it a day to make sure he isn't going to bother you. One day. Margo can let you know if he comes by."

"Devon..."

"Not today." He ran a hand up his face. "Stay here today."

"While you go work?" Hope cocked a brow. "I'm not saying I'm happy with how court went—God knows if I'll ever be able to forgive my mother for that letter—but Aaron won. He's on cloud nine. And like you said, the order was *paper*. I'm not less-safe at work today, especially when Aaron is busy celebrating my humiliating defeat."

Devon tilted his face toward the ceiling and closed his eyes, looking like a shell of himself, and Hope started to doubt the reason for his distress.

"Is there something else you're worried about?"

His throat bobbed. "I... Never mind."

Hope shook her head. "Right... Have a good day at work. I'll be at home this evening, so let me know if you want to come over after you get off."

"But..." He looked around the room, then gestured to the dog snoozing in the corner. "I have to let Apollo out."

"You can come kiss me goodnight before you head home if you want." Or crash in her bed for a couple of hours, as was his habit before Aaron ran her out of her apartment.

"You can't stay in your apartment," Devon said, taking a step toward her.

"Pretty sure I can. My name's on the lease, and thanks to both of my jobs, I can afford the rent." His paling face tugged at her heart strings, until she softened. "You'll be at the bar until closing anyway. Right down the road."

"Right..."

"So what point is there in me driving all the way over here? You're welcome to come over, and you can see where I am with your stalker th—"

"Tracking."

Hope smirked. "I'll be fine. The longer I wait to get back to normal, the harder it will be."

She walked out of his bedroom and toward the living room, retrieving her purse and keys from an end table.

"Is this a fight?" he said at her back.

Reaching for the door, Hope stuttered to a halt. "This is me going to work."

"But you're not coming back." He ran a hand up his face and through his hair; in the brighter light of the living room, Hope could see the bruising on his knuckles. Pacing away and back, his chest heaved. "I knew you wanted to go to work, but you were supposed to be here when I got back."

"Hey…" Hope walked toward him and caught his hand. "Talk to me. What's happening here?"

Wide hazel eyes locked with hers. "Nothing. Nothing. I'm fine." Devon looked down to their joined hands. "Sorry. I worry about you, is all. I'm fine. I'll figure it out."

Hope's brow furrowed. "Figure *what* out?"

"You know…Apollo, stopping by your apartment, all that…Just out of practice because I've gotten used to you being here."

His smile was mechanical.

"Okay…" Hope looked between Devon and the front door, an unnerving worry budding in her stomach. "I'm going to be late if I don't get going."

He smiled harder. "I forgot I have some things to take care of before my shift anyway." His throat bobbed. "Text me that you made it to work?"

DEVON

"That's great, Mom."

It had been two years since he or his mom had seen his tia. Five since his mom had traveled to Florida instead of wearing herself out playing hostess to his aunt at home. She needed the time away from work as badly as she needed time with her only other close family member. Devon did his best to drum up some enthusiasm, despite the cloying scent of roses invading his sinuses.

His whole car smelled like those fucking flowers—like Hope's apartment that day she'd hidden a similar bouquet in a trashcan. Then, Devon tied her up in his living room floor and scaled her walls because he wasn't cut out for—

The sound of breath rustling tissue paper pulled him back.

"Are you sure? I have three weeks of vacation saved up, but I'm only taking two."

"Why would I have a problem with it? I live twenty minutes from you, and I see you every other week. I love you, Mom, but I'll manage."

"I won't be here for dinner with you and Hope next week." She raised her dark brows. "You all did want to start our schedule again, didn't you?"

Devon ignored the pang at the mention of Hope's name, the niggling guilt that he'd gone on this pilgrimage while she assumed he was running errands and working. If she checked his location, she would find him half an hour from Cleary's and heading straight for five rolling acres of headstones—but she wouldn't check. She had no reason to think he wasn't where she expected him to be.

"Go, Mom." He glanced at his phone, then back to the road, the knife in his chest twisting. Of course, Hope wanted back into her own space. Fear was the only thing that had kept her at his house this long, and Devon would do best to remember that. Maybe, like Hope and his mom, he needed to get back to normal too. "Have fun for once."

"I wondered if you'd bring my future-daughter-in-law along today." She shifted in the passenger seat, the movement crinkling the paper engulfing the flowers in her lap.

Devon sighed. "I told you to stop saying stuff like that."

"I don't say it in front of her."

"Not in English..." he muttered. His mom smirked, dark brown eyes twinkling mischievously. "She's working today."

"Does that worry you? With the...troubles?"

He studied the familiar road ahead as he skirted past her question.

"Her boss is there."

"Ah... I see."

In truth, Devon wanted to let Hope in so badly it hurt, but he didn't want her caught up in his struggle. He didn't know a better way to handle this...*suffocation*. The twentieth anniversary of Kelly's suicide wasn't the straw that broke the camel's back, so much as another dump truck full of gravel onto a camel that he hadn't seen in weeks. Christ, for all Devon knew, the camel was dead.

And he couldn't understand *why*. Why was it so hard this time? Why hadn't he figured this out by now?

"You look tired, hijo."

"I'm fine, Mom."

How many times must a person tell a lie before they believed it? And in the case of this particular lie, would believing make it true? *Fine* was as subjective as pain, after all.

"You were always such a strong boy." She puffed out her chest and nodded. "From the first time I held you, I knew you'd be strong. Kelly came out floppy. They had to poke her to get her crying, but you came out *angry*. I'd never seen such fierceness in something so small. You needed it in our family." She fell silent for a time and then... "Sometimes, I think he was harder on you because of it."

Devon clenched his jaw and reminded himself to breathe.

"Your dad did love us...in his own way."

"He *owned* us. There's a difference." No matter how gentle her tone, he couldn't keep the harshness out of his words.

"You grew to be a good man, though. For all his faults, he had a hand in that."

A sardonic laugh crawled up his throat. "Yeah, right... He gets credit for— Never mind..."

He shifted his weight, refocused on the road. Catching his reflection in the mirror, he noted the myriad of dark circles, new lines, and exhaustion masking his face. His body ached. Though he gripped the steering wheel with knuckles marred only by a bit of bruising, he suspected he'd fractured the fifth metacarpal of his left hand while wailing on the bag overnight. Hit hard enough, and you'd punch through your girlfriend's bubble of protection, gloves or no.

Putting on the turn signal, he pulled into the cemetery and followed the curve of pavement to a quiet hill in the back. This was the hard part. Not now, when he'd keep it together—but later. After he left, the memory of this part of the day would break him. Then, he'd put the pieces back together. He hadn't come apart at the seams quite this bad recently, but he'd manage. Maybe it was for the best Hope wanted to stay at her apartment. If things got ugly, he could clean up before she saw.

He had stitched shit back up plenty of times through the years—the parts visible from the outside, anyway. Not the prettiest job, but it held until it didn't. Kept everything else out of sight. He didn't need help beyond the occasional ride home after he fell off the bar.

He didn't.

The next thing he knew, they were standing in front of Kelly's marker. Giving in to compulsion, he crouched and brushed away the smattering of leaves from the base. His mother stepped forward, depositing the extra bouquet off to the side before placing her spray of pink roses in front of the stone.

Kelly hated pink.

Devon turned away as his mother pulled out her rosary. He waited through the prayers and the whispered words—waited for the pain. Not the clean, bright sting, or the hot, purifying burn his darker side toyed with. His mother's pain was breathtaking, gut-wrenching. Viciously cruel and viscerally real. There was no redemption in her breaking. It welled in her until the dam crumbled, but the flood cleansed nothing.

Recognizing his cue in her hiccupping sobs, he turned back and opened his arms, wrapping up her smaller frame as she shook with grief. *Mother's grief.* The torture of a parent who kept breathing after their beloved child stopped. He'd watched her stand in hell for twenty years trying to pray Kelly to heaven. It never got easier.

"She's gone, Devon!"

Her knees buckled, and he adjusted his grip to keep her up, ignoring the tightness in his chest and his blurring vision.

"Twenty years!" Her keening lashed at his defenses. "Longer than I had her, my baby's been gone."

"I know, mama," he said, staring over her head at *nothing*.

She sobbed around prayers and pleas, as Devon pretended that he couldn't feel a thing. Better to be made of the granite of grave markers than soft flesh and a softer disposition. His mom was right about one thing. As terrible as his father may have been, he'd taught Devon more than a few life lessons.

Eventually, she quieted, and he hated what that meant.

"Come on," she said, sniffing and pulling away. Bending down, she retrieved the second bouquet—the red one—from the ground. Devon stiffened. "Let's go pay our respects to your dad."

Resisting the urge to turn back to the car, he offered her his arm. Then they were three rows down, his mother laying roses atop the winter-brown grass. She whisked her hands over the stone, brushing away debris that Devon didn't give a fuck about, before resuming her prayers.

All the while, Devon stared at a name he loathed. Beneath it, a September birthday and tomorrow's date hugged a hyphen that represented nothing but hurt. The only person that bastard loved was Kelly and only when he was sober enough to remember it. Kind of made sense that the asshole would die five years after her. Poetic, or something. Or it would have been if it had magically unfolded that way. A heart attack... A stroke... Spontaneous combustion...

Devon blinked and found himself in a memory. The steel resolve of cold calculation washed through him, followed by the sensation of his right-hand crunching into meat and bone. Warm blood sprayed over his fist like a morbid geyser—its metallic tang scenting the air. His old man's head snapped back on his spine, as his hands sluggishly flopped up to block a blow that had already landed.

Lay another hand on her, and I will kill you.

Get the fuck out of here.

Don't come back.

"Devon? Hijo?"

His mother's concern nudged at the edge of his perception, and Devon shook his head clear. "Yeah, sorry. What was it?"

"Lunch, before you have to get to work?"

He smiled stiffly and gestured back toward the car. "What do you feel like eating?"

"Let's go somewhere with fudge Sundays. We can share one."

His forced smile softened. "If Kelly were here, we'd need at least three, huh?"

"And we would still have to share!" Sunlight winked off her tears as her laughter rose. "She'd eat every bite but stayed so skinny. I don't know where she put it."

HOPE

Hope lay on her bed in one of Devon's abandoned t-shirts, her heart thundering. After an uneventful day of irrational angst over whether someone might accost her on her way to or from her car, it seemed unfair. The cozy-goodness of her pajama pants and fuzzy socks, the soothing monotony of picking constellation patterns out of her 1980s glitter ceiling... It should be enough to calm her, but her apartment felt like a silent, inescapable box. Three stories off the ground, with only one exit.

No Devon. No Apollo. Even Chloe was out for the evening.

Pushing upright, she inched to the window and peeked between the curtains into the street below. Vehicles rolled past, their headlights washing the road in illumination but never reaching the dark corners and deeper alleys. If she stared too long, her brain would mold those shadows into monsters.

"Screw this."

She turned to grab her phone from the nightstand, where it sat beside a digital clock illuminating 10:04 in glowing blue numbers. The phone buzzed before she got there, and Hope smiled.

She already knew who it would be. *Did you make it home? Do you need anything? Have you checked the locks? Checking on you.* All the ways her boyfriend said he loved her.

He would be thrilled to walk her to her car and follow her back to his place after he closed the bar. He probably wouldn't even joke about her aborted first attempt at returning to her apartment because he'd be too relieved to have her back.

Her phone buzzed again, and Hope's brow furrowed. Buzz number three meant a call, not a text. She launched herself at the bedside table. Catching sight of his name on the screen, she answered.

Noise. A god-awful din blared through the earpiece.

"Devon?" She all but shouted, quelling the assault on her eardrum by yanking the phone several inches away from her head. "I can't hear you."

Shit. Where could he be that sounded like *that*? Hope walked to her bedroom door, unsure where she meant to go or why, but then a voice came over the line. The racket made interpretation impossible, but she caught bits and pieces in a pitch higher than Devon's.

...need you to... can't get him... Fucking hell...

One *thump* later, the line quieted enough for her to make out the speaker.

"Hope?"

Her heart stumbled over the cold dread blooming in her chest. "Nix?"

"Yeah... Hey, I—"

"Is he okay? Where is he?"

The noise on the other end of the line echoed in the background, penetrating whatever door Nix had closed herself in behind and filling the empty space.

"On the bar." Hope heard a faint clicking sound—Nix's tongue ring sliding across her teeth. "He's on the bar, and I can't get him down."

Sometimes when I'm...having a bad day, I drink whiskey and stand on the bar.

Hope closed her eyes. "Oh no..."

"Yeah... Did he talk to you about...today?"

"He's Devon." She was already walking toward the living room. "What do you think?"

Nix's sigh distorted in the speaker. "Great... Look, I can't get him down unless I have the guys do it." Hope had never heard the feisty, pint-sized dominant sound so defeated. "I'd hate to do that to him. Not tonight."

Nix had all the details on why tonight mattered. She was a good friend to Devon—his best friend. She loved him like a brother, and she'd called because he needed more support than she could give. Hope was grateful...and still jealous.

"No, I can't imagine that would deescalate things." She cringed at the thought of the two massive bouncers forcing Devon to do anything.

"I'm not even supposed to be here," Nix said. "Lucas called me when he got to be a handful. He's already said some shit to Mark."

"But Devon loves Mark." Hope dug her tennis shoes out of the coat closet.

"Not when Mark tries to convince him to come down. He's... Well, I've never seen him like this before, and I've seen some shit with him. Believe me." She shouted over the escalating volume of the Cleary's war zone. "They'll tear this place apart if I don't get him out of here, but he's not feeling obedient. It's worse than August."

"What happened in August?" Hope shrugged a coat over Devon's t-shirt.

"Some jerk copped a feel, and his favorite patron went MIA." She winced. "Oh. Right."

"I know you've had a week, but this isn't the night I want to have them drag him down," Nix said miserably.

"I'm walking over. I'll be there in a minute."

"Thank you." Relief saturated her voice. "I'll have Alex watch for you from the door. Wait..." Hope paused with her hand on the knob. "Can you drive a stick?"

"Um... No?"

Technically, she could, but it had been about twelve years, and he might need a new clutch by the time she got her rhythm. Plus, it sounded like she had enough to worry about, without adding Devon's beast of a car to the mix.

Nix raised her voice above the increasing noise. "Then you need to drive. You can't walk anywhere with him, and the rest of us have to help Lucas shut this down."

"Okay—" A sound in the background that could've been a building collapse cut Hope short. Nix cursed.

"Hurry or there won't be a bar to haul him out of."

***

After a heart-pounding sprint to her car, Hope drove the three blocks between her apartment and Cleary's, where she parked in the fire lane and got out. She peered toward the unusually dark windows of the bar, confused by the lowered lights, until she realized what was going on. Innumerable body-shaped shadows drifted and undulated within, obstructing her view and blocking light from exiting. All the welcoming warmth of the place was gone, replaced by something unsettled that you could feel from the street. She locked her car and rounded the hood.

As Hope stepped onto the sidewalk, Alex yanked down the skull-printed gaiter and loomed over a blond dressed in running clothes. The woman looked out of place standing there at ten o'clock on a Friday night, wearing sweat-soaked, name brand athletic wear...in winter.

"I don't think you get it," Alex snarled. "We are closing; that means *people leaving,* not *more people going in.*"

"Doesn't seem like you're closing," the woman shot back.

"It would go a lot faster if I weren't wasting time arguing with you." Alex jerked his head toward Hope, indicating the door. She nodded and stepped past him.

"Are you fucking kidding me? You're letting her in?"

"Look, why do you even want in? I'd recognize you if you were a regular, and—full of offense, sugar—you need a shower."

"Don't act like this place has a dress code; she's in pajamas!" The outraged woman shrieked behind her.

Ignoring it, Hope shoved her way inside.

She'd never imagined so many people could occupy the space. And the volume... The kind of *loud* that distorted in your ears and vibrated the air. Some song about *pirates... sailors...?* It pounded through the speakers, sounding like an Irish jig made a baby with rock. People were everywhere. Shouting, sloshing drinks, packing the dancefloor, and swarming the bar.

The bar...

Hope looked beyond the crowd and spotted the reason for her pajama-clad outing. Devon stood atop the usually glossy surface, stomping, and singing, with a half-empty bottle in each hand. His face ruddy from exertion, his eyes wide and wild as sweat dripped over the tattoos winding up his arms and over his shoulders.

Where was his shirt?

Before she could process it all, a trashed guy in a ball cap slung his arms around her. He slurred something unintelligible over the noise, then tried to force his mouth to hers. Hope palmed his face, shoving his head back, as an infuriated Alex hooked the stranger around the waist.

"Alex?" Hope wiped her hand down her coat-front, grateful but surprised by the bouncer's sudden appearance. "Where did you come from?"

He looked at her like she'd grown another head. "The goddamn sidewalk. You just passed me."

"Yeah but—"

"Get him the fuck out of here!" he barked, as he wrestled the man who had tried to kiss her out the door.

"I'm working on it!" Nix shot back, breaking free of the crowd with Mark behind her. Without preamble, she grabbed the sleeve of Hope's coat and pulled her into the raucous mob. "It's a good thing you live close." Even with her yelling, Hope struggled to pick her voice out of the mayhem. "I can't get this under control with him up there. We need him down before someone calls this in."

Hope swallowed hard, shoving down her fear of what someone calling the cops the day after her ex left a court hearing with his rights intact might mean in this situation. She looked at Devon again, the bulk of him periodically blocking her view of the hand-painted *You won't like him when he's Irish* sign that normally hung well above his head. She'd seen plenty of *Controlled Devon*, *Dominant Devon*, and glimpses of *Vulnerable Devon;* but she didn't know the guy on the bar.

"If Mark can't get him down—"

How was Hope supposed to do it? Mark had known him longer; he was twice her size. She glanced at the bouncer hovering behind Nix, his usual easy smile replaced with frustration, and she felt a swamping sense of dread.

Nix propped her tongue ring in the corner of her mouth and canted her head. "I think he'll listen to you. There's always been one person who could talk him down, and since he's not interested in anything I have to say, I'm assuming you're the new *Devon Whisperer*."

Seeing him up there, so utterly different, Hope had serious doubts.

"What if it doesn't work?"

"Then Alex and me will handle it," Mark said, his voice brimming with grim determination.

Nix's face contorted. If Hope wasn't close enough to see her mouth moving, she wouldn't have caught what she said.

"He's barely hanging on as it is, Mark."

Hope gestured to the bar. "You call this hanging on?"

"So, what's the new plan?" Mark said, ignoring her question.

"Hope takes him to his place." Nix tipped her head in Hope's direction. "Apollo will need out and fed. One of you guys can help me drop off his car later."

"We need his car keys," Hope said. "I only have keys for his house."

Nix held up a familiar keyring and gave it a jingle. "He'll give his keys to anyone the moment he grabs a bottle. I had them before I managed to lift his phone and call you. So, everyone on board?"

Mark nodded. "As long as it works fast. We need him down, Nix. Now. And if Alex is involved, it's going to get rough. He won't tolerate his bullshit like we will."

"Pretty sure that's why Dev hired him," Nix grumbled. "But Mark's right. We need to get this done."

As Hope glanced up at the bar, Devon's gaze landed on her. He cocked his head, sank into a crouch, and tapped a finger on the wood beneath his feet. For the first time since she'd walked in, she recognized everything about him.

"Right..." she said weakly.

Flanked by Nix and Mark, she made her way toward him. Lucas stood backed up against the wall of liquor—Brandy beside—sheltering from the chaos. And then there was Devon...the catalyst.

Hope took a bracing breath and walked right into him.

"Devon, you need—"

He reached down and grabbed the front of her coat, then yanked her up with him—oblivious to the bottle he dropped in the process. Perception skewed by the unexpected change in elevation, Hope wobbled.

"Hey!" Mark protested below them.

Hope held up a finger, motioning for him to wait. She could salvage this. She hadn't planned to climb on the bar, but it wasn't like she'd expected him to abandon his post the moment she asked either.

"God, I've missed you," her very drunk boyfriend said.

Devon stepped into her. The remaining bottle in his hand pressed against her lower back, nudging her closer, as his other hand caught the collar of her coat and shirt... *his shirt*... yanking both to the side. Cool air and warm breath swirled over her bare skin, as he nipped and sucked his way from her shoulder to her ear. The bar raged around them.

"Small tastes." He mumbled against her throat. "If I devoured you, you'd be gone. But I want to. Can you tell how badly, darling? Can you tell?"

He smelled like cedar and sandalwood. Whiskey and sweat. Heat radiated off his scorching skin. Before Hope knew it, she'd wrapped her arms around his shoulders, skimming her fingertips through the damp hair at the back of his head.

Devon brushed his lips over hers, and someone let out a whistle, breaking the spell. Hope leaned back as far as she could manage with his arms around her, but the action pressed her lower belly more firmly into his growing erection.

Shit.

"We need to go home," she said, putting a hard stop to the tingle at the apex of her spine and refusing to acknowledge the one between her thighs. This was not the time or the place, and he was in no condition.

"This *is* home," Devon slurred. Releasing her, he pivoted toward the crowd, raised his bottle high and shouted. "Cleary's is home for bastards like us, aye?"

A wave of unease rippled across the adrenaline in Hope's blood as hundreds of hands and drinks went into the air—dozens of partially-full bottles of rum among them. A chorus of voices cheered *Aye!* back at their impromptu leader.

Devon thought he had control of this; he didn't even have control of himself.

He returned his attention to her, all red-rimmed eyes and smug satisfaction. "Until I throw them out." He smirked. "Nix tries to snatch it sometimes, but *this*..." He stomped the bar for emphasis. Hope looked down at the black scuffs left by his boots, and her heart lurched. "This is mine," he growled. "She's *always mine*."

"Devon, you have to stop."

"Ah... You've been talking to Nix." He giggled like a kid and took a swig. "You need to loosen up." Holding the bottle of Dead Rabbit toward her, he seemed to reconsider. Liquor licked up the sides of the bottle as he pointed at her. "This isn't even wine. Lucas! A bottle of our finest Cab Sauv for the lady! Hurry like your job depends on it because it does." He giggled again.

Lucas turned toward the shelves then back again, like some sort of glitching video game character. He stopped when Brandy put a hand on his forearm and shook her head.

"I'm fine, Lucas," Hope assured the young bartender. "I don't need—"

"Then dance!" Devon shouted, swigging whiskey like water. Without warning, he hooked an arm through Hope's and spun, the lights and sounds going tilt-a-whirl despite her sobriety.

"We need to—"

"Dance!" he demanded again, belting out lyrics he knew by heart.

She couldn't hear herself think over his singing, and the crowd grew louder right along with him. As Devon wailed something about a dancefloor in hell, Hope wedged her free-hand between them. A push, straighten, and yank later, she popped loose—and stumbled back across the bar, arms pin-wheeling.

She didn't have a plan for that part.

Nix and Mark reached up in her periphery on one side, and Lucas and Brandy scrambled to do the same from the other; but it was Devon who shot out a hand, caught her by a wrist, and pulled her flush against his body.

"Careful, darling." He purred into her ear, forcing the wrist he held behind her back and squeezing her tighter.

Hope shoved back from him, this time keeping her balance. "Devon Cleary," she snapped, trying to channel...well, *Devon*. "Get. Down."

Devon regarded her with irritated boredom. "I don't want to."

"When Mason has a hard time," Brandy offered, "sometimes you just have to grab him and go."

"I'm sorry, who is Mason?" Nix shouted over the din.

"Her kid," Lucas yelled back.

"Your four-year-old gets like this?" Nix gestured to Devon as he shook sweat out of his hair like a dog.

Brandy shrugged. "I mean...usually it's over leaving the playground, but same concept."

Hope tried again. "I said, get off this bar, Devon. *Now.*"

Devon smiled wickedly and swayed on his feet. He extended his arms out to the sides in invitation—liquor bottle still in hand. "*Make. Me.*"

"I'll fuckin' make ya," Mark grumbled from the floor, stepping closer.

Devon laughed at the big bouncer. "We both know that's not how this works, jackass. You can't make *me* do a goddamn thing."

"Not the place, Dev," Nix said.

Hope watched the entire situation devolve. Pretty impressive, being that she'd assumed they were at rock bottom when she arrived.

"Didn't ask you," Devon shot back. "I'm talking to this guy." He jabbed a finger at Mark. "If you want to do this, I'm game, but I'm going to embarrass you in front of *my whole family*!"

His voice rose with the last three words, earning a deafening response from the crowd. Most of this mob knew Devon. They didn't want the party to end any more than he did. They'd set off a brawl if Mark and Alex wrestled him off the bar now. Devon had to get down of his own volition, peacefully—and fast. But he was in no mood for reason and ordering him down worked as well as throwing gasoline on a fire. What did Hope have left?

The crowd pressed forward, buffeting Nix and Mark from behind.

"This is ridiculous," Mark snapped. "I'm getting Alex, and we're ending this before this dipshit ends up in jail."

No, Hope thought. This was all wrong. Everything about this situation was about to get so much worse, and she didn't know how to stop it unless...

"Sir?" she said, loud enough to carry over the commotion. Mark stopped short as Devon shifted to face her. "I want to leave, please."

Devon canted his head.

"If you want to leave, leave. I'm not *forcing* you to stay." He jerked his chin toward the door before his face contorted. "But call me," he tacked on. "So, I know you got home. Wait... Did you tell me you were coming? You're supposed..." Patting his pockets in search of the phone Nix had confiscated to call her, he pulled out the stone Margo had given him. He squinted at it. "The fuck is... Oh." Devon repocketed it and kept looking.

"Please, come with me. This is..." Hope looked around the bar, at the utter chaos in a place he always kept under tight control. "Wrong..." she murmured. "Let's go somewhere calmer, Sir."

Devon laughed, forgetting the search for his missing cell. "You realize this is all me, right?" He grinned, gesturing to the madness with his waning bottle of whiskey. "If you want *calmer*, you better leave me here, kitten." He brought the bottle back to his mouth but lowered it at the last second.

Hope wet her lips and started again, laying it on thick.

"Please, Sir. I changed my mind. Let me stay with you tonight. Put me to bed."

Devon shrugged; the movement so detached that it chilled her. Mark and Alex would snatch him right off this bar, and Devon's haven would erupt into a destructive brawl in the aftermath.

"Please, Sir. Let's go home."

Defiance filled his hazel eyes. Seconds ticked down toward the moment all hell would break loose. There was no way he'd budge—not with that look on his face. Except then, his defiance shifted to an amused smirk.

"Persissent...per...persistent little thing..." he chided. He leaned over and set the bottle on the bar, before climbing down and holding a hand up to her. "I can't drive," he said.

Hope followed him to the floor, ignoring the glass crunching under her tennis shoes. A moment after Devon steadied her, she found herself steadying him.

"I kind of figured," she said.

Nix, Mark, Lucas, and Brandy all exchanged relieved looks, as Hope pointed Devon toward the door.

"I know where I'm going," he said.

"Of course, you do, Sir."

He answered her with a side-eyed glare that would've served as a warning if he weren't swaying. Halfway to the exit, whatever had been keeping him upright ran out. Devon stumbled against her, and Mark appeared on his other side to help shoulder the load.

"This means nothing," Hope's inebriated boyfriend slurred.

Mark patted his chest. "Never does."

They met Alex, still manning the door, turning away any new patrons, and tossing folks as he could to maintain a modicum of control over the anarchy. As soon as he saw them coming, he joined the effort, taking Hope's place.

"It's about time," he snarled, as they broke out into the relative quiet of the street. "What took so long?"

"Trial and error," Nix said.

"What's that supposed to—"

"Darling girl," Devon drawled loud enough that anyone in a four-block radius could hear. "Did I ever tell you how badly I want to shove a—"

"Whoa there, big guy," Mark shouted. "Let's...uh...get you in the car so you can...uh... get her where she needs to be." He shrugged as if to say he was winging it.

They dumped Devon in Hope's passenger seat, and Mark buckled him in. Devon swatted at his hands and cursed a blue streak in more than one language, but he didn't throw any punches. The moment the door slammed, Alex rounded on Hope. He jabbed a beefy finger at her car.

"*That* is dangerous."

Hope glanced down at her passenger-side window and found herself staring into Devon's upturned face. His slitted-eyes fixated on her every move. She forced out a weak laugh.

"Because of the alcohol poisoning?"

"No." Nix stepped forward, crossed her arms. "Alex is right. You played subby to get him down, and he's fucking trashed." She glanced between the guys. "Maybe one of us should go with her."

"One of *us*," Alex said. "I'd take you in a fight against any man, any day of the week, Nix, but that don't mean I'm intentionally sending you to deal with this drunk bastard."

"Here, here," Mark chimed.

A black SUV crept past: both bouncers paused to track its progress.

"Fourth time I've seen 'em," Alex said.

Mark shook his head and spit on the sidewalk. "They're after something."

"Or someone..." Alex turned to Nix. "Someone needs to walk the girls out tonight. You included."

"Look, I go wherever I—"

"We make the safety calls when this jackass can't." Mark hooked a thumb toward Hope's car. "Those are the rules."

Nix rolled her eyes and cocked a hip. "You two are so dramatic."

"We're careful," Mark corrected. "And for good reason. You live in a bubble, cupcake. We keep it that way."

"Fine, but who's going with Hope? Unless you two have a massive love child that I don't know about, we're running short on bouncers."

Hope shook her head. "No one is going with me. You all need to get back inside and save his home away from home. It's Lucas and Brandy and a few college kids against a riot in there." As if on cue, a crash emanated from inside the building. Everyone cringed. "I can handle Devon."

Nix pressed her mouth tight, attention divided between Hope and the front of the bar. "If he gets…"

Alex threw his hands up. "You can't be considering—"

"The safeword we use is *red*." All three of them stared at her. "I've never needed it, but he reminds me all the time."

Nix looked to Devon in the passenger seat. "No version of Dev shy of *unconscious* would ignore a safeword," she hedged.

"And if he's unconscious…" Mark shrugged. "Well, she won't need one, will she?"

"You shut down Cleary's; I'll get him home," Hope promised.

Alex shook his head. "I don't like it."

"Ah, but you didn't see her in there." Mark clapped her on the shoulder. "Called up a demon, then charmed him right out the door."

"Yeah, well, let's hope we can handle the rest of them." Nix blew out a breath, gearing up for what came next. "Call if you have trouble. We'll drop off his car after we close. Thanks for coming." Then, the bossy pixie hugged her, a quick, uncertain squeeze.

"Thanks for calling," Hope said against Nix's ear.

Nix gave a knowing nod and pivoted on her heel. The muscle followed in her wake, with Alex glancing irritably back over his shoulder. As the three of them made their way inside, Hope headed for her side of the car. The music halted, cutting the commotion coming from Cleary's by half; and then the opening notes of *Closing Time* began and the wide windows brightened. A chorus of *boos* rang out; disappointed patrons filed into the street. Hope closed her door and shifted her attention to the pile of Devon occupying her passenger seat—half-naked and drenched in sweat.

"You must be freezing."

Her teeth chattered as she started the car and cranked the heat. Icy air blasted them making even Hope, in her coat and pajamas, shiver harder. Slumped against the door, staring up through the window, Devon chuckled.

"I don't feel a thing. That was the whole goddamn point."

HOPE

Aside from a heavy sigh as they passed that big warehouse close to his place, Devon didn't move. He was so quiet that Hope fretted over how she'd get him out of the car. That issue resolved itself when they reached his house though.

Pulling into his driveway, she parked; and Devon—not as *out* as he'd seemed—jerked to life. With the speediest clumsy fumbling Hope had ever seen, he released his seatbelt, found the door handle, and tumbled out onto the asphalt. She stared at the spot he'd once occupied for a solid three seconds before her congested brain put the pieces together.

"Shit! Devon..." She hustled to his side. "What are you doing?"

Devon stared up at the night sky, white steam swirling into the darkness with each exhale. Irritation twisted his features.

"Leave me here."

Hope sighed. "Get up. It's freezing out here." She grabbed a hand and pulled, but Devon yanked it back. Stumbling to his feet on his own power, he lumbered toward the house and up the porch steps.

"Thanks for the ride. Love you. Bye." He didn't spare her a glance as he spoke.

Then, without preamble, he dropped trou and peed right over the railing. Hope stopped mid-stride, her mouth falling open. She couldn't leave him like this—shirtless, pissing on a shrub in full view of his neighbors. He hadn't even realized he was locked out yet.

Zipping up, Devon turned his attention to the front door, grumbling as he searched the pockets of his jeans for keys he did not have. Hope urged her limbs into motion again.

"Where..." His head snapped up, surprise widening his eyes as he spotted her ascending the steps behind him.

"You're still here." His brows lowered in suspicion. "*Why* are you still here?"

Hope opted for that whole catching-dominant-flies-with-honey approach that had gotten her this far. "You said you'd put me to bed, Sir,"

Devon snorted. "*Please, please, please Sir...*" He rolled his eyes. "You didn't want to stay with me. You just wanted me down like the rest of them."

Having failed to locate his missing keys, he eyed the front window.

"I've got mine." She pushed past him. "Scooch over."

She opened things up before he could add a flesh wound to the night's festivities. Devon stalked inside, petted Apollo, then staggered to the patio to let him out. Despite his unnatural speed escaping the car, he fiddled with the deadbolt with the efficiency of a raccoon wearing mittens. The dog at his feet whined. Hope started toward them, ready to handle it herself, when Devon succeeded. Apollo bolted into the backyard, patio door hanging ajar behind him. Oblivious, Devon walked into the kitchen and began rifling through cabinets, as Hope watched warily.

"I'm fine," he groused, swaying on his feet. "You should go."

He hit paydirt in the back of the cupboard over the coffeemaker, pulling out a bottle of amber liquid. Prize in hand, Devon leaned his back against the fridge. A painful catching and rending sound followed him to the floor, his sweat-dampened skin grabbing the slick surface every few inches as he sank.

Staring at him there, half-naked, covered in sweat and debris from his tumble in the driveway, clutching yet another bottle of liquor by the neck, Hope decided that, even if she had wanted to be alone at her apartment, Devon wouldn't have a snowball's chance in hell of getting rid of her.

After Apollo pushed his way back in, she latched and locked the door, dumped a scoop of kibble from the bin into the dog bowl, then marched into the kitchen. She filled a glass with cold water and held it down to Devon.

"Trade."

He scoffed. "I'm not trading for *that*."

"Yes, you are."

"Or what?"

"Or I'll take up jogging. At night. In poorly lit locations, along Aaron's beat."

Devon growled, and it was all she could do to keep from laughing at him. "You're a fucking brat," he said; but he relinquished the bottle, and she forced the glass of water into his hand.

"Drink it all," she ordered. "You'll thank me tomorrow."

She settled on the floor beside him as he chugged with a grimace. Figuring *why the hell not?* Hope twisted the cap off the confiscated whiskey and swigged. Smooth fire raced from her tongue to her gut, burning through tension on the way. He was a mess, but she'd gotten him home, inside, and hydrated. Even if he slept on the kitchen floor, the worst of it was handled.

Devon passed the empty glass from hand to hand. Hope reached over and caught it as it slipped.

"Never saw you drink whiskey," he said, as she set the glass aside.

"Yeah, well. You made it seem so fun."

"I'm supposed to be alone."

"You would've smashed out a window if I'd left the last time you told me to go."

"I'm supposed to be alone." The sentiment wasn't any sweeter the second time.

"Devon, half an hour ago, you were leading a sing-along from the top of the bar, and you wouldn't come down. You didn't want to be alone then."

"That's different," he bit out.

"Right..." Hope took one more sip from the bottle before setting it by the empty glass, out of his reach. "You'll hang out with all your nameless friends, but not your girlfriend, huh?"

"My girlfriend wanted to stay in her apartment like a big girl, and I decided to be okay with that."

"Oh." She swept a hand in his direction. "Is that what this is?"

His narrowed eyes slid to her, and Hope expected to be told to leave again.

"Too quiet here," he mumbled instead. "I can hear... You don't need to be here for this. You should go."

Trashed as he was, something in his tone sounded crushingly serious.

"I can't do that. You aren't safe alone right now, and I can't spend all night worrying about you."

"You didn't care that I was going to spend all night worrying about you."

"Devon..."

"Give my bottle back."

Hope sighed. "No."

He shut his mouth and bounced the back of his skull against the refrigerator door; Hope winced with every thudding impact.

"What are you drowning?" she asked. Devon pulled in a ragged breath and stopped whacking his head long enough to shake it. "You can tell me. What happened tonight?"

The sound he made landed somewhere between laughter and anguish. "I fucked up. Obviously." Hope put a hand on his arm; he flinched away from her touch.

"I can see that you're hurting, and I think it's about more than where I planned to sleep," she said. "Talk to me. Help me understand."

"You say that, but you don't know. You wouldn't even be here if you knew." He weighed that for a few seconds before continuing. "No, that's like...smart. Easiest way in the world to get rid of you. The kicker will be whether you come back."

"Devon—"

His laughter chilled her. "No, no, too late now. Let's do this." He clapped his hands together, rubbed his palms. "Today, marks twenty years since Kelly died," he announced.

Hope blanched. "Why didn't you tell me this morning?"

"Tell you I fall apart every year over something that happened two decades ago?" More laughter. "Yeah... that's manly as fuck."

"I told you I would stay."

"But you shouldn't have to." His head turned toward her, cheeks pink and eyes shining. "How hard is it to drive Mom to the cemetery once a year...watch her pray and cry over my dead sister?" He shook his head. "*Twenty years,* and I'm still not over it. And you need me to be better than this. You have a stalker that no one seems to give a shit about, and I'm too drunk to stand right now. I couldn't keep you safe if I tried. What the fuck is wrong with me?"

"Nothing. Nothing is wrong with you. Grief doesn't have an expiration date. I'm so sorry—"

"Why? You're always apologizing for shit you didn't do. Not like you shoved a bottle of pills down her throat. You didn't fuck an uncosh...un..." He shook his head again, chewing over the word tripping up his inebriated brain until his tongue cooperated. "...*unconscious* girl, while people laughed."

Hope recoiled from the content, from his crude delivery. And then she watched his defenses falter, feeling slipping through his cracks.

"I mean...she wasn't...*unconscious*." He managed the word more smoothly the second go. "Not exactly." Devon's brows bunched, as he remembered details of a scene a brother should have never laid eyes on. He scrubbed a hand over his face. "She made sounds. Little..." He trailed off, a violent shiver running through him.

"So, you take your mom every year?" Hope asked, leading him back to a less triggering part of the story, selfishly hoping that it would keep him talking. Devon nodded.

"I hold her up." He chewed his lower lip. "Because I'm *fine*."

No wonder he'd ended up on his bar clutching two bottles of whiskey. Hope wanted another pull herself.

"She's lucky to have you."

Closing his eyes, he slammed the back of his head against the refrigerator so hard that Hope squeaked. He took a slow, deep breath, glanced at her out of the corner of his eye. "I take her to see Kelly." His throat bobbed. "Then, I take her to the other grave."

Angst fluttered in Hope's chest.

"Devon Colin Cleary. *Senior.*" He turned away from her and spat, as if he needed to get the name out of his mouth.

"Your middle name is *Colin*?"

It seemed like such a trivial detail when he'd spent the twentieth anniversary of his sister's death reading his own name on the grave marker of a man he *hated*.

Devon made a derisive sound.

"Beloved father and husband... That's a goddamn lie. He beat the shit out of Mom more times than I can count. His daughter ate a bottle of pills to escape, and his son killed him five years after that." Tears brimmed in his eyes as he laughed. "He's the one who broke us."

"You...you didn't kill your father, Devon." Hope reached toward him, then hesitated, afraid to bridge the last inch. "He died in a car wreck. It wasn't your fault."

His smile sluiced down her spine like ice water.

"I know how to throw a punch," Devon slurred. "But that's a secret. *Shhh...*" He pressed a finger to purple lips—too numb to realize he was freezing. "*I* took Mom to see Kelly that day. *I* took her to dinner. He was already drunk. He was always drunk when it mattered, and he was more a bastard when he'd had more than a few..." Devon shook his head clearer. "Or less than a few... He was *always* a bastard." He pressed the heels of his hands to his eyes, then scrubbed them on his jeans. "Shouldn't have been my job," he mumbled.

"No, it shouldn't." Giving in to the desire to touch him, Hope stroked his bicep, his skin cool and clammy under her hand.

"*First, fives, tens...* They matter." His eyes narrowed as he mulled it over. "*Eighteen* because she was eighteen. *Nineteen* because she didn't make it to nineteen."

Hope nodded. "That makes sense."

"It was *five years.*" Devon pinned her with a meaningful stare, then turned away in disgust. "That one counts. He should've spent the day with her. He should've taken her. That's what a father is supposed to do, or a husband, or whatever…"

"You're a good son, Devon. You take good care of your mom, even when you shouldn't have to." His body quivered beside her, and she would have gone for the throw on the living room couch, if he hadn't spoken.

"He thought he could put his hands on her again. People always putting their hands on people…" She watched his attention wander, agitated eyes skimming empty space but seeing something else. "I know that. I should know that… I'm sorry. I keep fucking it up. I'm sorry."

"You didn't do anything." Hope brushed her fingers through the hair at his temple; he jerked away.

"R…Right… I didn't *do* anything. I turned around when I was sup…supposed to watch you."

"Are you talking about what happened on the dancefloor that night at Cleary's?" Darkness rolled over him in confirmation, as she struggled to follow his disjointed train of thought. "Devon, you got there before Alex, and you were farther—"

"It never should have happened. Like Aaron in that parking lot. It never should have happened. *I* let it happen." He shivered harder.

"No…" Hope reached a hand toward his hair again. With a lurch, he scrambled two feet away from her.

"Stop petting me! You don't get it. You don't understand. I knew something wasn't right with Kelly. I knew Dad was too gone to drive. I knew to watch you on the dancefloor. I knew your piece of shit ex was trouble. It's like you said, I did *nothing*."

Deep, aching pain hung in the air between them. Devon's chest heaved in quick, ragged breaths, as he curled into himself, trembling, and muttering a punishing string of self-loathing that Hope couldn't quite make out. Her eyes stung with unshed tears and rage filled her to bursting.

A broken child—that's what sat before her. A scared little boy who had convinced himself long ago that if he tried hard enough, he could control the world. Because that was the only way Devon knew to survive. Crawling toward him, Hope hooked a hand under his chin and nudged his head up.

"Hey you..." She might want to throttle a few people for the state of him right now, but she'd be soft for him. "Come on. Hot shower. Warm bed. Things are always better in the morning."

Grabbing him by the hand, she hauled him upright. To her surprise, he stumbled after her without complaint. He didn't protest when she started the shower, or stripped his jeans, or even when she got naked herself and stepped in with him. He stank of sweat and alcohol. You could lick him and come away tipsy enough to ignore the mouthful of salty leaf matter. The water carved clean lines through the grime that had peppered his torso since his graceless exodus from her car. Devon stood there; unfocused eyes trained at the level of her collarbones.

Hope studied his dark circles, purple lips and the fine pattern of goosebumps texturing his ink. Freezing, filthy, and exhausted. And she intended to take care of him. Bloodshot hazel eyes met hers, expressionless, as she grasped the sides of his face and tipped his head back under the spray.

"Let's get the dirt out of your hair and rinse you off," she said, squirting a dollop of shampoo into her palm.

He stared at her, as she rubbed circles all over his scalp, coaxing the shampoo into a rich lather. His lids drooped, tension flowing down the drain with the filth of the evening. Devon's head lolled as she rinsed, careful to shield his eyes from the stinging suds. Next came bodywash, which felt a lot like washing a car because he stood so still. She was reaching past him for the shower cut-off when his eyes popped open, and his entire body stiffened.

"I know how to throw a punch," he said, the words slow and uncooperative in his mouth.

Hope pulled back her hands, hesitating. "Let's get you—"

"I didn't want to deal with him." Water dripped off his lashes, the tip of his nose. "I wanted him *gone*." A cruel smile whispered across his features. "Do you know the last thing I said to him? I told him that I'd kill him before I let him touch her again. I told him to get the fuck out of there and never come back. That was the last thing I said to my father, and I meant every goddamn word of it."

His smile faltered, and he blinked several times. Hope framed his face between her palms and pulled him down until their foreheads touched.

"I don't blame you one bit," she whispered, before pressing her lips to his.

Five minutes later, she had him tucked into bed, butt-naked, with towel dried hair dampening the pillow. It was the best she could manage, given that he'd all but lost the energy to stand as soon as he stepped out of the shower. But as Hope felt the steady rise and fall of his chest, his heart thrumming beneath her palm, the way his hands limply clutched her borrowed t-shirt, she decided her best was exactly what he needed tonight. Even if he was terrified to admit it and had no idea how to ask.

HOPE

Hope jolted awake—one leg thrown over pillows that smelled like Devon. She squinted against the weak light spilling through the shades, then scrambled off the bed to find her boyfriend.

In the bathroom, all evidence of the night before had vanished. Towels left on the floor hung on rods. Discarded clothing no longer lay strewn about. Despite the mess of organic matter that had fallen from his jeans when she stripped him, the tiles were spotless. Worry skittered along her nerves.

Padding into the bedroom, she intended to dig out a pair of pajama pants, before continuing her search; but a pungent odor made its way into her sinuses, and she followed her nose to the top of the basement stairs instead. Devon's wolf tattoo came into focus as she stepped into the dimness. He scooted over when she reached him, and she settled beside him on the second step from the bottom. The chillier air of the basement seeped into her exposed legs, as Devon wordlessly offered her the joint in his hand.

"Uh...No thanks."

He shrugged and took a hit, holding his breath as he tamped the lit end out on the concrete floor. He exhaled a cloud of smoke, eyes fixed straight ahead.

"I figured if you stayed through last night, your reaction to a little weed would be the least of my problems this morning." He placed the remainder in a tin and shoved it beneath the step.

"How do you feel?"

He flashed her a rueful smile. "Better than I deserve. The ibuprofen has almost kicked the headache, and I expect the nausea will settle down shortly. Thank you."

"I didn't—"

"You did. You didn't have to come, and you didn't have to stay." He fidgeted with a lighter—fuel racing from one side of its translucent-red encasement to the other, as he flipped it end over end. "I'm sorry I ruined your night. More than that, I'm sorry that I ended up wasted. It bothers me that I was in no state to help if you had needed me."

Hope's brow furrowed. "You were trying to manage the anniversary of a significant trauma alone."

"But there are bigger things going on."

Hope smirked at him. "I'm pretty sure that makes it *more* difficult."

Devon flipped the lighter again. "I thought I could get through it without making it your problem."

She placed a hand on his back, relieved when he didn't pull away. "The worst part of my night was seeing you hurting and not knowing why or how to help. I'm not afraid of your dark days.

Sometimes, they're going to overlap mine. Please, don't lock me out next time."

He exhaled a small breath through his nose. "I love you, but you still don't get it."

"I get that you blame yourself for a ton of stuff that isn't your fault. Last night, you seemed convinced that you killed your father, among a host of other things you had no control over. I know there's a part of you that believes that."

Devon laughed. "Not *a part*. That's a thing I know. Every inch of me knows it." He turned to look at her, dark circles lighter after sleep, hazel eyes no longer rimmed in red. "Sometimes, when I'm drinking, I feel bad about it. That's the only difference between last night and this morning."

Hope shook her head. "You kept saying that you knew how to punch, but your dad died in a car crash. It had nothing to do with—"

"I *do* know how to throw a punch. Which is why I know that it's my fault he's dead." Hope's brow furrowed as he went on. "I made a *choice*. I knew he couldn't drive; I didn't care. I hit him in the nose, so it would hurt like a bitch and bleed like a stuck pig. I pulled it because I needed him conscious enough to leave. I couldn't leave Mom there alone with him, and I needed..." He trailed off, his throat bobbing as he swallowed.

"What?"

His eyes went to hers, then to the lighter in his hands. "You know what I needed."

An electric tingle buzzed across Hope's nerves.

"I stashed my phone in my locker. By the time I finished working my way through two subs, he was dead. The ER doctors called it after midnight, but he was unresponsive when the EMTs got on scene. His headstone has today's date, but he died five years to the day after Kelly. It's the reason Mom lets me get away with one trip."

Devon fell silent, flipping the lighter, studying it too closely.

"No." Hope shook her head. "I'm not letting you have this one."

He stopped toying with the lighter and faced her. "Excuse me?"

"You don't get to claim that you killed your father because you punched him in the face hard enough to get him to leave your mom alone but not hard enough to knock him out. That's ridiculous. Your parents were adults, and you were what?" She did the math in her head. "A traumatized nineteen-year-old boy? It's bullshit, Devon, and I don't accept it."

His mouth twitched, and then he laughed. He laughed and laughed and...

"What's so funny?"

"Sorry," he said, snickering. "You were saying all that, and I imagined trying to explain the same thing to you and..." He giggled. "What the fuck is wrong with me?"

Hope fought an unexpected grin. "Do you want my professional opinion or the girlfriend version?"

"Wait... You're telling me that I still have a girlfriend? Even after last night and..." He gestured between them. "Whatever this is?"

She swatted his arm. "You aren't getting rid of me that easily."

Devon put a hand on his sternum. "I *sang* for you. I pulled you up on the bar, then nearly dropped you off."

"I'm shocked you remember that part, to be honest. Do you also remember your combat roll out of my car and pissing on the shrubs or had we reached black-out levels by then?"

"The azaleas?" He cringed, and Hope laughed harder. "It's not funny. They're cursed. I've replanted two since I bought this place."

"Maybe because you keep peeing on them."

He waved it aside. "That's like twice a year."

"Yeah, but you put in two bottles of whiskey and somehow produced nine thousand gallons of pee."

"If I drank two bottles of whiskey, I'd be dead."

"Well," she bumped his shoulder with her own, "you were wearing as much as you drank, and you did drop the one bottle when you hoisted me onto the bar. The mystery remains. How did you make so much urine?"

"Beats me." He smiled that slow smile, then got to his feet. Pocketing the lighter, he offered her a hand up. They climbed the stairs at an easy pace. "I should've started dating a therapist years ago," he said. "I could've avoided a lot of hangovers."

Hope's eyes widened, but with Devon ahead of her on the stairs, only the wolf noticed. "Well, it's not like—"

"One conversation with you, and I see how ridiculous this stuff is. R&R should give you a raise." He turned at the doorway and winked down at her, before pulling her up the last few steps and toward the hall.

Hope smiled uncomfortably. People didn't heal a lifetime of deeply buried trauma in a single conversation. It didn't work that way, but it could be a start.

"Thank you for talking to me." She squeezed his hand. "It means so much, but I do think you should talk to Dre sometime. Or if you don't want to talk to him, maybe—"

Devon glanced back over his shoulder, leading her down the hall. "You really want me talking to Dre? Your new coworker might find out what a freak my girlfriend is."

Hope chuckled. "I want you to talk to whoever you'll feel comfortable with. You need more than me as a sounding board."

"I go to group," he reminded her.

Tugging her to a stop in his bedroom, he grabbed her hips, peered at her from beneath dark, sleep-tousled hair. Hope's heart stumbled in her chest, tripped up by the overwhelming swell of affection she felt when she looked at him.

"I love you," she said, wrapping her arms around his shoulders. "I don't want you carrying a bunch of guilt."

Devon scooped his hands behind her thighs, hitching her legs up around his waist. "Mmm... I don't want to carry that either." He stepped across the floor. "I'd prefer to carry you right over to this bed." He lowered her back into softness. "Skim my hands under the hem of this shirt." He did just that. "Torment every inch of you until the only thought left in your head is how good my cock feels in your pussy." Hope gasped, and he chuckled, tugging off her panties. "We don't need these anymore, do we darling?"

"N...no, Sir," she managed.

Devon reached for a condom from the nightstand, then pushed down his joggers. Sheathing himself with quick efficiency, he nudged her thighs open and slid inside. "I'll never get enough of the way you feel," he said against her ear, voice sweet as honey and hot as the whiskey she drank on his kitchen floor the night before.

The night before...

Hope tried to focus on her lover—an act that should have been effortless as Devon palmed the back of her head, pumping into her. He was okay, she told herself. Maybe not a hundred percent, but...functional. He sounded like himself. He smelled like himself. Cedar and sandalwood, with a faint hint of something else. The joint he hit to settle the nausea; she realized. Cedar and sandalwood and...*weed*.

"Where are you, darling?"

Hope braced her hands on his biceps and tucked her face into his neck. "Here," she answered, even as thoughts of him on the bar, the epicenter of chaos, nipped at the edges of her mind.

"You're distracted."

"I'm trying," she murmured back.

It felt lovely—him stretching, filling, then retreating. Her body hummed with pleasure, regardless of her noisy brain.

"Let's try harder..."

He flipped her to her stomach, shoved her face into the bed, and yanked up her hips. The air whooshed out of her lungs and anticipation cascaded along her nerves. Devon splayed the fingers of one hand low on her rump, letting his thumb slip between her lips, dipping into the hot, wet, pit of her. He then slid that thumb upward, circling the pucker of her ass, as he seated his cock deep in her core once more. Hope wiggled and mewled.

"Ah..." he all but growled. "Now, I've got your attention. And look at my view..." He began moving again, his slick thumb teasing all sorts of sensations from her as he did. "Are you blushing, darling? You blush so pretty for me."

Her face felt like a furnace, and every nerve in her body terminated in a place where he touched her.

"If you're planning to stop me," he gritted, "now's the time to say yellow." Then, he *spat* on her.

Realizing what he'd done, Hope jerked. Her thoughts flip-flopped between the knowledge that it was either one of the filthiest things a guy had ever done to her or the most erotic, as his warm saliva slid south. Coating his thumb anew in the spit dripping down her crack and resting the broad pad against one of the most sensitive spots on her body, he waited for her response. Hope knew what he was planning, and she had zero desire to stop him.

Devon circled, circled, then gently pushed the tip of his thumb against her tight ring, demanding entry.

"Come on, darling," he murmured.

Hope panted, a warm tingle gliding from the back of her skull to where Devon played between her legs. She needed to let go, but...

"Sir..."

"Let me in, love. It'll feel so good," he crooned, prodding at her until the tip of his thumb breached the threshold. Backing out... Back in, to his first knuckle... Meanwhile, he throttled the pace of his thrusting, dragging the head of his cock along her internal nerves with decadent slowness as he spoke. "Almost there... God, you're so tight here." He tutted. "Can you imagine trying to fit more than a finger in this little hole?"

Hope's entire body shuddered and in he slipped. Thumb buried in her ass, cock in her core, her mind melted into static and sensation and...Devon.

"There's my good girl," he said, satisfaction potent as heroin threaded through the words.

It felt *too good*. Hope was too full, with too many sensations, too many tingles; and the pride in his voice did something weird to her insides that made her feel like she might explode.

"Oh, darling... I think you're going to come for me."

Hope drummed the tops of her feet against the mattress, the tension inside her coiling tighter and higher. Devon kept crashing into her, one hand gripping her hip for leverage, and a thumb right up her butt, and— The orgasm flared through her, a cleansing release of so much amassed energy that his grip was the only thing keeping her up on her knees.

"That's it, baby. That's what I wanted." Having ensured her pleasure, he increased his pace. "Someday," he said, between punishing thrusts, working his thumb in and out of her ass, "we'll get my cock in here." Hope groaned. "Oh...are you going to come again, love? You like the idea of me fucking your ass?"

Hope panted feverishly, unable to form words that wouldn't matter anyway. Her body betrayed how much his suggestion turned her on by gripping his shaft in another pulsing hold.

"*Fuck*." Devon buried himself deep, tipping over the precipice with her. "Fuck, kitten, you feel so good."

***

Devon slid out of her and off the bed in one fluid motion. Hope sank to her stomach, quaking. Turning her face so she could breathe, she peered up at him. Without a word, he yanked the comforter over her, then strode toward the bathroom, joggers halfway down his ass.

Lurching to the edge of the bed, Hope pulled the blanket around herself and perched on a tush that felt...*funny*. She spun the bracelet on her wrist as she waited. After the sounds of condom disposal and running water quieted, Devon appeared in the doorway with water spattering the front of his pants.

"Ah... Breakfast?" he said.

"Um... Sure."

She gathered clothes and headed for the bathroom. Reemerging, she found him in the kitchen, skillet already heated, coffee brewing. She sat at the table, watching him toss an empty milk jug into the recycling bin. He'd ditched his sweatpants for jeans and a black button-down while she was in the bathroom. He already had his boots on.

Hope scrunched her toes together beneath the table.

"I thought you'd take off this morning," she said, as he popped two over-easy eggs in front of her.

"Hmm?"

"You're dressed for work."

"Yeah, well..." The corners of his mouth curved up. "I made a mess of things last night."

He headed back to the stove, where he shoved the cast iron skillet in the oven. Hope glanced at her lone plate.

"You aren't hungry?"

"I'll eat when I'm sure my stomach won't revolt."

He brought her a cup containing a ratio of forty-percent milk/sixty-percent coffee. Standing beside her, he swigged from his own cup—working entirely too hard to swallow.

"Are you sure that's a good idea?" She gestured to his coffee.

"Ugh... It's a terrible idea, but the caffeine is nonnegotiable. I won't stay late today. I'll try to leave by eleven."

Hope tapped her phone screen and frowned at the illuminated 8:03.

"In the morning?"

Carrying his empty mug to the sink, Devon laughed.

"Yeah...no. I'll be lucky to have the main floor functional by the time we open."

"But do you need to stay all day?"

"Getting the doors open on time is the bare minimum. I'll have to sort out the bar that I trashed in between customers and the weekly bookkeeping. It's going to take time, but it's fine. I'll handle it. You can relax here with Apollo."

Hope traced the clasp on her bracelet. "Just so you know, this feels like you're avoiding me."

"I had a thumb up your ass and my cock in your cunt half an hour ago."

"Because you wanted me to stop talking," Hope countered. "Because you are *avoiding* me."

His cheeks pinked.

"We talked. I told you I'm fine."

Hope raised her brows at his sharp tone.

"*Fine* people don't sound this defensive, Devon."

"You sound like Nix." He huffed, shaking his head. "This isn't defensive. This is *annoyed* because my girlfriend is accusing me of avoiding her, despite the fact that she's been sleeping at my house for the last two weeks."

Hope looked to her barely touched plate of stupid, over-easy eggs, and decided that if she wanted breakfast, she could get it herself. Scooting back her chair, she stood and stormed toward the living room.

"Wait, what are you doing?" The alarm underlying his words said he knew he'd screwed up.

Hope pulled on her shoes. "I'm going home. I can settle in during daylight. It'll make tonight easier."

Devon circled the kitchen counter, following after her.

"Hope...wait."

"No." A tremor started in her fingertips, crawled up her hands. "You're right. Regardless of the circumstances, we haven't had a break from each other for weeks. I need time to think. Maybe you do too."

His eyes widened. "About what?" Hope looked at him meaningfully. "About us? You need to *think* about *us*?"

She pulled in an unsteady breath. "You once told me that you didn't blame me for my walls, but that you were tired of standing outside of them. Right here, in this room." She looked at the spot on the floor, where she'd knelt for him, because it was easier than looking him in the face. "You had a bracelet made from the rope you used." Her words were barely a whisper. "Do you remember that?"

"That's different. Aaron was stalking you and—"

"This hurts. Can't you see that? It hurts me to know that there are whole sides of you—huge, important sides—that you don't trust me with. I'm watching you struggle alone, when you have so many people waiting to support you. I can't be this close to you and this far away at the same time. It's killing me."

"What is it you think I'm hiding?" He took a step toward her, his face set in hard lines. "You know me better than anyone on the planet."

"Do I? You've been upset about more than Aaron for weeks, but it took a gallon of whiskey for you to tell me why you ended up on your bar last night."

"I didn't call you; that was Nix."

"Oh, believe me, I know. And if she hadn't, who knows what would have happened to you. You are falling apart in secret." She chewed her lip, her fingers finding her bracelet as she weighed the next sentence on her tongue. "And there's at least one coping mechanism that you've sworn off because of me. One that's way safer than freaking alcohol poisoning."

"The one where you break up with me?" Devon laughed manically. "*That* coping mechanism?"

"Look..." Hope rubbed her temples. "We got together at a stressful time. Aaron started his crap right after we started dating, and you had an extensive trauma history already."

His cheeks flushed crimson. "Despite our chat earlier, you aren't my fucking therapist."

"Trauma bonding is a thing, Devon."

"I'm not *trauma bonded* to you," he snapped. "I'm *in love* with you."

"I'm not saying that you aren't. I'm saying that real intimacy is uncomfortable sometimes. It means digging deep and communicating; and not everyone can handle that level of vulnerability. Not everyone wants to..."

"Yeah? Well, you couldn't handle Edge," he shot back. "How's that for communicating?"

Hope's mouth fell open. "That's the best you can come up with?"

"Maybe it is. I'm a shit communicator, remember? Or...and hear me out... Maybe I'm saying things just fine, but no one is listening. I've said over and over that I don't want you at Edge."

"Why, Devon? Tell me why."

"Because you can't love him!" Shock flooded his face, and he took a step back. "*Me*," he corrected. "You can't... It's..."

"You mean *Demon*."

The color, once angry and red, leached out of him. Hope wet her lips.

"Devon, I know that side of you exists. I also know that you aren't a monster out there hurting people against their will. You value consent and autonomy more than anyone. I'm not going to stop loving you for being yourself."

"You've never met that side of me. Not really. So, *respectfully*, you have no fucking clue what you're talking about." Something pained lay beneath the gravel in his voice, something raw and wounded that reminded her of the way he'd rocked on his kitchen floor, the horrible things he'd said.

"Then, show me."

Devon backed up another pace.

"You should stay here. You'll feel safer than you did at your apartment, but you'll still get a break from me."

"Devon..."

"I have to get to the bar, but you should stay," he repeated, moving to the front door.

"We aren't finished talking about—*Wait*." She said it to his back as he walked outside.

Mumbling something to himself, he reached behind the porch planter and pulled out his keys and phone. Being that whoever had dropped his car off the night before had parked behind Hope, she wouldn't have been able to execute her own dramatic exit anyway. At least, not without first asking him to move.

"This is what I'm talking about." She followed him to the Charger, and he slid into the driver's seat. "I'm trying, and you're running."

"I love you." He fixed his eyes straight ahead. "I already told you that I have to go."

"You can't suppress core parts of your personality forever," she said. "It won't work."

He looked her direction, and her heart fluttered. She only needed a moment—like on the bar. Yes, Devon was stubborn but not rigid to a fault. He'd pulled out of his destructive choices the night before. She leaned forward a fraction, one hand braced on the edge of the car door, and the other against the roof.

"Come home after Cleary's is up and running. We can talk things out—maybe even check out Edge this evening. You head there when things are hard, right? I want the opportunity to know you, Devon."

His gaze softened only for a moment.

"Cleary's is my life, and I trashed it last night. That's my priority today. Everything else is irrelevant."

"*Irrelevant?*"

"Step back, darling."

"Devon."

"Watch your hands."

"Are you really—"

"Move. *Now.*"

Stunned, Hope stumbled back from his car, and Devon slammed the door on their conversation without another word.

DEVON

S hame kept his head down when he heard the muffled jangle of keys, the soft swish of the door's bottom edge across cement. He leaned closer to the bar's wooden surface and scraped at a scuff with his thumbnail.

"You're in early," Nix said, re-locking the door and walking toward him.

"Makes two of us."

Setting her things atop a barstool that Devon had righted half an hour earlier, she looked around. "I assumed I'd have a mess, but it looks like you've handled it pretty well."

Scuff removed, Devon slid his fingertips over the wood until a sharp divot caught a pinky. Bracing his hands on the bar, he sighed. "Not all of it."

She bent and grabbed something from the floor, then placed a rogue shard of glass on the bar. "It'll buff."

"Not this time."

Picking up the glass he'd missed while sweeping, he dropped it in the bin. It chimed musically, getting reacquainted with its brethren. Nix's brows drew together over unlined-eyes, and Devon thought about how rarely he saw her fresh-faced. Without makeup, she looked deceptively innocent—for someone capable of bringing a grown man to his knees.

"What's going on, Dev?"

"I'm—"

"If you say *fine*, I will fucking throttle you."

Devon inhaled, exhaled, then looked up at his friend. "I fucked up."

"What did she say?"

"So, I say I fucked up, and you assume I've screwed things up with Hope? Not the schedule, the ordering, Apollo's dietary needs... Nope. Just straight to *Your girlfriend hates you.*"

"She said she hates you?" He watched one of her dark brows ratchet upward; her full lips quirked to the side. He sighed.

"She said she needed time."

Nix's eyes widened. "Like...to think about your relationship? What the fuck, Dev? Because you got drunk on the anniversary of your sister's suicide? That's cold as—"

Devon shook his head. "Because I cut her out. She thinks I'm *hiding* from her. Thinks I'm using her as an excuse to stay out of Edge. I was too drunk to keep my mouth shut last night. I tried telling her I was fine this morning, but she thinks I'm supposed to drag it all up again, I guess. She was about to leave." He dug beneath the bar for another towel. "Then shit went sideways, and I came here." Devon kept the rest of the story to himself. He wasn't telling Nix that bullshit about his *You can't love my alter-ego* slip-up; it made him sound certifiable. "What? You aren't going to say anything?"

Air puffed from her nostrils—an anemic laugh. "Only that she's right." Devon shot her an annoyed glare, which she dismissed. "Simmer down, Demon." She smiled when Devon's chin inched up of its own volition. "She's not done with you; she's...giving you a nudge."

"What does that even mean?"

Nix lifted a shoulder. "You've been using her as an excuse for a lot of things. Not talking to her because it might upset her. Acting like Edge is out of the question because of her. Hope isn't a delicate flower, Dev. She's kind of a badass, if you haven't noticed."

"She's had enough on—"

Nix's venomous expression cut him off before she opened her mouth.

"She walked in here last night with zero idea what was going on because *you* didn't think she could handle your bullshit. You put her at a disadvantage, and she handled it anyway—on a really shit week for her, might I add. You yanked her up on the bar, in all your drunken glory, and Hope didn't even flinch. She is *the only reason* that Alex and Mark didn't drag you out, kicking and screaming—which also makes her the only reason this place isn't a pile of rubble. You think a few overturned tables and marks on the bar is bad? Your *family* was more than willing to throw down on your behalf, dip-shit." Devon's cheeks heated; he dropped his gaze. "That girl stood in your storm and guided you out, and you act like she can't handle you. It's insulting, to be honest."

"Maybe it's better this way. If I can't hold up my end of things—"

"Oh, so we're moving on to self-deprecation?" She propped her tongue ring in the corner of her mouth. "Great, let's do that. You can act all pitiful, while she moves on."

Devon narrowed his eyes. "At least, I love her enough to let her."

"Wow." She shook her head. "Did you really set the bar at *abusive-stalker-ex* and think that anything above it was a win? That's like...on the floor, dude."

He found it harder to breathe with every word out of her mouth.

"Christ knows I deserve it, but you are killing me right now."

"That's not me, boyfriend. That's your conscience, and it's going to get louder when she lands at Edge without you. I bet she runs into Nosh the first night. That prick can smell fresh meat a mile away."

His head snapped up.

"Oh..." She chuckled. "That got someone's attention. Hey, big guy."

Devon's back teeth ground together, a muscle in his jaw twitched. Hope was a cautious creature of habit. It didn't matter how upset she was; there was no way in hell that she'd walk into Edge alone.

"She wouldn't do that."

"You sure? I can't see her going back to vanilla partners, and she wouldn't know where to find—" Nix trailed off, gesturing to Devon.

Me, Demon whispered in his head. *She'll go looking for something like me.*

"Two seconds ago you said she wasn't breaking up with me, and now you're saying she's going to end up in a scene with Nosh. Make up your goddamn mind."

"Make up *yours,*" she countered. "Go talk to her, like she asked. It's not rocket science. You got yourself into this situation, so go get yourself out. I can handle the bar. Everyone's broke, hungover, or in jail after you pull a pub night anyway."

Devon pulled in a grounding breath. "Maybe you're..." He trailed off as his phone vibrated in his back pocket. Pulling it out, he glanced at the notification. "That little brat," he growled.

"What did she say?"

Devon shoved the phone at Nix, the automated notification that Hope had left his address still emblazoned across the screen. She canted her head, studying it.

"Where do you think she's going?"

"Somewhere behind a locked door, if she knows what's good for her."

Nix smirked. "You need to go deal with that, Dev. Now."

"If I go now, it looks like I'm only going because she left. What happens the next time she's pissed? I'm not letting a bratty-sub manipulate me into jumping through hoops while she does whatever she wants."

"Except this *bratty-sub* is your girlfriend."

Without a better response, Devon opted for, "No."

"She's going to keep pushing buttons until she stops trying altogether. You don't want that, Dev. You love her."

"This is your fault, you know. You had to go and call her."

"I couldn't get you down. What was I supposed to do?"

"Let me deal with my own problems, or at the very least, don't dump them on my girlfriend!"

Nix smiled like some kind of carnivorous flower—pretty and deadly. "Have you considered... Oh, I don't know... Working through your shit so it isn't *anyone's* problem anymore? You're on the board of a nonprofit that offers free counseling for people in your exact situation. One of those counselors is a close friend of yours. If you don't want your girlfriend playing snake charmer, designated driver, or therapist, start taking better care of yourself."

His face and ears were on fire, and the collar of his work shirt was strangling him.

"R&R's resources are for *victims*, which I am not." The towel in his hand whipped against the bar with his final word. Nix raised a brow, saying nothing. "*I'm fucking not,*" he barked.

Chucking the towel in the trash, Devon rounded the bar. He stormed toward the hall, until her voice pulled him up short.

"You need to decide how much you value that lie before it's all you have left."

A sneer curled his upper lip when he pivoted to face her. "You give a lot of fucking advice for someone who doesn't know what they're talking about."

She crossed her arms and cocked a hip. "You have a lot of fucking problems for someone who has access to all the support in the world."

"The next time I fire you, don't bother showing up for your next shift."

Nix shook her head, an incredulous laugh bubbling out of her, as Devon seethed. "Whatever you say...*boss*."

For several seconds, Devon's awareness shrank to the sound of his labored breathing and the numbness crawling through something too similar to regret.

"I'll be in the office," he said. "Stock the well."

"Yes, sir," she said sweetly.

A flurry of racing heartbeats later, he ducked behind the safety of a door. Sinking into the battered rolling chair, he stared at the army-green desk, its surface littered with receipts, rogue invoices and utility bills. Multicolored lasers danced across the screen of his sleeping laptop in the exact spot Hope sat the night he'd convinced her that after dark strolls could be dangerous—using mostly his tongue.

Then, Aaron had watched him walk her home...

He stood back up, paced in the tiny space. Anxious energy bounced through his body like an arcade ball.

He was fine.

More than that, he was *right*.

It was everyone else who wouldn't let his past die.

Devon only drudged it up on occasion. He didn't need help for a problem that didn't exist, so long as people let him handle things his way.

And sometimes on anniversaries.

And occasionally when something happened to someone he cared about.

"Christ."

He pulled out his phone and typed a text before he could change his mind.

HOPE

Halfway up the first flight of stairs, Hope startled and spun. Behind her, Chloe pushed through the entry door with grocery bags hanging from both arms.

"Hey." She tilted her head, blond bun flopping. "Sorry, did I scare you?"

"No, I'm fine. You off?"

Chloe nodded as she caught up to her, and they started up the steps together. "Yeah, but I'm meeting some girls from work for a bachelorette thing this evening. You want to hang out for a while before I go?"

"Sure." Unlacing her keys from her fingers, Hope opened her door.

"I'll put these up, then come over," Chloe said, then she disappeared into her apartment.

Hope stepped into her own and closed the door, her hand hovering over the deadbolt. It looked silly, paranoid, locking a door in the middle of the day, when her friend would need through it a moment later. Still, chill bumps raised along her skin, prickling under the fabric of her sweater—that familiar sensation that something was coming for her...or already behind her. The door-knob turned, and Hope staggered back, whipping her head over her shoulder toward her empty living room, then back before her friend noticed.

"I assumed you'd be at Devon's," Chloe said, as she crossed the threshold.

"Why?" Hope cringed at the annoyance in her voice. It wasn't Chloe's fault that she was having a bad day.

"I don't know." Chloe lifted a shoulder. "It's only been a couple of days since court and that went...not great."

Hope shrugged. "I need to get back to my life. The sooner I do, the easier it will be."

"But...now? You can't give it a few days to see if Aaron behaves?"

"Yes, *now*." Huffing, she urged herself into motion, retracing the same steps she'd taken upon arriving home from work the evening before—the same steps Devon had taken before they ended up fucking on her couch the day after the fitting. "I haven't slept here in weeks. Last night, I was going to stay, but I ended up pulling my boyfriend off the bar."

Chloe trailed behind. "What do you mean *off the bar*?"

"He doesn't talk about shit," Hope said. "He bottles it up until he can't, then he gets wasted."

Chloe caught her arm. "But...on the bar?"

"Singing, dancing, and picking fights."

"So, he's that kind of drunk. Get some liquor in him, and it's trouble in paradise." Chloe released her, then followed Hope into the tiny bathroom.

"Did we ever have paradise? Aaron was screwing with me before I met Devon." She wrenched back the shower curtain. "And Devon has been fucked up since he was five."

"Five? Hope…"

Ignoring the concern in her friend's voice, Hope stormed into her bedroom and opened her closet.

"Wait… Are we searching your apartment?"

Hope sank onto the edge of her bed. Chloe perched beside her.

"Yes, because I'm having an obnoxious trauma response that I can't seem to shake, and my hardheaded boyfriend isn't here to do it for me."

"What happened with Devon?" Chloe asked, draping an arm around her.

Hope leaned her head on her friend's shoulder. She wasn't mad or sad, just…tired. So tired of being afraid for herself, for him. So tired of all the things he wouldn't say, but she stewed on anyway.

"I don't even know. One minute, he was making me breakfast, and the next, I was leaving. Then, he left instead?" She shook her head, trying to make sense of how it all fell apart. "I came here because I thought he might walk over from the bar when he got the notifications." The embarrassment of desperation warmed her cheeks; Chloe's brown eyes filled with sympathy. "He's all about getting behind my walls, but he slams the door in my face when I get near his. What am I supposed to do?"

Chloe blew out a breath. "I guess you have two choices. On the one hand, you can let him shut you out and hope that he comes around on his own."

Picking at her bracelet, Hope remembered the anguish on his face in the shower—*I know how to throw a punch*—the anger in his driveway—*Move. Now.*

"If I do that, I'm worried that we won't make it. That *he* won't make it."

Chloe squeezed her into her side. "The other option is that you get louder; communicate with him in a way he can't ignore."

Hope rolled her eyes up and over until she was looking her best friend in the face. "So, make more drama."

Chloe winked. "Bingo."

"I am a therapist. I don't make drama."

"Are you serious? That's your whole job description. You all drag stuff up and shine a light on issues all the time." She bumped Hope. "You just do it in a more controlled way than most people."

"So like...good drama?"

Chloe grinned. "Exactly. Drama that ends in hot, angry makeup sex."

DEVON

"**I**'m proud of you."

Devon looked down at his picked apart BLT, the heat he'd grown accustomed to over the last few hours flushing his face again.

"Rude to have you drop everything on a Saturday, though."

Dre leaned in. "The universe worked this out, although I'm sure my kids disagree."

Both men chuckled. Dre's *kids* were a nine-to-eleven-year-old youth basketball team, who were currently missing their game after two-thirds of the roster came down with a stomach bug. The puking freed up Dre's Saturday to deal with Devon's nonsense.

"You start where you can. Next time, we'll get you on the schedule."

Devon looked up. "Next time?"

"Ah…" Dre smiled. "This is probably how Hope felt when you assured her that a single conversation with your girlfriend had erased your trauma." He cocked an eyebrow. "Yeah, next time. Next week. I'll figure out where I can work you in and text you."

Devon brushed invisible crumbs from his lap.

"I don't know—"

Dre put up a hand. "I'm going to stop you right there. You spent the last couple of hours trauma dumping all over this cafe. No wonder you're struggling, man. You have a lifetime of physical, mental, and emotional wounds, and you've barely processed any of it. Even better, your one solid way of working through things is also a deeply ingrained shame-trigger for you." Devon's back molars ground together; Dre crossed his arms and rested back in the booth. "What is that?" He gestured in Devon's direction before tucking the hand behind his other arm. "What's going on in your head right now?"

A redhead. One with alabaster skin striped with pretty pink scars. A year ago, Devon spent three consecutive nights at Edge, painting that girl a mural of red, blue, purple, and green. Every painful feeling pried out of his chest and marked on her body—left for her to heal. He had only needed a willing chalice to dump darkness into, and she'd obliged, *repeatedly*, because he had what she needed too. He hadn't even taken her in the playroom; the first two nights he hadn't even known her name.

Then a month later, he met Hope.

And two months after that, Edge stopped cutting it.

But he couldn't say that aloud.

"You say that like BDSM is some kind of healing, connecting thing," he said instead.

Dre's brow inched up again. "Isn't it?"

"Well, yeah. For some people, but—"

"But not for you," Dre finished for him. "Never for *you*. Everyone else is allowed to work through their trauma, let go of their shame over who they are or what they couldn't control. Everyone except Devon Cleary, right?"

"It's not the same."

"It doesn't *feel* the same," Dre countered. "Do you think you're the first guy to have this issue? They raise us on this shit, man. *Man up. Don't cry. Control the world, or you're a pussy.*"

Devon looked him in the eye. "I beat the shit out of people that I barely know, Dre."

"People who consent. People who, for whatever reason, are seeking the kind of treatment that you are skilled at providing. You do it within a strict framework of rules that the man who raised you wouldn't give a damn about."

"Be great if you could not bring my dad into my sex life."

"We aren't talking about your sex life, though, are we?" Dre raised a brow. "We're talking about the way you fulfill a need for control—a thing you were denied for most of your childhood and adolescence."

Devon scoffed. "Bit clinical."

"My relationship with the DSM seems to mirror your relationship with BDSM." Dre reached for his sweet tea. "Scratch that. The DSM still needs work." He sipped.

"What in the world are you talking about?"

Across the table, Dre laughed. "The DSM is an imperfect book, detailing diagnostic criteria for psychiatric disorders. Look it up later."

Devon rolled his lower lip between his teeth. "And it talks about BDSM?"

"Used to," Dre said. "Y'all had a diagnosis until the fifth edition."

"See," Devon held out his hands, "I told you I'm screwed up."

"Eh, they sorted it out eventually." He sipped again. "I look at other resources, anyway. There's all kinds of stuff out there on the therapeutic benefits of power exchange and the like. Even some papers exploring BDSM through the same lens we use for orientation. It's a fascinating topic."

"Not sure what I'm supposed to do with that information."

Dre hitched a shoulder. "Given that I'm a therapist, I use it to better understand some of my patients. You'd be surprised how often kink pops up in trauma counseling—especially when that trauma intersects with sex. You, on the other hand... Do whatever you want with it. The point is that sometimes we need a thing, even if we wish we didn't. Nothing is perfect. We're all just out here journeying toward *better*. You said you didn't start having qualms about BDSM until you started having feelings for Hope. Does that mean you didn't care about the wellbeing of your previous partners?"

Devon straightened. "Of course not."

Dre nodded. "But Hope is different," he prompted.

Pushing his destroyed sandwich around with a finger, Devon pulled in a breath, then slowly released it. "Hope is... Everything. The idea of letting her see me at my worst is terrifying."

"Do you imagine it would be worse than her getting you off the bar and taking you home?"

He swallowed.

"Well, not exactly."

"Worse than when you walked out on her this morning because you were afraid to talk to her?"

"No..." he hedged, "but those are like apples and oranges."

"Fair enough." Dre inclined his head and waited until Devon reached for his soda. "How about worse than when you *bought a flogger* because you were pissed off that a customer you had no connection to—"

Devon's glass clacked against the Formica tabletop; Dre hid his smirk behind the performative dab of a child-sized napkin.

"I can't believe I told you this shit."

"Indulge me for a minute," Dre said. "Imagine what it would look like if it didn't go terribly."

"It *would* go terribly."

"Come on, Dev. *Try*. What if you were fully yourself with Hope? With *you*? Imagine taking her to that club that you so desperately need to visit, and her not hating you after. Imagine getting to a place where you are so secure in who you are that you don't hate yourself afterward either; you don't even worry that you might."

The low, thrumming music of Edge whispered in his ears, alongside the snap of leather on flesh. Devon shuddered.

"This feels so fucking vulnerable," he whispered.

Depositing the napkin on his empty plate, Dre nodded. "Connection is vulnerable. It's also foundational. You can't…" He trailed off, smirking as Devon laughed. "What?"

"Sorry." Devon shook his head, struggling to quiet his laughter. "Go on."

Dre grinned. "You first."

"You said *foundational.*"

"I did."

"And my old man owned a construction company," Devon said, giggling again.

"Ah." Dre nodded. "A lot of talk about foundations, I take it?"

"All the damn time. That bastard went on and on about the importance of a solid foundation. How every step had to go right, or there would be issues down the line. You can build a palace, but if the foundation's off, it's worthless—a disaster waiting to happen." Devon noticed a tapping sound, then realized it was his leg bouncing beneath the table. With a steady breath, he willed it still. "Kind of wish he'd put more effort into ours. I mean, mine." He forced a smile.

"Nah," Dre shook his head. "I think you meant what you said the first time." Devon stared at a wilting piece of lettuce on his plate. "But here's the thing, Dev. You're here. You are surrounded by people who care about you. And forgive me if I screw this up; I've never built a thing in my life. I'm not saying it isn't a hell of a job ripping out cracked cement—finding a way to hold up the whole damn building while you do—but if you can't be secure on the foundation they gave you…if you spend every moment worrying that it's going to collapse beneath you, sucking everything you are into some dark pit... *Pour a new one.*"

HOPE

Wearing the same slip of a skirt and silver crop-top that she hadn't returned to Chloe five months earlier beneath her woolen coat, Hope studied the warehouse from the backseat of a small car that smelled like onions. She had no idea if she'd dressed appropriately. She wasn't even sure she had the right address, though the location made sense. Of course, Edge was located a few measly minutes from Devon's house; and, naturally, despite them driving past it together multiple times a week, the most attention he'd ever drawn to the building was huffing in its general direction while drunk.

"Here?" Her chauffeur had the accent of a guy who should be driving a tractor instead of a ride-share.

"Um..."

Hope fiddled with the bracelet on her wrist, then stopped herself. The lot was half-full, but without any sort of signage, she had no way of knowing for sure. She imagined walking into nightshift at a factory wearing fishnet hose and *fuck me* heels and cringed. Having turned off Devon's location sharing and alerts before leaving her apartment, no one knew her whereabouts. Well... except for her driver. He seemed safe enough, even if his eyes bored into her in the rear-view.

As Hope considered her sanity, a woman in knee-high stiletto boots and booty shorts sprinted in front of their idling car and pulled open the door without hesitation. A disorienting pool of black-light-indigo illuminated the rope patterns woven into her tights as she disappeared inside the warehouse.

"Ma'am," Hope's driver said, "I don't think—"

He was young and polite and about to have a white-male-savior moment. While Hope appreciated the sentiment, she didn't have time for it. She came looking for a demon, not a knight in a Toyota Corolla.

"This is it, thanks." She pushed an extra five bucks at him and shoved out of the car before she could change her mind.

The temperature assaulted her, a fine mesh of goosebumps dotting her exposed skin. Perhaps donning the same outfit she'd worn on that fateful trip to the Cleary's dancefloor, paired with the fishnet thigh-highs sawing between a few of her toes, took things too far.

Everything else is irrelevant.

On second thought, toes were overrated, and freezing was a peaceful way to go. Someone should come up with a better design for fishnets though. Like maybe a bit of sheer hose lining the end or something. That would probably look weird with strappy shoes—and now she was stalling in front of the door to a public dungeon by considering the design flaws of fishnet hose of all things.

Hope feigned confidence, as she followed a woman bundled in a parka through the door and into a small, sectioned off lobby. Muffled music droned deeper in the warehouse. People in apparel ranging from street clothes, to club attire, to fetish wear and beyond walked toward a velvet curtain, flashing cards at a behemoth of a man dressed in leather pants and a neon pink chest harness.

Hope swallowed hard. She did not have a card. She did not know how to get a card. She did not want to out herself as an outsider by asking someone *about* the cards.

"First time, miss?"

Shit...

Hope turned to find a guy wearing a glittery shirt, topped with a harness matching the doorman's, enviable eye makeup, and cat ears. She nodded; Kitty Ears grinned.

"Hit that table for the legal stuff." He pointed a stiletto nail that faded from neon green to fuchsia at a table covered in stacks of stapled documents, printed on bright pink paper. "Read it carefully because the rules matter here. Take it over to Tandy when you've signed everything." Her feline companion gestured to a woman at the register dressed in... tape? Yep... Blue tape, pink harness, and a collar with a heart-shaped tag. Hope spun the clasp on her bracelet, refocusing on her sparkly guide. "She'll relieve you of fifty bucks or so, and then you can journey down the rabbit hole." Kitty Ears winked. Chloe would love him. Hope missed Chloe.

"Thank you."

"Anytime, miss. Play safe."

It turned out that *the legal stuff* consisted of a nine-page document specifying rules, dungeon etiquette, scene protocols, privacy, substance use policies, sanitation, safety and consent practices, and the banned usage of recording devices beyond the lobby, outdoor spaces, or private rooms. Hope skimmed the section headings. Her hand hurt from all the initialing and signing as she approached the tape-clad Tandy at the register.

"First time, babe?" Tandy said, as Hope relinquished her signed packet of legal jargon. So much for slipping in under the radar. Everyone tagged her as the new girl the moment they saw her.

"Uh huh."

"You on your own or...?" Tandy raised a brow and let the question drift.

"I'm, um, meeting someone."

Someone who would not be a happy camper when he arrived. She knew goading him wasn't productive. It wasn't *positive communication* or *conflict negotiation* or *anything* she'd learned in college. But like Devon had pointed out so succinctly that morning, she wasn't his fucking therapist.

Once the plan had formed in her head, she also couldn't seem to stop herself.

Tandy skimmed through the packet, checking signatures and initials. "If it's somebody you don't know well, you can let the DMs know to keep an eye out for you. A lot of new people like to start out here, so they aren't alone." She straightened her spine and lifted her chin. "Mistress is very particular about our safety protocols."

Hope thought of Devon, barefoot in black cargo pants in his playroom full of gear.

"I know him pretty well, thanks."

What she did not know was what *DM* meant in this context, though she doubted it had anything to do with social media messaging or tabletop role-playing games.

"Alrighty. I need your ID, shug."

Hope produced her license, which Tandy pored over, checking the dates and picture, before handing it back.

"It's fifty for a one-night membership, seventy-five for a two-week trial, or—"

"Just tonight, thanks," Hope said, tapping her card against the reader, siphoning off cash she should save.

Tandy nodded. "Can I put a wristband on ya?" Hope extended an arm, and Tandy ran a finger over her bracelet. "Oh..." Her lashes fluttered as she looked Hope in the eye. "Can't cover that up..." Grabbing Hope's other wrist, she affixed a neon pink band. "All set. Teddy will let you into the dungeon." Tandy gestured to the guy manning the velvet curtain. He did not look like a *Teddy*.

"Just double checking... It's okay for me to use my phone out here before I go inside, right?" Hope motioned to one of the reminder signs hanging by the curtained-off doorway.

"Yes, ma'am," Tandy said. "Phones are allowed in the lobby, so long as you don't take pictures of other patrons without their consent. The wristband lets you come and go for the evening, so feel free to step out if you need."

"Thanks."

Tandy did a shimmy that sent her tape covered breasts swaying. "Play safe, miss."

Hope stepped into an out of the way corner. A tiny wave of guilt hit her when she pulled out her phone and saw the string of notifications. She ignored Devon's because if she started talking to him before she went inside, her whole plan would unravel; but Chloe's text was another story.

I just got a text asking if you were with me. I told Nix you weren't, but since you have a stalker, please let me know you're alive.

Hope smiled down at the screen, which promptly illuminated with a *Where TF are you???* from her brother.

Shit. She sent a response to Chloe.

I'm good.

How do I know this isn't Aaron pretending to be you?

Hope laughed. *Chill 3F.*

It is you!!!

Yeah, and I'm fine. Just…communicating more loudly. Can you let JJ know I'm alright? Just got a text from him too.

NP. Where are you?

Hope bit her lip, looked around the lobby. From over by the door, Kitty Ears fluttered his color-tipped fingers in a wave.

I'll tell you later, she sent back to Chloe. *Keep you out of trouble. Just let JJ know I'm okay. Devon can figure it out on his own.*

Chloe returned a smiling devil emoji and another of a cat blowing a kiss.

With that sorted, Hope opened the last remaining thread of unread messages. Not sparing them a cursory glance, she sent back one of her own. Then, she approached the man at the curtain.

DEVON

A frigid breeze ruffled Devon's hair, the sum of quick steps over smooth sidewalk. Clutching a stack of warm papers in his left hand, he cut through the darkness with singular focus.

He'd stopped by his house to take care of Apollo, deal with the morning's dishes, and...procrastinate. Eventually, he headed to Cleary's, slipped in the back door, and printed off the information he carried now. Not because he planned to take her tonight, he told himself, though his brain tossed out a different idea— Pulling her into a private room. A hand between her shoulder blades, pressing her down onto a table or bench. The other flipping her skirt up. So simple.

"Fucking perv," he mumbled, shoving the fantasy down as his cock stirred in his jeans.

"Excuse me?"

His gaze snapped toward a passing woman.

"Uh..." Gesturing to his head, he kept walking. She'd either think he was talking into an earbud or loony. He didn't care which, so long as he got a leash on his desires before he got to Hope.

Tonight was for talking, mending—no matter how much he wanted to put her in a tiny skirt and defile her.

Devon glanced down the alley by her building as he passed. *Smart kitten*, he thought, spotting her silver Prius beneath a streetlight. He jogged up three flights of stairs, running through the script in his head. *I'm an idiot. I fucked up. You deserve someone who will talk to you. I never should have left.*

Reaching her door, he knocked, waited and knocked again.

Nothing. Not even the sound of the television or her moving about, and her walls were thin as parchment. Devon's brow pinched. Pulling out his phone, he fired off a text.

`Can we talk? I'm at your door.`

He stared at the message, waiting for any indication that she'd read it. Ninety seconds later, he called.

You've reached Hope...

His pulse doubled. He knew she was there. The last notification he had was her arriving at her apartment at 10:37 a.m.

He texted her again.

`If you don't want to see me, I'll head home. But if I don't get a response, I'm going to let myself in to make sure you're okay.`

He strained his ears for the sound of buzzing through her door. Two minutes oozed by like molasses, and when she hadn't so much as opened the message, Devon pulled out his keys.

"Hope?"

He called her name from the doorway, feeling out of place. Not a single light shone; the apartment sat silent as a tomb. Devon's mouth went dry.

"Hope?" he called again, his own voice echoing back at him.

Devon surged forward. Napping, he decided. In her room, fast asleep... But she wasn't. His fruitless search took less than twenty seconds and turned up nothing. Returning to the landing, he crossed the hall and knocked on Chloe's door, even though something in his gut told him she wasn't going to answer either. At the same time, he stuffed the papers in his hand under an arm, pulled up a number, and dialed.

"If you're calling to fire me, I will hand your keys to this guy sucking down Guinness and walk out." Nix's voice overlayed the sound of drunken laughter.

"Is Chloe working tonight?"

"What makes you think—"

"Fucking hell, Nix. I don't have time for you to act like you don't know."

The other end of the line quieted. "She's out with some of her work friends. A bachelorette party or something."

Devon scrubbed a hand up his face and through his hair; the stack of papers clattered to the floor.

"Christ..." He bent to grab them. "I need to know if Hope is with her."

"I can text her and let you know what she says."

"Do it. If she doesn't respond, call."

"Dev..." Her voice turned serious. "Do you think something happened to Hope?"

"I... No." He shook his head, but not hard enough to make it true. "She's just pissed at me. Text Chloe. I'm going to check the shared spaces in her building. I'm sure she's here somewhere."

"Okay. I'll let you know when I hear from Chloe."

Hanging up, he bolted down to the main entry door and deeper. Skipping the last three steps, he landed hard. A man loading a washer startled, his basket of dirty clothes tumbling to the basement floor.

"Sorry." Devon breathlessly waved his now-dilapidated stack of paper, before folding it into quarters and cramming it in his back pocket. "Have you seen a woman down here? Thirty-ish. Brown hair. Gorgeous..." Why did he say that? Because she *was* gorgeous, and Devon couldn't fucking find her. "Probably looks like she's in a shit mood because her boyfriend is a moron."

The guy's eyebrows lowered. He smirked and shook his head. "Sorry, man."

"Fuck."

Devon pivoted, taking the stairs two at a time until he reached Hope and Chloe's floor—as if standing between their two doors would somehow ensure that the two of them were shoving dollar bills into the g-string of a male stripper together. His phone buzzed.

Not with Chloe. Chloe says she doesn't know where she is. I texted JJ too. He's working. Hasn't seen her either.

Devon stared at those words as the blood drained from his face. He had nothing left. Hope's car sat outside. There'd been no notification of her leaving the building. He should have gotten a notification, but maybe there was a glitch? Tech glitches happened.

Go get her.

"I'm trying," Devon whispered, typing out another text to Hope.

I'm using my stalker app and coming to fucking find you. If you don't want to see me, TEXT BACK NOW.

Not waiting for her reply to his *shouty-capitals*, Devon pulled up her contact and navigated to the map. His eyes searched for her smiling face in a digital bubble that...didn't exist. The cold panic of a million unspeakable things seeped into his body, freezing him in place.

It had to be Hope, right? She was mad at him, so she turned off the location sharing. But she wasn't at Cleary's, and her car was right outside.

Where else could she go without her goddamn car?

Aaron could take her.

His hands trembled.

Aaron could hurt her.

The air turned to syrup.

Aaron could—

Devon flinched violently as his phone pinged with a text alert. A video, it said. From Hope. Proof that she was fine. That he was losing his goddamn mind, but she was *fine.*

He likes pictures. Videos are more fun.

Nausea rolled in his gut, cold sweat prickling his skin. He felt fourteen... Fourteen and terrified to watch a video that would be every bit as horrific as he feared.

Not a child. What if she needs you? You are not *a fucking child.*

Tapping the screen, his eyes skimmed details—six seconds of exposed skin, fishnet fabric, the heels she'd worn as he fucked her on his bar the night he told her he loved her. The band around her wrist was a shade of pink that Devon would recognize anywhere.

"Come and get me, Sir," she said, over the familiar beat of droning music.

The edges of Devon's vision went red, then black, as his frantic thoughts coalesced.

You fucking brat.

"You fucking brat."

HOPE

Smack! *"Ow!"*

Having ditched her outerwear, rather than swelter in the club's warmth, Hope clutched her coat. Hyper-awareness teased every inch of her exposed skin. On stage, a brunette in acres of black latex rubbed a hand over a rosy bottom.

She had kept her head up and her eyes down as she traversed the warehouse, passing pieces of equipment that reminded her of Devon's playroom and various sitting areas on the way. She wanted to watch a rope scene, but the spectators made her nervous—so many bodies pressed close to a floor-level spectacle. You couldn't see without getting into the thick of ongoing conversation between people who knew each other by name.

The unmistakable sound of something connecting with flesh drew her to the stage; and, since going farther would get her into an area of painted cinderblock walls and closed doors, she decided this was where she'd stay. Stages were logical places to wait and watch, after all, and because of the raised platform, people hadn't crowded so closely. In fact, Hope stood alone at the front edge, her view unobstructed.

The spanker doled out another light tap; the owner of the tush wiggled and squealed. Hope's brow furrowed. She'd watched them for a while, but the intensity hadn't changed. It seemed to be more of a sensual thing than an ouchy-thing for these two.

"Like what you see?"

Hope turned toward the voice, looking up into the face of a dark headed guy around her age. He wore jeans and a long-sleeved t-shirt. His build reminded her a bit of Devon, but his eyes were green. Having been mesmerized by the couple on stage for untold minutes, she had no idea how long he'd been there. The guy grinned and offered his hand.

"Nosh."

Extracting an arm from beneath her draped coat, Hope shook it.

"Hope."

Nosh smirked. "Wow. Your real name, huh?" Hope opened her mouth, but Nosh went on. "No worries, princess. I won't tell. You should pick something if you don't want your name getting passed around, though. People see new faces, and they start talking. You need someone to show you the ropes or—"

"I'm fine," she said too quickly.

Nosh's grin widened. He leaned closer, hooking his thumbs in the front pockets of his jeans. "I only bite occasionally."

"I'm waiting for someone."

Donning the same flimsy armor that women had used for centuries, she turned, scanning the area for her usually overprotective boyfriend—the one who had left her standing in his driveway that morning and could not get from Cleary's, home to change and let Apollo out, and then to Edge so quickly now.

Turning back, her eyes locked on a new arrival, standing diagonally from her along the stage's side. The lighting washed out the details of the mask and dark clothes, morphing them into an intimidating void that all but jumped out at her. She took a step back, stumbling as one of her heels caught the tip of Nosh's shoe. He caught her elbow, steadying her before letting her go.

"Whoa there, princess. You okay?"

Hope looked from Nosh, back to the masked stranger. It was no different from the other fetish wear she'd seen since she walked through the door, but something deep in Hope—the part of her that saw hooded figures in empty alleys—didn't like the way the mirror-black eyes gave the impression that the person beneath could be staring at her, and she wouldn't even know.

"Yeah." She forced a smile. "Sorry. Just clumsy. Thanks."

"Masks and clowns," Nosh said, nodding.

"What?"

He grinned and tipped his head to the newcomer. "A lot of folks are afraid of masks and clowns. It's the idea that it could be anyone under there. A murderer. A rapist. Your brother..." He pointed to another masked figure, this one with ears and a muzzle. "Or maybe it's just a guy in a pup hood, who likes to be called a good boy, then bred for hours." He shrugged. "Some people like it, and some people hate it. Then, you've got the people who don't like it but play with it anyway. They get off on the fear."

Hope imagined a body pressing into her. Black-void eyes staring down at her. The scent of cedar and sandalwood in her nose and whiskey and honey in her ears and... Her stomach fluttered. She tugged the hem of her skirt.

"I can see how someone could get into that," she said.

Nosh crossed his arms and settled in. "You picked the right spot to wait for your friend." He gestured to the women on stage. "Bunny and Gidget are both switches. If they start taking turns, those two could go on for hours. Plenty of entertainment while you wait."

The whacker delivered another swat. Hope bit back a laugh, and Nosh cocked a brow.

"That funny to you, princess?"

"No, it's just..." She waved a hand toward the pair. "Obviously, they could do that for hours."

His brows went higher, and Hope realized that she'd piqued his interest far more than intended.

"She's not even trying," she said, not helping matters. "To hit her hard, I mean." And...now she was insulting their scene, which was probably a no-no in that giant packet that she hadn't read. She huffed out a sigh. "It looks like they're having a great time."

Nosh chuckled. "I take it whoever collared you has a heavier hand than Bunny."

Hope put a hand to her throat. "Oh, I'm not..."

"Collared?" he finished for her, tilting his head. He bit back another grin. "That can't be right. You might be new here, but you talk like a painslut. Either your eyes are bigger than your ass or someone forgot to fill you in on a few things. You mind?"

The brush of fingertips down her forearm accompanied the question, as a quiet sense of warning prickled through Hope. Nosh caught her hand before she could process it, running a thumb over the silver clasp atop her wrist. The space around them grew louder, the energy escalating.

His gaze swept up from the bracelet Devon had gifted her for Christmas, settling on her face. "Not all collars go around your neck, princess."

"That is not yours."

Hope's eyes widened at the familiar voice behind her. She jerked free of her new acquaintance, and her back slammed into a solid body. The scent of cedar and sandalwood wafted into her nose, and Devon's too-quick breaths tickled the back of her ear. When she turned around, the rage on his face burned.

"Hello, Sir."

"Darling," he replied through clenched teeth. "What the fuck are you wearing?"

"I—"

"*Ho-ly* shit." Nosh clicked his tongue. "You collared the princess? Demon returns to his forsaken domain...with a toy."

Devon looked at him like he wanted to kill him, but instead, he linked a hand around Hope's wrist and started walking.

"Wait, I..." She trailed off as she realized that he wasn't pulling her to the exit, but deeper into the club. "Where are we going?"

"What? You don't already know? Didn't plan this far ahead, darling?"

"Daddy Demon?" pealed a childish voice, as they approached the hallway lined with closed doors at the back of the warehouse.

Hope looked around in confusion. "Are they yelling at you?"

Devon gave his head a swift shake, let go of Hope, and plastered on a fake smile like it was his job to look pleasant and non-threatening.

"Daddy!"

The voice melded with pounding footsteps echoing down a stairway to their right, and then a blur of pink and blond slammed into Devon so hard that he stumbled back a step. A woman. A woman in a freaking tutu and pigtails... Hope watched her wrap her legs around his waist as he hooked his arms beneath her ruffled-panty-covered ass.

"Daddy, Daddy, Daddy, Daddy, I *missed* you!"

She sounded like a five-year-old with a sugar rush, and punctuated every word with a bounce, before grabbing his head and smashing a kiss to his cheek—wiggling like a live wire the whole time.

Hope's face was on fire as she struggled to grasp what was happening. Devon had spent most of the day avoiding her, but he was looking at the kindergarten cos-player like she hung the moon.

"I missed you too, Minnie."

He shifted the woman...*Minnie* sideways, propping her on a hip, despite her being way too big to be held like that. Hope's whole body buzzed with something ugly that had nothing to do with Minnie.

"Who's dat?" Minnie asked, pointing to Hope and swinging her pink sneakers because... why wouldn't she?

"Yeah, *Daddy*," Hope said, "who's—"

"No." Devon cut her off in a snarl. "You're the one who came here. You don't get to do *that*."

Hope's eyes widened, and she closed her mouth in stunned silence.

"Curious, aren't you?" Devon said, turning his attention back to Minnie. He tapped a finger on her nose, before plopping her down. "Unfortunately, curiosity often gets little girls into very big trouble. Isn't that right, sweetheart?"

"Yes, Daddy." Minnie stared up at him, twirling her tutu side-to-side.

"There's a good girl."

Hope fumed.

"Now," Devon said, "go tell Mommy I'm home. I won't be long, and I do not want to be disturbed."

"Will you come cuddle?" The real tears in Minnie's eyes set Hope's teeth on edge.

"Not tonight." Devon glanced to Hope, a flash of hazel eyes before he looked back to Minnie, like she was the most precious thing he'd ever seen. "Daddy isn't feeling very cuddly right now, but I'll come cuddle soon."

"When?" Her pink sneaker stomped the floor in time with the demand, and Devon sighed.

"Later this week, if I have time."

"Promise?"

He looked to Hope again, pressing his mouth tight and canting his head in a universal *Look what you've done.*

"I promise. Now, go on, baby."

With another quick kiss and a swat on the butt, Minnie skipped off into the crowd chanting *Daddy's back* in an unnerving singsong voice, looking for her *Mommy.*

"Fuck," he murmured to himself, running a free hand up his face and through his hair. "Now, I'm lying to littles... It's like you're determined to drag out the worst parts of me."

"Well, apparently Minnie is immune to your crappy—" The words died on her tongue as Devon stepped into her face.

"I'm saying this *once*," he growled. "I don't fuck Minnie. I don't do scenes with Minnie. There is no way in hell I would ever *date* Minnie. And if she had any reason to believe that I wanted to do any of those things, she wouldn't get within ten feet of me. When she asks to cuddle, she's asking for a guy to hold her without letting their goddamn hands wander because she spent the wrong half of her life with men who let their goddamn hands wander."

Hope sucked in a startled breath. "Oh..."

"Oh? That's all you have to say? Just...*oh.*"

"I'm...sorry."

He stepped back from her, shook his head. "Not yet, you aren't."

Then they were moving again, Devon pulling her into the hallway lined with closed doors. He headed for a skinny guy dressed like everyone's definition of a porno dominant—but with a neon pink chest harness on top.

"Finally get off cleaning duty," Porn Guy was saying, studying his boots as he scuffed the floor. "And now I'm stuck back here when—"

"Open a room," Devon said. "Any room."

The guy didn't even look up as he droned out a response.

"Leave the room how you found it. All bodily fluids must be cleaned using the provided cleaning solutions in the supply cabinet. Failure to comply with any rule will result in immediate removal from the premises. A DM will remain in the hallway at all times for your safety and inspect the room after you finish. House safewords?"

Uninterrupted moments passed before Hope realized that the last statement in Porn Guy's string of information was meant to be a question.

"Answer the man, darling," Devon said, a dare in his tone.

Hope looked at his hand around her wrist, her heart beating faster with every second she scrounged her memory for scraps of information from the pink packet she'd skimmed. The only thing that had stuck with her was the phone and recording rules Tandy had reiterated.

"Go on…"

He stared at her like she was taking too long to dig her own grave. Hope wet her lips.

"Um…"

He cocked a brow.

"Today..." Porn Guy said, finally looking up. "D... Demon..." he stammered. "I'm so sorry. I thought you'd be on stage. You're always on the stage—"

"Door," Devon snapped, staring at Hope with soul-searing intensity.

"Yes, sir...er..." The poor guy took a bracing breath. "Sorry, Demon. Which one, Demon?"

A muscle feathered in Devon's jaw, and his hand twitched against Hope's wrist.

"Any. Fucking. Door."

"Yes, Demon." The man fumbled with a keycard, eventually opening a room. "S..so sorry for the delay, Demon." He bobbed his head in some sort of weird bow, then scooted several doors down, where he waved at them with a big, lopsided grin.

"Is he terrified or starstruck?" Hope stared at him, baffled. "I can't tell."

"Un-fucking-believable..." Devon murmured, shoving her into the private room and slamming the door.

***

Hope looked around at the small space, her heart hammering the backside of her sternum. Eyebolts protruded from the sides of a padded table. A storage cabinet, hamper, and trash bin lined one wall, a row of chairs another. She dropped her coat on one, while Devon kept his back to her.

Away from the crowd, with the music muffled, she took a breath, then another. Emotion packed her body to bursting, antagonized by her own behavior. She'd gone too far. This was too much after the last few days. And even though she knew that, Devon was right; she couldn't yet bring herself to regret it.

"Red and yellow." His voice, a constant source of comfort for Hope, was so detached that it sent a shiver down her spine.

"Wh..what?"

"The house safewords are red and yellow," he repeated. "The same ones I gave you from day one. Like a stoplight... You'll find most people in the community understand that system. Continuity makes people safer."

He turned, hazel eyes raking over too much exposed skin. Hope fidgeted with her bracelet, tugged the edge of her crop-top toward the skirt that a stranger once stuck his hand up. The room shrank.

"You would have known that if you hadn't lied about reading the packet you signed to get in."

His feet inched wider on the concrete floor; hands fisted at his sides. The tattoos on his forearms undulated over tensing muscles, before disappearing beneath his rolled sleeves.

Shit.

"I wasn't going to...*play.*" She wrung her hands. "I didn't think it ma—"

"When a *rape* and a well-negotiated CNC scene look like the same goddamn thing, it fucking matters."

"I don't know—"

"*Consensual non-consent*," he said with an insulting degree of enunciation. "When someone *rapes you* out of the goodness of their black heart."

Hope shut her mouth, swallowed. Devon's upper lip twitched.

"There are people in this building who will assume you are having the time of your life, while someone *breaks you*. Did you notice the way that guy fawned when I shoved you in here? Do you think he'd open that door for you, kitten, or jerk off in the hallway to your screams?"

Hope pressed her thighs together, arousal smearing between them, despite her unease.

"Devon..."

He moved so fast. One moment he was standing with his fists at his sides, the next his hand encircled her throat, yanking her forward.

"Devon isn't here," he said through gritted teeth. "I am."

"Wait." The single-word plea choked out of her, and her eyes went wide.

"*No.*" He plowed forward, grinning wickedly. Hope grabbed his wrist as she stumbled backward, tripping in her heels. "There are rules for a reason, darling, and you're about to learn what happens when you break them."

Keeping that grip on her throat, he shoved her the last step. Her back hit the cinderblock wall, knocking the breath from her. Before she had time to recover, Devon pinned her with his body. His free hand dug against her belly; cold metal scraped her skin, and the buckle of his belt jangled. Hope squeezed his wrist tighter, her fingertips tingling.

"I'm going to fuck you against this wall," he said in her ear. "Then, I'm going to bend you over that table and stripe your ass purple. I'll do it like I fucking hate you; so, by the time I finish, you can tell yourself we're on the same page."

"D... Sir," she stammered, her breathing stilted.

"Last. Chance." He glared down at her. "Spit it out, kitten. Make me let you go."

"I won't..." she managed, face burning and eyes watering, "hate you. I *can't*."

A muscle feathered in his jaw; his exhale fanned over her face, as tears slipped down her cheeks.

"Give it time."

Releasing her throat, Devon bunched her skirt around her waist. She knew what he was seeing when he hesitated. The thigh-highs, the lack of panties. Every item of clothing she put on—or didn't put on—had been a calculated choice to instigate his darker side into something she hadn't been able to get out of safe, supportive, boyfriend-Devon. The one that feared letting her over any walls, lest she scale them all. He looked back up at her with something that would have passed for disgust in his eyes—if his cock weren't smearing precum above her navel.

"Brat."

He hoisted her legs around his hips and thrust hard. Hope cried out with the impact, her back crushing into the unyielding wall, as he seated himself deep.

"You goddamn brat," he growled again.

He slammed into her over and over, sweat dampening his hairline, eyes wild. All Hope could do was hold on and take it. His fingers dug into her thighs. Her breath rushed out with every brutal stroke.

"Such a fucking brat. Such a..." His rhythm faltered. Emotion that she never would have anticipated from a demon choked his words, and then— He confessed. "I didn't know what to do. I thought he had you. I thought..."

Hope wrapped her arms around his shoulders, pulled him close. "Take it, Sir," she said. "Take what you need."

With a flash of hazel eyes, Devon caught her beneath the knees and folded her in half, spreading her wider for his use. Their heaving exhales mingled, swirling down her collar, hot and damp. The sting of each blow stole her breath, as her clit smashed into his pubic bone.

"Fuck..." He panted. "*Fuck.*"

Hope cried out as he bottomed out hard, and as she did, Devon glanced over his shoulder to the table. He shivered, and Hope saw it so clearly—the *need* in him.

"Whatever you need."

He shook his head. "I don't."

"Punish me, Sir."

She barely got the last word out before he tore her away from the wall and planted her belly-down on the table—her heeled-feet on the floor. Wetness dripped from her aching pussy, down the inside of her thighs, trailed to the concrete beneath her.

"Punish you?"

He yanked his belt free; Hope's chest heaved.

"Purple stripes," she said before she lost her nerve. "Like you hate me. Like you promised."

Like he needed.

The belt sliced through the air with a sickening whistle; her scream ricocheted off the walls. He swung again before the echo faded, laying a second stripe below the first. Hope's entire body jerked with the impact, her screech ringing in her ears. Behind her, Devon let out a shaky breath. He tangled a fist in the skirt wadded around her waist, then settled in.

Stripe after stripe. Scream after hoarse scream. The word *red* bounced around her skull like a lifeline, and Hope clenched her jaw to keep it behind her teeth. To make him proud. She'd earned this, and he needed it... And then it all went fuzzy—deliciously, absurdly fuzzy in a way that made every nerve in her body buzz.

Devon laid down another lash, and instead of wailing her distress, Hope *shuddered*.

"Oh no." She whimpered, muscles tightening, core twitching. "No, no, no..."

"*No* is not a goddamn safeword here, and you fucking know it."

A slicing blow landed across the backs of her thighs, just below the swell of her ass; and it was over. Her legs went rigid. She *groaned* as her pussy grabbed at nothing. Tears splattered the table, and a wracking sob tore from her chest. The belt hit the floor, and Devon's hand slid onto her hip as he squatted behind her, staring into her pulsing cunt.

"Are you... Did you just..."

Hope pressed her face into the table, unable to stop her hiccuping sobs. Tutting, Devon pushed to his feet.

"What am I going to do with you?"

Pick the belt back up seemed the most logical choice for a brat who broke rules, then got off during her punishment; but the front of his jeans brushed the backs of her legs, instead. Hope's misfiring brain rolled over the rhythmic, fleshy sound that accompanied his heavy breathing, then he planted a hand by her ribcage a split second before hot liquid spurted onto her stinging flesh.

"Stay," he ordered, his voice rough.

She couldn't move if she tried.

The cabinet opened, and then a soft towel swiped the insides of her thighs, dabbed at the cum crawling down her tender ass. The sounds of spraying and the scent of cleaner followed. Rustling. Crinkling. His belt buckle scraped the cement as he retrieved it from the floor. Hope's mind swam, but her body flinched.

"Shit, it's okay. I'm..." His hand touched her back—the lightest of contact. "I'm going to get you up, okay?"

The room pitched, and then Hope was staring into his eyes. Her lip wobbled.

"It was an accident," she snubbed. "I didn't mean to come."

"Hey..." Devon cupped her cheek, brushed a thumb through her tears. "Cry about your ass, not your orgasm." He frowned at the skirt encircling her waist. "You can wear my shirt," he said, working through the buttons and slipping it off. "It's long enough to cover you." He forced a smile, as he fed her arms into the sleeves, fastened a few buttons. "I know you're a mess right now, but we need to get out of here before the club gets busier." He draped her coat around her shoulders.

"I didn't drive."

"Yeah, I know. How did you get here?"

"A Toyota Corolla," she mumbled.

"A..." He blew out a breath.

"It smelled like onions."

Devon looked skyward, then snatched her up. Hope wrapped her legs around his waist, her pussy dripping down his bare stomach. After adjusting her coat and his shirt until he'd covered her, he walked out into the dungeon.

Music droned around them; whispers followed in their wake. Hope saw Nosh leaning against the stage, lots of people she didn't recognize at all. Devon ignored Demon's name a dozen times, as Hope fought to keep her eyes open against the dragging exhaustion in her limbs and the soothing sway of his body. She was weightless. Floating. And pressed against the safest thing in her world. The rest could be sorted in the morning.

"Almost there, kitten."

The low words tickled her ear. Hope opened her eyes for one last view of the sprawling warehouse then jerked. Devon's arms tightened at her sudden movement, and he shifted his feet for balance.

"Christ... Darling, I have you."

Hope buried her face in his shoulder, peeking out at the masked figure in the crowd behind them. Her heart thudded against Devon's chest as he carried her through the lobby and out into the cold.

HOPE

Hope lay cradled in softness, pulling in deep breaths of cool air. The pillows crammed in around her, the comforter over top, they cocooned her body in a way that left her floating in a haze of delicious perfection. Then came that sound again...

"Ungh..."

With effort, she lifted her head and peeked over the pile of fluff, toward the source—a dull pain throbbing in her muscles with every movement.

Devon lay atop the blankets in sweatpants, instead of his usual bedtime boxers. A bit of light from the bathroom illuminated his furrowed brow. He looked as if he'd nodded off while leaning against the headboard. Hope looked down at herself, noted the t-shirt he'd put her in, the way he'd tucked her in, but wasn't touching her. And then, memories from Edge came crashing back like a tidal wave.

The look on his face as he slammed her into the wall—fucking her like ownership and punishment had merged into a single overpowering act at the order of a Demon. Was punishment fucking a thing? The throbbing in her groin made it feel like a thing—one that, intense as it may have been, hadn't sated his hunger.

No, fucking her like that had been an appetizer, she realized now. Hope wondered if their relationship up to that moment—when he shoved her onto the table and pulled off his belt—had been much the same. A starving man, snacking on her, while desperate for a meal.

Small tastes...

She thought of the first searing stripe from his belt and swallowed, her throat scratchy and raw. All of Edge heard her, but no one interrupted—as he'd promised. Lick after vicious lick, until she had done the unthinkable. Normal people did not come as their pissed off boyfriend laid into them with a belt, right?

Shit.

"Please..." he mumbled beside her, snagging her attention.

As Hope narrowed her eyes at his sleeping form, Devon *whimpered*—a sound so unlike anything she'd ever heard from him that adrenaline dumped into her veins.

"Hey," she whispered, nudging him.

She heard the wet sound of his mouth parting, the ragged inhale that followed; but the rest of his body lay still as a statue.

"I'm sorry. I don't want to." His voice was thick, air sawing in and out of his lungs. *"Please be okay..."*

Hope pushed herself more upright, the panic in his voice chilling her blood.

"Don't make me. Don't make me. I can't. Please, I can't—"

"Devon!" she snapped.

He surged off his back, nearly head-butting her on the ascent. Then it was his hands everywhere, skimming her body like when he'd gotten to the tailor's shop.

"Is this me?" he mumbled, eyes glassy with sleep. "Are you, you?"

Hope scooted close on her knees. She caught his wandering hands and squeezed them tight.

"You were dreaming."

"I would never do that." His watery eyes pleaded for her belief.

"Do what? Dev—"

He cut her off with his mouth, a feverish kiss meant to erase something that they needed to deal with.

"I don't have to hurt you." He trailed hurried kisses down her jaw, her throat, as he lowered her back. "I swear."

Devon shifted down her body, pushed up her t-shirt and spread her thighs. He lapped his tongue over her once, twice…

"Devon," she managed. God, his tongue felt good. Hot and wet. Sliding over her in languorous strokes.

"It won't matter if you don't know the safewords; you'll never need them."

Hope's head jerked up. She stared at his dark crown, dipping between her thighs as he licked and sucked. She'd come if he kept going—come for the person he was pretending to be—and everything about that felt wrong.

"Yellow."

He pulled away in an instant, the juices of her arousal wetting his chin in the low light.

"Wh… What?"

Hope took a deep breath. "Yellow," she repeated.

Devon shook his head. "So, you'll safeword when I'm eating you out, but not when I'm shoving you in a private room and pulling off my belt?"

She put a hand on his cheek, kept her eyes trained on his.

"This hurts worse."

He stiffened like she'd slapped him. "But..."

"No more fake Devon." Her eyes stung, and her voice wobbled. "I know this is scary for you. It's not easy for me either. But I love you, and I want all of you."

"Hope..."

"Demon too."

He rocked back on his knees, out of her reach, swiped a hand over his mouth.

"Darling..." Whiskey and gravel filled the word.

"Both or neither. Those are my terms. I don't care if it's fucked up. I don't care if no one else understands. I won't settle for half of you."

"You can't mean that." He shook his head. "You're purple. *Again*. I hit you with a belt, Hope, while the rest of Edge listened to you scream."

"And I came for you."

He ran his hands through his hair. "I should have dragged you to the car."

"But you didn't."

He blinked at her, his chest heaving.

"You didn't drag me to the car, Devon, and I am so glad for it. I'm going to say something right now, and I need you to listen. Really listen and consider what I'm saying, okay?" She waited for his minute nod, then went on. "We've had negotiations, right? You know I'm fine with impact play, restraints... You know I know our safewords."

"Yeah, but—"

"What made tonight different?"

"I was..." he huffed. "*Uncontrolled.*"

"Really? So uncontrolled that you stopped to teach me the dungeon rules?"

"Because you didn't fucking read them."

Hope bit back a smile.

"So uncontrolled that you reminded me of the safewords? Prompted me to say one before you even started?"

Devon scoffed. "Demon likes to break things. I just wanted to hear you scream them."

"Then why did you stop?"

He stared at her.

"I think," she ventured, "that you might be having that thing happen with the hormones and stuff." Hope knew that the *stuff* in his case was emotional, and Devon struggled with emotions on the best days. "Like when I started panicking at R&R on New Years."

His brow furrowed. "You think I'm *dropping.*"

"I do, and I think that's been going on for a while. You're suppressing things you need, because you're afraid of what happens after. Right?"

He shook his head. "Doesn't matter. I..." Hope crawled toward him, and he trailed off. "What are you doing?"

"Helping," she said, her voice quiet and soft. "Like you helped me." She leaned in, brushing her mouth against his, straddling his lap. "I love your sweet side."

Devon exhaled a shuddering breath.

"Hope, I'm hard right now because I had a nightmare about belting you until you bled. I'm not *sweet*, and I don't think you should—"

"I wasn't finished."

She reached between their bodies. Devon groaned as she dipped a hand beneath his waistband, gripped his erection and pulled it free. Running a finger through the precum at his tip, she watched his lips part as she brought it to her mouth and sucked.

"Mmm...you taste sweet to me," she murmured, shifting her body to align herself. His eyes caught hers in the low light, boring into her as she sank.

"*Fuck,*" he breathed.

Hope cradled his head in her hands, pulled herself flush against him.

"I love it when you lick me." She raised her hips, lowered them again. "I love it when you fuck me." She repeated another controlled rise and fall. "Apparently, I even love it when you belt me... at least enough to come for you, Sir."

"Christ," Devon whispered. Hope smiled over his shoulder, stroking herself up and down his shaft in an unhurried pace.

"I love the way you *own* me. Every inch, Sir. Every. Single. Inch. Write it on my body. Cum, marks, blood... I don't care, so long as it comes from you."

His fingertips skated beneath the t-shirt and up her ribs. Hope caught his hands, pulling them down to her bruised ass. She pressed her palms into his fingers, until she hissed at his grip on her flesh.

"You give me what I want," she said, grinding into him, her words stilted with pleasure.

"Pain? Possessiveness?" Even as he said it, he couldn't keep the raw lust out of his voice. Hope rocked against him, forcing his cock so deep that her pussy ached. "*Fuck...*" He groaned again. "Too greedy for your own good."

"You give me what I need, what I never knew to ask for," she managed, addicted to the slide of her throbbing clit against him. "You are my pleasure and my pain. You are my safety. Please, Sir," she said, surprised by the tears rolling down her cheeks and onto his shoulder, the unmasked vulnerability surging within her. "I'll try to be good for you, but don't stop loving me like this."

The honesty in her words soaked Hope's already slick cunt. Devon's erection pressed harder against her inner walls. He pulled off her t-shirt, tossed her off into the pillows, and climbed up her body, resheathing himself with her on her back.

"Thank you, darling," he purred against her ear, before his voice turned to stone. "But I'll take it from here."

Snatching her hair, he bowed her spine as his other arm shot under her back for support. Everything hurt. Hope's rear burned as he slammed into her; her body ached at his restrictive hold; and her heart... Her heart fluttered in her chest like the wings of a hummingbird.

"I love you," she sobbed, realizing that he wasn't the only one in need of reassurance and connection. "I love you so much."

"I'm here," he gritted out, pumping into her like their lives depended on it. "You have all of me too, and I promise you that as long as you want me, nothing is ever, *ever* going to change that again."

Hope shattered. Devon stayed deep, letting her ride it out before pulling out to finish on her stomach. Staring down at her trembling body, he swiped a finger through the spunk by her navel, then gripped her chin with the other hand.

"Going out like that, without telling me or anyone else," he said, brushing her hair out of her face with the heel of his palm, "you will never, ever do that again. Do you understand?"

"Yes, Sir."

"Who do you belong to, darling?"

"You, Sir."

"That's right, sweet girl. Mine."

He caught his lower lip between his teeth and skimmed a sticky line from the edge of her right eyebrow, up toward her hairline before completing some sort of up and down zigzag and scooping his finger through the goo on her belly again. The next line he drew was straight. Hope's mouth parted as she realized what he was doing. Marking his territory. On her face. In *cum*.

"All mine," he said, kissing the tip of her nose. "And you will not take unnecessary risks with what is mine—which includes turning off the stalker app, taking rides from strangers in Toyota Corollas that smell like onions, lying about reading the protocols when entering public dungeons, and letting *livid* dominants drag you into private rooms." Hope grinned, cheeks squishing against his fingers. "What?"

"Location sharing, Sir."

His mouth twitched. "You are a brat."

"But I'm your brat, right?" She pointed to her forehead.

"For as long as you'll let me keep you." Releasing her face, he flopped down beside her on the pillows. "If you ever forget that, you can bet your sweet, purple ass that I will remind you. You can clean up the rest, but this," he pointed to the drying writing on her forehead, "stays until morning, understood?"

"Yes, Sir."

"Good girl. Now, go back to sleep. It's early and late at the same damn time."

DEVON

Holding a re-purposed lunch meat container which housed two of the world's ugliest cinnamon rolls, Devon shifted his weight. The cursing and the releasing of locks subsided, and then, Nix peeked up at him through a crack in her front door, squinting into the late-morning sun.

"Oh. It's you. Did you find Hope?"

"Yeah, she's at my house."

"Then I assume you're here to fire me, since I won't be needed for a search party."

Devon toed the floorboards with the tip of his boot. "I wanted to apologize for being a raging asshole."

"You wanted to, huh?"

He met her gaze head on. "I'm sorry."

Nix sighed and pushed the door wide, revealing a pink onesie, dotted with giant strawberries.

Devon jolted back.

"What the fuck are you wearing?"

"Pajamas, dipshit."

"But it's…" His eyes bounced from one berry to the next as his brain struggled to make sense of what he was seeing. "*Pink*."

She put her hands on her hips and shifted her stance, rainbow-oil-slick toes inching over the rug. "Are you judging my jammies while asking for forgiveness?"

"No, I just thought you were allergic to anything that didn't scream *Goth Femme Domme*. You wear that black lace getup with the corset to the pajama parties at Edge."

"And you think I wear that at home?"

Devon opened his mouth, closed it. Nix rolled her eyes.

"We all have layers, asshole."

"But…strawberry layers?" His grin got the better of him. "Like a parfait?"

She screwed up her face and crossed her arms, shoving a bushel of berries toward her chin.

"Get in here before I make a parfait of your face."

Devon strode past her. "It sounds like you're offering to shove your boobs—" His head whipped forward as her palm connected with the back of his skull. "*Ow!*"

"It will be a bloody parfait, made of one-hundred percent jackass, and my *berries* will not be involved."

Devon rubbed the sting, chuckling, as his friend stormed toward the kitchen. Berries bounced everywhere. While he sat at her breakfast bar, Nix poured coffee.

"Here," she said, putting a cup in front of him before taking her seat. "Even though you don't deserve my coffee."

"Thanks." He sipped, reveling in the way that, despite its stimulating properties, coffee was comforting. Or maybe the comforting part was the bit where he had apologized to Nix, and she hadn't told him to fuck off yet.

"I didn't plan on entertaining visitors like this." She swept a glance down the front of her outfit. "Unfortunately, a remorseful grump of a Dom, with atrocious timing, showed up on my doorstep with a container of lunch meat."

"Cinnamon rolls." He pushed the lidded tub toward her. "Mom's always putting leftovers in these things for me."

She eyed the container. "Cinnamon rolls?"

Devon nodded.

Popping the top, Nix frowned. "What happened to them?"

"Sorry, I made them before Hope woke up this morning. I tried to keep them warm, but the icing melted off in the oven." He looked at the gooey mess in the tub. "I kind of...scooped it back on."

Nix shrugged and took a bite. "Oh my god. This looks like garbage and tastes like heaven."

"Right?"

"So, if you managed to not only find your missing girlfriend but get her to your house last night, why are you here?"

"Penance, mostly."

"I thought you were cured of religion."

He shrugged. "Some parts stick with you."

She took another bite. "You didn't have to drive over. I would have forgiven you over text. You have important things to worry about."

Devon canted his head. "You're important."

"Yeah, right..." She laughed, and Devon didn't love the way it made him feel.

"You are."

"Fine," she brushed it aside. "*More* important. Like the woman who fled your house yesterday morning, then went missing."

He wet his lips, ran a fingertip around the rim of his mug. "She wasn't missing so much as she wasn't ready for me to find her. She texted a video from Edge right after I talked to you."

Nix's mug clanked against the bar. "Holy shit."

"Yeah." His laugh was humorless. "Told me to come and get her."

"And I'm guessing Demon took that as a personal invitation?"

Without a towel, Devon settled for sweeping nonexistent crumbs off Nix's counter. He hitched a shoulder. "Being mad was easier than being afraid."

Nix smirked. "Shocking."

"Right?" He laughed, then... "When I got there, she had on that outfit from August. Nosh was running his shit excuse for game, touching her like it wasn't any big deal."

"I told you—"

"I know." If he started dwelling on Nosh, his blood pressure would start climbing again. "I should have taken her out as soon as I found her, but I pulled her toward the private rooms..."

Nix's eyes rounded to saucers. She groaned. "No... Dev..."

"And Minnie tackled me on the way, which Hope...reacted to." He rested his elbows on the counter and rubbed his temples; Nix cursed. "The dickhead with the keys didn't even check that she knew the house safewords before letting me in a room with her... She didn't, by the way. Well, she did...but she didn't know she did, and that was terrifying too—the idea of her in a goddamn dungeon with zero understanding of the safety protocols. She looked at me like I was speaking Russian when I said *CNC*."

Realizing he'd started gesticulating at some point, he pressed his palms to the granite.

"Fuck."

Devon nodded. "Yeah, that about sums it up."

He shuddered at the memory of that last lash of his belt. Hope's muscles tightening and core pulsing. The wet heat of her sliding against his stomach as he carried her to the car.

"It wasn't pretty," he managed.

It was fucking gorgeous, Demon countered.

Nix slapped her hands on the counter. "And you run here?"

Devon's spine snapped straight. "*What?*"

"Dude, you can't keep doing this running-away-from-hard-conversations crap. No matter how hot the sex, it won't make up for—"

"I didn't run." He shifted his whole body to face her. "I talked to her this morning. Talked for hours, over fucking cinnamon rolls that I made when I couldn't sleep. Apparently, I'm a guy who makes cinnamon rolls now? I don't understand what she's doing to me."

Nix's head tilted further and further. "So, instead of *hitting things*, you opted for *baking*."

"I know it sounds weird."

She blew out a breath. "No kidding. How did the Minnie thing play out? Was she jealous?"

Devon chuckled. "Minnie or Hope?"

Nix lifted her cinnamon roll in a toast. "Touché. But I meant Hope. Minnie's jealous of the attention."

"Turns out, they aren't very different on that front. Hope was jealous because she'd spent all day trying to get me to acknowledge her after I called her irrelevant, then I scooped up Minnie and played daddy the moment she appeared."

Devon heard a *whack*, as a jarring impact erupted on his shoulder.

"Goddammit, Nix." He glared at her. "Stop hitting me." He rubbed the pain.

"You called her *irrelevant*?" she said through clenched teeth.

His face heated. "I told her that Cleary's was my life and everything else was irrelevant."

"Jesus fuck, Dev."

"I wanted…to get away. So, I said something that made it easier." His body reacted to a swift movement out of the corner of his eye. Nix's fist smacked into his palm, the catch more instinct than skill. "Look, I know I fucked up. You don't have to beat it into me. I knew it before I left the bar yesterday." Hell, he knew it before he left the house, but he still went, and it would take time to forgive himself for that mistake. Devon shifted on his seat, blew out a breath, and released her hand. He left his own hanging in mid-air, waiting for the next attack. "I met with Dre. I'm meeting him this week too, like...on the schedule or whatever."

Nix lowered her fist. "Like...therapy?"

"I go to group," he reminded her.

"You know what I mean, Dev."

He shrugged stiffly. "Yeah, I guess. Whoa..." He steadied her as she wrapped her arms around him, slipping off her chair in the process. "We hug now?"

"Shut up, cabbage."

Devon snickered, pink fluff tickling his nose. "You were right," he said, even though she would bring it up when they were ghosts in the great beyond. "Every time you urged me to talk to Hope, to Dre, to *anyone*... You were right. Getting Hope when I wouldn't get off the bar—that was the right call, and I was an ass about it. I've fired you or wanted to fire you way too often lately, when I should have taken your advice." He swallowed hard. "You're my best friend. You're like...a sister." Devon waited for the pain to dissipate, while Nix went the kind of still that told him she knew how much it hurt. "I'm sorry."

She sniffed and patted his back. "No worries."

"That's it?"

Scooting away from him, she smiled. "Yep. I'm right; you're wrong. You're a sorry asshole, but I forgive you. That simple." She re-perched on her chair. "So, how are you and Hope? It can't be too bad if she's at your house, right?"

"It's good; we're good." And he meant it in a way that turned the tension in his muscles to putty. He smiled into his coffee. "I'm taking her back tonight."

"You're kidding. How did that happen?"

"Would you believe it was the result of talking about our feelings over ugly cinnamon rolls?"

She opened her mouth in an approximation of shock. "You *are* kidding me."

He hitched a shoulder. "I was hoping that, if you weren't busy before your shift, you might help me with something." He sipped, pleasant bitterness washing over his dry palate. "I was thinking of getting something for Hope, before we go."

Her dark brows tightened down. "Go on…"

"Dre suggested that I imagine taking her to Edge and everything being fine. I ended up printing Edge's documents before I went to her apartment last night. I thought we'd talk about it and ease toward it."

Nix parked her tongue ring in the corner of her mouth. "Your girlfriend torpedoed that ship."

"Threw us into the deep end, for sure," Devon agreed. "But before I realized she was missing, I was trying to do what Dre suggested. I was thinking she'd look good in…you know…" He cleared his throat. "One of those skirts that's…" He circled a finger in the air. "*Twirly*?" Devon realized he'd caught his lower lip between his teeth and quickly released it. "Or…whatever."

"Devon Cleary... Are you asking me to go shopping?"

His face heated. "I wear cargo pants. Even if I didn't have a drawer full, I could pick them up anywhere." Nix flipped her tongue ring, alternately revealing the top and bottom balls as she wiggled on her seat. "Forget I—"

"No fucking way. You asked, and we're going. I know the perfect place, too. They open at noon."

HOPE

Tipping her head back, Hope cursed...*conditioner*. Though only minutes had passed, it felt like years spent rinsing—years in which she could hear only the once comforting sound of rushing water and couldn't keep an eye on the silvery mass of Apollo lying in the bathroom doorway. She swiped a hand over the glass. Her tension eased when she spotted her sentry—butt facing her, head resting on his paws beyond the threshold. Gathering her hair at the nape, she squeezed out excess water, chiding herself for her fear. And then his head popped up.

Hope straightened, her mind bouncing between exits and towels, weighing the likelihood of finding a useful weapon as her heart rate doubled. It wasn't until Apollo's tail thumped the floor in the lazy welcome rhythm he reserved for people he recognized that she started to settle. If someone were about to go psycho on her in the shower, Apollo would be much more excited; he loved meeting new friends.

"I'm home," Devon called from the front of the house.

She poked her head out. "In the bathroom."

He stopped in the door jamb by Apollo, staring at her. "You...took a shower."

Hope shrugged. "It's not a big deal. How did things go with Nix?"

"Good." He glanced around the bathroom. "I'm sorry I took so long."

"It's fine. I wanted to wear my hair wavy tonight, but it takes a while to air-dry."

His throat bobbed. "I love your hair wavy. Looks like I already got my hands in it."

Hope was aware of every drop of water crawling down her skin, the way her hair prickled at her scalp. There was a palpable anticipation in the air—one both of them could feel.

"Are you about finished in there, darling?"

"Since you're back, I think I'll go ahead and shave."

"When you're done, we have some things to discuss." He dropped into a crouch by Apollo. "You stay here, buddy," he said, ruffling the dog's ears before he disappeared into the bedroom.

Hope emerged twenty minutes later—smooth from her shoulders to the soles of her feet, every inch of her buffed, polished, and moisturized. Her damp hair wafted a fruity-floral scent and hung past her shoulders in loose, drying waves. Devon pushed up from his seat on the bed. His stare darkened as his eyes skimmed down her naked body; then, he offered her a bag.

"No bra. No panties," he said as she reached for it.

Hope pushed aside the tissue and peeked inside, then met his gaze.

"You bought me clothes?"

He smirked. "I wouldn't say that."

She sat on the bed and pulled out the first item—a short, black skater skirt. The fabric fell in liquid ripples, and a scent that could only be described as *expensive* perfumed the air. Hope looked at him with raised brows, then fished out the next scrap of fabric—a long-sleeved top. Black, soft, and missing the bottom half.

"I bought clothes that I wanted to see you in." His eyes sparkled with wicked amusement. "Nix helped. I don't know how sizes work for you all—it's all numbers or letters or both, and an *M* in this thing is twice the size of an L in that thing."

Hope giggled. "That sums it up."

"Go on, kitten." He wet his lower lip, tipped his chin toward her. "Let's see."

Hope noted his jeans and russet-colored, long-sleeved tee. "Now? We aren't leaving for hours, right?"

Devon nodded. "You're getting dressed now, so I can park you on my lap while we go over rules."

She rubbed the soft fabric of the top between her fingers. "Are you changing?"

"I have a feeling going over dungeon etiquette will get you all drippy. Probably shouldn't arrive with you already smeared down my thigh, huh? Ah... You're blushing again." He grinned as she put a hand on her cheek. "Edge opens at eight. I say we go early, get in before there's a crowd to battle through. I'll change before we leave. Now, show me what I bought."

Hope pulled on the skirt, then the top. She tugged the front, but every time she released the hem, the edge snapped up to flutter beneath her breasts. Her nipples pressed against the thin material, called to attention by the chilled air on her exposed stomach and legs.

She gave her hips an experimental shake, fabric teasing along her thighs. Peeking behind herself, she caught a glimpse of purple stripes below the inadequate length of the skirt. She looked to Devon, who was looking at her like he wanted to eat her alive.

"Are you sure I should wear this? People can see."

"You look so pretty, darling." His voice was molten honey. "Everyone who sees you tonight will be jealous, for one reason or another."

Hope fidgeted with the skirt's hem.

"Okay, but I need a bra," she said, fingers dancing along the underside of her breasts. "And underwear."

Devon crossed his arms. "You didn't feel the need for knickers yesterday."

"That's because I was trying to…"

"Piss me off?" He arched a brow, and his grin was *feral*. "Congratulations. You succeeded. This covers as much skin as the outfit you wore last night. More, actually. This has sleeves."

Hope looked down at herself, finding no valid argument. Devon stepped closer.

"It turns out that, when I'm not seeing red, I *like* the idea of my fingers brushing your weeping cunt every time I slip a hand up your skirt." He skimmed a fingertip along the edge of the fabric;

her pussy pulsed with need. "Be careful of your tantrums, darling. They give me ideas." Smirking, he pointed to the bag. "Keep digging."

Hope reached in and pulled out a package of fishnets. "Really?"

He shrugged. "I liked them. You'll wear your boots," he said as she plopped onto the bed, and began pulling on one thigh-high, then the next. "I love your heels, but I want you stable on your feet. And one more thing..."

Hope stood, smoothing the fabric of her skirt. "I hope it's a floor-length trench..."

She trailed off at the sight of the jewelry box in his hands—cherry red like the box he'd used on Christmas Eve. Swallowing hard, he popped open the lid, showing Hope the contents.

"Is that a..."

Longer than her bracelet, with the same black rope, the same silver bales... The only thing missing was the circular clasp, and she had a feeling she was already wearing that part.

"You could call it a choker," he said.

"Except it's a collar."

One given to her by a man who was *very, very dominant* by his own admission... She could call the thing a *kazoo,* but it would still be a collar; and as Nosh had said the night before, not all collars go around necks. Hope touched the matching rope around her wrist, heart hammering in her chest.

"So, Nosh was right."

Devon's eyes hardened. "No. The bracelet is a bracelet—one that has a certain look, sure, but you can't collar someone without their consent. If I wanted to put you in a day collar, there would be a conversation—one full of rules and expectations. It's a commitment." He looked down at the box. "Stacy made this one first, then I thought a bracelet might be a better fit."

"But now…" Her voice lilted upward, full of tentative hope.

"I want people to keep their hands off you tonight. This achieves that goal. You could take it off after—like a *play collar*. It matches your outfit."

The pragmatic way he said it stung more than it should. Obviously, he didn't want to put a symbol of commitment on her the day after she'd pushed him to his breaking point.

Hope forced a smile. "Yeah…okay."

She nodded, and Devon reached for her arm, removing her bracelet and slipping the circular clasp through one of the bales on the collar. His hands brushed her shoulders as he fastened it around her neck, foreign and familiar at once.

"It's perfect." His voice contained so much satisfaction that the words sounded dirty; Hope reminded herself it was just for play. "Give me a twirl, good girl."

Hope executed a dainty pirouette, then curtsied. "Is it everything you dreamed?" she said, looking up at him.

"Oh, love." Devon caught her wrist and tugged her toward the hall. "You overestimate my imagination." At the kitchen table, he settled her in his lap. "My fantasies could never compete. Now, let's talk."

"We already did, and I haven't changed my mind." She started counting things out on her fingers. "No penetration with body parts or otherwise. No membrane contact. No—"

"Not about my scenes—assuming I even end up doing one. We need to talk about you. You can't go in a dungeon without reading the rules. It isn't safe."

"I get that now, and I'll be with you this time."

He trailed fingertips over the fishnet fabric on her thigh. "What if I was the problem and you didn't know who to ask for help? What if the sanitation requirements weren't stringent enough, and you caught chlamydia from a chair? A poorly monitored dungeon is one of the few places something like that could happen."

"Devon—"

"What if there were a live feed online, and you signed a release you didn't bother to read?"

"You wouldn't go to Edge if—"

He caught her jaw and turned her head to face him.

"You aren't hearing me. This is a rule. A forever and always rule. It's a rule if you're with me. It's a rule if you *hate* me. It's a rule if I'm struck by lightning and no longer around to go with you; and, it is not specific to Edge. I don't care who you're with or how much you trust them, Hope. I mean it."

"Didn't you just say that rules and expectations were a different conversation?"

He groaned. "Give me this one, darling. For once in your life..."

"Okay, okay... Yes, Sir."

Devon blew out a breath. Releasing her face, he tapped on the stack of crumpled paper on the table.

"Thank you. Now, front, back, and sideways, Blush."

Hope craned her neck to look at him. "*Blush?*"

"I figured you might want a name for anonymity. Given how often you turn pink, I thought I'd give Blush a try. No good?"

"Well...no. I think I like it." She also could have used it twenty-four hours earlier.

"We can change it if you want, or if you have something else in mind."

"Demon and Blush," she said, trying it out.

The corner of Devon's mouth twitched, and something possessive kindled in his eyes. "Blush and Demon," he countered, tapping a finger on the clasp at her throat.

Hope shifted on his lap. "Demon made me Blush."

He leaned in, his exhale heating the side of her neck. "If you want to play word games, Demon can make you do all sorts of things." He dipped a hand between her thighs. "Start reading, Blush."

HOPE

Despite his grin, Devon's face was beet-red. Perched on a massive pink beanbag in the room affectionately known as *Minnie's Cuddle Puddle*, with Edge's music humming under her feet and creeping in through the walls, Hope hid her laugh behind a hand.

"Minnie..." Devon wheezed. "Daddy's gotta breathe."

On his back, Minnie bounced, the bottom of her purple onesie digging deeper into her butt with every wiggle. If Hope were wearing panties, she'd have to pick a wedge...sympathetically.

"Sorry!"

"Sure, you are." He chuckled, patting her forearm.

His gaze landed on Hope, and something changed in his body language, in the expression on his face. Another person might not have noticed, but Hope recognized the tensing of muscles. The hunger. She took a slow breath, trying to head off her racing heart.

They'd been at Edge for half an hour. Half of that time they'd spent navigating the lobby and the logistics of adding Hope as the included *plus one* on Devon's account—a novelty, as he'd never brought someone, much less permanently added someone. Tandy spent a fair amount of time bowing and murmuring *yes, Demon*; and when they got to the curtain, Teddy had reminded Hope of the house safewords and how to alert a monitor if she needed help before letting them in.

Once past the curtain, Devon had beelined across the floor and up the stairs for the Cuddle Puddle, but judging by the expression on his face, *Demon* was about finished visiting Minnie. Devon shifted, hoisting the woman on his back around to the front, then plopping her down. He held out a hand to Hope and pulled her to her feet.

"We need to get going," he said to no one in particular.

Minnie rushed forward and hugged Hope. "Thanks for coming to my Cuddle Puddle, Blush."

"Thanks for having me."

Minnie twirled a braided pigtail around the end of a finger. "Will you come back to visit?"

Hope smiled. "I'd love that."

Devon dropped a kiss on Minnie's cheek, then tugged Hope out the door, spinning her back to the wall and caging her with his arms as soon as they breached the hallway. Cedar and sandalwood filled her nose, heat soaked into her front. Devon stared at her throat, her mouth, then shifted focus to her eyes.

"Thank you for that," he said.

Hope squirmed, her bare back pressed to the wall, her nipples pebbling against the thin, black fabric of the cropped long-sleeved tee he'd given her.

"I didn't do anything, Sir."

Someone giggled, and Hope glanced over in time to catch a woman, standing a few feet away, pointing her direction. Spotted, the stranger dropped her hand. One of her companions popped their eyebrows, while another stifled a laugh. It wasn't the first time since their arrival that Hope had gotten the impression that someone was laughing at her.

"You told Minnie that you liked her shirt."

Hope focused on Devon, trying to ignore the strangers. "It was cute."

One of his brows rose. "It had crotch snaps and a glitter unicorn."

Hope lifted a shoulder. "Purple is my favorite color." When Devon kept staring at her, she went on in a hushed voice. "She covered up with that blanket when I walked in with you. It's weird enough being the new girl with the god of pain."

"God of pain, is it?" He smirked.

"I don't want Minnie feeling uncomfortable because of me."

Hope had the discomfort covered for everyone—maybe more than the night before, as unlikely as that sounded. At least she had hurt feelings and adrenaline on her side that time. Arriving alone, she had been a nameless newcomer, but put her next to Devon... She became a lamb in a wolf's den. Unaware of her thoughts, Devon trailed his knuckles down her cheek, shoulder, arm, snagging her hand and leading her back the way they'd come.

"I'd say you succeeded." A guy in footie pajamas stepped aside as they passed, tracking Devon with a deferential bow of his head. "She dropped her blankie and asked for a piggyback ride."

They reached the top of the stairs, and Devon released her hand, offering his arm for the descent.

"It was kind of funny watching you—all black cargos and intimidation—beg her not to choke you out," she said. Devon laughed.

The stairs spat them out where Minnie had tackled him the night before; but this time, instead of heading for the private rooms, they paused amid the smorgasbord of skin and fetish wear. The same wild energy that had followed her boyfriend through the dungeon doors one day earlier swirled through the warehouse in a self-sustaining reaction amplified by the masses. Perhaps that was why she felt so uncomfortable. Demon's presence altered the entire vibe of the dungeon.

"I told you he'd be back."

The comment came from a guy in jeans and silver hoops through both nipples.

"What's with the girl?"

Nipple Rings' companion scrunched up her nose.

"Lolli said he carried someone out last night."

"Yeah, but he brought *this one. He picks people up; he doesn't* bring *them."*

"Look what she's wearing."

Hope's fingers brushed the choker.

"Forget what she's wearing, look at her thighs…"

Her gaze caught on Nosh, who shook his head at the floor, chuckling.

"Darling?"

"Sir?"

"...marks on marks...no idea...hard lesson..."

She glanced around then back to Devon, painfully aware of the laughter erupting nearby. "Sorry, I didn't hear you. What did you say, Sir?" More laughter. Hope tugged the back hem of her insufficient skirt.

Devon tipped his head toward the wooden structure where she ditched her coat the night before. The same couple resided beneath it. The man's greying head bent, as he passed a length of rope behind his partner's back before arranging it above and below her breasts. There was a surety about his movement that spoke of years of practice.

"You want to watch Bight do a tie?"

"His name is Bite?"

Devon smiled. "B-I-G-H-T, not *bite*." He snapped his teeth after the second version of the word. "It's a ropey-term."

"Oh... Right." She made a mental note to look it up later.

"To be fair," he said, scanning the room, "it could go either way around here."

When his surveillance reached the stage, he hesitated. One foot inched away from the other, and his chin lowered. The back of Hope's skull tingled. Then, Devon swallowed, blinked, and looked down at her.

"So, um, how about it? His ties are clean, intricate..."

"That sounds time consuming."

His tongue passed over his lips. "We have all night. We'll make time for anything you want to see."

"What if I want to watch you, Sir?"

"That's a question," he said, stalling.

"Did you know that most questions are statements in disguise?"

"I seem to remember asking you the same thing, the first night I took you in the playroom."

Hope smiled up at him. "So maybe I'm making a statement."

He glanced toward the stage, then back to her. "If I'm about to *break something*," he said, looking at her, "you have to tell me."

"*Disruption or interference with another party's scene will result in immediate removal from the premises.* Page six."

"It's page two, and you know this is different—"

"Sir..." She caught his hand. "I'm playing with you. I'll let you know if it's too much, but I don't think that's going to happen. Trust me with this."

His chest rose and fell in a rush...and then he flagged down someone in a neon pink harness.

"Get Maeve to the stage. Let the staff know it's about to get loud," he said.

"Sure thing, Demon."

The monitor, not as flustered by the local legend as others, nodded and walked off into the crowd, lifting a walkie-talkie to his mouth. A moment later, the club's droning beat changed to something dark and familiar. Devon stared after him, before banking toward a section of lockers to the side of the raised stage.

"Do they always do that? Change the music..."

"Yes."

"Why?"

"Because I like this music. Uh... sorry. I'm getting..." He gestured toward his head, and though he didn't finish the sentence, Hope understood. "The music sets the mood. People know what to expect when it changes. I'm going to have Maeve stand with you, if that's okay. I think you'll like her, and I trust her."

Hope nodded. "Okay, Sir."

He grabbed a combination lock and spun the dial, barely looking as he selected the numbers. The lock popped open with a *clunk*; Devon hooked it on the top edge of the door. As he ditched his shirt, a woman in booty-shorts and a mesh top scurried up to them. She dropped to her knees.

"Line up," he snapped.

"Yes, Demon. Thank you, Demon." And then she crawled, *crawled* to the stage, and settled behind two people kneeling at the stairs.

"Um..." Hope looked between them and Devon, as he unbuckled the belt he used on her the night before. "When did..." He cinched it tight, and her mouth parted, relentless tingles cascading down her spine. "Are they waiting for..." When he caught her eye and yanked it free, her train of thought went with it.

Shit.

He rolled the belt and put it in the locker atop his discarded shirt; then fished out a second belt, draping it over his shoulders.

"Didn't notice them earlier? The first two have been there since we got here."

"I guess..." Hope studied their attention to posture, their lifted chins and downcast eyes. Three kneeling submissives who wanted her boyfriend to choose them. "I didn't realize there would be a line."

Devon leaned into the curve of her throat; her fingers went to the clasp of her collar.

"The one in front," he said, directing her attention to a fair redhead, "she goes by Firefly. Tiny, but I work up a sweat breaking her." His breath tickled her ear, heated fingertips brushed her spine. Hope shuddered. "Molly is the one we just saw, the one at the back." He rested his chin on her shoulder and sighed. "I have to throttle more for her, but she makes pretty sounds."

"What about the one in the middle?"

Devon chuckled at her breathless curiosity.

"Look close," he said.

Hope let her gaze wander over the stocky, blond guy wearing only red lace panties.

"I feel like I know him from somewhere," she mumbled.

"*Pim*," Devon corrected. "You feel like you know *Pim*."

She turned to look at him, her eyes wide. His smile was cautious.

"I think he would have been fine with me saying that I knew him and how; but I wasn't sure, and he was at work. I'm not trying to out anyone at their day job."

He studied her face, waiting to see how she would react to the revelation that the guy on his knees had sold them cellphones.

"He looks...sturdy," she managed.

Devon's lips parted, and his eyes focused past her, zeroing in on the man kneeling several feet away.

"Pim's a hardcore masochist. He loves pain like wires got crossed in his brain."

"Which is satisfying for you," Hope said.

His face flushed. "I'd like to think it's satisfying for everyone involved." He looked to the line again. "Molly will be fastest, least intense of the three. The other two might be something to build up to, but—"

"Choose Pim."

Relief and desire saturated him, and then, his shoulders fell. "I'm not sure that's a good idea."

"Pick him because I'm still pissed off that he let you pay for my phone."

"So, you think I should punish him for the phone fiasco?"

"As a personal favor, Sir."

"Demon, dearest?"

They both turned toward the woman striding toward them. She wore a neon pink button-down with a ruffled collar and a houndstooth pencil skirt. A silver whistle sat nestled in the surplus fabric on her chest, and her iron-grey hair twisted into a severe bun. In her hand, she held a short crop.

"Maeve."

Devon opened his arms, and the woman, two inches taller than him in her bright pink stilettos, kissed both of his cheeks.

"Darling," Devon said as he stepped away from her, "this is Maeve, the Mistress of Edge and my longtime friend."

"And Minnie's mommy," Hope said, dipping her head and offering a hand.

Maeve smiled, crinkling lines at the corners of her eyes. She clasped Hope's hand. "Some of Minnie's little friends do call me that. What can I call you, poppet?"

"We're giving Blush a try," Hope said.

Maeve bent at the waist, her lips hovering over Hope's knuckles. Her dark eyes cast up to her face, and her breath warmed the back of Hope's hand. "Mmm... *Blush*... How pretty. Demon's never brought a guest, and we don't have anyone using that name. It's a pleasure."

"The pleasure is mine," Hope managed.

Devon's chest brushed her back, and his whispered words tickled her ear. "And that is why we're calling you Blush."

Maeve straightened, her shrewd eyes cutting his direction. "I'm sorry I only saw you in passing last night."

Devon brushed it aside. "I had my hands full."

"Indeed. I'll be glad to have you back on stage. Your girl has a beautiful voice, but some of the newer patrons aren't used to more intense scenes; especially when they can't see the source."

Devon looped an arm around Hope's waist. His thumb caressed her bare stomach, and humor warmed his voice when he spoke.

"Someone complained?"

The Mistress's scarlet lips stretched into a feline smile. "Someone *expressed concern*. My poppet said you were in a state when she saw you. You drowned out the music, and you never use a private room. Something get into you?"

"Mostly this one," he said, nipping Hope's ear. "And a little Nosh."

"I see..." Maeve tapped the crop on her palm. "Anything I need to address?"

"I think it's handled, but I would appreciate it if you could hang around for a bit, keep Blush company while I'm busy. Maybe explain anything she isn't familiar with?"

"I'd be delighted." The Mistress inclined her head and offered an arm to Hope. "Right this way, poppet."

Devon pressed a kiss to her cheek. "Remember, darling."

Hope slipped her arm into Maeve's. "Red and yellow, Sir. I remember. Remember about the phone."

Devon's grin was wicked.

***

"Everyone has their own rituals." Maeve glanced down at her. "I'm sure you know that, of course."

Beside the stage, Devon, torso bare, a hand gripping each side of the belt draping his neck, sauntered past the line of kneelers. Hope's heart surged as he stopped at Firefly—the dainty thing with bright red hair. From her spot at the front lip of the stage, she could see faint, pink scars lining the woman's exposed skin. She wondered how they got there, when it didn't appear she could reach some of them.

As if he'd heard her, Devon's head pivoted on his spine. He winked at her, then moved to the stocky blond guy in red lace knickers—Travis, AKA *Pim*. The redhead wilted as Pim folded forward, pressing his face to the ground between Devon's feet.

Dropping into a crouch that nearly had him sitting on the back of the guy's head, Devon spoke softly. Two broad backs—one an expanse of warm, unmarred skin, the other bearing an image of a wolf—vibrated with words that Hope couldn't hear.

"Oh, it's Pim." Maeve's voice warmed. "He'll be delighted. He loves pain." She craned her neck. "They're negotiating. It won't take long. They do this all the time. Are you excited?"

Hope nodded, then swallowed. Devon pushed back to his feet, towering over the group on their knees in the same way he towered over her in his playroom. Except this wasn't his playroom. She could feel the rest of Edge at her back. The sound of footsteps, the swish of rope or jingle of restraints softened to near-nothing.

What could be heard shared a common theme. *Can't believe it. He's back. Demon...* Every eye on the main floor watched the stage. The weight of their collective gaze bored through her to get to what they wanted.

"They're starting," Maeve said, pointing with the crop.

Pim clamored up the steps on hands and knees; Devon prowled behind. With a booted foot, he shoved a short, padded bench to the middle of the stage. He addressed the crowd with the same enthusiasm he'd use behind his bar or from the top of it, as Pim crawled toward the bench behind him.

"Mistress Maeve has informed me that I may have upset some folks last night. Maybe you heard a little ruckus?" The crowd laughed, and dimples dotted his cheeks. "Consider this a warning for anyone with... *delicate sensibilities...*" His head pivoted, looking over them all. "If a little screaming is more than you can handle, I suggest you check out the more secluded sections of the club for a while."

He turned and—as Pim was about to climb onto the bench—grabbed an ankle and hauled him back. There wasn't a countdown or a signal that it was go-time. Devon simply snatched him. Hope covered her mouth as the other man's body hit the floor a few feet in front of her. Devon, no… *Demon* chuckled. Circling Pim's prone form and crouching at his head, he dug a hand into thick blond hair and lifted, arching Pim's back until they were eye to eye.

"Pim, Pim, Pim…" He sighed. "You've forgotten your manners."

"May I get on the bench, sir?" Pim said in a strained voice.

"Oh…" Regret colored Maeve's voice. "Pim…" Hope looked from her to Devon, as Devon canted his head.

"What did you call me?"

Pim's face paled. "Demon…"

Devon clicked his tongue, sending shivers down Hope's spine. "That's not what I heard. How many lashes for being a filthy liar?" He twisted the fist in the other man's hair, eliciting an agonized groan that sounded suspiciously like a moan. The water pooling in Pim's eyes glittered.

"Sir," he whimpered. Hope pulled in a ragged breath. Heat flushed her skin. "I called you *sir*."

"I don't…" She glanced to Maeve. "Is that a problem?"

Maeve toyed with the silver whistle at her throat. "Obviously. He's *Demon*." She laughed. "They all know better than to call him…" Her mouth opened in an *O*. "*Interesting…* You don't know that rule."

"What rule?"

Maeve shook her head and gestured to the stage. "Watch what happens next, poppet."

Hope did as instructed, looking to where her boyfriend sat on his knees a few feet in front of her.

"Am I your sir?" Devon asked, disgust coloring his words.

"No, Demon. You are Demon, and I am yours."

Pim wasn't allowed to call him sir? The rule that everyone seemed to know except her, was that you don't call Demon *sir*? Sweat dampened Hope's fisted hands. She looked around self-consciously.

"Pim means right now," Maeve said. "It's a scene thing, not a—"

"I get it," Hope managed. And she did, it was only that she'd never watched something so violently intimate from the outside, and Demon was just getting started—Pim wasn't even on the bench yet. Plus, she was learning *rules* that her boyfriend had never mentioned.

"I asked a question."

She tensed as surely as if Devon had been addressing her.

"How many times should I hit you for being a filthy liar, and how many more for being a useless fuck who makes me repeat myself? Do you think I have time to repeat myself to useless fucks, Pim?"

"No, Demon. *Ahh!*" Pim shouted as Devon, who looked chillingly detached from the whole thing, twisted harder. Hope swiped a hand across her forehead, pressed a palm to her chest wishing someone would turn down the thermostat or open a window; the warehouse was stifling.

"Answer the question, useless fuck."

"As many as you want and double for my mistakes, sir." Pim's eyes popped open as his repeated slip registered. "Demon!" he shrieked.

"I don't understand," Hope said to Maeve. "If he likes pain, why's he trying to comply?"

Maeve lifted a shoulder. "It would be over in a couple of minutes if he didn't; neither of them would get much out of it."

Hope let out a ragged breath as Devon stood, dragging Pim halfway to his knees before dropping him again. Pim made no effort to catch himself. "Useless..." Devon mumbled. "Get on the bench, before I kick you off the stage."

"Yes, Demon. Thank you, Demon."

Pim rushed to obey, while Devon paced behind him, periodically looking at Hope before glancing away. Every muscle in his body coiled with visible tension, begging for release. He wasn't the only one...

He pulled the belt from his shoulders, doubled it over, and trailed the loop along Pim's spine as he passed. Hope wet her lips, a mirroring sensation caressing her own back. Then, without warning, Devon squared up to the side of the bench and brought the makeshift strap down across Pim's shoulders with a *crack* that stole the breath from Hope's lungs.

The echo of leather hitting flesh silenced every other sound in the warehouse. In the momentary vacuum, Hope heard the soft gasp of Pim's pained inhale as he filled his lungs; and then, all of that air left his body in a primal wail.

Devon rolled his shoulders—tattoos undulating over flexing muscle. He smirked at her, then brought the belt down again and again. Hope couldn't tear her attention away as the blurred barrier that separated Devon and Demon faded to nothing.

Sweat dampened his hairline, now, his cheeks going pink. Pim oscillated between screaming, grunting, and a chilling silence. The whole thing disoriented Hope. The warehouse buzzed with electric energy generated by the men on stage, but another energy rattled through her bones, left her breathless.

Devon switched up his target, laying a stripe across the back of Pim's thighs. Pim announced his distress on a guttural sob that morphed into an unmistakable moan. He pushed up from the bench, his body fighting for escape even as he seemed wholly invested in the beating he was taking. Devon shoved him back down, smug satisfaction evident in every line of his body.

"Get off that bench again," he said, voice dripping a challenge that likely helped him earn his name. "I dare you."

Maeve laughed, delighted. "You did a number on him, didn't you?"

"What?"

Maeve arched a brow and pointed with her crop. At the same moment, Pim screamed from the stage, the timbre jarringly panicked. Hope whipped around to find Devon, a knee on the other man's back, laying into him with a vengeance.

"I told you to stay down," Devon growled.

"I'm sorry, Demon! I'm sorry! Please!"

Pim's eyes rolled back. He sagged on the bench. Devon's next lash landed without reaction, and Hope gripped the lip of the stage, wondering if the submissive had lost consciousness.

"Pim's in heaven now, hmm?" Maeve said, unbothered. "But Demon needs the feedback. He'll wait, see." She pointed with the crop as Devon shoved upright. He paced the length of the stage behind Pim, wrapping, then unwrapping the belt around his hand. He looked...annoyed.

"What's he—"

Hope flinched as he brought the belt down twice across the myriad of angry welts marring Pim's shoulders. Each impact landed with an ear-splitting *crack* that Hope half-expected to draw blood. Pim jolted back to life.

"Yellow! Yellow! Yellow!" He shouted in quick succession before realizing what he'd done. "No! Sorry Demon. I didn't mean it."

"Demon has the stomach to push him past his limits."

Hope startled, turning toward the voice to her right. She blinked down at a smaller-statured man in skintight jeans and an *Assume Nothing* tee. She had no idea who he was or where he'd come from, but the guy kept talking.

"Pim needs the approval as much as the pain. He doesn't want to safeword."

"Who are you?" she asked.

The guy, who couldn't be past his early twenties, grinned. "LB," he said, offering a hand which Hope shook. He tipped his head toward the stage. "Pim's mine."

"And you've been watching this..."

"I've been here since they lined up." He rubbed his palms together. "I mean, look at them."

"Oh..." Hope managed. "Will Dev... Demon stop if Pim doesn't safeword?"

LB shrugged. "Hasn't yet."

"It's a running thing with them," Maeve piped in from down the line. "Demon's good at gauging where to start, but he's after their breaking point. He makes it clear in negotiations. It turns people on, the idea that he's going to push them. Most tap out early because of it. They know he won't stop unless it gets unsafe, and even then, he's going to berate them for making him call it. There's nothing to aim for. You're never going to please him by outlasting him because he's never *done*. Pim thinks he'll make it to the end one day, but he won't."

"Filthy fucking liar," Devon ground out. "You aren't worth the twenty seconds it'll take to wipe your sweat off this belt." He slapped the leather against Pim's butt with no force at all. "Pathetic."

Pim's floodgates opened. Gut wrenching, gasping sobs tumbled out in answer. Tears streamed down his cheeks before he buried his face against the bench. Devon tapped him again, barely a swat. The man spasmed and cried harder. Everyone watching knew this was over the moment Devon decided to end it. No matter how much Pim wanted to stay on that bench, his body was done. Hope brought a hand to her mouth as Devon glanced her way. A flash of emotion crossed his face, too fast to interpret.

"It's all the endorphins," Maeve explained. "Demon's making fun of him with those little pops, and Pim is... Well, think of it like tenderizing meat." She laughed in a ladylike manner that shouldn't fit the moment. Hope found the sound unnervingly erotic, which was a whole other mindfuck. How was this situation so off-putting and enthralling simultaneously? "Pim's very soft right now," Maeve said.

LB snorted. "Oh, I guarantee he's not soft."

Maeve giggled again. "LB will end up cuddling him for hours in one of the rooms, while Pim uses his cock as a dummy."

LB groaned. "He gives the best head when he's this far gone."

"This is..." Hope trailed off as Devon walked to Pim's head and settled on his knees. "What's he doing now?" She glanced at LB and Maeve, but both were transfixed, tiny creases between their brows as they watched.

"If I didn't know better," LB said with a laugh, "I'd think Demon finally got the memo about Pim's subspace head. I don't think he fucks guys though—just the degradation and impact stuff. Unless he's branching out?" He looked to Hope.

"I...I don't think so."

His face fell. "That's what I thought. Oh... here we go..."

"Pim?" Devon said.

Pim rolled his head from side to side, still sobbing into the bench. He didn't look up.

"Eyes up, Pim."

The second order was steeped in an authority that made most of the dungeon inch up their chins. Pim complied, too, his lower lip trembling. This guy didn't want to safeword, but he was so done. Devon looked to Hope, checking that she was watching. His throat bobbed.

"Are you giving up now, when I only need two more things from you?" He said it almost sweetly, and Pim's eyes lit with a glimmer of renewed determination. He sniffed.

"I wasn't giving up, Demon."

Devon smiled, a mask for some other emotion he hid. "Shut up, filthy liar," he said playfully.

"Yes, Demon."

Devon grabbed Pim's hair, wrenching his head sideways. This left him facing the front of the stage, three feet from Hope. Her nails bit into the wood as Devon leaned forward and rested his cheek atop Pim's. Hazel eyes lit with fervor bored into her, as a second pair, the rich brown of melted chocolate, fixed on her as well. Hope stopped breathing.

"You see that pretty, impatient little thing by your Dom?" Devon said, pointing with the hand holding the belt.

"Yes, Demon."

"She's the reason you'll sleep on your stomach tonight. Thank her for your tears and snot, Pim. For the fact that *clothes* will hurt tomorrow. Thank her for every mark I left on you, and the weeks they'll take to fade."

Hope could feel her pulse in her clit, and it was really, *really* distracting.

"This is fucking hot," LB stage-whispered.

"Go on, now." Devon jostled Pim's head, staying cheek to cheek with the all-but-broken submissive. "Then we'll have one more task, and I'll let you up. I promise." A wicked smile flashed over his face, something Pim couldn't see.

"Yes, Demon." Pim cleared his throat. "Th... Thank you for my marks, and my pain, and umm... snot, miss."

"That's a good boy," Devon said soothingly, rolling back on his haunches. "Such a good boy." Pim shuddered with pleasure. To Hope's dismay, she shuddered too.

"I'm about to bust a nut in my pants right now," LB declared. "He never talks to him like this. Why is this so fucking hot?"

Hope's brow furrowed.

"Last thing," Devon said as he stood.

Pim squirmed in anticipation of a finish line he'd never crossed. You could *feel* his excitement; but something in Hope's gut pinged a warning on the phone salesman's behalf. Devon canted his head and smirked. When he spoke, the softness of the order didn't negate its power.

"Say *red,* Pim."

"But Demon—"

Hope jumped as Devon whipped the belt against the back of Pim's thighs. Alarm and confusion flooded the sub's face as his scream bounced off the walls. A giddy murmur went through the crowd, the entire place reacting to the show.

"Say *red,* Pim," Devon demanded, placing a fresh stripe below Pim's panties.

"Holy fuck this is the hottest thing I've ever seen," LB said, as if he hadn't already made that point. "This is better than porn."

"You *promised...*" Pim said between sobs.

It was the wrong response.

"Are you calling me a liar, filthy liar?"

"No Demon! I'm sorry, Demon!"

"I told you I needed two things, and then you could go. Can you not count to two, Pim?" Devon swung again.

"He was never going to let him up," Maeve murmured. "Not without breaking him."

"Say *red.*" Another vicious blow sliced through ragged cries.

"Say—"

"Red!" Pim squealed, bringing Devon up short on a backswing. "Red, Demon! Red!"

He drummed his hands and feet on the floor, breath hiccupping out of him. Devon closed his eyes and turned his face to the ceiling.

"See, Pim," he said, breathing hard. "It was easy."

Pim whimpered as Devon walked to the front lip of the stage. His knuckles whitened and the leather groaned in his grip before he dropped the belt to the wood. Hope stared at where it landed, inches in front of her on the chipped surface. She looked at his boots right beside, then followed the lines of his cargo pants and bare torso until she settled on his face.

The moment they locked eyes, he bowed.

DEVON

Bent at the waist, Devon kept his eyes on Hope. His head buzzed, and his body tingled. Sweat cooled on his skin, as Pim sniffled behind him. Satisfaction ran alongside the blood in his veins, and he couldn't remember the last time Demon had been so...quiet.

But the other details began to break through. The way Hope chewed her lower lip and crossed her arms over her breasts. The paleness of her face, paired with the pink patches on her cheeks. Maeve's expression told him he'd outdone himself, but Hope was...

Fuck me.

Devon straightened and stepped off the stage.

"LB?"

Though he addressed Pim's partner, he stared at Hope. *Hope.* His whole fucking world, and he'd risked her for...*this.* Bile rose in the back of his throat.

"I've got him, Demon." LB already had a foot on the stairs, on his way to retrieve his pet. "Go do what you need to do. So good to see you again, man."

Devon mumbled a response as he took Hope by the wrist and led her toward the private rooms. He detoured around some jackass in a mask, taking up way too much room, then swore. For reasons unknown, the same useless prick had the keycards.

"Red, yellow, that one."

He jabbed a finger toward the room they'd been in the night prior, as the incompetent DM spluttered apologies. The guy crammed a card into the slot, and the moment the door opened, Devon had her inside. He turned to Hope, took her face in his hands.

"Never again," he said. "Nothing in the world is worth losing you, Hope. Nothing."

"Devon..."

"I mean it. I'll get on my knees and say it, if you want. If this doesn't work for you—"

"*Sir...* I mean..." She shook her head. "Sorry. I don't know what I'm doing here."

Devon watched the color creep into her face, her namesake splashed across her cheeks, growing darker with every beat of his heart. The column of her throat bobbed beneath the collar he'd put on her. He took a step back.

"Hope, what's going on?"

She wandered away from him, trailing her fingers along the table he'd bent her over before pulling off his belt. He'd screwed up. Too much too fast, and now he didn't know how to fix any of it.

"You gave me a pass, and I didn't even know it."

Devon froze. "I don't..."

"People have been laughing at me since we got here," she said.

"No…"

"Yes, and after you got on stage, I figured out why."

She looked over at him, one hand fumbling with the rope around her neck. "If you don't like being called sir, why didn't you tell me?"

"Is that why you looked upset when I finished?

"It's part of it."

"What's the rest?"

"Do you have any idea what you look like up there?" Blue-green eyes glanced his direction. "The look on your face? The way you move?" Another tentative peek, but this time laced with yearning that settled in his groin like a roving hand.

"You promised to stop me if—"

"I didn't *want* to stop you. I wanted…" Her chest rose and fell, her lips parted.

Oh…

"You're blushing."

"So are you," she said softly, pressing her thighs together.

"What did you want, darling?"

Say it.

She wet her lips, tugged the hem of her skirt. "I wanted…"

Say it, pretty girl…

"I wanted *you*." She shook her head. "I wanted up there with you. I wanted you to *want me* up there." Something dark and hungry hummed through Devon's veins. "But that's ridiculous, of course. I couldn't handle another hard scene tonight."

"Yeah..." He reminded himself to breathe.

"See? Silly, right? I just wish people would stop laughing at me for being the only person who doesn't know Demon's rules."

"What if it didn't have to be that kind of scene?"

She grinned. "That was what you needed."

"And I got it because you gave it to me." He reached for her hand, and then the door handle. "Now, we're going to go get what you need."

"Wait, what are..." Hope trailed off as he led her into the hallway.

"Belt's on top of your locker," LB said as he and Pim passed, heading for a private room of their own.

"Thanks, man. Um..." He slowed, turned back. "Pim?"

Pim stared at him, glassy brown eyes still wet. "Yes, Demon?"

"You were great tonight. Thanks for the privilege."

"Really?"

"Yeah, Pim. Really."

Beside his partner, LB grinned and nodded his thanks.

Devon kept walking, tugging Hope to the stage stairs, and up. He released his hold on her and pulled a chair to the now-empty center—turning it away from the crowd. Intertwined with the music, voices rose and fell behind him as he sat. Devon had no doubt that everyone in attendance was confused by his current behavior, and that was the point. They all thought they knew him so well, when they didn't know him at all.

They'd catch on soon enough, though.

Hope stood in front of him, facing the crowd at his back. She fidgeted.

"Eyes on me, darling." When she tore her attention away from their growing audience and focused on him, he continued. "Trust me."

It wasn't a question, but she nodded anyway.

"Come here." He patted his knee and watched her throat bob as she walked toward him. "The other way round," he said, as she went to sit. Hope eyed him warily. "I won't let them see you," he said softly.

She straddled his lap, looking down into his face as her own reddened.

"What are we doing?" she whispered.

"Making a point." He slipped a hand between them and brushed his fingertips at the apex of her thighs. His digits came away slicked with her arousal, and his cock throbbed. "You weren't lying when you said you wanted up here with me."

"It's going to get on your pants," she said against his ear, already breathing faster.

"Good."

Reaching farther under her skirt, he probed a finger between her lips. It took no effort at all to slip inside her. Her pussy opened like the petals of a flower. A slick, wet flower.

"S..." She stopped, glanced behind him, then reconsidered. "Demon?"

The tentative nature of her sweet voice tightened his sack and heated his blood. She wanted to be good for him—to do it right. And Devon, Demon, *both of them* needed her and everyone else at Edge to understand that she was the only one who could.

"They can't see," he reminded her. "But I'll stop if this is too much; just say the word."

The murmur from behind them died away, Edge's clientèle enthralled with the sight on stage. Most of the crowd had watched Demon drag out safewords on dozens of occasions; the bravest screamed *Red* for him any time they got up the nerve to play.

None had ever seen him do anything like this.

"Look at them, darling. Are they watching?"

"Yes," she hissed.

"Maeve looks flushed, yeah?" Hope nodded, panting. "She's always polished, but the cheeks give her away. Turns into a cherry when Minnie's eating her in the Cuddle Puddle. Right now, she's thinking that your pussy's occupied, but your mouth is available, and she's sad that I don't seem willing to share."

Hope whimpered, hips rocking minutely.

"Impatient little thing," he chided, knowing she couldn't help it. "And Nosh," he said. "He looking?"

"Yes," she said.

A possessive satisfaction thrummed through him as he nipped her shoulder. "Good. Who else?"

"The women who laughed when I called you Sir upstairs. Mask Guy, Kitty Ears, Nipple Rings..."

Devon chuckled at her nicknames.

"Not laughing now, are they kitten?"

"No, Sir."

She ground her hips into his hand.

"They're busy wondering how this little blushing vixen turned a sadistic bastard into a pleasure Dom." He stroked his fingers along the front wall of her pussy as he spoke—thick, clear fluid pooling in his palm, as saliva pooled in his mouth. It took every scrap of his self-control to keep from unfastening his cargos and thrusting up into her bare. Fuck, it would feel so good.

"Who do you belong to?" he said, loud enough for the crowd.

"You, Sir," she whispered, just for him.

Devon grinned and kissed her throat, the rope collar sandwiched between his lips and her skin.

"They can't hear you, kitten, and I want them to hear you."

Hope rolled her lower lip between her teeth, then repeated loudly, "I'm yours, Sir. Every... *Oh*..."

The words died on her pretty tongue as Devon rubbed a thumb over her clit. Anonymous whispers threaded through the throng at his back. When she flopped against his chest, clinging to him, Devon pulled his hand free and scooped under her from behind. Whether she had forgotten that people were watching or no longer cared, she greedily rocked against his erection. Devon pushed the fingers of one hand into her needy cunt, hooking the middle finger of the other in her taut little ass for more control. His hands moved with her pelvis, the sensation of feeling her take her pleasure shorting out his brain. There was every possibility that he'd come in his cargos, and he didn't fucking care.

"Tell them, baby. Tell them again, in case they didn't believe you."

"Every inch of me," she managed, glassy eyes staring over his shoulder, grinding against him as she did, "is yours, Sir. Only yours."

"There's my girl," he growled. "Such a good fucking girl. Do you know why they're all staring at us, even though they can't see a thing beyond your face over my shoulder?"

"N...no, Sir." She kept rocking, rocking...

"Because they get it now," he managed. "They understand why no one got to call me *sir*, before you, and I'll still check anyone else who tries." Her hips bucked. "Come for me," he said. "Come for me in front of all these people, and I'll tell you what they've already realized."

He felt the roll of her belly against his own, the languid, serpentine undulation of her body as she tried to comply. His cargos were soaked, and her muscles fluttered against his hands with her threatening orgasm. The scent of her arousal perfumed the air and touching her was touching fire.

"So close," he told her. "You're so goddamn close, I can smell it."

"I need..." Her breath hitched in his ear. "I can't..."

But she was trying. Holy fuck, was she trying. With a quick shift, Devon pulled the finger out of her ass, replacing it with the thumb of the hand whose fingers were palm deep in her pussy.

"S... Sir!" She shouted at the added intrusion—an exclamation that the audience didn't miss, and Devon worried that their reaction would yank her away from the edge.

"Now, darling. *Now*."

Before she had time to register the increasing volume in the warehouse, Devon snatched her hair, yanked her head to the side, and sank his teeth into her shoulder, hoping that the pinch of pain would tip her over. He was right. Her ass and pussy grabbed at his fingers in frantic, pulsing waves, as she groaned *Yes, Sir*, for the entire dungeon.

Devon released her hair but left the hand buried in her holes. *His holes.* He stroked her back, loving the way her body twitched and rippled with aftershocks, as she snuggled into him. Pride and love and satisfaction hummed through his body like a drug. Someone killed the stage lights, plunging them into dimness that felt like privacy. The sounds of normal activity resumed bit by bit, but Devon stayed where he was, holding her as their breathing slowed.

"They realized," he said into the curve of her neck, "that you get to call me *sir* because you own me."

DEVON

Devon wasn't sure what was more surprising: the fact that he had awoken from a deeply satisfying dream in which he'd been showing Hope how to use a belt-sander, rather than some horrific nightmare about beating the shit out of her; or that the sound wrenching him from that slice of mundane goodness was an obnoxious chirping that he couldn't remember his phone ever making.

He scrambled for the offending device, tapping the screen until the racket died. Beside him, Hope lifted her head.

"Is that your alarm?"

"No, it's…" With bleary eyes, he squinted at the screen, then shoved himself upright. "Fuck."

"What's wrong?" She moved to follow him, before Devon eased her back down.

"There's an alarm tripping at Cleary's. I need to see what's going on." He pulled on the joggers and t-shirt he'd dropped beside the bed. "You go back to sleep."

"I can go with you."

She said this into the pillow. Devon smiled at the back of her head.

"No, baby. It's almost three in the morning, and you have to be up for work. You sleep. I'll make sure everything's okay, then come straight back. It'll be fast."

She rolled to her side. "You promise?"

"Promise."

She grabbed his hand, squeezing. "I love you. Be careful."

Devon smiled to himself, kissed her forehead. "I love you too, darling. I'll be home as soon as I can."

Leaving her in bed, he threw on his boots and a coat. Then, he was on the road. He would have hated leaving her on the best of nights, but after making her come, on stage, in front of an audience... It was a special kind of torture, which had him more worried about the woman in his bed than whatever had tripped the alarms at the bar.

At least, until he smelled smoke.

Red and white lights flashed against the faces of buildings, reflected off windows. Devon's heart beat a violent rhythm all the way to his toes. Parking behind a firetruck, he got out. A maybe five-foot person in a parka hustled toward him, with a firefighter on their heels.

"Dev!"

"Nix? Why are you here?"

She held up her phone, her face alternating between red, white, and that *lit-from-above* harshness that came from streetlights.

"You aren't the only one who gets alarm notifications, dude."

"Okay, but how did you beat me?"

"I was close," she said. "I'm also a manager and on all the accounts, and probably the executor of your will, so they already talked to me. This guy says he knows you." She gestured to the man towering over her, swathed in protective gear and reflective tape. Devon took a closer look.

"*Baker*?"

The firefighter nodded. "Fire's out. Confined to a small area."

Devon scrubbed his hands up his face and through his hair. "Thank you. That's...good."

Nix reached over, and to Devon's utter shock, she grabbed his hand. "They..." She took a deep breath. "They busted out one of the front windows."

"It gave us the fastest access," Baker explained.

Devon nodded. "Windows can be replaced easy enough."

"There will be a ton of cleanup with the smoke and water," the firefighter went on.

More nodding. "If we start right away," Devon said, "it shouldn't be too bad." Nix squeezed his hand, so he looked down at her, then back to Baker. "What aren't you saying?"

"Tell him," Nix said.

"Devon, I don't know how to say this, man, but someone set that fire."

Devon felt like his brain was sloshing in his skull, then realized he was shaking his head. "No, that can't be right. The building's old. It's got to be a short or something."

"You had the wiring redone when you bought it," Nix reminded him. "You said it had to be up to code for the loan and insurance stuff."

"Yeah, but people don't intentionally burn small businesses in freaking Asheville. That's insane." When Nix's expression didn't change, Devon looked to Baker, as if the guy who made this off the wall suggestion would be the person to retract it. "That's insane, right?"

Baker put a hand on his shoulder. "The investigator folks will talk to you about it, I'm sure. But since I know you, and you don't seem like the type to torch your pride and joy for insurance money, I thought you might want to hear it sooner."

"Someone started it *intentionally*," Devon repeated.

Baker nodded. "Looks like they *Molotov-cocktailed* the center of your bar." Devon struggled to hear anything over the buzzing in his ears. "My guess is they used something off your shelf. It wouldn't take out the whole place with crews so close; but they made one hell of a mess. You'll have to rip out the whole bar area."

"You really pissed someone off this time," Nix said.

Devon pulled his hand from hers and put it on his chest, where his heart pounded beneath his coat. Something felt *wrong*.

"Or it's random," Baker said. "Some kids making trouble… Hey, you okay, man?" He zeroed in on Devon again. "The damage isn't that bad. It could have been a lot worse."

But Devon was having a hard time giving a shit about the damage because Baker was right—it *could have* been so much worse. He shifted from foot to foot, widening his stance, clenching his fists over and over to ward off the unnamed discomfort thrumming through him.

Something feels wrong...

Nix looked at his hands, her brow pinching; so, Devon shoved them in his coat pockets to hide them from view. His right knuckles collided with something cold and hard, and he wrapped his fingers around the stone that Hope's boss had given him—the one that was supposed to be full of peace and protection or whatever... He squeezed until his nails stung his palm, but it didn't help.

Something feels wrong.

"Yeah, it does," he mumbled.

"What does what? You're being weird right now, Dev."

Something is wrong.

Devon stumbled back a step as his concern solidified into a battering ram of *knowing*. He looked from Nix to Baker.

"I think...something's wrong."

"Well, yeah." Nix gestured to the collection of emergency personnel and vehicles in front of Cleary's.

"Nix, the bar is yours." He turned and walked back toward his car.

"Dev, wait..."

"I'll be back as soon as I can. She's yours."

HOPE

Apollo made a gruff doggy noise; his tags jangled. Hope rolled to her back. She wasn't sure how long Devon had been gone, but the time on her phone read 3:32 am. She considered sending him a text to check-in, but Apollo's uncharacteristic restlessness took precedence. She put the phone back on the nightstand and turned to Apollo.

"Need to potty?" In answer, the dog walked to the doorway and growled softly into the hall. "Well, you don't have to be rude about it."

Hope scooted to the edge of the bed. With goosebumps dotting her skin, she pulled one of Devon's sweaters over her head and hobbled down the hallway behind Apollo. He sniffed around the living room, then over to the door that led to the garage, grumbling the whole time.

"You sure are in a mood," she told him, rubbing her arms against the chill. "He'll be home soon...I hope."

Hope opened the patio door a fraction. Apollo circled the dining table, then bolted into the darkness, that same unnerving growl rumbling deep in his barrel chest as Hope latched the door. She stared after the pup, careful to keep her gaze sweeping, lest a monster manifest in the backyard.

As she waited, she felt a *pull*. It wasn't in the darkness beyond the patio doors, but toward her periphery. She imagined a mass rising on the other side of the counter, looming in silence. Her pulse sped; her breath quickened. She turned toward the kitchen, taking in the hulking shadow, as her heart slammed in her chest.

Usually, they appeared as she kept staring or disappeared when she looked at something in her periphery head on. But this was different. Hope's imaginary monster looked...*solid*. Faint light from the kitchen window highlighted the soft folds of a black pullover, the hard lines of the mask from Edge.

"I'm fucking losing it."

The shadow chuckled, and her blood turned to ice at the familiarity of the sound.

"A...Aaron?"

"Babe."

"How..."

"Nice of Ash and Dr. Dickhead to drop off your car, but you should be more careful about where people leave your keys. It would be so easy for someone to pop the lock on your shitty apartment door...make copies...leave the originals where they found them... And they aren't only *your* keys, are they? Does your boyfriend know you're so careless?"

"You broke into my apartment." Hope tried to breathe as the pieces of a disturbing puzzle snapped into place. "You followed me at Edge."

He took a step forward, bringing him to the edge of the counter that sat between them. "You ruined my life. We are nowhere near even."

Hope tugged down her sweater, as if the fabric could keep her safe. Her brain rolled through possible routes. The door behind her went to the garage, but it was packed with stuff and didn't offer a fast escape. She wasn't even sure where the light switch was located or the button for the door...

"Devon will be home any minute," she said.

"I don't think so." Aaron laughed and took another step. Hope matched it with a step back. "I made sure we'd have time to play."

Terror churned in her gut. "Aaron, what did you do?"

"Don't worry. He's fine. I just wanted a little privacy. I'm not the filthy exhibitionist here."

He took another step toward her; Hope shifted toward the living room. The front door had two locks, and she wasn't certain she could open them quickly enough to get away from him. She needed a way to slow him down *and* a way out. Her phone would be helpful too. If she could grab it from the nightstand on the run, she could call for help.

"Do you like my mask, babe?"

"No."

"Mean..." He rubbed a gloved hand over his sternum—gloved because...*fingerprints*. "I thought you liked it. You kept looking at it when you were writhing for the crowd—or was that show all for me?"

"I didn't know that was you."

"Not sure I believe that, babe."

"Nothing I do is for you, Aaron."

"Nothing?" He cocked his head, canting the maliciously grinning mask. "I bet you'll run for me."

He lunged, but Hope bolted out of his reach. Her soles smacked the hardwood floors in time with his pounding steps. She heard Apollo whine from outside, as she pivoted into the hall. Hope raced for the bedroom, betting her life on two locks. If she could get through the bedroom and the bathroom doors in time to lock them behind her, they should buy her enough time to climb out a window and get to a neighbor's.

Back on the patio, Apollo had figured out that the thing triggering his instincts was inside the house—and he was losing it. Snarling and barking punctuated the repetitive impact of his big body against the glass. The dog who would never hurt a fly sounded ready to rip out a throat.

Hope dug harder, her legs already spent from two nights of debauchery. She could feel Aaron bearing down on her as she cleared the bedroom doorway, turned, and shoved with all her strength. A half-inch shy of closing, her forward progress halted as he slammed into the wood. Hope stumbled backward, tugging Devon's sweater lower, as Aaron flipped on the lights. He pushed back his hood, and a head of blond hair appeared above the mask.

"Nice." He looked around the room. "Good choice, babe."

"Aaron, don't do this."

The mask tilted to the side. "It really pisses me off when you say shit like that, you know. You act like I'm a monster, but you *love* a fucking monster, don't you, whore?"

In the background, Apollo whined desperately. His nails raked the glass; another thud of impact echoed when he hurled himself against it.

"Maybe that was the problem all along. You're too fucking sick to be treated as well as I treated you."

He moved as he spoke, corralling her away from the doors, away from the nightstand with her phone. Hope looked over her shoulder, searching for a weapon, a way out, anything... Aaron tipped up the mask and smiled at her. He pulled out a gun.

"Don't do that," he said. "If you start doing things that I don't like, I'll have to start doing things that you don't like. Don't make me do things that you won't like, babe."

Hope held up her hands.

"Wait..."

"Knees," he barked.

"Wh...what?"

He shoved the gun in the back of his waistband and stormed toward her. Hope scrambled back until she collided with a wall.

"Do what I fucking tell you, you stupid fucking whore!"

His fist connected with the wall an inch from her head, his forearm dominating the left side of her periphery. Hope froze, staring into eyes full of malice.

"That's what you want, right?" Bits of plaster sprinkled the floor, as he pulled his hand free. "Someone to *make you.*"

"He doesn't make me do anything."

"So, you're saying you *let him* defile you?"

"Aaron..."

"You let people *watch?* You walk around showing off the bruises that you *let him* leave on you; but you press charges if I so much as look your direction, is that what you're saying?"

"Aaron, it's not like—"

"You were supposed to be my perfect wife. Pretty and pleasant and well-fucking-behaved. And you ruined *everything*." He wrapped both hands around her throat and squeezed in a way Devon never had. His face contorted in disgust. "What good are you now? You're filthy. So, get on your fucking knees, and convince me that something so *filthy* should be allowed to breathe."

"P...please..." she managed. His face reddened and hold tightened further. Desperate tears tumbled down Hope's cheeks. She tried to scream, plead, say his name, but nothing came out. Air, blood... None of it moved like it should. Her nails gouged her own flesh in an effort to pry his hands free.

"Get on your fucking knees!" he shouted, oblivious to the fact that the only thing keeping her on her feet was his grip on her throat.

Hope clawed at his gloved hands, panic ricocheting through her body. She tried to knee him, but her leg weighed a ton.

Devon is going to find me dead on the bedroom floor.

She recoiled from the thought but couldn't change it.

He's going to find me dead.

Tears streamed down her face. Her lungs sucked against the brick wall in her throat.

On the bedroom floor.

Her vision darkened, and her body tingled. Instead of clawing at Aaron's hands, she found herself limply grasping his wrists.

On our bedroom floor...

A faraway shattering sound echoed through the house—one that Hope was too far gone to identify. As the world shrank to nothing, air rushed back into her lungs and blood flooded her brain. She landed hard on her knees, staring at the back of Aaron's legs.

Her thoughts were sludge, and her skull felt like it might splinter apart as she tried to make sense of the freight-train tearing through the hallway, bouncing off walls and scraping against the floor. Her oxygen-deprived brain struggled to process what it meant until Aaron dipped his hand into the waistband at his lower-back, pulled out the handgun, and pointed it toward the bedroom door, aiming low.

Hope pushed unsteadily to her feet.

"Stupid mutt. Dead mutt," Aaron muttered, as Hope silently reached for the only weapon at hand.

The boxy head that breached the threshold looked nothing like the pup that cuddled a one-eared teddy bear to sleep each night. Hellhounds would back down from the snarling mass of silver muscle, peppered in broken glass and streaked with blood. He looked every bit the dog of a demon. Teeth bared. Ragged ears back. A ridge of fur stood on end from his head to his tail.

Such a good boy...

Hope aimed and swung, whipping the belt buckle across Aaron's temple with a satisfying *CRACK!* His startled scream rivaled the gunshot, and when a bullet hole appeared in the wall opposite her, Hope knew he'd missed his mark.

Aaron turned to her, blood welling from a gash by his right eye. "You stupid—"

Apollo latched onto the back of his calf, tearing viciously. Another round fired into the floor.

"No!" Hope screamed.

Aaron stomped free of Apollo, then kicked him hard beneath the chin. To Hope's horror, the pup went down like a seventy-pound sack of potatoes. The breath that she had fought for so desperately moments earlier, went right out of her.

"You hit me in the face with a fucking belt," Aaron snarled, storming toward her.

Hope tried to skirt past him, but he caught her sweater and yanked her back against his body. His arm came up around her throat catching her in a chokehold that she had no hope of escaping.

"I warned you," Aaron snarled. "Start doing shit I don't like, and I'll start doing shit you don't like." He was digging for something in his pockets, keeping one arm locked around her throat. "I know how to take the fight out of a stupid whore."

"Let me go!" She stomped the top of his boot with her heel—cried at the pain, while he laughed at the futility.

"Keep trying, babe. It's fun."

She twisted and squirmed, unwilling to give up. Then, all she could see was *Devon* running toward her down the hallway—eyes wide and terrified.

"He has a gun! Get down!" She screamed, but he kept coming.

"Shame," Aaron said against her ear. "Just when we were getting to the best part."

He leveled the gun with his free hand. Hope thrashed, trying to push the muzzle off course, worried she might make it worse. Gunshots. One... Two... They might as well have been aimed at her chest for the way her heart constricted with each resounding *BANG*; but Devon didn't so much as flinch.

"Fuck," Aaron grunted.

A look of anguish crossed Devon's face as hot metal brushed Hope's temple. He flung his arm forward as if reaching for her from too far away. It was heartbreaking...the utter desperation on his face...the knowledge that it wouldn't change a thing.

Then, Aaron jerked. Hope didn't know what startled him, only that it gave her the opening she needed to tuck her chin and bite the shit out of him. He ripped his arm away from her, and she tumbled to the floor, as Devon barreled through the doorway. He grabbed Aaron's wrist, pushed the gun to the side, and slammed a fist into Aaron's face so hard that the sound of the impact turned Hope's stomach.

Another gunshot sounded—splintering wood from the closet doorframe, as her ex's head snapped back, and blood spurted from—*everywhere*. His eyes rolled, and his body crumpled. The mask that had been atop his head clattered free as Devon rolled him to his stomach and straddled his prone form. Hope felt like she was watching a movie, like she wasn't even in the room, as Devon slid the handgun across the floor toward her and began digging through Aaron's pockets.

"There's no safety. If he twitches, point and shoot until you're out of bullets."

Hope looked at the gun, back to Devon.

"Of course, you fucking do..." he snarled, yanking a bundle of metal from her ex's back pocket.

Handcuffs...

"He... Why would he bring those?"

Even as she asked the question, Hope knew the answer. Devon glanced her way, and the expression on his face made it hard to breathe. Refocusing on Aaron's limp body, he yanked an arm behind his back until something popped.

"You never deserved her, asshole, and you will never touch her again."

Hope sucked in air in quick gasps, as Devon latched cuffs around wrists and ankles, then bowed her ex until he was hog-tied. Leaving Aaron face-down on the floor, he stumbled toward Hope, dropping to his knees in front of her.

"Are you okay?" He skimmed cautious fingertips down her sleeves, up her bare thighs. "Did he..."

Hope's chest tightened; tears burned her eyes. "You came back." She lunged at him, wrapping herself around him. Devon stroked a hand over her spine.

"I'll always come get you, baby. You know that." He leaned into her more heavily. "Shit…" he murmured.

"What is it?" She couldn't catch her breath, so the words came out choppy. "What's wrong?"

"It's okay. It's going to be okay, but I need you to listen." Devon kept running his hand up and down her back. So calm. As if they weren't sitting on the floor amid glass and blood and bullet holes, with Aaron unconscious and handcuffed on one side, and Apollo—

"Apollo!" Hope jolted as she remembered. "He smashed through the patio door when Aaron choked me. It's the only reason he let me go."

"Fuck…" Staying close, Devon pushed her hair out of the way to get a better look. "You're bruising. We need to get you checked out fast."

"I'm alright."

"Until you have a swollen airway…"

"Aaron kicked him in the head when he bit him. I think he's unconscious."

"*Apollo* bit him?" He blew out a breath. "Surprised Aaron didn't shoot him."

"Well, I hit him with your belt, so he missed."

Devon chuckled weakly. "That's way hotter than it should be. Is he breathing?"

She looked over at the steady rise and fall of the massive silver chest.

"Yes," she snubbed, "but he's bleeding from the glass."

"Good girl. We'll get him fixed up."

Devon's hand slid down her back and rested on the floor behind her butt. Warmth soaked one sleeve of her sweater; worry seeped in with it. The room smelled tangy and metallic. His face was white as a sheet.

"Devon..."

"It's okay," he repeated.

He rolled onto the floor next to her, the action shifting one side of his coat to reveal a crimson stain. Hope looked down at herself, found a matching shade saturating her uncomfortably warm sleeve. She brought a hand to her mouth.

"Holy shit. He...he *shot* you."

His lids drooped before he forced them back open. "I punched him harder." He smirked at her. "I know you're shaken up," he said, groaning as he pulled out his wallet, "but I'm getting a little dizzy here. I need you to listen." He pushed a Visa smeared with blood into her hand. "Call Nix. You'll have to use your phone; mine is in the living room, on the line with 911. Tell her there's a magnet on the side of the fridge with the afterhours contact number for Apollo's vet. Cost isn't a concern, just get him healthy. Tell her the bar can wait."

Tears flooded down Hope's cheeks. "Why can't you tell her?" she demanded.

Devon closed his eyes and sighed. "Because I'm pretty sure I'm about to pass out. Believe me, I know how inconvenient that is."

"No passing out. Eyes open." She pressed her hands to what she hoped was the source of his bleeding. Nothing was spurting, but blood oozed at a steady clip.

"I appreciate the effort, love," Devon mumbled, "but I don't think you have enough hands. Bastard caught my hip, too."

"Wh...what?" Her attention shifted down his body, colliding with a second patch of blood soaking up from his right hip, across his lower belly, down one side of his joggers... "Oh my God..." Her pressure on his shoulder faltered, and she felt a warm gush between her fingers. "I don't know..."

"Just pick one and stick with it, I guess."

A visual search of their immediate vicinity gave her nothing useful. She looked from the spreading patch lower on his torso to her bloodied hands on his shoulder. Not enough hands. Not enough...

"Wait... I have an idea." Hope swung a leg over. Devon's eyes fluttered open, staring up at her as she squeezed her thighs.

"I don't think I'm dying, but if I were, *this*—with you wearing nothing but my sweater and my collar, straddling me in our bedroom—would be a good way to go. Just gotta ignore the rest of this mess..."

"Devon, please don't pass out. I'm freaking out right now."

"Doing my best, darling. Doing my best."

DEVON

The air smelled of antiseptic, and the lights were too damn bright—filtering through Devon's lids, turning everything a bloody red that pulsed in time with an obnoxious beeping from far away.

Hospital.

The realization slammed into him, speeding his heart and constricting his muscles.

"Hope..."

Hands pressed into his chest as he shoved up.

"It's okay. Lay back. You're alright."

Some of the panic leached out of him at the sound of her scratchy voice. Devon opened his eyes and found her leaning over him in bubblegum pink scrubs, an off-white blanket wrapped around her shoulders. Colors that shouldn't be there dappled her skin from collarbones to jaw, including a perfect ring just off-center—the clasp. Aaron's grip had pressed the clasp of her col...*choker*...into her throat.

For a moment, he was breathless...and then he remembered that someone needed to look her over. He looked around the room—a generic ER room housing little more than his stretcher, a chair, a cabinet with a sink. Not a medical professional in sight.

"Your throat..." he rasped, before clearing his own.

"It's fine."

"They need to check." He patted his hands around, disrupting an IV line and sending a box of tissues into the floor. "There should be a call button or..."

Hope's brow pinched. "They did some kind of soft tissue pictures. It looks bad, doesn't feel great, but the doctor says it's superficial." She brushed her fingers through his hair. "You don't remember?"

"I..."

Devon shook his head, trying to grab onto something beyond his mental reach. How could he forget something so important? He remembered her on her knees in the bedroom floor. Skimming his hands over the bruises on her throat, her naked thighs. *Christ...*

He opened his mouth to ask a question that he wasn't sure he could stomach the answer to. "You're wearing scrubs," came out instead.

"You bled all over me, then insisted they put me in the first ambulance. I didn't have time to change."

"Second," he corrected. Because instead of leaving Aaron choking on his own blood, like he deserved, the paramedics had taken him first. A cop tagged along.

"I see you remember some things." Her mouth lifted at the corners, then fell. "The question you're afraid to ask..." she said.

Devon dove into that gorgeous blue-green that made him feel like tranquility might exist in some alternate universe. "Yeah?" he managed.

Hope took his hand, looked down at their interlaced fingers. "He didn't."

"He *didn't*," he echoed, his breathing uneven.

"I'm banged up and bruised, a few cuts from the glass, but that's all."

Devon nodded as he processed. "Okay... Um... Apollo?"

"The vet said he has a concussion and a few of the lacerations needed stitches, but he's okay. They're keeping him until tomorrow to be safe."

He blew out a relieved breath and searched his faulty memory.

"I didn't faint."

Hope winced. "No, you stayed conscious all the way to the ER. Too mad to pass out, they said."

Someone knocked, then the door opened. Chloe appeared in the doorway; one shoulder propped against the jamb.

"Oh good. I see our patient is awake again."

"*You.*"

She grinned. "Yes, Mr. Cleary?"

"You fucking drugged me."

Chloe stepped inside and closed the door. "This is my house, Dev, and you wouldn't behave."

She crossed the room in a few strides, and he found himself sandwiched between Chloe in her electric blue scrubs and Hope in that sugary pink—which he now realized she had likely borrowed from her friend.

"He asked about my throat and Apollo," Hope said.

"Well, yeah." Devon shrugged, winced, reminded himself to move more carefully. "Someone tried to murder both of you, and I'd kind of like an update."

"It's the Versed. *Bandage check...*" Chloe announced and pulled down his hospital gown. She glanced at the gauze on his shoulder and hummed her approval before re-situating the gown. "He doesn't remember the last time he was awake."

"The last time? What do you mean *the last time*? How many times did you drug me?"

"Just the once," Chloe said.

"It wore off pretty fast," Hope added. "You were pissed again, but then you fell asleep."

"I fell asleep? Just...*fell asleep?* When you look like you do, and we're in a hospital and..."

"And that's normal?" Hope asked to her friend. "He forgot that whole conversation."

Chloe nodded. "Wild, isn't it? People always swear they'll remember, but they never do."

"Will he remember this?"

"Of course, I will. Wait... I will, right?" Devon looked between the two of them, but they seemed more focused on his body than anything he was saying.

"Oh yeah. The meds are long gone. I already made up a goody bag of dressings and some heavy-duty antibiotic ointment for his hand. I can always take a look if anything seems infected. We'll print some care instructions, but the doctor wants to make sure he's hydrated before you go. If he'd lost any more blood, she'd have to keep him overnight, but as it is, you should be out of here in a couple of hours."

"I can't believe he doesn't need stitches," Hope said.

Chloe raised her brows and nodded. "With this kind of injury, stitching things up is an invitation for infection. *And the hip…*" She yanked the blanket down and his gown up.

"*Whoa!*" Realizing his boxers were MIA, Devon cupped himself with a bandaged hand.

Chloe tilted her head. "Well, that's where our positive Throckmorton came from…"

"Throck-what?" Hope leaned further over him.

Devon's face heated, as Chloe gestured to his pelvic region.

"It's a radiology thing. They did films to verify the bullet didn't clip bone. Showed his dick pointing to the side of injury. Basically, his penis is all *Ouch. Help. Boo-boo here.*"

"Can you stop talking about my penis? I didn't get shot in the dick, so no one needs to look at it."

Hope patted his shoulder. "She saw it all when you were out."

Devon glared at Chloe. "The first time or the second?"

She covered him back up. "The time I drugged you, and we cut your clothes off. Round two was all you—a six-hour power nap that your body desperately needed. If you can sleep that soundly in an ER, you should get more rest. As for your dick… Sorry. Bodies are like...the sun while I'm here. I see them every day. No big deal, even when you're packing a—"

"*Chloe*," he snapped.

She grinned. "Your bandages look good. Nothing's bleeding. Aaron managed to shoot you, *twice*, and you did more damage with a fist, so congratulations."

"And they brought him *here*," Devon snarled, pushing himself upright as he remembered. "She was coming *here*, and they brought him anyway."

"Stop flailing before you start bleeding again." Chloe shot a look over her shoulder, toward the door.

Hope's hands fanned against his chest—birdlike brushes as if she knew he was about to detonate. "It's okay..."

"It's not!"

When he refused to lay down, Chloe rolled her eyes and inclined the head of the stretcher to meet his back.

"How can you all not see that?" He looked to Chloe, to Hope. "They brought you and dropped you off with him."

"That's not how it happened, and you know it," Chloe said.

"I don't care! He tried to fucking kill you, Hope! Then they chauffeured you to the same damn hospital!"

"You should keep your voice down, before another two milligrams of Versed finds its way into your arm," Chloe warned.

She reached for the IV line, and Devon grabbed her wrist, hissing when a searing pain shot through his shoulder, hip, and hand.

"Wait...I have to be awake, Chloe, please. That's like...bare minimum. I have to be awake."

"Dev…" Her brown eyes softened. "Look, at my hands. They're empty, see? I'm not giving you anything; I'm just checking, so I can chart that I did. But I *do* need you to calm down."

"I just…" He glanced at Hope, then back to Chloe. "I need to stay awake."

"I hear you," Chloe said. "I need you to hear me too, okay?"

Devon nodded, and Chloe smiled.

"As soon as we get another bag of fluids in you, you get to go home with Hope. Aaron will stay here, cuffed to a bed, recovering from the surgery to put his facial bones back where they belong. The one that I can't tell you about because that would be a HIPAA violation…understand?"

"He's…"

"Not even conscious. More sedated than you were when I drugged you." She winked at him. "You hit him really hard, Dev."

Hope kissed him on the forehead. "He knows how to throw a punch."

"Sounds like Marden had it coming."

Devon looked toward the new voice and saw Detective Imani Neely peeking through a crack in the door.

"Detective Neely," Hope said. "Did you need something else?"

"I'd take Devon's statement, if he's up for it, but I was mostly checking on you for Mom. If you'd prefer, I can come by in the next day or so for the official business."

Devon sighed. "If it's all the same to you, I'd like to get it over with. I've got a home and business to clean up when I get out of here."

"Alright." Neely pulled out a clipboard. "Tell me your version."

He rattled off details, as Hope held his hand and Chloe flitted in and out of the room. When he was finished, Neely handed him a pen so he could sign the statement. As he passed it back, she shook her head.

"The whole thing is unbelievable. Breaking into Hope's apartment and copying her keys... Disguising himself with a mask to stalk her through that club... Starting a fire at a secondary location to get you out of the house, then attacking Hope. It sounds made up."

"I was there for it, and I feel the same," Hope agreed.

The detective shook her head. "I guess it just goes to show that people lose it sometimes. He's a cop; he knew there was no getting away with this or coming back from it."

"I think he cared more about making sure I was punished than getting away with anything."

Devon reached for Hope's hand, pressed a kiss to her knuckles.

"There is one part of your story that I don't get, Devon," Neely said.

"What's that?" He wracked his brain for details he'd left out but came up empty.

"You went back home."

Devon shrugged, and his shoulder sang. "You ever get...I don't know...a *vibe*, detective? Like an inner voice that tells you something is off?"

Neely nodded and smiled. "I'm a cop, so..."

"Something felt wrong, so I went home."

"While a fire crew was at your business?"

He rolled his lower lip between his teeth and nodded, a smile tugging at the corners of his mouth. "Priorities, detective."

Neely shook her head and held up the clipboard. "I'll get this into the file. We'll be in touch with any new questions or information on hearings and such, and you know how to reach me if you need anything."

"Yes, ma'am."

"Oh, I almost forgot." Neely patted her pockets. "We found this in the floor while collecting the shell casings and all." She dropped the piece of quartz into his hand. "Figured it got knocked off a table in the altercation, and I didn't want it to go missing. I know Ms. Margo's rocks are special."

"I appreciate it," Devon managed, staring at the stone, failing to keep his voice and breathing steady.

He lost track of the rest of the conversation, attention glued to the lines of black lancing through milky-white. It wasn't until Hope lowered the rail on her side of the stretcher that he realized they were alone.

"Are you okay?" she asked. "You seem shaken up."

"I threw it." He rolled the stone over in his palm, closed his hand around it. "When he..." Devon swallowed, shook his head. "He was shooting at me, and that was fine."

"Devon, don't—"

"It's true. Even if I got hit, even if it was the last thing I did, I *knew* I could make it through that door. I only had to hit him once." He grinned at her, until it faltered. "But then, he put the gun to your head. I wasn't going to make it. I was too far away, and I had *nothing*. He had a gun, and I had a goddamn rock. I threw it, because it was all I had." He rolled the stone again. "I guess Margo's right. It's protective as fuck if you throw it hard enough."

She surged toward him like a dam breaking, collapsing onto his chest. With the adrenaline from the attack all but spent, it hurt like hell—the good kind of hurt. A reminder that he was alive, and she was squished against him, warm and breathing. He wrapped his arms around her and squeezed her tight, determined to hold on until she let go. Her chest shuddered against his, and tears wet the side of his jaw and neck as she crumbled.

"It's okay, baby," he said into her hair. "We're okay, right? We're okay."

HOPE

They stood on the sidewalk in front of Cleary's. Because nothing ever moves as quickly as you want in a hospital, it was already nearly 4 p.m. Hope had on Chloe's pink scrubs and a jacket from *lost and found*, and Devon—coat-less—wore a green set of scrubs from some sort of surgical attire vending machine. She didn't know how it worked, only that Chloe needed to return them for credit ASAP. It was kind of hot, the way his tattoos crawled up and under the sleeves. Unfortunately, she needed about a week of sleep before she'd have the energy to play doctor.

Thanks to the efforts of her brother, her car made it to the hospital before Devon's discharge. With the vet keeping Apollo overnight for observation, the next pressing concern was the state of the bar. Devon hadn't seen the damage himself, and he wouldn't be able to rest at home until he did. Granted, Hope wasn't sure he'd rest after either. She squeezed his hand, watching his gears turn in profile.

"Someone boarded it up," he said.

Plywood covered one of the massive windows at the front of the bar. A sign taped on the door read *Closed for repairs*. She suspected that part was Nix's doing, but she had no idea how she had managed to haul plywood in her tiny car; someone helped.

"Baker said the bar is a lost cause." It was the third variation of that statement that Devon had made since they left the ER. "I bet the floors are ruined. It's been what?" He glanced skyward and bobbed his head, calculating. "Twelve hours or more in water? More before I can make a dent in it..." He groaned. "They were original to the building."

Hope knew how much that stung for him, the pride he had taken in the beautiful details.

"We can get help. It's not like you have to do it all alone."

He glanced at her side-long and she knew all the things he wasn't saying. *His bar. His mess. His responsibility...*

"Best see what we're working with." He took a fortifying breath, walked up to the door, and slid the key home. Sunlight glinted off the gold lettering as he pulled.

"Boss man!" came a boisterous shout as they crossed the threshold.

Devon stopped cold, with Hope right beside him.

"*Lucas?*"

"I called him because he was the only one with a full set of keys," Nix said. She sat on her knees in one of the booths, leaning over a board with a paintbrush in her hand. Soot streaked her face, her clothes. "Not that it mattered at the time with the massive hole in the front." She glanced up. "You all look terrible."

Devon stared at her, as Hope swept her gaze across the room. Two massive dehumidifiers hummed, and the air smelled faintly of smoke and liquor. She had expected a disaster, but the space was...clean.

Hope tugged his hand. "Devon, look."

It wasn't one of his controlled assessments. This time, his attention jumped from one area to the next, without rhyme or reason. He let her go and stumbled forward, turning in a circle. There was damage, sure, but the brass gleamed. The floors, while in need of a good mopping, were bone-dry.

"How..." He turned to Nix. "You were at the vet for hours..."

"Ask Lucas," Nix said. "I came back after they said they wanted to keep Apollo. Got here about three hours ago."

Devon turned to the young bartender.

"Well," Lucas said, "I know you don't like the floors wet. When I saw how bad it was, I called Mark. I didn't know what to do about the fire part, but I know how to clean up water—just not when there's this much." He looked around, shrugged. "I couldn't do it fast enough alone."

"Kid called Mark; Mark called me." Alex said, carrying a fresh box of towels out of the stockroom.

Devon blinked at him in stunned silence.

"We rented the dehumidifiers and hauled them over," Alex went on. "Spent a few hours getting the place dry. You probably think it fucking stinks in here, but you're wrong. I will never get that stank out of my sinuses," he grumbled.

"You all... The floors... The..." Devon spun slowly, taking in the space again.

"Many hands make light work."

Hope's head snapped toward the familiar voice coming from the hallway. Dre flashed a smile. "Oh, let me grab that." He stepped past them and propped open the door.

"Dre," Devon said, shuffling himself and Hope out of the way of traffic. "You're supposed to be at Redact and Recover."

Dre laughed. "My first couple of appointments had something come up," he said.

"But, how did you even know? Did you...?"

Hope shook her head when he looked to her. It hadn't crossed her mind to call Margo until she was already forty-minutes late for her own shift, and the singular text she'd sent to Monique only said that she was sorry, but she wouldn't be in for a few days.

"That's on me. I was his 9 a.m." A guy Hope recognized, but couldn't place, walked through the door, carrying the front-end of a length of wood.

"*Baker*?" Devon said.

One of the Locker Room guys... No wonder he looked familiar.

"Place was a mess, and you took off like you left the oven on." He winced. "Fuck, that's like the firefighter version of a dad joke, huh? Anyway, when you called...Nix was it? Sorry. I suck at names." Nix waved a hand in acknowledgment. "I realized you might need help covering bases."

"We're in a rec softball league, so covering bases is kind of our thing," the guy on the other end of the load said as he cleared the door. Hope knew this one—a J-name. She had nodded when Devon introduced them at R&R, because her hands were full of lunch. She looked over to see color flushing Devon's face.

"Josh," he said, inclining his head.

Mark wandered in behind them and swore under his breath. "Look, I did the driving, and I loaded that thing myself. They met me out back to carry it in. Don't go thinking I'm the only one not helping."

Hope laughed, a shaky, watery laugh.

"When Baker called, I got in touch with Josh and a couple of the other guys," Dre explained. "Made pretty good time, I think." He lifted his chin. "Syd and Monique were here this morning, too. They wiped down all the fixtures."

"And JJ and Ashley," Nix chimed. "Glass removal, then they helped with the furniture, the walls. Every surface in here was covered in soot and water. Greg and Ashley are coming back when Greg finishes at work."

"I had no idea all of you were here. No one mentioned it," Hope said.

Nix put down her paintbrush and scooted her project forward and inch. "We all figured you two had enough to worry over, and I don't know if you've noticed, but Devon doesn't accept help easily." She parked her tongue ring in the corner of her mouth and flashed him a wry smile. "So, what do you think, boss?"

Hope stared at the tabletop—read the same words that had hung over Devon's head since the day she'd met him. Her chest burned.

"Nix..." Devon's eyes shimmered, and his throat bobbed.

"You better like it because we aren't trashing it. This is Cleary's. We need the reminder that no one likes you when you're Irish."

Devon sucked in a breath. "I know it's a little singed," Nix went on. "You get all up in your head about things being perfect, but I think the scorched-look gives it character."

"It is perfect. All of this is..." He cleared his throat, struggling to speak. "Um... Thank you, everyone."

"Don't thank us yet," Alex said, dumping ice water on the warm and fuzzy mood. "Your bar is fucked."

Devon walked to the bar, the only part of the building that they hadn't yet touched. He circled around behind and took his place, pressing his fingertips into the charred surface.

"That wood you brought in..." he said, not looking up.

"Cut to fit from a guy Mark knows," Alex replied. "We got lumber for underneath too. A couple of coats to seal it, and we can open. Just didn't want to pull out the original without your permission."

"Truck's in the back lot," Mark said. "I can scrap this one if you want to rip it out now."

Devon shook his head. "No."

Hope's brow pinched. "Devon..."

"I'm not scrapping it."

She reached for his hand across the bar. Black smudged her sleeve, the edge of her palm. "Devon, this is burned clear through in the center. Two-thirds of it is *coal*."

Hazel eyes drifted up from the bar top, locking with hers. "With everyone here, I can get it off in one piece."

"And do what with it?"

Devon shrugged. "One step at a time. I'll figure it out later. I just need a little...help...to get it home."

A body appeared beside her. Hope looked over to find Alex with his arms crossed, frowning at the bar.

"Gonna be fragile," he said.

Nix popped up on Hope's other side. "Could you strap it to the new piece to haul it? Like a splint?"

Mark bumped her with a hip. "You might be onto something, cupcake."

"You'll need some rope," Lucas said.

"*I've got...*" Nix, Mark, and Alex trailed off simultaneously. Hope bit back a laugh.

Devon chuckled. "Best use Mark's, since he'll be the one hauling it."

"You all are so adult," Lucas said. "Here I am, biking to work, and you all have vehicles and tools and rope for tying down whatever you're hauling."

"Bless your heart," Nix mumbled.

Devon grinned at the baby-bartender.

Alex headed for the door. "Let's get this bitch strapped down and transported. I need to head out."

Mark caught up to him, clapping him on the shoulder. "You got a hot date?"

"More like a headache," Alex shot back.

DEVON

It took years—fucking eons—but the bar was in one very damaged piece, propped on sawhorses in his garage. With Mark and Alex doing the heavy lifting, a piece of plywood had been tacked over the missing patio door, hiding the view of police tape. It was more help than Devon liked to accept, but he couldn't let Hope die of hypothermia one night after Aaron tried to choke her to death, and you couldn't heat the place with a gaping hole in the back.

He wanted the house to stop feeling alien. To take off his shoes, take a hot shower, fall into bed with Hope and sleep for days... Instead, he stopped beside her in his living room. He followed her line of sight to the hallway, the light sparking off rogue shards of glass.

She shivered.

"It'll warm up soon," he promised. "Just needs time to regulate now that things are closed up."

"I wish Apollo was here." She glanced Devon's direction, then away. "Doesn't feel like home without him."

Devon swallowed the lump in his throat, unsure if this building could ever feel like home again. "Would you rather stay at your apartment? We could—"

"No. We're both exhausted. We're here." She glanced toward the dining room, back to the hall. "I just...need a minute."

"Do you want to talk about it?"

The column of her throat—slender and covered in bruises he would see in his nightmares for decades—bobbed. She exhaled a shuddering breath.

"Apollo knew something was wrong. He's never like that—growling and pacing." She sniffed. "I thought he was upset because you left. I let him out back." Her eyes locked on the sheet of plywood, then drifted to the shadows of the kitchen. "He... he must have been crouching behind the counter."

A chill crawled up Devon's spine, and his heart squished in his chest. He'd come so close to losing her. Another Kelly, but infinitely worse. Something...unsurvivable.

Her hand brushed her throat, and her brow creased. She grabbed the bottom edge of her adopted jacket and pinched the fabric. "He asked if I liked the mask because I looked at him."

"Christ... I'm sorry." The words felt so empty, but he kept saying them. "About Edge, about taking you on stage. I didn't think. I should have—"

"What?" Blue green eyes cast his direction, sparking with humor. "Magically known that my ex was wearing a mask and standing in the audience? Even you aren't that good." Her nose scrunched. "We smell like blood and hospital and smoke. You think we could go clean up and sleep a while? I'm so tired."

"Come on." Devon held out a hand, ignoring the crunching underfoot as he led her to the master bathroom. Flipping on the light, he peered inside. "Leave your shoes out here, so we don't track glass in."

Hope slipped them off and stepped over the threshold, and though Devon wanted nothing more than to follow her, he thought better of it.

"I'll get clothes, while you shower."

"You need to wash off too."

He sighed. "I don't have the energy to tape all this up again." He inspected the gauze wrapping his right knuckles. "I'll grab a whore's bath and—"

"A what?"

He flashed her a tired smile. "Are you even from here? I'll wash up in the sink."

"That cannot be the politically correct way to say that." She emptied her pockets, pulled off the scrubs she'd borrowed from Chloe, and dropped them in the hamper. Devon chuckled.

"Do you have a problem with sex workers?"

"No."

"Concerns over my hygiene?"

"Well, no..."

"Get in the shower, love."

While fetching clothes, he tucked Margo's stone into the top drawer of his dresser, sandwiched between black fabric and a velvet jewelry box. He sent a text to Nix arranging Apollo's transportation the next day. Then, he went to work at the sink.

Devon had his head under the faucet, doing a shit job of one-handed scrubbing, when Hope, naked and warm from the shower, pressed into his side. Her hands slid into his hair, and he relinquished the job—melting into the sensation of her fingers tracing a million tiny circles along his scalp.

She cut the water when she finished and palmed his crown to keep him from clipping it on the faucet as he ducked out. Draping a towel over his head, she rubbed briskly, then looped it round his shoulders, tugging both sides like the lapels of a coat. Every breath he took pressed his chest to her forearms.

"Thank you. It's, um, hard to wash your hair one-handed."

"My pleasure."

She dropped her gaze, the way she did when she was anxious about saying something, or flustered by something Devon had said to her.

"What is it, kitten?"

"Um..." She gestured to her things on the counter. "They made me take off my jewelry for the imaging."

"Well, they had to see what was going on, love."

A tube of lip balm rolled into the sink as Hope grabbed the collar and held it out to him. "Could you help me put it back on?"

Devon looked at her, still naked, with injuries smattering her body, offering him a *collar*—one that she knew was meant to be a collar. "I can get your bracelet, if you'd prefer."

Hope held it out further. "Sir, please?"

"It's a lot more conspicuous than your bracelet."

"I know."

"It comes with rules."

What the fuck was wrong with him? Was he trying to talk her out of it? Because that would be peak-idiot.

"I know," she said patiently.

He threaded the length of rope around her neck, careful not to catch his taped knuckles in her hair. "I think I'm supposed to make a show of this; not fasten it on you after you ask, standing in the damn bathroom." The silver circle rested in the hollow of her throat. His fingertips brushed her collarbones.

"It's good enough for me, if it's good enough for you, Sir."

"Any time I'm with you is good enough for me, darling. You let me know if you need help getting it off."

He handed her a sweatshirt and shoes because of the glass, then led her back through his bedroom and down the hall, stopping to open the playroom door. Wincing as he went, he sank into a crouch and shined the flashlight from his phone across the hardwoods. Satisfied the glass hadn't breached the door, he stood and left his boots in the hallway; Hope followed suit.

The bed, with its monstrous frame, loomed in the center of the room. Devon's assortment of gear lined the wall in neat rows. He closed and locked the door, shutting out the chaos of the rest of the house. Turning to Hope, he reached for her hips, pulled her closer.

"Sorry, I know it's cold. It'll be warm under the covers."

"Are you...trying to seduce me?"

"Christ, you have a lot of faith in my stamina." Her brow pinched, and the corner of his mouth quirked upward. "I'm trying to put you to bed, Hope."

"You said that's not what this room is for," she whispered.

"Yeah, I did." He ran his knuckles down her cheek, annoyed by the bandages muting the sensation. He tipped up her chin. "Unfortunately, I lack the energy for more than breathing right now, and the house is full of glass and bullet holes. This is the best I have to offer tonight."

She wrapped her arms around his waist and folded into him. Devon scooped her up, ignoring her protests and his aching body as he carried her to bed.

HOPE

Hope peered out from the cocoon of the playroom. Sunlight flooded into one end of the hall from the living room; artificial light from Devon's bedroom illuminated the other. She had a feeling that she'd been asleep much longer than intended and didn't remember the need for shoes until she was already washing her hands in the guest bath.

Looking down as she returned to the hallway, she found the floors clean. The walls on the other hand...those were a different story. Her stomach churned at the sight of the reddish-brown smudges—evidence of Apollo's desperate effort to reach her while she fought for her life. Despite the warmth, she hugged her arms around her midsection, squishing the soft fabric of her sweatshirt as she padded forward.

In the bedroom, a trashcan occupied the spot where Apollo had fallen, and a broom leaned against the dresser where Hope had snatched Devon's belt. She brushed her fingertips over her tender throat, until she reached the rope cord, finding a grounding sense of security in that tactile connection.

Various items—tools, a bucket of drywall mud—were strewn about. The scent of pine cleaner hung in the air. The floors were spotless, except for a rogue bullet hole. Devon lay face-down on the bed, boots hanging off the edge. White gauze peeked out from the waistband of his sweats over his right hip, matching the bandages encircling his left shoulder, cutting across the palm of his limp right hand. The wolf on his back rose and fell with his breathing.

Lucky, she reminded herself. So damn lucky.

Hope heard a faint jingle, and to her surprise, Apollo's boxy head lifted from behind the mass of Devon's body...*and* promptly dropped like a cinderblock onto his bandaged shoulder.

"Oh..." She rushed forward a step, but stopped when Devon grunted, groaned, then rolled out from under the dog and onto his back. "You okay?" she said softly.

His eyes popped wide, and he shoved off the bed, scrubbing his hands over his face and through his hair. He frowned when the tape caught and yanked it free, leaving one side of his hair sticking straight up.

"Sorry. I must have dozed off. Didn't mean for you to wake up alone." He moved toward her, stiffly, and pushed her hair behind her shoulders to get a better look. He brushed a thumb down her cheek, across her collar. "How are you feeling? Is your throat bothering you?"

"I'm okay. When did Apollo get here?"

Devon glanced at the dog as if remembering.

"Couple of hours ago. Nix went and got him for me after the glass was up. Good thing, too. Flurries started right before she got here, and it's sticking."

Hope frowned at a spot of fresh-red on the front of his shoulder. "You're bleeding."

He grabbed his bicep and rolled his arm forward to inspect the bandages. "Eh... Pissed it off sweeping. Not getting any bigger, though."

"How long have you been up?"

He shrugged. "Awhile. I couldn't sleep."

Hope sighed. "You should have taken the pain meds. You would have been out cold."

"It's not bad," he told her.

"Really? I can't imagine scrubbing up blood was fun."

Devon laughed. "Sweeping was worse."

"Devon..."

"It had to be done, so I managed. You walk around barefoot or in socks; Apollo doesn't have shoes, and he couldn't come home until the glass was gone. Like you said, the place doesn't feel like home without him, and the roads aren't getting clearer."

Hearing his name, Apollo rolled to his back, sprawling on the king-size mattress where he was not allowed to sleep. Hope walked over and sat beside him. His tail thumped as he snuffled his nose against her hip.

"Is he high?" she asked, running a hand down his flank.

"As a kite." Prying the lid off the bucket of plaster, Devon winced. "They sent him with meds, and he was due for a dose when he got here."

"So, you medicated the dog, but not yourself?" She raised a brow. Devon glanced at her, dipping a putty knife into the bucket with the same hand he'd smashed into Aaron's face.

"I took some ibuprofen."

"Devon, you were shot."

He rolled his wounded shoulder, before turning a bullet hole into an innocuous smudge of fresh plaster.

"I'm aware, but I need a clear head. I have work to do." Hefting the bucket to the other side of the room, he sized up the spot where Aaron put a fist through the drywall. His shoulders slumped, and he cursed under his breath. "Putty isn't going to cut it for this one." He peered into the void in his bedroom wall, grumbled something about wishing Aaron had found a stud.

"You got the glass up, got Apollo home. The rest of this can wait."

Hazel eyes flicked her direction, before refocusing on the wall. "It can't."

"It's a few holes," Hope said. "R&R survived with a hole in the bathroom for weeks."

"That was a leak." He gestured to the offending damage. "This was a fist."

"Does that matter?"

"Hell yeah, it does. You aren't sleeping in a room with fist-holes in the wall, Hope." His muscles tightened, tension rippling through the wolf on his back. "Are you…" He scrubbed a hand over his face, took a heavy breath. "Do you think you'll be able to stay here after what happened? Because if you can't, I need to know."

Hope's brow furrowed. "So, you can take me home before the roads get bad?"

Devon turned to face her, canted his head.

"So, I can sell it."

"Sell *your house*?" She stared at him; mouth parted.

"I can clean the floor. I can fix the door, the walls. I managed to get the dog home before you woke up." He tipped his chin toward the snoring lump of Apollo beside her. "I'll paint this bedroom any color you want, but none of that matters if you can't feel safe here. We aren't living in a home where you can't feel safe, love."

"W… we…?"

He stuck the putty knife in the bucket, then walked over and knelt in front of her, resting his hands on her bruised knees as he looked up into her face.

"You make enough to stay in your apartment," he said. "And you survived Aaron."

"I was rescued from Aaron," she corrected. "First, by my brother, then Apollo, then by you. And every one of you got hurt in the process."

Devon shook his head. "JJ already told everyone how you saved him right back. Apollo would have had a bullet in his head the moment he cleared the door. I wouldn't have made it through the hall if you hadn't fought so goddamn hard. You're a fucking fighter, Hope. You don't have to stay with anyone, not for the money, and not for the safety. You get to choose, and I know that, in the past, sharing a home hasn't been your thing; but if you wanted…" He pressed his teeth into his lower lip for a moment, then went on. "You could choose to live with me."

"That's so sweet," Hope said, reaching for the hand with busted knuckles, taking it in her own, "and you're also kind of trauma-tized."

"Are you about to suggest that I'm trauma bonded to you again?"

Hope giggled, but her eyes misted. "It went so well last time," she said. "But seriously…we almost watched each other die in this very room yesterday."

"I told you I'd sell the house."

"That's reactive."

"Spout all the therapist bullshit you want at me. If it's what you need, I don't care if it's reactive."

Hope narrowed her eyes. "If you invite me to move in after this huge, scary thing, and I jump on it, I'm taking advantage of your emotional state."

Devon shook his head. "See, that's where you're wrong. I've been biting my tongue so hard I taste blood for weeks. Since back when Aaron was quiet, and our lives were normal. But it's too soon, and you don't do live in relationships. I thought you'd say no, or worse…get scared. Run." He looked up from their joined hands, and Hope lost her way in a forest of green and gold. "You might not be willing to take advantage of my fragile emotional state, darling, but I'm not above taking advantage of yours right now."

"You want me to live here?"

"I want to live where you live, and your apartment doesn't allow pets over twenty-five pounds. I checked three weeks ago, back when we weren't living in crisis."

"You're kidding."

He shrugged, smiled tightly. "I love you when it's calm, too, Hope. When your defenses fall away...but when you need those defenses, I want to be right beside you, helping you hold the line. I want to wake up with you every morning. Kiss you before I fall asleep each night. I want to be with you."

"Purple," she said.

Confusion and mild panic shadowed his face, and his hand twitched in hers. "I don't know if that's some kind of safeword or..."

Hope laughed. "It's a color—a pretty, purpley-grey."

Hesitant understanding bled through his confusion. "Paint?" he said, voice tentative. "For..."

"Our bedroom." She looked around the space and nodded. "I think it would look beautiful with the floors, Sir."

"Our bedroom," he repeated, easing up from his knees, leaning over her, and pressing his mouth to hers.

Dear Readers,

Thank you, again, for coming on this journey with me. I hope you enjoyed Hope and Devon's latest adventure as much as I enjoyed sharing it with you. Early in the writing of Edge of Ruin, I became aware that The Edge Series is about far more than Hope and Devon. Instead of wrapping it up with a neat bow, I wanted all of these characters to get their happily-ever-after. That means telling their stories.

So, if you want to find out what Alex is up to on the mountain, how Brandy ended up a single mom with singular focus, whether Baker can ever heal from his trauma, or the number of flavors in a Nix-parfait...stick around. Or maybe you're just curious what Devon has in mind for that slab of charred wood in the garage. No judgement here. The Cleary's crew and I would be happy to have you. Now, about that mountain...

All my love,

Lennan